Co-Wife

(A woman's live-in relationship with a gay)

Pradipta Panda

FROG BOOKS

ISBN 978-93-52017-37-9
Copyright © Pradipta Panda, 2016

First published in India in 2016 by Frog Books
An imprint of Leadstart Publishing Pvt. Ltd.

Sales Office:
Unit No. 25-26, Building No. A/1,
Near Wadala RTO,
Wadala (East), Mumbai – 400037, India
Phone: +91 96 99933000
Email: info@leadstartcorp.com
www.leadstartcorp.com

US Office:
Axis Corp, 7845 E, Oakbrook Circle,
Madison, WI 53717, USA

Disclaimer: The views expressed in this book are those of
the author and do not necessarily reflect the opinion of the
Publisher.

Editor: Apoorva T and Cora Bhatia
Cover: Ananya Aiyyer
Layouts: Chandravadan R. Shiroorkar

Typeset in Palatino Linotype
Printed at Repro Knowledgecast Limited, Thane

DEDICATION

To

My friend, philosopher, protector Jagga,

The Lord Jagannath

ABOUT THE AUTHOR

Pradipta Panda was born in 1976. A thinker and an entrepreneur, he portrays lively characters in a simple way in the story. His previous successful books are *Under One Roof* and *In God's Wishlist.*

He completed his post-graduation in Journalism and MBA in HR. Presently, he is working at Bank of India.

Your valuable comments will certainly help the think tank to narrate more lively characters among us.

Feel free to write to him on social media.

Acknowledgements

My sincere thanks to:

Lord Jagannath to whom I dedicated not only book but also my life. I always feel blessed. It is all his, the success and the failure.

Mamta, my wife, a source of eternal love and my true inspiration.

My sons: Akash and Abheek, my pride and my joy.

Cora Bhatia, the editor, to whom I feel greatly indebted to. As I feel she is a true editor and mentor, who took great pains to go over my manuscript and give me her suggestions about how to improve the manuscript and cleaned up my language to bring it to what it is now.

Uzair Thakur, the coordinator, deserves my genuine gratefulness for all efforts to bring out the work in time.

And the entire Leadstart team: CEO Swarup Nanda, Malini Nair and Amrita Jagtap.

PRELUDE

This story would have never been written if the Delhi High Court's July 2, 2009, historical verdict had not come out to decriminalize homosexuality and if I had not become pregnant. At 32, I remain single and never miss to read 'Diary of a single girl' in Times Life, on tenterhooks as the fable reflects my being single.

Coincidences are always inverted in my life. I confirmed my pregnancy on July 2, 2011, when the concerned man was celebrating the anniversary of the pride parade, pulsating with drumbeats and rainbow hue masks adorning his eyes, at Jantar Mantar. His face was beaming with pride and joy and my shine of motherhood progressively faded.

I phoned him in the evening; he was in a café at a party, in Hauz Khas. He responded to my call, but came back very late that night; it was almost morning. His excitement and pleasure were not yet over. I had not told him of my pregnancy over the phone. I wanted to surprise him with this news face-to-face, so I could get a closer look of his exhilaration. Caught up in a mixture of emotions, I waited and waited for him, until the wee hours for his arrival. I was stuck on many probabilities, unsure of what would be his reaction.

I announced the secret carefully. I was surprised, as he too was overwhelmed with happiness. He hugged me and showed his care for me. I mixed my ecstasy with his throbbing thrill and we slept without much discussion, as my eyes were full of dreams and my heart came out from uncertain boundaries. In the morning, my eyes refused to open up from the leftover dream. It was Sunday, my motherhood needs care, and the caring man still slept beside me. I slept awaiting his love and care from his fatherhood.

However, he woke up and left, without saying a single word. I was hurt as I was expecting plenty of care and thoughts from him, as it's natural for a woman. Especially a pregnant woman needs lots of love and care from the would be father of her child.

I asked, "Are you going?"

He nodded and answered, "Plenty of things are pending because of my involvement in the pride parade. Let me complete some of it today and my website needs updating as well."

"You have not thought about me? I need to discuss a lot with you," I asked again.

"Yes, yes...you were saying something in the night. It is great. Who is the lucky father?" his voice was spontaneous and vehement.

I was dying for death in that moment. He departed and I kept on watching him with tearful eyes.

With many ambiguities, hesitation and a little hope, I kept on rolling days with the baby in my womb. I wanted to make closer of our closeness, so that we could feel and each other's breath and intimacy. You can only hide a pregnancy from others, until about four months, not beyond that. I needed settlement. I could not be single with motherhood, much longer.

On the eve of the fourth annual Queer Pride Parade, he came to me with a guy, who happened to visit my home, several times with him and is his now close friend, a younger guy than us.

He called me, "Pranami, this guy loves you and wishes to marry you."

I was clueless at his sudden move. When I asked he didn't answer and now he had brought a man, who wanted to lay claim being the father of my child. It was hilarious and I refused to listen to what he said, as if I was deaf.

After a few minutes, getting back my consciousness, I asked, "He must be a member of your queer group and preparing for the mega event tomorrow?"

"Yes, but what's wrong with that?" he questioned back.

"Does the man know I am pregnant?"

"Yes, and he loves you not just today, but from the day he saw you first."

"Certainly, I wouldn't like you to be the father of my child," I replied aloud, and the guy watched us as if we were third world's creatures.

Again, the coincidence of a date comes to play in my life. The next day, again happens to be a Sunday, November 27, 2011. I admit myself for an abortion with the help of a doctor friend. While he fluttered with a colourful mask and vibrant pleasure adorned his face, I was in the labour room with unbearable physical pain that was intensified with a broken heart.

CONFESSION OF
THE OTHER CHARACTER IN OUR LIFE

Vardhman Karla

Hi, I am Vardhman; I am a gay. I am a country boy from Hukumatpur, a village of Ludhiana, Punjab. I am a Charted Accountant and work at Ernst and Young, Gurgaon. I cannot say when and how I became gay, but gradually I was inclined towards it. But I must confess that I fell in love with Pranami profoundly, the day I first saw her. She has neither the heroine-like figure of the present era, nor a flat belly nor a curvaceous figure, but she has the looks and the elegant beauty of the older age heroine, 'Madhubala'. It takes just a glance; a single look to understand that kind of beauty—a single unbroken rice-like figure, well built, bulky, yet extremely charming.

Now, the clashing question is, whether I should be gay or straight? So, am I bisexual?

I am a boy from a small town where attracting the opposite sex is the natural phenomenon. Earlier, I wondered and had long drawn-out conversations with my friends about what it was like to be a gay. Then anal sex was fun to me and we often laughed with the sexual orientation one gay must encounter before discovering it in me. I started loving my boyfriends and was jealous towards girlfriends. I had to accept my friend's alienation and society's prejudice.

13

It was hard to accept me as a gay. It needs plenty of courage and audacity to fight among friends, families and relatives.

Why was I in the mass? I was single man proclaimed as a gay among my childhood friends, why so? I asked myself a thousand times to get the answer. I pampered myself in it and I loved it. Then I asked while others lived a meaningful and prestigious life, why couldn't I, what difference did it make to me?

Few friends suggested it is science, but how can science tell me what I am? I mean I've had boyfriends, rather say gay friends, and I love Pranami, who happens to be straight with no link to the group. Earlier, too I would attract girls. So, I don't have a gay gene and I don't believe in science.

What is the role of science in gayness? To me, it is purely a state of mind.

Now I stand at a crossroad, think more and act less. I have joined the party and activities of gays, but dream of Pranami and think about having a happy family with her.

As a butterfly transgresses from stage-to-stage, my wishes and acts also change from phase-to-phase. We were enjoying sex both ways; top and bottom, now I feel it's better to be the bottom. People love and care more about the bottom. And who in the world does not want to be loved?

I know Pranami loves Manav, Manav loves me and I love Pranami. It gives a complete cycle definition and boosts my hope for a better relationship among us. But Pranami hates me and hates my relationship with Manav and it seems obvious.

In the love story of gay and straight, between Manav and Pranami, I am very much in the novel. Adds some spice to their love and makes it more interesting to formulate a love trilogy. Watch out for me in the Pranami and Manav's love life in the swinging and bouncing of a relationship...

CONFESSION OF
MANAV'S MENTOR

GOPAL MENON

Hi, I am Gopal Menon, History Professor in DU and hail from the south. I proudly proclaim I am a gay and enjoy my life as gifted by the almighty. I don't have any concern in the love trilogy, but gradually I am involved in Manav's life as a guru and his mentor. He likes my ideology which is inspired by my fightback with society and loves me. I saw true love and passion in his eyes and my weakness, where I found true love I saw god in it. I am impressed by his nobility.

Manav rushed to me when I was attacked by some protagonist at Lalit Kala Akademi. I am a poet and write about gayism in an open forum of a leading daily newspaper. Let me clear it all. I am not intended to spread 'dirt' in society. I am by nature a poet and love nature as it is… I am involved in the awareness campaigning of gayism. If you are a gay or lesbian then don't hide yourself. By doing so, one criminalizes his birth and god.

Gay life is not all about sex. Non-stop sex and same sex shopping are not what it means to be gay. To me, it is only love, a formation of true love. The gay community should not be judged by news reports about gay pride parades, with rainbow hues and colourful masks or any excesses of few college students, during spring breaks. Sometimes, it is said relationships just don't happen with gay men. Gays want sex, not relationships... people always misquote the fact. There are people who have been going out with people for years and stay for years. It seems like exactly the same relationship between the opposite sexes.

May I ask what distinguishes the difference between gay and straight?

There is one and only difference, in the case of straight, a man's genital is inserted into a female's biological genital, whereas in the case of a gay, the man's organ is inserted into another man's organ. Who can define which is natural and which is unnatural? It is only a mental state. Love exists in both cases. As far as children and hierarchy are concerned, 98 per cent people are straight people, compared with two per cent gay people.

But the percentage gradually increases.

And it means, gayism is both an art and a science, natural and man driven.

There are many ifs and buts over gayism and homosexuality in the air, long debates in parliament and court. But I have nothing to do with it, we have shown the world about our pragmatic step to deepen and strengthen our love. My love is my friend and colleague Mr Arvind Goswami. We enjoy our gayism, but do not stay together and this is our specialty, balancing society and our love life.

The world can be conquered by love only. So, be in love always, it won't reprimand you...

You will know more about me in Manav's narration...

I am very much in Pranami and Manav's love life.

Manav Agrawal

Hi, I am Manav and proudly proclaim I am a gay. I am an IIT Delhi alumnus and work in Ericsson, Ghaziabad. I secretly run a gay website. I want to see the gay world rising and rising at the top of the world. I wish everyone to come under the LGBT group and enjoy sex as part of nature. My requests to the total population...don't hide yourself, if you are gay, lesbian or bisexual come out with pride, you will be happier in life. My message is to the entire LGBT group...remember one thing, you are not alone, many people out there will understand your feelings and it will be wafted across the group. This is how my website *myrelationship. com* works. What matters is not to run and express swiftly wafting voices among groups but to help people come out from stress, which is the role of my website. May I ask a simple question to the whole of humankind, 'What is the cost of life?' Until now, I do not have the answer, and whatever answer I received is not satisfactory. It differs with every human being. Naturally, everyone placed their dream as the cost of life, to be a doctor, engineer, architecture or entrepreneur. But it's the dream about where one's happiness is placed. Okay, you have your dream and ambition fulfilled, then after that? One new resolution and what about those who missed the line? Happiness, is it the cost of life? That is where I stand now.

I am the kind of a man that always thinks extreme. It is axiomatic; I see the whole world as gay and lesbian. Every human being possesses some homosexuality; in some, it's hideous, in some people, it's dormant and few expose it bravely. Those render on heroically get their due course of love and affection. And those that don't come out from their hideous places suffer tantrums and stress. My website works for them.

However, the difficulties associated with accepting gay feelings and coming out, mean that many gay people don't identify themselves as gay, until much later in their life. They carry on their life, as our society wants them, but at a certain point, they fail to perform the natural verdict and search for their happiness. This contradiction has labelled them off as a failure to bring certain admiration into their life.

Our society has progressed enough to talk on sex, but certainly, it has not accepted homosexuality. Unfortunately, straight people hate gayism and lesbianism. The court's verdict certainly does not change the human mind. It needs a thorough knowledge of the science behind gay people. The wiring of our brain occurred in the womb itself and the hormones development is not in one's hand. The brain and hormone controls our sexuality. So, once the controlling agencies are not in one's hand, then how can he or she be blamed for the desire?

What is love and how it happened I don't know. Pranami always says she loves me. It is being said love transforms one to a world of hues, where pleasure is abundant and happiness is plethora. And love is the panacea for all remedies.

But my pleasure and happiness is in my website. I love to be with gay people. In this circumstance, how can I tell her that, I love you? But I have concern for her; share my sorrows and happiness with her.

Watch me in the novel with the aspiration of love and Pranami in my life...

ME

PRANAMI SHARMA

Hi, I am Pranami, a graduate from IIPM. This is my story and thoughts. I am craving for the gay man, Manav. But I am straight. I stay single in Shri Ganesh Apartment, Plot no 32C, Sector-7, Dwarka, Tower–II, First Floor, Room no 108, facing the Vardhman City Mall. Our ancestral house in Green Park was sold out. I started my career with Standard Chartered Bank, Basant Kunj branch, near PVR, earlier Priya Theatre. Now I work for HFFC bank and am positioned as the branch manager at its Gopinath bazaar branch, Delhi Cantt, among the most admired and respectful Indian Army personnel. Being a branch head, responsibilities and errands are much more. But I enjoy being short of time, I like to be fully engaged, 24×7 to kill my time, I feel I should not have spare time so that my inner thoughts come out and I become transgressed. I am a Facebook fan that shows me 'in relationship' in my profile, though my relationship is in infinity. At an average, every day, I receive two to three friendship requests on Facebook. I care for them and increase my fan base. Guys post porn photographs, praise me and propose to me even proposing marriage, though they all know I am in a relationship. Few old friends are inclined to grab me, take advantage of my singlehood, though they are married. To my surprise, one day a Major, who happens to be in my Facebook friend list and a customer in my branch invited me for a coffee and proposed to me...

What would have been my answer, one can easily guess. But when I narrated it to Manav to tease him, rather to know his thoughts, he promptly replied, "Yes, Pranami, you get married to him. What I have heard is that these army people are very caring and love their wives and respect their ethos and emotions. You will enjoy your life and freedom, I bet."

I don't know where he gathered this information. But working for the last few months in a cantonment area, I am sure Manav is not saying anything absurd.

This is not one instance; a single girl gets many offers around the corner with many hues, marriage is only one facet of this kind. Lovemaking, live-in relationships, dating and entertaining are other facts. A single girl continues to be a passing fad for all ages of malehood. I say all ages of the male group because few films of love with older women and young adults like 'Leela', 'Freaky Chakra' 'Ek Chhotisi Love Story' make young men with ages much younger than me, feel the same craving and I hope that I can be part of their experimental love life. College-going, young men men with silver grey moustaches presume that I am a woman in distress, in need of love and care, and they imagine further intimacy, which will lead to a sexual intercourse. It's the filmy effect.

But my love is for Manav. So, I accept the naked truth of homosexuality. Some people, we could say most people do not have their first homosexual feelings or experience until they are well into adulthood. And Manav was not born gay and I bet no man is born as gay, as there are no such parameters to judge as a born gay. We have had many evidence of our love. So, I still wait for a miracle to happen and I will be out of speculations...

The dream becomes a nightmare if not worked and I repent being late. Nevertheless, it will be too late to make him revert, as he needs to mingle with the community...

And watch out for me in the novel among the band of gay's...

1

My heart has never transgressed beyond Manav.

To me, love is what my heart wishes. And relationship is where all five W's and 1 H (Why, Where, When, Who, Whom and How) gets its answer.

We all know love when we feel it; otherwise, it is always in the air. It amazes when your childhood friend swiftly became your lover and you feel it, the teasing days become memorable and every single moment exciting. It is the reason why friends' started being jealous of me, when I was in class IX. Before the screenplay, in the background I struggled a lot, fought with my thoughts and wished to make him my boyfriend. On those days, to define what-is-love was difficult; the definition of love was still in its infancy. Before proclaiming, 'I am in love', I also asked myself thousand times the very common question, "How can I tell I'm in love? Am I really in love?" But it was not an easy question to answer. Finally, I unravelled the mystery saying, "Yes, I am in love. I am in a in a relationship, what else? I am proud being in love."

"Who doesn't want to be loved? But it was still a long debate, which lasted for several days, when I expressed myself among the girls. Friends did not accept it easily, but when they believed I am in a relationship they all started becoming jealous of me. It's natural for girls as the 'why not I factor' bites them.

There will eventually be a large community of loveologists (scientific students) who specialize in love, especially those who have experienced it in school; those who define what-is-love and are able to offer important contributions and suggestions, asked me tens of thousands questions initially, both of a suppressing and depressing nature like, "How can you say he loves you? It is just friendship. You are not able to distinguish friendship and love."

Then the question changes, "Has he ever said that he loves you or it is one-sided?"

They tried to convince me equalizing many facts, "Love is always a controversial and sensitive subject. Teenage love is very dangerous, families never accept it and then heartbreak destroys both career and life."

When I neglect everyone and go ahead with my die-hard attitude, loveologists soften their stance and speak in a tangible way about love and my relationship, "How do you feel with him, is it marvellous?"

Love is a sensation through the physical, mental, emotional and spiritual senses. It is compassionate, romantic, generous, heartfelt and funny and heals all things. Love is the master key that opens the gates of happiness. Love stretches your heart and makes you big inside. God blesses you both and prays for the longevity of your love.

I won the battle and received the nod from the so-called loveologists as well as friends. That time I was sure love is not easy and realized why it is being called a 'bed of roses' the thorn bites and its feeling is sweet too, but it has tremendous power, power to transform a rock into a river. Falling in love with a senior guy, handsome and muscular gives one the upper hand and proud moments among friends.

I fought with my world to make Manav my boyfriend, but up to now, he has not told me, 'I love you' and there is no hope for it later as well.

Those initial love days were marvellous,

First discovery of love,

One sided love with many ifs and buts,

Waiting for his every moment,

Escape from class to play basketball with him,

Senior girls teasing and jealous,

Family get-togethers,

The exciting day, getting nods for our relationship from family,

The outing for movies and parties…

The sensational electrifying and thrilling days were only on commemoration.

Gone are those days.

--Ω--

I was on leave for a week after the abortion. On Monday, the beginning of the month, I joined feeling fresh; it's rush time for the bank as most Army personnel's salary is credited here. I had observed a long queue in front of the ATM, while entering even before the bank opened. It's usual at the beginning of the month and I was habituated to the rush, but today unknowingly, I was scared of the mob, because of those eight days of leave, I had spent alone in my home. Suddenly, so much rush made me sick of it. The same scenario existed inside the bank also and unfortunately, two colleagues Diksha and Rasmita were on leave. Rasmita's leave was expected, she had gone for maternity leave and Diksha was on a day's urgent leave.

My deputy, Gaurav Sharma, who shared my surname explained the reason, "Madam, Diksha requested for one day leave. Her boyfriend is in Delhi and they planned to dine outside and go for a movie."

25

"What about tomorrow?"

"Her boyfriend is going back today. His flight is in the night, at 9 p.m., Kingfisher Airlines. He is going back to Chennai; he came here on a business trip. No local boy, madam. He is a Chennai boy that was the reason that she badly needed one day leave. Diksha will join tomorrow hundred per cent."

"You are pretty updated about her, Diksha told you all this?"

Yes, madam. she never lies," replied Gaurav.

I won't be so harsh on these sentimental issues. The staff will think being single, I am against love or betrayed from love. And neither I am against love nor betrayed from love, as I am still in love. Despite my abortion, my proclivity towards Manav has not ebbed; rather sympathy has built up for the man.

I told Gaurav, "You join the second teller counter; let the rush be minimized."

Gaurav joined without uttering a word. The queue divided into two and was shortened. I made Savita move from personal manager customer information counter to insurance and investment counter and took her place. The move was intentional as Savita was slow with her answers and the queue would increase.

"Madam, where is Mr Praful Dash?"

"He is sitting at counter number seven."

Customers never come directly to their problems. They prefer the man with whom they did the last transaction. Mr Dash must have been in this seat, when the man approached.

"Madam, my account shows a deduction twice of ten thousand, whereas, I withdrew only ten thousand," asked the second man in the queue.

"ATM withdrawal?" I asked.

"Yes."

"Which ATM and when?" I asked again. asked again.

"Yesterday, Madam, near Pusha road from the Canara bank ATM; I got two SMSes from the bank regarding my withdrawal and the amount was deducted twice as well. I then took a mini statement...it shows the same."

The man tried to show his mobile for the SMS and narrated all the events he encountered with the mini statement slip.

"Tell me your account number," I said.

Instead of his account number, he gave me two ATM slips one mini statement and one ATM withdrawal slip of Canara Bank. Almost 99.9 per cent people don't remember their account number.

"Tell me your account number, a ten digit number mentioned in your cheque book?" I repeated my question and clarified it too.

"Oh," was the man's first reaction and then he took out the chequebook from his bag.

I checked the account; yes, two deductions were made on the same date and within few minutes' difference of time.

I told the man, "Your account shows two deductions at the same date and the same time, it could be a database error. Please write an application illustrating your transaction and give us just two working days to solve your problem. By tomorrow evening, you will get an SMS alert."

I gave him a blank sheet and told him, "Please give the application to counter number five."

The third man showed a deposit slip with a cheque.

"Sir, please drop it in the cheque drop box."

"No, I want the counter slip with a signature and the bank stamp," the man insisted.

I took the slip from the man, put the round stamp and signature, and while returning the counter slip and deposit slip said, "Please check the account number properly and drop it into the cheque drop box, please."

Now, the man agreed.

The next man was about to say something, when the attendant Gopi interrupted, "Madam, your phone."

It was still ringing; it showed Manav calling...the phone was kept in my cabin table in silent and vibration mode. I wanted to pick it up quickly looking at the rush but that moment the vibration stopped and the display showed three missed calls. All were from Manav. Again, the phone started vibrating; it showed once again Manav calling.

I kept it aside and asked the man, "Yes, sir?"

"I want a bank draft."

"Sir, please fill up the draft form and give it to counter number five."

I called Gopi, Gopi, give a draft form to sir."

The man had more doubts, moving from his position, he asked again, "I need a draft that will be drawn from SBI, Bangalore, where my daughter is studying. Is it possible?"

The 50-year-old man was confused and probably making a draft for his daughter for the first time. Sometimes, a man narrates everything without even asking a single word.

"DD's are not made for a particular bank," I said.

Ni, I need a SBI draft," the man insisted.

"This is a different bank and we can't make a DD of SBI."

The man looked puzzled and hopeless, "Then what can I do, shall I go to SBI branch?"

Even though people do banking for 30 years, they are not aware of many factors of banking. I understood what he wanted to do.

Don't worry, sir. You an account in our branch?" I asked.

"Yes...it is my salary account; my account no is 0137852..."

I interrupted, "Your daughter's account no is in...?"

"SBI Koramangala, Bangalore," he completed the sentence.

"What we can do is we can make a DD, which will be in favour of your daughter's name and payable at Bangalore. Let your daughter deposit the DD in her SBI account and it will be credited to her account without charging any extra money from your child. Why go to SBI? Or you can transfer the money direct to her account through NEFT but it is chargeable, though a nominal amount whereas the bank's commission is waived for making a DD from your salary account." I tried to make the man understand about the bank ethos.

"You will not charge any amount for Demand Draft?" asked the man. Though puzzled, his face gradually brightened up.

No, sir. I mentioned our bank gives this facility to salary account holders. What is the amount, sir?" I asked.

"Fifteen thousand," the man promptly answered.

"No problem, sir. It will be free of charge and it's better you go for DD."

I looked for the next man in the queue, but the previous man had not gone still had doubts, "Madam, one last thing. You said something about money transfer. Will you please explain? If it is feasible, I will transfer it."

"You ask at counter number five He will explain everything to you and will do all the needful for you, whatever you want to do, DD or transfer."

The man left the counter with the DD form that Gopi gave him. It happens, people try to save that nominal amount too, so the man preferred DD over NEFT.

The phone rang again. Manav was calling and the next man quietly stood and reviewed me.

I asked, "How can I help you, sir?"

"Sure, please help yourself and take your call. It may be the same caller who repeatedly calls you, he may be in trouble. I have been watching you for the last fifteen to twenty minutes that you are attending the customers and neglecting his call. The caller may need you girl...take his call, we can wait."

I looked straight at the man, retired Army personnel. I had interacted with him many times at the branch. These men are always kind and candour in their approach. The man stood and waited for my response. He was so much older that I could not overreact with him. Without a choice, I took the phone and abruptly thought I would answer him, "I have a life also; I am liable to many people standing in front, to my service, to the bank and to the organisation who gives me the employment. So, please stop calling me repeatedly."

But before I could answer something from my thoughts, the phone stopped ringing. This was an excellent opportunity; I switched off the phone. The man looked pleased as I obeyed his order.

I asked, "Sir, tell me how I can help you?"

"Miss Pranami, I would like to open a account."

Few people speak straight and it always pleased me; no madam, no girl or woman business, they called me by name and it sounded good.

"Sure, sir. It's nice." My words were as pleasant.

"You may think why was this old man interested at this stage to open a share account. Actually, I thought why not try this out? Many people have tried and failed, but they never stopped. They fall down, wake up and then try again. Why is it like the suspicious tempting apple? Let me also see what is in it? Why leave any stone unturned in life? I will gain market knowledge as well as the time kill machine."

His words sounded like vibrant laughter that added a spark to the surrounding. He spoke loud and clear and his joyous words caught everyone's attention.

A smile erupted in me as well, step, sir. Certainly, our bank will help you and educate you about the market.

I called the investment banker; she deals with all mutual funds and demat accounts.

"What are the requirements for this?" he asked.

"Photocopy of PAN card, cheque and photographs."

"That's all?" he enquired further.

"Certain signatures and declarations will be needed."

"Yes, madam..." Smita waited for instruction.

"Sir wants to open a demat account so please help him."

I said to the man again, "Sir, please go with her. She will help you out with the entire formalities."

"Thank you, Pranami." The man left.

"Welcome, sir." It was my turn to be polite.

The next man was desperate, probably the previous man, the retired Army officer had taken more than the expected time.

"Madam, on Saturday I had deposited thirty-thousand into my account, but it has not credited to my account."

"Tell me your account number."

"0372115001...the account is in Ahmedabad, Gujarat...is this the reason for the delay. On Saturday, while depositing the server was down," the man kept on asking.

I checked the account, "Sir, the amount is credited to your account."

No, I did not get the SMS," the man was reluctant to believe.

Hello, Pranami. How are you?" a sweet voice appeared addressing me.

"I am fine. How are you, madam?" She is the wife of senior Army personnel and a good investor in mutual funds.

I offered her a seat, "Madam, please sit."

"Thank you." She obliged, but the man had not moved from his position.

"Sir, the amount is credited; you can check it through the ATM."

He repeated his words again, "But I didn't get the SMS."

"Sir, the amount was credited at 2 p.m., and why you didn't get the SMS I can't say."

"Please check my mobile number, if it is properly fed or not...9731355758." People always suspect the bank is at fault.

"It is right, sir; your mobile may have been switched off or out of reach at that time, for a long period, your service provider's server may have some problem, there are many possibilities." I gave a probable reason, the man moved, but unhappily.

"What happened, Pranami, today you are sitting at this counter?" the woman asked.

"There was a rush in the early hour, so I just sat to clear some of the crowd; two staff have gone on urgent leave. Give me few minutes, madam. I will clear them and we will move to the cabin."

"I am comfortable. You just carry on. Last week too I came. On Wednesday, Mr Sharma told you had taken a week long leave...Did you go somewhere?"

She tried to be cosy. If I answer her queries, she will further dig out all eventualities. There were two people in the queue now, so I answered, "Just two minutes, madam. Let me clear them, then we will sit comfortably and talk."

The next man wants to open an account, "Just wait," I said to him and looked to the other man, "How can I help you, sir?"

"Nothing, madam. I came with him," the other man indicated the first man. "He is with is with me," the first man confirmed. I called Mr Praful from counter number seven.

"Yes, madam..." He came quickly.

"He wanted to open an account," I turned to the woman, "Let's move to my cabin, madam. Sorry to make you wait."

"Sure, madam." Mr Praful gave the account opening form to the man, even before taking a seat.

No, Pranami... I enjoyed watching you while at work, I like women who are highly professional."

The woman got up to move with me. Before picking the mobile, I gave a final glance from the corner of my eye to both the guys at the counter. What is the necessity of two men coming to open an account?

I finally asked, "Do you want a single account or a joint account?"

Single account, madam. I am still a bachelor, not married yet," the man replied.

I am not supposed to ask him this type of question. The sooner I leave the seat the better. But it's the Manav effect that I was bound mentally. I started suspecting everyone might be homosexuals.

He always proclaimed, "You just see, Pranami. One day, the world will take a stride and men will love men, women will love women."

He even says, "People will come to your bank for opening joint accounts to secure their future."

How funny. But Manav was not funny at all, he had this vision. Now I start looking through his eyes, both guys are young and share time together.

The sooner I left this place the better it would be for my mental state.

I said, "Gopi, two cups of coffee ... in my cabin."

The woman had a penchant for coffee, and never said no to it.

--Ω--

The woman started from where she stopped, "Had you been somewhere, Pranami?"

"No, I was here only."

She started relating again, about how she came last week, what time and what the day was, not finding me in the office she asked Mr Sharma and left, then where she had gone, etc. I was thinking of Manav. He should not call on the bank's phone, finding my mobile switched off.

I was thinking in line of the retired Army personnel. Manav must have some urgency or is he in some problem? I should have attended his call; I regretted not taking his call. He had not called me from the last Queer Pride Parade.

On that Sunday morning, he asked me over the phone, "Are you joining us, Pranami?"

Shameless, I had already taken the appointment for an abortion. That was the last we had spoken, a very short call.

Over my silence, he had said again, "Come at least to cheer up. Many people come out in our support also." I did not listen to him and dropped the call.

Gopi served the coffee. The woman in front of me stopped talking and started sipping the coffee. I switched on my phone.

Over coffee, I asked, "Madam, you have not said why you came today?"

"Nothing so specific," with a little pause she said again, "I had planned for some investment. Actually, the market is so volatile now. I am afraid hat to do!" to do!"

Madam, don't worry. The market is at its bottom position now, you will not lose anything. How much have you planned for investment?"

"Around ten lakh."

I touched the call bell; Gopi came in to take instructions. I told him to call Smita. Smita came within a second, "Yes, madam..."

"You have not called Madam for any investment."

"No, she called me twice," the woman answered.

Smita then said, "Madam also came once, but actually she was waiting for you."

"Now tell her what to do. Madam is ready to invest ten lakh, but she is worried about the market condition. I was just suggesting why not go with few blue chip companies," I said.

"I was telling Madam the same thing. She is not going to lose anything based on the position of the market, and I am here to tell her about the everyday scenario. What we will do is that we will not put the amount in a day and we will cautiously invest in it batchwise."

The woman looked enthusiastically and listened to Smita carefully.

"Someone suggested intraday trading; it is a lot of profit making. Why not we try for it?" the woman put the question in Smita's court.

Smita looked at me; she waited to see what I would suggest? The customer has a tendency; they listen to everyone, do what they planned but behave as if they are completely dependent upon the expert advice. It is for their backup, if something goes wrong.

"It is nice, madam, but the risk is more. We will go for it, let you get accustomed to the market a little more. It is not wise to enter into intraday trading when the market is volatile and the rupee has its all-time low value against the dollar. Except few, the global market is down sliding."

"Okay...I have full faith on you," she agreed.

Smita, take madam with you and she has a demat account," I said.

"Every day spare a few minutes for Madam to update and take suggestions. Check out today's market condition and if it is down, purchase a few shares."

The woman was extremely pleased. She got up to go with Smita and said, Thanks, Pranami. It is up to you how you care for me."

"Don't worry, madam. You are in safe hands."

--Ω--

I was desperately waiting when she would move. I looked at the phone immediately; it showed a new SMS. SMS alert showed three missed calls from Manav. Again, I regretted; I should have taken his call. I started guessing probabilities, what could happen to him. His calls were always short and precise. He never makes gratuitous calls. He is in trouble and must be in need of help, that's why he called so many times. I kept on guessing and waited for his call. These minutes made me impatient. No, he hasn't given a call again.

So, I finally called him.

Suddenly he spoke, "Where are you, Pranami? I called you so many times."

"I am at the bank."

"Why in the hell's name did you not take my call?" he seemed a little irritated.

"It is the rush hour, inflated first week of the month, and besides, two employees are on leave today. Putting aside all my regular work, I also sat at the counter. I can't take your calls in front of a crowd standing in queue at all counters."

"What's wrong with you? Why can't you Manav was a bit surprised.

"You won't understand; you never take my job seriously. Tell me why you called?" I had no hold of my emotions; there were movements in front of my cabin and people were standing to enter.

"I need your car today," he said without any formality.

"Why? What happened to your car?" I was astounded, so I asked two questions simultaneously.

"I have it, but it has been giving me problems for the last two days so it is not wise to take it for a long drive. It needs complete servicing or some spare part change."

Mystery continues as he never speaks in tandem. Speculation arises where and what is the need, but I had lost the moral ground to ask, so answered quickly, "Okay, but why so many calls? You could have come and taken it. Where need the need arise to ask me? When did you care for me so will do today?"

"I needed to confirm. You may have a commitment or may have planned to go somewhere."

With suppression, I giggled, "You know I don't go anywhere, other than up and down to the bank."

"Okay, okay...you have not asked where I am going."

"No need, have I ever asked?" I raised the question mark to him. Though my heart wished to ask him where he planned a long drive and why, and who else were going? But my ego hurt to ask.

But he answered quickly, "I am going to Alwar, about 165 kms away, to interview a high school teacher for the website. I will let you know everything when we meet in the afternoon. I will be back in Delhi by midnoght. Tomorrow, I have to go to office as well. I will come around 3 o'clock and pick your car and I will leave my car with you."

Before he dropped the call, I managed to say, "Listen, don't bring your car. I will manage with a taxi, but you give your car for servicing today itself."

"Okay and thanks, Pranami. I was worried," he said and disconnected the call.

2

Manav reached sharp at 3 p.m. The last I spoke to him was three hours ago. I was worried about him, though I continued my routine jobs. Stress mounted and it would exist until he took the car, then I would be relieved.

He said from the door and looked exuberant, Pranami, let's for a cup of coffee. I have many things to tell you."

Any other day, I would be the happiest sharing coffee time and listening to him.

"CCD is in the other part and far too. Even if there is a chance, I cannot leave office and go for coffee with you. People in Gopinath know me very well and I can't hurt my image. You sit down first. Gopi will arrange coffee for you," I seemed cooler than other times.

Manav was not left with another option.

"Have you eaten lunch?" I asked.

"No, I did not get time." Manav looked at his watch. He must be running short of time. The more he delays, the more are the chances that he may be caught in the the traffic rush. I instructed Gopi for two coffees and a sandwich for Manav and then asked, "Will it do?"

"Right, but do it first..." Gopi on his way back heard it, so I need not not tell him and he replied, "Sure, madam just two minutes."

"You were saying you have many things to say me," I broke the silence after Gopi departed.

"Yes, yes, we have not met for few days. Really there are certain issues I need your help on, but see there is a constraint of time."

He knows my weak point. I love talking to him, so impatiently, I devoted my ear and heart to listen to him.

He continued, "And I need to reach there on time, the old man goes walking around 6 p.m., in the evening. That is the only time which he promised that he could spare some time for me, away from Alwar's eye in its suburb. Besides, he has to return home by 7 p.m. So, I have only 40-45 minutes to interact with him."

My first reaction was a terrible snarl, "An old man?" as I felt it was the nuisance of the young generation.

"Exactly, and he is suppressed by family members, his wife, and grown up children. His every moment is being watched and monitored. Think of how much he is humiliated!"

"Then why did he fall into it? A family man having been married for so many years, rather his family must be feeling ashamed?" It's my natural reaction as I feel it's an individual's fun making.

"Again, Pranami, I told you it's not in anyone's hand, it is intrinsic rather natural..." He stopped as Gopi entered with the sandwich and coffee. He nibbled the sandwich and took a sip of coffee as Gopi left, and then started his unfinished advocacy. "It really kills every moment, every day, until the man comes out about what he is and when one comes out before dying people start evading him. Where does one do harm? Instead of being attracted to a woman, one is attracted to a man? But the difference is one can choose for women, but in the case of a gay it provides limited options."

"What, what does it mean?" I was bemused by his last sentences.

Manav smiled, looked at his watch and said, "I will talk about this topic another day. It is an interesting mail that I received few days ago. I will make you read it and you will come to know how the veracity of imagination transgresses from the virtual to real." He always babbled like this, which was difficult for me to understand.

He did not allow me to ask any more, and stood up finishing the coffee with a long sip, "Let me go, if I reach late, it will be useless."

I gave him the car keys and he came out from my cabin. I waited for a while and followed him. Few things were causing me restlessness and needed an immediate answer; otherwise, the petulant mind will remain agitated and before he got into the car I asked, "Are you going alone?"

"Yes. Who will come? Today is a working day."

I had my answer, but Manav was confused about my query and asked, "Why, is anyone supposed to come with me?"

"No, it's nothing, you go and drive carefully," I came back. He was about to say something, but I didn't wait.

--Ω--

Manav was not as what he seems today; we had wonderful days of love. From whatever extent I could go back to the past, I remembered that Manav was always with me. But when I was aged three, my father had told me that his family had come to stay at 12C and we lived at 12D.

My juvenile question was, "Where did they stay earlier?"

"Can't say, my child. They purchased this flat and came to stay as our neighbour."

"Can I play with him?"

"Sure, they are our neighbours and we have to share many things with them. Subham is already friends with Pranab."

These are few lines of Papa I still remember. Subham is my elder brother and Pranab is Manav's elder brother. I was really amazed; they were such good neighbours, who had two sons of our ages Subham Bhai can play with Pranab Bhai and I can play with Manav.

Mama sometimes cautioned us, "Don't hurt them, they don't have a mother, who stays with them like your Mama stays always with you."

"And the aunty, who stays with them, is not their mother?" I asked.

"No, she is their Bua, their father's sister, a widow."

"Then where has their mother gone?" I asked, as the information had not quenched my thirst yet.

"She has taken a divorce and stays separately."

That moment, Mama felt that she had informed us much more, more than what I was supposed to know and changed the topic. At that age, I didn't understand what divorce is, but what I could gather out from the discussion was 'their mother stays separately from them and they are to be sympathized with.' Moreover, this thought still carried with me; I could not obviate from his demands and always felt he needed sympathy.

We both went to the same school, 'Tagore Shree International School, Vasant Kunj' and shared the same bus. Most interestingly, Subham Bhai and Pranab Bhai were studying in different schools. No one studied in our school, so no watchful eyes and cautious commands were given like my other friends whose siblings were studying in the same school.

I enjoyed his company. Manav was one class senior to me and the best all-rounder the school had. He played basketball, football, handball and cricket. He had good command on musical instruments as well, and played the piano the best. When and where he practiced amazed me. Even after school hours, we played in both our gardens and he had no musical instrument at his home. So I take it is intrinsic and god gifted. But the beautiful thing was most seniors with all juniors had respect for me and I felt I earned this because of Manav, as he shared vital time with me and accompanied me to school too.

It is very difficult to say when and how he became my boyfriend from a childhood friend. But there were instances where our love story was a hit.

--Ω--

Loveologists had not given the nod, until a bizarre occurrence struck the school. As per their view, nothing could be said about love, since the boy was the neighbour of the girl. It is obvious and customary, as both were always in touch and there may be a feeling of love too, but it's not actually love. Our mixing up, sharing thoughts and taking notes are all ordinary in the eyes of the love masters.

It all started with the piano class. As we grew up, many factors suffered, many matters differed which were common to us, especially our play. We used to play in the evenings, in either his garden or mine. Suddenly, all this stopped one day, when Manav started going to the JNU Campus or IIT Campus to play basketball or tennis. He was a boy and no longer was he bound with girls' garden games. I had no right to stop him from outdoor games. But gradually, he started coming home late in the evening and I found less time to interact with him. I was left with only school time talks and that was confined to very specific times and topics surrounded with friends.

I was desperately looking to spend some time with him and I got the opportunity when I enrolled for piano classes. Every day, practice was in progress for the annual cultural program. As Manav was good at piano, the piano teacher gave him a free hand.

The piano teacher was in charge of the complete functioning of the cultural program and very often, left the class, so Manav was given the task of taking our class and making us learn. I was delighted to be trained by Manav.

Manav changed into a different person while teaching. He was filled with enthusiasm and took utmost pain to make us understand. He had a common dialogue those days, 'Put more zing...put more zing', which he used to add in all fields. I still laugh when I think about the memory; when he said, 'Put more zing...' It made other's laugh too, but it had no impact on him. He tried inspiring us, saying, 'Put more zing...'

I noticed in class that not only me, but another girl, Archana Mallick, a professor's daughter from JNU also enjoyed his company as I used to. If you consider someone as a rival then it is necessary to know her background. My intensity of suspicion increased, as she was from the same class and section, and shared the front bench with Manav. I was shocked; I was living in a fool's paradise. I had never thought someone else could also love Manav; my supremacy in the world was lost. Filmy girls like me are more suspicious. I prefer movies and soap operas to games and music. When Manav started going to the JNU and IIT campus, instead of playing with me, I switched to more movies and soap operas. The inherent suspicion from soap operas made me more insecure. Manav loved a short hairstyle and that bloody damsel had it. Boys always love to see the neckline and back neckline naked and if a string is attached to it, it adds to the imagination. I am sure this is exactly what Manav must be experiencing. He was free to watch her back neckline every moment.

Immediately, I cut my long hair to short, with layered bangs and curls and I was amazed how well it suited me. Yes, Manav noticed it too, but not in the way I was expecting.

Manav just asked, "Why did you cut your long hair?"

"For you, I know you like short hair," I answered him.

"Who told you? You look good in long hair, but this is still better," he commented.

From that day, I have the same hairstyle and do not feel the necessity to change it. Rather, the parlour girl grew into a woman, but I hadn't changed either my hairstyle or parlour, until I shifted to Dwarka.

However, this was not enough to extinguish my suspicion. The girl was from the JNU Campus and Manav went there every day either to the JNU or IIT campus, maybe only the JNU campus. I changed my routine and started cycling with him to the JNU campus.

The first time I urged Manav to let me cycle with him, he looked blank, but he did not refuse to take me, just asked me, "What will you do there?"

"I will also play something..." To get Manav, if the need arises to play, then certainly I was determined to play anything.

"It's better not to go there; you are not from the same campus," he replied.

However, this reply made me adamant to accompany him; I smelt something fishy.

"Why? I will not disturb you or do you have any other motive in not taking me?"

Reluctantly he accepted, but later, when I faced the consequences, I realized why he was reluctant at first.

For the first few days, I was merely a spectator to his matches. I was the only one watching him play in the basketball court. Soon, I bought a badminton racket that I felt was the best game for a girl like me to play. Unfortunately, despite my best efforts at the game, I lost every game I played. I was neither aware of rules nor I did I derive any pleasure in the game. The only reason I played the game was Manav. While one of my eyes was always fixed on him, the other looked around to find Archana. My heart always feared if she also comes to watch Manav playing, then what? However, I was fortunate that she was not interested in this line of race.

The cultural program ended, but I did not have much success. While I was stuck here at the JNU campus, I was fixed. Some people watched me as though as I was a fantasy. Few boys started teasing me and commented on me, my attire and other things, poking fun at me. Boys usually have a perverse attitude, where they look at girls, as though they are things instead of girls, especially if they are not from their area, community or their campus and it was obvious that I was not from their campus. I now understood why Manav was reluctant to take me with him. Nevertheless, it was too late; the Mahabharata had started already.

On that day I was not playing, but rather watching Manav from one corner of the basketball ground. A guy touched my breast and pushed me to the basketball pole. He pushed me so hard, I just screamed and was terrified at his move; he not only pushed me, but pressed me with the pole and kept on pressing me with his body. I sensed the hardness of his body; he said, "Get out of this guy; otherwise, I will throw you out of his life."

I was so terrified I did not hear all his words. Only later, I realized what he meant.

However, Manav was well aware of his move. Manav was cautious and knew of the guy's intention; before I could say something (though I was not in a condition to ask anything), he threw the guy out of my reach. A filmy style fight started. He was a senior guy and from the campus, so he was at an advantage, as other guys joined him.

Manav was well built and man as he was, he could at most tackle about two to three boys; they were more than ten of them. Manav received the thrashing of his life before my eyes and all I could do was stand by as a spectator. More than 10 minutes passed, before his friends from the campus could come to his rescue; some professors on their evening walk rescued Manav. By then, the damage had been done.

Manav returned like a wounded tiger and I could not even bear to look at him. I was the cause for everything that happened. I blamed myself; I knew all this happened because of my suspicion about him.

He lied to uncle, telling him it happened in a road accident, as a speeding car hit his cycle from behind and sped away after hitting it. To lend truth to his story and make it appear real, he damaged his cycle. Uncle and Pranab Bhai questioned the story. Since I was the prime witness, my verdict would be believed as the truth, so I nodded my approval to Manav's story and narrated it in the same way that he had told it to them. Uncle took him to their family doctor to attend to his injuries.

--Ω--

When rivalry exits love manifolds itself. The chapter ended for a few days. Manav stopped going to the JNU campus and nobody opened any dialogue about it. Meanwhile, I became a detective and started enquiring about the truth behind the entire episode.

The truth that came out was fascinating enough; Rakesh, the guy who hit me was Archana's boyfriend. He was studying for the first year in BA, doing his history honours at DU, Ram Lal Anand College. The campus boy loved Archana and she was dating him. But where I fitted into their love trilogy is still a mystery. That day, I was convinced that there is always an element of truth in what one hears. In Delhi, every boy or girl always has his or her backup ready, if plan A fails, they are ready to execute plan B, C or D.

I was only an excuse that Rakesh used to take his revenge on Manav.

Revenge and jealousy became engraved in me. I was waiting to spit my vengeance on her and the day arrived soon enough, during the preparation phase of the school's Annual Sports Meet. Though I was the worst player in any sport, I enlisted my name for basketball and badminton. No matter how bad a player I was, my participation could not be refused. I knew Archana would participate, at least, in these two events and Manav was the champion of the school, so he participated in all events.

In game periods, I participated more in basketball. Archana, undoubtedly a good player, also joined the game. The practice was a mix of boys and girls, where senior players as well as Manav provided playing tips. Manav and Archana were fortunately in the same house, but both played in their own category. The participation in the event would be house wise and boys and girls would play separate games.

As the event days grew closer, we practiced more. I had more interest in Archana, rather than the game, I was searching for the moment to take my revenge; the question was when and how? I was there only as a watchdog for Manav to protect him from the demon, Archana Mallick.

As long as we girls participated, we were fine; Archana and I shared eye contact. However, on the eve of the mega event, I retaliated; I slapped her hard that it echoed ten times around the ground. Everyone froze, wondering what happened. Immediately, the sports teacher took hold of me and marched me straight to the principal's office. Our judgement began. I was happy and proud, I had managed my payback and it came at the right time, when every student of the school was present. But Archana was red-faced, trembling in anger as she did not get the chance to hit me back; I was immediately taken into custody of friends and the teacher.

The judgment bench comprised of the principal, class teachers, sports teacher, physics and biology madams. The principal's office became the courtroom and I was accused of the charges; one, serious misconduct with a senior, that is, manhandling; two, not obeying the ground rules and violating the sportsman spirit; three, being an obstacle while a game was going on. For one act; three charges.

The case began:

The principal asked me, "Pranami, you slapped your senior, Archana. Is it true?"

First, I looked at her and boldly answered, Yes, sir.

That's what I wanted; let everyone know why I slapped her. If she thinks she is the only one who knows how to play a gimmick then she is wrong. She had never thought that her gimmick would bring such trouble; she became pale faced.

The principal was agitated hearing my intrepid, answering 'yes' without any penance, perhaps, his thought wobbled between the pros and cons and he said again, "You have violated school norms and it's of a serious nature."

"I know it, sir."

"Then why did you slap her?" asked the principal.

Before coming to the principal's office, I had thought I would not disclose the truth, as unnecessarily things would be exaggerated, but seeing Archana's daring and heroic face, I changed my thoughts and decided to confess. She was proud about the way she felt she took revenge. Now she will become pale-faced when the truth is unveiled.

"She kissed Manav."

Now I confessed the truth. My answer was stunning and astonished everybody; they could not have expected such an answer. All the jury members looked at each other. They wanted to laugh but they could not.

"Call Mr Manav," the principal ordered and the sports teacher stood up and opened the principal's office door. At a glance, I saw all the students gathered outside the door in pin-drop silence.

Manav came inside and the principal repeated, "Is what Pranami's saying true?"

"What is she saying, sir?"

The principal hesitated and the sports teacher took over from him and asked, "Did Archana kiss you on the basketball ground?"

"Yes, sir," Manav replied firmly.

"You can go now," the sports teacher gave the order, but the principal asked him to wait, "No stay back," and Manav came back.

"Pranami, you love Manav?" asked the principal.

"Yes, sir," I replied confidently.

"You, miss Archana, you also love him," the principal wanted clarity and I won the battle.

She hesitated, looked from top to bottom, thought many times before answering and it worked for me. Meanwhile, the principal asked me, "This is why you slapped her?"

"Yes...sir," I gained courage and confidence, as if I had won the Manav battle, without any bloodshed.

Then I narrated everything; starting from the piano class to the JNU campus fight about Manav. I spoke about the boy Rakesh, Archana's boyfriend. The story seemed interesting to them and they all listened patiently; in between, the sports teacher had just gone outside once. By the time, my story was over, Manav's father, Archana's father and my father entered inside.

The principal sent us out and a long discussion continued with our fathers inside. School normally ends by two, but the discussion was on until three thirty, and again we were called inside.

The principal announced his verdict, "This time, I am leaving you with just a warning on request of your fathers. Tomorrow you three, collect your warning letters from my office. Further, repeat of this or any mischievous activity will be dealt seriously and may lead to rustication, understood?"

"Yes, sir," three voices came out simultaneously.

"You may go now." We were out of the office in seconds; few minutes after, our fathers came and took us with them.

The next day at school, everyone's lips were sealed. We collected our warning letters and promised not to repeat it again or commit any type of nuisance in life. I got my revenge in style and things spread in whispers. The loveologists accepted we had love.

--Ω--

On returning home, Papa did not ask me a single question, he just drove our new Opel Astra. Mama was surprised to see both of us, "What happened? Father and daughter have come in chorus. Pranami, you are so late today, why? Is everything fine? Will you go back to office again?" Mama threw all her questions simultaneously to Papa and me. Papa did not answer a single one.

I was terrified about Mama's reaction; even Papa had not expressed his view and what would Bhai think! Quietly, we finished our late lunch.

After lunch, when Papa sat with his paper, Mama asked again in irritation, "Will someone tell me what happened?"

Papa, this time, gave a smile and said, You know, your daughter is in love. She has chosen the groom and simplified our way. The principal called me to school. We were coming from school.

Mama was stunned; her initial reaction was, "What?"

"Yes, she chose Manav as our son-in-law."

Papa narrated the story as the principal narrated it to him. I ran away to my room to hide from all this, and soon went to sleep.

I fell fast asleep and Mama woke me up, "Get up it's 7 o'clock already."

No one in my family asked me any more about the incident and did not restrict me from mixing up with Manav. Our love was licensed. Often, when we went out for movies, I also saw Archana and Rakesh going out together to Priya and the newly built PVR shows. The feeling and thoughts of those days were amazing; we would watch movies in the front row, when the tickets cost just Rs 8 and we watched every new movie with our pocket money.

That time, I thought I took my revenge, but later, I thought I must thank Archana, as I was safe and confident of my love only because of her. No one asked me about this, which meant all my family members accepted our love.

Once at PVR, while entering for a movie, I was behind her and expressed my gratitude, "Sorry, Archana, I regret my misdeed, but I thought I must say thanks to you. Because of you, we became so close and our family gave the nod, we are now free birds. So, thanks."

She wanted to say something, but the checker interrupted, "Madam, your, get it checked there," he indicated to a female security. The time had not come for her to say the uttered words.

3

Deepa Mehta's controversial film 'Fire' was released in Delhi. As a filmy girl, I had a strong desire to see the most hyped movie of that time. The problem was how to see it? There was enough written in the newspapers about the controversy, so I couldn't tell my family that I wanted to watch the movie. Mama would straightaway refuse.

At that time, I did not know about homosexuality and lesbianism. Conversation was widespread on these issues, after its release, and colleges and schools were not spared about the controversy. Once the film gets controversial, the curiosity to watch it spirals.

I asked Manav to accompany me, but he flatly refused, "No, it's not good to watch. My father, uncle and aunty will not accept it."

"Okay, we will go without their knowledge," I said. I acted bravely and he was behaving like a shy boy.

"No, we should not watch it."

"Why, what is there?" I asked curiously, expecting that he must know something.

"It shows the love of Sita and Radha; two mythological characters' lesbian love, which our society does not accept. People protest about it," Manav tried to convince me not to go.

I asked, "Do you know how?"

"No, how do I know?"

"Then let us watch it, what is the harm in watching it?" I asked.

"Nothing," Manav agreed there was nothing wrong in watching the movie; rather, we would satisfy our curiosity.

"I have to see it," I proclaimed, rather urged.

We planned to see it at 'Ragal'. Because it does not fall in our proximity, so no family member, friend or relative could recognize us easily, as we usual watch movies at Priya and PVR.

It was our bad luck, it happened to be 3 December 1998, a school day, where I had to skip my class and Manav his IIT coaching. The same day Bajarang Dal attacked the theatre; they pulled down hoardings, tore posters and cut the screen, and beat up the viewers. The movie was screening at the point, when the kiss scene was happening between Shabana Azmi and Nandita Das. (The picture was screened up to this, when the Bajarang Dal attacked.)

Viewers rushed to save their lives and we did the same. One man from the mob beat up Manav. He slapped him a few times, but Manav did not do anything in return, which was unlike his character. When the man came to slap me, Manav pushed him away and we rushed to take shelter in the toilet.

We waited for two hours in the pungent smell, until the police took over and controlled the mob. Around fifty more viewers came out from the toilets and junk places, frightened. Among the viewers were Subham Bhai and Pranab Bhai. When our eyes made contact, we all gazed down.

--Ω--

No one told the family the truth; we were all in the same mess. Then the analysis phase began. I felt sorry for Manav.

He was again the worst victim, and he was beaten because of me.

Again, he told a fake fable at his house. The bruises were due to a scuffle between Arnab and him over some tricky issue in the coaching class. His Bua was not ready to believe him, "Is this for Pranami?"

"No, Bua, where does Pranami come to my class? It was due to a silly issue."

"Tell me what the issue was? If not Pranami, then some other girl, Deepa, Rohini," his Bua teased him.

"Stop, Bua, I told you it was a silly issue. Arnab sits beside me and yesterday, his chemistry book fell down from the table and a few pages came out, so he scolded me for this."

Manav acted so realistically on the fake tale, as if it had happened in exactly in that way.

"If the guy sits beside you, how he can be so hostile? He must be your good friend, there is something fishy. I don't believe you." His Bua was not ready to believe him.

"Then you ask Pranami."

"Where does Pranami come into the picture?" his Bua was shocked.

"She was present there yesterday."

"Yes, that's what I want to hear," his Bua was happy to catch us on the wrong foot. Bua presumed that Manav made up this story as an excuse to cover another story.

"It's okay, son. Now tell me what really happened?" his Bua asked again.

Manav looked at me; Aunty (Manav's Bua, I called her Aunty) asked again, "Nothing to worry, son. Tell me the truth."

Manav was about to tell the truth on hearing her assurance. I stopped him by winking at him, and said, "Actually, Aunty that guy Arnab tried to abuse me. He is his good friend, but said some words like 'sexy bomb' and 'sweet explosive' about me, which he didn't like and so he slapped him and the fight began."

Aunty guffawed loudly, I was stunned. Had my fake been caught or what? After few minutes, when she stopped, she said, "Why be afraid of this, he is your boyfriend and lover, how can he endure such comments about you?"

We looked at each other again.

Aunty said, "It happens...new generation...young blood... your friends may not know your exact relationship...but don't hide the truth." We were pleased as Bua accepted this story.

"Manav was afraid to tell, you may think rather..." I said.

Aunty interrupted, "Nothing to worry, I will stand behind you."

We were rescued with pride. Happy that no one knew what had happened in the cinema hall. The glee of being rescued seemed more prolific with Aunt's standing behind our love.

But Manav did not say a single word about this. I was expecting a big thanks from him.

--Ω--

I was amazed and bragged about the 'fire' punch line in class. Everyone craved to know more about the movie, so 'Fire' made me popular overnight. When something is banned or is in high demand, the passion increases automatically. I was the first girl to see the movie in my class.

Indrani Banerjee must have asked me the same question, at least five times, "Tell me why they do it?"

No one at a juvenile age analyses things, they are just carried away with the present pleasure, I replied, "When their husbands are away from home or asleep, they do it."

"Was it shown how?"

"That is the beauty of art making. If they show everything how can you develop your imagination? You fool; it is a secret for every individual." I wanted to believe and behave as if I was the most knowledgeable person.

Indrani did not seem satisfied with my answer; she was looking for some dramatic and detailed answer.

I inquired about this from Leela, "Oyee...what happened to Indrani? She is repeating the same query as if I know everything on lesbianism."

She smirked, "Simple, either she is a lesbian and perhaps practicing it."

"How can you say this?" my curiosity to see a live example increased.

"She is!" Leela emphasized.

"You know about her! Any evidence."

Leela laughed, "The entire class knows it, and how are you such a fool? Don't you see she is interested only in girls? She was caught in the act with her neighbour."

"Ohaa I see," I frowned in surprise.

"You don't know anything," Leela smirked again.

"What?"

"You confine yourself within Manav. How could you know all this?"

"What happened, tell me?" I was curious.

"In Manav's class, there was a guy, who is a gay," said Leela.

"Let me ask Manav."

"Yes, you better ask him."

"What is his name?" I asked.

"Alfred Pinto."

I felt embarrassed; I had very little knowledge about my surroundings.

The next moment, I asked Manav, "You know Alfred Pinto, is he a gay?"

He paused, but my curiosity didn't allow me to wait, I asked again, "Is he a gay?"

"I don't know?"

"Why you don't know, the entire school knows and both of us are not aware of it, we have not even sensed this?" I felt sorry about my ignorance.

Manav smiled, "Is it mandatory to know all this?"

"Yes...yes, we must know about our surroundings, girls think that I am a fool and they are much ahead in this regard."

I felt sorry for me not being in the world.

--Ω--

When I started digging, many things came out, who is doing what, who had done what, and who is in a relationship and with whom? I was astonished, girls kept their relationships secret; I am the only odd one, who proclaimed it.

Sagarika loved Dipankar, Pritish loved Swati, Raghav loved Sangamitra and many more; they were from my class only. Juniors had their own ways. The exception was Kiran from my class twelve; she loved a junior boy. Usually, girls love either the same batch mate or a senior guy, but she was the exception.

Leela was the source; she had come closer to me among my friends. She had done almost everything and had all the answers to all queries. I always pretended how she knew all this? When I asked, she simply smiled, but my question was not answered, which meant that I would not quit so I asked again.

"It is just like yar," said Leela.

I seemed more confused, "It is not just for me?"

"You keep your eyes and ears open, and you will know things."

Things are always easy for a professional. I preferred to be a listener.

Leela continued, "You know, Pranami, Sagarika is dating Amlan."

"She has a love break?"

"No break up. She dates both Dipankar and Amlan."

"That's interesting but how do you know?" authenticity was necessary, otherwise, things would be counted as gossip.

"I did not believe it, but I saw her with Amlan and they were too intimate."

"Maybe she had a breakup with Dipankar?" I asked.

"Yar, I told you that's not true, as the next day, I saw her with Dipankar."

It's awesome, yar. How beautiful, two at a time, two loves! I was amazed about the wild thought.

"It's not love, it's danger!"

"Whatever maybe, yar. As long as things are going her way, everything is fine."

Leela and I became very close those days; she gradually came up with her story too, as girls are never ashamed of sharing their sex life between them. They find fun in sex. She was in a relationship with her neighbour, Rohan. Our relationship had common grounds, so our companionship progressed without obstacles. Rohan was five years senior to her and was doing his MBA in IMT, Ghaziabad. He made daily trips up and down in DTC and Blue line buses.

"When did you share your feelings?" I always asked her, as for me to be in a relationship meant your love had to be with you at all times.

She answered, "We have entire nights and holidays."

"How do you manage in the nights?"

"On the rooftop," she said.

Leela lived in the crowded area of Munirika; their rooftops were conducive for love, as they touched each other, with no gap between house to house.

Every day she told me what happened the previous day, what they talked and did. The next day, she said Rohan touched her, and next he kissed her cheek. Rohan advanced faster touched her breast and kissed her lips. Moreover, within a few days, they had even made love to each other.

She told me everything, where he touched her first, how he begged and how she made him crawl, everything.

"You know, Pranami; guys agree to do anything, before appealing for sex."

She shared many encounters and experiences every day. I was enthralled and fascinated to know her secret. That's why I said girls are never timid, discussing their own sex life and actively participate in sex gossip; perhaps boys too love to show off their sexual exploits and experience to show how manly they are. Boys always discussed where they touched and where they kissed their girlfriend. But Manav seemed to be a different gene from all of them.

Everything that I heard from her, the next time I met Manav, I narrated everything to him. I had enough gossip to talk for long hours about it with Manav. Sometimes, he listened and sometimes he did not, but I never failed to talk about this subject. His coaching class ended by six in the evening; I waited for him in front of the institute. Then we took a walk in front of the IIT institute gate or sat in the DDA Park in front of IIT, but had never tried to go inside the IIT campus and play as we did earlier. Both gradually lost interest after the fight day with Archana and Rakesh.

Sometimes, we went to 'Dadi Poti Ka Gumbad', it was less crowded and historical.

One day, I asked Manav, "You know about Sagarika and Dipankar?"

"How would I know? They are from your class and I left school such a long time ago!"

"So what, you know many of them! How couldn't you know about Sagarika and Dipankar!" I was irritated and hoped that he should know this too. It was one way of expressing a girl's love, as when a girl gets angry the boy softens in his stance.

Manav said, "Promise, yar, I don't know any of them, but what is the matter?"

"You know Sagarika dates both Dipankar and Amlan both?"

"So what, what's wrong in it?" he questioned my curiosity, I asked the question as if something had happened to them and again this irritated Manav. Girls always have an upper hand in love. But I was not in a mood to leave the discussion there and quit.

"So, it seems normal to you?" I asked again.

Here, I played a contradictory character. What I wanted to ask had not come out as it should have. I got on with the flow of that moment and it was not at all good for a girl in love with two persons simultaneously.

I asked because it expresses deep emotion. Questioning or asking about some other fellow was just a way to measure our own love too.

Manav read me very fast, "Amlan is from your class?"

"No, he is from a different college."

"So there is no contradiction. Sagarika activates her Plan 'B' with Plan 'A'."

"It is nice na...no spare time...always in love, when no Dipankar it's Amlan and when Amlan no Dipankar," my tone was full of excitement.

Manav stared at me for a long time and then replied, "Are you planning something like this or what?"

"Shut up," my voice was hard and furious. Manav never expected I would be so angry. When a thing comes to my jurisdiction, it's only pure love no adulteration. I didn't digest jokes too, because neither I could think of anyone beyond Manav nor was I ready to listen about anyone's name attached to him.

The next moment, I got up and started running...

"Wait, Pranami, I was just kidding," Manav kept on rushing after me, but I did not turn back that day.

He came to me in the night, but all my family members were present and he could not talk only to me. Papa asked him questions of his competitive exams and career. He kept on replying Papa and finally left; I did not head to him.

Before he departed, Papa had given him the chance, and asked him, "You came for some specific job Beta or you want something from Pranami...Pranami...Pranami..." Papa had asked for me, as I was not around them in the entire conversation and it had not happened before.

I had been hearing all the conversation and immediately made my appearance before Papa, but he answered, "It's nothing, Uncle, I came to meet all of you. It had been a long time since I spoke to you all and I didn't find time between my preparation and coaching classes."

"It's nice to see you, Beta. Now you go, it's late at night, Beta, you need to study hard," said Papa looking at the wall clock; it read 10.30 p.m.

He left saying good night and my anger increased, why didn't he say a single word to me despite of knowing I was angry.

The next day I waited for him in front of his coaching class.

He came saying, "Sorry, Pranami. I was just kidding, you became so serious. You know the entire night I was not able to study and sleep properly; today also, I didn't focus in class. Specifically I came to say sorry yesterday night, but Uncle caught hold of me...and you did not bother about me also!"

My anger disappeared; I became cosy with him and forgave him.

His study and life were important to me as well, but I didn't say it. That's the reason girls are very concerned, when you love, you love the boy's ambition and desire and it's not vice versa.

4

It was 12.45 at night, when the doorbell rang; it may have rung several times, before I really became aware of it. I was in deep sleep after the day's hard work. Who can it be at this time of night knocking at a single girl's door? I guess it cannot be an outsider; whoever it is must be from within the compound, maybe a sozzled man or someone very notorious. It had happened earlier. Guys, even a married man, knocked my door late at night. There was one motive and thought, a grown-up single girl maybe desperately in need of the company of a man. They were fortunate I had not reported it to the security or police. First, I thought about not opening the door, let the guy go disappointed, but he would come again.

Could it be the security? Yes, security personnel cannot be avoided maybe something mischievous may have been done and the security man was trying to call me up. But he could give a ring on the intercom?

I started thinking many ifs and buts, pros and cons and other probabilities. After the repeated ringing of the doorbell, the guy started knocking the door. I finally decided to open the door; nothing wrong could happen to me, it is a double door system so I got up. The closer I came to the door; I heard the guy call me by my name, "Pranami...Pranami..." then he knocked the door and pushed the doorbell.

It was Manav, at this time Manav's appearance made my heart beat faster, I promptly opened the door. I regretted that I should have told him not to return the car at night, as I would too manage by taxi the next day. However, whenever he comes late at night, he normally would call me and told that me he was coming.

Is someone calling using Manav's tone? Any possibilities are possible for a single girl. First, relatives, friends and community and when they fail, they take the help of outsiders and leak the news that I am single to tease and see the consequences of how I fight, rather how long I can fight before I succumb down to their fantasy with easy prey to all the dishonest men. It's the natural phenomenon in our society.

With many thoughts, I opened the door and it was Manav only. I was quite relieved.

"You were so deep asleep, I was knocking for the last ten minutes," Manav asked, while entering inside.

"Yeah...it was a hectic day," my expression showed that I am still in sleepy mode.

He put down his bags and loosened the shoelaces, all in slow motion.

I said, "You should have called me and what is the need to return the car so late at night?"

He smiled in reply and taking his bags entered into another bedroom. Nothing is hidden from him and there's nothing to guide in the place. He opted to sleep in the other bedroom, so it's his wish. I gave him one of my pyjamas and T-shirt so he could change. He did not mind wearing my clothes when he did not have anything to change into.

He took out the laptop, camera and other items from the bag and put them on the bedside. Probably, he would not go to sleep, as he had work to do. So he opted for the other bedroom.

I asked, "Have you eaten something?"

"Yeah...don't worry, I had my dinner. You go to bed, you are tired enough."

In the drawing room in the green nightlight, it was not noticeable, but it is very visible in the bedroom, Manav had a swollen face.

"Have you been beaten up?"

He preferred silence, without answering me. My heartbeat was fast enough and I asked, "Have you been beaten up again?"

"It's nothing; few people gathered in the end, probably, they had an eye on the headmaster. In the end, when I was coming back, they came like a storm and went back just like that; I did not even see anyone's face."

"This is the fate you deserve," I said to myself, but was worried about him. He opened up his shirt and trouser to change, he was never ashamed before me of anything, so there was no need of a bathroom to change his clothes, so that I should move away from the place to allow him some space. There were bruise marks over his entire body, as if they had whipped him. I could not control myself and I touched his body on the red swollen marks.

"Ohaa..." he screamed in pain.

"They have whipped you like an animal?"

"They used some sort of bamboo sticks, but sorry they damaged your car as well."

"Have you taken any medicine?" I was more bothered about him than my car.

"It's okay, no need to go to the doctor," Manav opened a bottle of black vodka 'Absolut 100'.

"It's very cold even in December this year," he advocated for the need to drink vodka. He had a penchant for black vodka and scotch.

"Pranami," he called me, "please give me a glass, a bottle of water and a slice of lemon, if you have it."

I came out from the room without saying a word about the glass and water. Meanwhile, I was thinking of making some warm water and nursing his wounds, so that he gets some relief from the body pain, but he preferred vodka to nurse his pain to me. I was disappointed.

He called me again in a louder voice so that I could hear him from kitchen, "Pranami, please bring some snacks, a mixture will do."

I provided all the four requirements that he asked. When I reached with his stuff, he had already settled down on the bed with his laptop, "Thanks, Pranami...and you go to sleep it's already late. I disturbed you. You also need to go to the bank tomorrow."

This concern increased our relationship bringing it closer. He is supposed to go to office tomorrow as well. He needs better sleep than me, to wake up earlier than me, to drive down to Ghaziabad. I am sure he has not taken leave or shown some medical problem though I cannot say? Once he sits down with his laptop, certainly, he is not going to sleep soon.

However, I had not asked him anything; he disappointed me so much that I left the room.

Before I crossed the door, he called me again, "Pranami, switch on the Wi-Fi."

"It's already on," I said, without turning towards him.

"Thanks...close the door."

I obeyed him, closed the door with a bang, and showed my frustration. However, it did not affect him.

--Ω--

I did not get any sleep; Manav was working on his recent interview of the schoolteacher, for posting it on the website, right now. He took time for the interview, neither did he become gay overnight nor did he suffer the trauma today, but what was the hurry to post it so urgently? Besides, I cannot ask Manav this question.

Once I had asked and he replied right away, "You will not understand, Pranami, you are not a gay or lesbian." The answer was so simple that I had not tried to intervene anymore between him and his penned down words. Perhaps, he is right I do not carry the empathy of lesbianism, being straight. If he feels that only a victim suffers the pain and no near and dear ones, then let him feel so, I was adamant not to clarify that close ones too suffer the same pain. So, I hardly visit his website; initially, when he started up, for few days I was a regular visitor to the site, but then I lost interest. It seems all the same stories; it maybe because I am straight, but I heard the site has gained a lot of popularity.

Sometimes, I feel he has an aim in life and he has dreams for it. However absurd the dream maybe, but I do not even have that. Without an aim, I cannot dream suitably and do not get a proper sleep. Until morning, I was upset and annoyed with him, but from the moment, he took my car I started thinking of him and now I felt a desire to get him in my bed. Very soon, I forgot that I lost my child because of him. I was hurt, when he preferred vodka to my care and service. And it was not that we had not slept together. Many times and on many occasions we have had sex. Those moments remain beautiful, but when I have memories of our way of lovemaking, the other guy automatically appears in them.

He has slept with that guy Vardhman as well. When I think of them together, a cold wave passes through my entire body, sizzled with thoughts that paralyse me. In the middle of the night, when I am unable to sleep, their postures horrify me and on many occasions, they chose my home to perform their lovemaking, as they are safe on a neutral venue. Manav took me for granted for all sorts of his mischief.

The horrifying thoughts of my life rewind. I changed my side, open my eyes; I am sleepless. The darkness of the room does not haunt me; I can see all types of assets and feel the brightness of the dark. Amazingly, I do not feel the darkness; I am an inhabitant of the darkness, for far too long.

Even after all sorts of wayward deposition in life, I can never hate him. Many times, I have thought and tried very hard to hate him, but finally, realized how disgusting I was that I would never be able to hate him. That is why still I desire him in my bed.

Again, I closed my eyes; this will change the direction of my thought process. This I experienced during those beautiful loving moments, when we had those loving days of our love, when we had many sleepless nights making love every night and yet we felt as fresh as ever, in the morning.

Romantic love cannot just happen with physical contact. One thing I am sure about my experience, to get into the world of romance just close your eyes and build your romancing world. I bet no other romance will be more amazing than this. Certainly romance never happens with eyes wide open.

Dream as long as it's in your control; the feeling is fabulous, even without sleep. I wanted to go back to my happy days of love, where we spent years and years in each other's arms. Both our families took our love as juvenile desire and this helped us to be closer. I grew up fast and became a perfect woman with possessions to lure a man. Time passed rapidly and happy days seemed like minutes. We passed school. Manav got into IIT and that too in Delhi. I was happy that I would not miss him. But he opted to stay in the hostel after the first year and I went to Kamala Nehru College for Women at Defence Colony. Manav was always a bright student and I was always an average, filmy and a dreamy girl. I neither tried for any competitive profession nor was I interested. The attitude of mine worried my family. At one time, Papa was nervous about what I would do in my life. Love is okay, but life needs some professional degree to back you up in life, as monetary independence is necessary. Papa used to say, your husband may earn in ten figures, but when it comes to independence and ego, one must possess some professionalism. Papa suggested that I should do my MBA after my graduation and had me admitted, at IIPM, one of the best business schools. I felt great and happy to be in Delhi with my love Manav.

--Ω--

I was able to think back about all this and fell asleep. In the morning, I got up early as well. Normally when the maid comes I usually wake up to open the door, this is the routine I follow and she makes tea for me then I rush around doing some other work. She comes regularly at eight. I avoid breakfast, so I have sufficient time to reach the bank on time. The other reason to skip breakfast was that I was getting fat.

But I woke up in the morning, at six, while it was still dark outside. I had barely slept for two hours; still I was fresh, exuberant and enthusiastic just because of charismatic previous time that played late night in my mind. I looked for Manav to check whether he is still awake or asleep. I am free to open his room. He had slept covering himself with a quilt on the double bed, face down and both hands stretched with gadgets scattered beside him. I loved to look at him sleep like this in his crazy postures.

I am carried away with my thoughts, as if this night had transformed me. While putting the water and milk to boil, I switched on my laptop, and hurried to check his posts. Yes, it was there, he completed it and then went to sleep. I just glimpsed through the contents to confirm it is the same post of today. I am not a regular viewer of the site. A long time ago, I had been to his website maybe a couple of times. There are plenty of changes in the style and design. I shut down the laptop and get ready with tea.

"Hello, Manav, wake up I have brewed some tea for you."

He got up suddenly, "What is the time, Pranami?"

I was not sure of the exact time, "Sometime after six," I said noticing his anxiety, so better not tell him the exact time.

He relaxed a bit.

I asked him, "Why do you want to know the time?"

"I have to go to office."

"There is enough time, first drink your tea." I sat down on the bed, with two full cups of tea.

"Just a moment," and he entered into the bathroom. That was normal, but he took only one minute to come back.

Taking the first sip, he said, "You have made it?"

"Why, who else is there to make it?" I threw the question back at him. I was confused whether he was asking it in the right sense or the wrong sense, because I have not tasted it yet.

"It's awesome." I feel shy like a teenage girl and drink my first sip.

"Really, I am not joking, Pranami, it's awesome."

I thought it is the transformation effect. It tastes good; perhaps our casual body was in need of some spark. But the euphony enhances my self-esteem. I made the tea the way the maid makes it for me. It is the same red label tea and I put in the extra five ingredients she puts in while boiling water, ginger and other spices, as shown in the TV ad of the same red label tea.

Silently, we sipped the tea until the last drop disappeared from the cup. At night, two things crossed my mind. One, why is he gay? And the other thing he loves me, shares everything with me and had sex with me, still he proclaims himself as gay. I need to find out the science behind it, the science behind the gayness.

In the silence, our eyes made contact, there is still love and care for me in his eyes and that's what why I am with him early in the morning in search of it.

I asked, as soon as we finished the cup, "You have not told about the school headmaster?"

Manav was dazed. As I never asked about his stories, obvious surprise erupted in his eyes.

I said again, "You were too disturbed in the night, so I didn't ask. I mean what is the story of the headmaster and did he also get beaten up?"

Manav smiled, probably seeing my curiosity and said, "No, he was not beaten. The headmaster said these people were hired goons and sent by his wife so they would never harm him. His wife always kept a watch on him, and knew of our secret meeting. So, she fixed everything in advance."

"How terrible?"

"Not as terrible as his life. My pain has gone; the bruise marks will go in one or two days, but the mental trauma the headmaster passes through is more painful. He is in close arrest in his own family, such as the gaffer has committed a gaffe of a serious nature."

"Why does he not protest, he is a learned man and must know of his liberties?" I asked.

I wanted to prolong the conversation and enjoyed talking to him. The dark was distant by the emergence of light. It's morning and Manav kept looking outside, many times. He was in hurry to pack up. I noticed his intensity and engaged him with my questions, which he simply cannot avoid. Though the sunrays have not fallen on the glass to penetrate into the rooms, it was not too late. Sunrays kissed my side of the room first, when it was visible in the gap of Vardhman City Mall and the other building. It rose from the gap and I kept waiting when the golden rays will illuminate us.

"It is not so easy, Pranami, social bonds are circulated in one's blood and very difficult to get rid of it and in this northern part of our country people won't hesitate to take the headmasters life."

"Who will take his life, his wife?" I asked to lengthen our conversation.

"Why not, even his children may do that. He is very insecure; they threaten him many times and might kill him one day."

"How ridiculous, he is the man of their family, he built the family and they don't have any respect for him?"

"Why will they respect him? According to their view, he is an evil and sinful man who deserves no sympathy and love from anyone."

"It is you who admits this?"

It is his nature. He never accepts social boundaries. His wish and work are his happiness.

I asked again, "Is he not aware of the law?"

Manav laughed. "Law is not at all applicable in social bonds."

I am delighted to hear all this from him, as at least he is now thinking of social bondage. My prayers have worked.

Manav continues, "I am not saying his wife is on the wrong side. What she is doing is best suited to taking care of their social life and providing a healthy life to her children. But my point is why you don't give freedom to the man who serves them like a slave for so many years."

This time it is my turn to laugh and I laugh loudly. "What freedom does he need, freedom of sex?"

"Not exactly, give freedom to his life, at best, think about what he wants, otherwise, he will die and that's what his family wants now."

I can very well ask Manav about the headmaster's sex life that normally goes hidden in all cases. These people have a sole desire for sex and they fidget to grab it in all their consciousness. I was completely sure that once I asked, Manav would not hide anything from me, but I was not at all in a mood to discuss sex. The golden rays tries to penetrate the window glass. I opened up the curtain of the window and allowed all of us to make a complete bath of it. I really feel more cherished when the rays touch my body. It is fabulous to have a golden ray bath after a sleepless night. This is where Manav slipped away from me.

He got up from the bed, I caught his hand and made him sit again, "Don't go, soak in the pleasure of the sun light, grab it in both hands, your entire day will be absolutely magnificent."

He obeyed me, but looked at me with eyes wide open. It was in our loving days when I used to make rightful commands and he would abide by it all. He must have been flabbergasted with my act, as it was not in me for the last many years.

The golden era is back, I merged in the golden rays with my eyes closed. It felt as if after so many years I had some happiness. I closed my eyes and started grasping the golden sun light through the glass; the room filled with love aroma seemed fantastic. From the last three years, I was staying in this place, but never ever sensed it.

"Pranami, let me get ready; otherwise, I will be late," Manav asked, he seemed agitated and it showed in him for the last fifteen minutes.

"Right, you get ready and let me arrange some breakfast for you."

I left the room without giving him a chance to speak. He came out of the room within forty minutes and with all his gadgets, fully prepared to leave.

I was waiting for him at the dining table; he asked, "Really you have made something for me?"

His expression showed he was not expecting that I could serve him anything at the table. I can best cook Maggi or serve bread at breakfast. He does not like Maggi, so I was left with only one option, which was bread and butter.

He was happy having his breakfast. So after one bite, he asked, "Are you not having breakfast?"

"No, I have not even brushed."

Actually, I felt heavenly feeding him, my hunger was satisfied seeing him blissful.

Halfway through his bites, he screamed, "Oh...shit...I have forgotten to tell you, you will need a mechanic for your car."

"Is it so badly damaged, any problem with the engine?"

"No...no, it's not crashed. There are scratch marks. The goons hammered the body, no internal damage; otherwise, how would I have travelled so far?"

"It's nothing. You told me in the night as well."

"I thought you will be upset about it. You love your car very much...I know how obsessed you are about it."

He was relieved, as my expresion was not fanatic. He is right; I loved my car very much. It is the last gift Papa gifted me in July 2008 'the Honda CRV' just a month before his demise.

He finished breakfast and got up to depart, just at that time the maid arrived. I was possessed and became cautious. These people carry plenty of thoughts and imagination.

Manav uttered the day's last sentence, "Okay, Pranami. I am going."

"But how will you go?" I asked, while he collected all his gadgets.

"I will take an auto to the metro station and then go by metro," he replied simply.

"No, you take the car."

"But how will you go?" he asked.

"I will manage by auto."

My voice was firm, so he could not argue with me or show any reluctance in accepting my offer.

I handed over the key and said, "Drive carefully, it's the rush hour and give me a call when you reach."

He nodded and departed quickly, as he was late and I came back just as quickly as I was also getting late.

The maid asked, "Didi, shall I make tea for you?"

She must have seen the utensil.

"No...I have had my tea," I told her and entered into the bathroom.

I quickened the speed and came out from the bathroom really soon; otherwise, I would be late and I do not like to be late for office. Especially as I did not want to spoil today's mood.

5

The title read, "Conflict in mass with bouquet of sweet romance."

The proclivity to read about his recent post made me restless throughout the day. Unfortunately, I did not get a single moment free to open up the website *myrelationship.com*. The entire day was fabulous; I worked with plenty of energy and enthusiasm. I reached the bank before time when the sweeper was sweeping all the rooms, the staff started coming after fifteen minutes of my arrival. The work acceleration was faster and the investment was more than any normal day. I sold out more than ten life insurance policies and more than twenty applications were received for credit cards. Two house-building loans, three personal loans and two car loans were approved. It gave me immense pleasure and doubled my joy, a satisfying working day. I wondered and fasten the words 'the mind controls the entire body'; otherwise, with a sleepless night; probably, the day would have been sloppy and sluggish.

But I left the bank at six, when things came down to routine. My appetite was agitated to read the post. Manav called me after reaching his office. He is always obedient; it is the reason despite of all odds that I still love him. As soon as I reached home, I switched on the laptop and settled down to read.

The content read:

He walks slowly with the breeze and talks gently; nothing seems so vivacious inside him. But when he opened up, there is a tornado crafted passionately and ready to spew poison inside him. As we continue with our conversation, I realize a sharp and loving mind lies behind the innocent looking face.

When Delhi coloured to celebrate pride parades, he went dormant and grounded himself. Earlier he used to cry, cry like a baby missing the occasion. He is not far away from the heart of the country and always remembers the days he had been in Delhi with his partner. They escaped from the village and flew to Delhi in support of their relationship.

"Delhi is to Delhi in support of their relationship. care there," said the school headmaster. *The other guy is a 'general shop owner' in his village. Unfortunately, the other guy is not techno savvy and very frightened of their present condition. However, he manages and updates the partner of the changing world.*

"This is our love," said the school head master, *"we loved talking for long hours. We are no more juvenile lovers with illogical thoughts. So we preferred to talk of the world and Sorbhoday also updates himself."*

The high school headmaster, Sambhu who teaches maths and science is in love with a general shop owner Sorbhoday, how amazing. However, they are not teens, in the village; they are gaffers in their lateral age. Sambhu has three children, the elder one aged eighteen and the younger one twelve, whereas, Sorbhoday has four. The elder one is sixteen and the younger one is just four.

Three years ago, they flew to Delhi to strengthen their love. They stayed fifteen days in Kotla, but their family then searched them out and the misery in their life began. First, they were beaten up badly, in front of the entire village and then kept under house arrest.

The high school headmaster has a government job; he goes to school and comes back under surveillance. He has high blood pressure and diabetes. When the doctor advised him for a walk, he would do this for an hour, in the evening.

When I asked, "This tense and confined life will further degrade your health."

He replied fretfully, "Who cares. Everyone, every family member wants our death. If it comes in a natural way its fine; otherwise, one day they will all kill us."

There is lot of pain and distress in his voice.

"How can they kill you, there is the law. This community and government will certainly help you."

Mr Sambhu smiles grimly at the question and vehemently lacerates his emotion, "Certainly not, social justice is over and above our law of court."

Sambhu was married when he was nineteen to a girl of sixteen, before he discovered he was a gay. Time forced him to fit into the normal and customary role of a husband and father.

Answering how and when he revealed himself as gay, he said, "I never got pleasure having sex with my wife and was never inclined to have sex with a female. Instead, I fantasized a male body, when I was engaged in sex with my wife. The ecstasy of having sex that I enjoy with a male body was not possible with a woman. I was keen and felt an attachment to men rather than grown-up women. Before deciding if I was definitely gay, I experimented with my thoughts and emotions. I watched 'A' rated movies, read 'Debonair Magazine,' stood in front of photographs of naked women and fantasized sex with many film stars, but the impact was the reverse. I was more inclined to a male partner."

The life of Sorbhoday is more or less the same. He also performed the duty of husband and father, produced children *and cared for them, earned money and saved for their future, educated them and dreamed of their prosperous life.*

It is not education or high society's fancy desire. His heart, mind and body are prone to have sex with a male. What is the fault in him, if god has made him like this, aspiration will also reciprocate in the same manner. God nourished the desire in him and provided the way out.

Mr Sambhu said, "Think simply, why did he become a gay when all sources of straight means were available and also provided him a life partner, his wife? It was because of God that he was born in my proximity. It was god's wish, nothing else, otherwise it could not have just happened in small towns like Alwar."

They think their love is heavenly and god's desire.

"Even Sorbhoday's life is worse than me; his stance is like a donkey, who works with no pride. We have not seen each other for more than a month. He comes to his shop, but his wife accompanies him and she does not let him move an inch away from her watchful eye. Sorbhoday does not know to use computers or the internet, so he stays like a frog in the well. I communicate to the world. Certainly, after few months or days, no one will find Sambhu and Sorbhoday. It will be all over, so before we meet our fate, let the world know our story, our love and inclination."

He groaned in despair. His voice reflected the horror and fear of losing his life and love.

That's his story, the other side of what people know, where betrayal and infidelity lacerate every moment and thought of one's life.

This is proof that to be a gay is very tough. First, the man struggles within himself about the reason he became gay, a single abstracted soul among thousands. When he has come out from that stance after a courageous fight and struggle to announce to the world that he belongs to the other community, and is declared as gay, friends and family alienate him. A treacherous life waits ahead...very few people succeed and survive, while the maximum number succumb at various stages.

There is nothing wrong in being homosexual; nothing changes other than one's sex life. He/she works, thinks and has the right and reason to live in society. When the entire world heeds to hedonism and there is a free talk of sex in the air, why are homosexuals away from the ecstasy?

I read this post not once, but four times. He had a message and it was loud and clear.

--Ω--

A two-minute power failure made me aware of the contiguity; darkness surrounds me, both inside and outside. It is eight in the evening.

I sat for almost an hour reading his website. I knew the story. Manav had narrated everything about Mr Sambhu, but I read it four times to find out the state of Manav's mind. I wanted to see how far he had flown within these days and presumed where he will land.

I felt like having coffee, as the entire day I had not eaten anything because I was tense. First, I entered into the kitchen. The maid had made dinner and I needed to put it into the oven, but suddenly I felt a strong desire to have tea at the tea stall. I locked the home, picked up my phone and walked out. A cold wind was blowing; I wore a T-shirt and trousers, with a scarf around my neck.

The roadside tea makers make good tea and sipping it on the street, standing with men, as the nodal point of their haunted gazing eyes, who try to make fun of me, sometimes raises confidence to encounter them and the advances feeling of adventure within me. The tea maker know me, so the comments were made in the initial days, when I became a resident of Dwarka. But now people just stare at me. In today's stance, I have the affinity to read these hawk eyes, to get confidence in my new avatar.

The tea stall man served tea in a glass, in the traditional style. The tea was good, it felt good because I am blossoming and seem weightless. With the tea glass in one hand, I phoned Manav. I felt the desire to be his shadow, always. Moreover, being far apart, the phone is the medium to get in touch.

He responded soon, "Yes, Pranami, tell me what happened?"

"Nothing, I want to confirm where you are."

"I am in office, is there anything that you want?"

I am a little surprised, though I am not wearing a watch, I guess the time must be eight-thirty and he is still in office.

In the same surprised tone, I ask him, "You are still in office?"

"I had a meeting at eight. I just finished the meeting and you called. I am leaving office. Are you at the bank? Tell me why did you call me?" he questioned.

"I left the bank early, at six and was reading your website."

"Really?" his laughter echoed over the phone. He could not believe that I would surf and visit his site.

"Yes, I read the entire story and I called to congratulate you. It is amazing and fabulous."

"Are you joking?" he asked surprised.

"Not at all."

Meanwhile, I finished tea, a little boy took the glass from me and put it in a bucket for washing. I searched my lower pocket to pay the tea stall owner, but realized that I do not have any money.

"Just one minute, Manav," putting Manav on hold, I searched again, but it was a mock exercise, as I had not brought any money with me.

"Sorry, Bhai, I have forgotten to bring money, if you send the little boy I will give it to him," I told the tea stall owner.

"No problem, madam, give it some other day," the stall owner said politely, and got engaged in filtering the tea to the kettle.

I went back to my phone conversation, "Yes, Manav, where were we? I was telling you about your post."

"You tell me where are you and what are you doing?" Manav interrupted.

His anxious tone pleased my heart; yes, I am going in the right direction.

"Nothing, I came down for a cup of tea and had forgotten to bring money."

"Tea at this time?" Manav was surprised.

"What else vodka or scotch? If you were here, I may have considered to give you company," I taunted him.

"Don't joke, tell me where are you?" his concerned tone thrilled me; I was on the right track.

"Nothing, I told you I just came down for a cup of tea and you know sometimes, I do come down for a walk or some street food."

He seemed convinced.

I asked again, "We were in the middle of our discussion; tell me why do you write about gay people?"

He was stunned and bemused; he never ever expected a question of this sort from me, as he preferred to be silent on the phone.

But I repeated my question, "What do you want to extract by writing on them?"

He again preferred silence.

I said, "Are you listening?"

"Yes, I am listening."

"Then why don't you reply?"

"What to tell you, Pranami, you know everything."

"I don't know anything, Manav. I really don't know."

I was talking, while on the move, a little ahead of the tea stall, at the crossing, about fifty meters away from the apartment's main entrance, a motor cycle braked heavily. I nearly had a collision that the motor cyclist avoided; it was my fault.

I had not looked around and walked freely, "Sorry," I uttered to the motor cyclist.

"Madam, please, look before you step out and please don't cross the road with your mobile switched on," the man advised, which I overlooked and walked away.

Manav heard the brake sound and my sorry, probably the advice of the motor cyclist, "What happened again, Pranami, what did you do?" he was worried.

"It's nothing, I missed a collision, lucky enough, but where were we?"

"Pranami, is this the time to talk. I am tired and want to leave office and you are in a crowded place."

"I am just few steps before my home, is it fine, now can we talk?"

"To give them exposure," Manav said, as he was finally crushed with all the questions.

"Exposure of what? Sex or love?" he preferred silence again over my question, but I said again, "you know, your TCOWYA (To Come Out What You Are) method will lead some people into danger and particularly Mr Sambhu, the high school headmaster will become an endangered creature for his family."

"How can you say this? Maximum people will extend their supportive hand in rescue of them and it has been proven." Manav gets irritated; I turned in my key and entered into the house.

"You have already mentioned that Mr Sambhu feels life's insecurity. Now when he gets exposed, will his family tolerate it?"

"We will talk on this subject some other day, Pranami, or let me call you on reaching home."

"Sure you will call me?" I asked.

His grim face blossomed, "Sure, Pranami, sure…" and the call was disconnected.

--Ω--

Again, after dinner, I visited his website. Let me make it clear to you all, after a three-hour thorough study of the website, having visited every page and all the links, I felt if you are a gay, lesbian, transgender or have a live-in-relationship you will enjoy the site. Nothing was left out for the common and straight people. The website's appearance had changed a lot, from the first time that I had visited it. There is a home page and five other tags: About us, in relationship, know your partner, join us and feedback.

In the home page, there are photographs of gay guys and paintings of various poses of male nudity.

The tag 'About us' is just one small page of three paragraphs and he writes about his motto, ethics and aspiration for the gay and lesbian sexuality. TCOWYA summarizes in three paragraphs about the life and fundas of gays. I am sure earlier he had given the tag 'About me' the sole proprietor of the website. Who joins him in running the website? A big question mark rises in me, is it Vardhman, his partner nowadays?

The tag 'in relationship' are stories of people like Mr Sambhu and his love, placed list wise with headings and each story is hyperlinked to the concerned page.

The tag 'know your partner' is an interesting one. Here the thoughts, encounters, experience and science of homosexuality are enumerated, diversity of personality and great change of thoughts.

'Join us' tag welcomes the gay man to the group. A user ID and password are provided to enter and sign up for the new user. I had signed up as a new user. Six questions are to be filled in the boxes: name, profession, address, mobile number, valid email ID and category. In the category field of the dropdown menu, it displayed, gay, lesbian, bisexual and transgender. And then the submit button. I filled all the requisite data to know what comes next, but did not submit it.

The feedback tag is meant for people's opinion about the site and how it has helped them to come out from atrocities that they faced in society.

Overall, after navigating all links and pages of his website and then comparing it with other gay websites, I can mark it as 'very good' category. There is absolutely nothing for straight people, but some straight people may exist like me, who may be wondering about and are haunted for love from a gay or lesbian.

Along with science, he put lots of his experience and thoughts in it.

--Ω--

He did not call the same night, neither the following day. On the same night, I had a sound sleep and the following night, , again I started navigating the website. Nothing new has been added overnight, but I was still amazed to read the absurd stuff in the 'know your partners' tag.

There are ten answers to a question, different views from different angles said because of varied perception. As I navigate, the questions do arise in bold and underlined, such as, what is homosexuality? Do gays differ in attitude from straight ones? Who indulged in it most? Is a homosexual safe from HIV? Like this, many other questions and their probable answers. Giving a pass to all, I was stuck in a point, which reads, "What is the age factor in homosexuality? Is gayism just a phase young people go through in India?"

There is a brief two page report on it. It is worth narrating the gist of the report.

There is no age boundary for homosexuality. Evidence exist that more people at an older age indulge in homosexuality. The reason being distress in their sex-life with their spouse and not getting pleasure from the present sex life is a strong reason. There is another reason that cannot be evaded, which is experimentation and fun. In these cases, older people get involved with the younger people.

Coming to the young generation of India, gayism or being homo may be a passing phase of age. No one knows for sure what makes someone gay or lesbian. There is no accurate science behind gayism or homosexuality. People may have many theories, but it is based on a certain study, on a certain group of people. People often realise that they're gay when they're very young, very few people observe later in life. Many people ask themselves at some point during their teenage years: am I gay? Whether they are gay, bisexual or heterosexual time tells. At a certain age, sex hormones start pulsing through our bodies. The sex in the air and culture ramifies these desires to experiment. This is the time our body tries to quench the desires of sex without even knowing what is sex. And it is the time boys or girls stay apart from the family or create a distance from family. They get knowledge, but not the proper stuff to satisfy the strong sex desire, which further amplifies. Here they start experimenting with available resources such as with friends, neighbours and dear ones. These practices are more in hostel life, and have the tendency to eliminate the cause, when in contact with the opposite sex. For those who decide that they are, it can sometimes be hard to tell other people. However, if this is the case, it is better to be sooner than later make the society know about you.

The same night, I wished to call him and ask some questions about the website, but his phone was out of coverage area. I tried for another three to four times and went to bed. Soon, I was fast asleep.

In the morning at 4.15, I got a call from him, "Hello," I answered the call, but was still drowsy.

"You called me in the evening; around ten, I received five missed calls," asked Manav.

I was irritated to be woken up from my sleep and soon realized there was something fishy.

With the support of my pillow, I raised myself a little bit and said, "Where were you, your phone was out of reach?"

"I was in the hospital and there was no signal in the basement. Just now, I came out from the hospital and got the SMS about your five missed calls."

"What happened?" I was terrified.

"Nothing happened to me, it is the old guy of 303. His son is not here and the old man suffered a heavy cardiac arrest. Luckily, the old lady raised an alarm in time and we brought him to the hospital," he said with smile, as he knew of my scared and concerned nature.

"Okay, how is the old man now?"

"Fine, survived...I was there until now, but I have to go to office. As he is out of danger, I thought I would take a nap before office."

"Who is there with the old man?" my tone was very concerned, as only the victim knows how painful it is to be alone in hospital. It happened to me; a woman in the night in Delhi is hopeless and hapless for all concerns, and his wife was an old woman.

"Few relatives arrived at the hospital around 3 o'clock. Things are manageable. Moreover, his son had gone to Mumbai and will land in Delhi within half an hour," clarified Manav.

"Right, you go fast, as you will get for sleep for a maximum of two to three hours." I looked again at my watch.

"It's okay; you tell me why you called me."

"It's nothing important or urgent so we can talk later," I said.

"Are you angry at me? That day I promised to call you, but was so tired that I could not even think I was capable of handling a phone call. Sorry for that, Pranami."

"I know, so don't be sorry and go."

"Tell me...you have pardoned me?"

He was being melodramatic, I said anxiously, "I am dropping the call; you go and have some sleep."

He did not say anything and cut the call immediately. After that, I could not get sleep again.

--Ω--

I had lost my parents in this condition, both in Delhi's chilled winter night and cried alone on the lap of Manav. The first to go was my mother, on a Gurgaon road when a speeding BMW hit our Honda Accord. The driver was injured but survived. Papa was out of state, on a business trip to Bhutan and Shubam Bhai had already left us and was on the verge of settling with his friend in America. He had studied in America and never thought of coming back.

The Delhi police called me; they admitted Mama at RML hospital. It was all over when I reached the hospital. But I do not know how Manav knew about it; he reached with two of his friends. He undertook all the formalities in the hospital and mortuary. I kept on weeping; Papa was able to reach the burial ground.

The following year, in January, Papa came back from office late and was preparing his drink, when his first heart attack occurred.

While preparing his drink, he said, "Pranami, my girl you have your dinner as I will be late."

If I had my dinner alone, Papa would carry on taking his pegs. So, I walked down to his room angrily to stop him drinking anymore, but before that, I heard Papa's painful Ophs...sound, and the sound of broken glass. He fell down on the floor.

I took him to AIIMS. He recovered a little, talked very less, but tears always flowed from his eyes. We don't have many relatives in Delhi, they are far and distanced. Just after an hour, Manav reached at AIIMS. I had been searching for him desperately, but I had not informed him.

He had a home, but he stayed at the IIT hostel, and gave it on rent, as his parents and brother were all dead.

Seeing Manav, Papa called him near as if he had frantically searched for him.

Papa tried to speak, his expression was clear but his words were broken. "It's now all over to you. There is no one to care for Pranami. I failed to tie her knot. I am leaving it to you." Papa tried to put his hands together in a sign of request and begging Manav to take care of me, but was unable to do so.

Manav replied firmly, "Why are you worrying uncle, you will get well soon." He believed Papa would get well soon, but Papa would not believe it.

Papa nodded reluctantly, he needed affirmation. A dying man always needs safety and security for his loved one.

Manav said again, "I promise, uncle…" Papa was satisfied.

Papa called me near him, he was unable to talk anymore, and his tears showed he felt very sorry for me. His soul would never get peace. As a father, he had not arranged to settle me.

If Manav was not a gay, Papa would have settled me with him. Papa knew the naked truth of gayism in him and was worried about me rather than him. My juvenile love was in a mess because he was gay and this would remain as a black spot in my entire life.

Manav assured Papa again, "Don't worry, uncle. I will always remain truthful to Pranami and take care of her." Papa looked pleased with his promise.

Papa survived until morning, before that, he asked for Shubam Bhai, after all, he is the eldest son, of our family and as per ritual, he is supposed to give fire to the dead body.

Manav replied, "He has already boarded the flight, and will be here soon."

He had informed Shubam Bhai, but when? I was bewildered. I had forgotten to inform him, but Manav did it. I asked him shockingly, "Did you inform Bhai?"

"He had already boarded the flight, but didn't get a direct flight, coming via London, so it would take time. The flight would land in Delhi at midnight, if the weather is good."

All winter this problem always exists. The fog causes flights to be delayed or cancelled.

He had done everything what was I supposed to do. The call from god cannot be delayed because of the weather and it will not wait any longer. Papa died in the morning with a heavy heart not having his son around in his last moments. In his final time too, his loving son was not present by his side. His eyeballs moved in search of his son. Any stone heart melts down in the end and Papa was very soft hearted. The reason may be his earlier resolution to throw away Shubam Bhai from our home and not to see his face until he left gayism and live as a straight person.

Shubam Bhai had not come for Mama's ritual, but for Papa he called me from London airport, "Pranami, I am coming."

"It's all over Bhai."

"No problem, wait for me. I will give fire to Papa, make arrangement for the body to stay in the mortuary." I simply recited the words to Manav.

With the doorbell ringing, I opened up eyes. Golden sunrays were penetrating the glass and falling on the bed, but today, I had no intention to grab it. It was the maid's time. The RML Hospital and AIIMS scenes gradually faded away from my mind and Papa, Mama, Shubam Bhai and Manav's face disappeared and my confused and frightened face ebbs away.

Entering the house, the maid asked, "Didi you want some tea?"

For the last two days, she used to ask whether to make tea or not, suggesting I had taken tea.

"Yeah...make it a little strong today. I have a headache."

She was happy, as my earlier days had come back.

--Ω--

The following day, on Friday, I woke up early again, made myself tea and sat on the balcony. Let the sunrays not through the glass to reach me so I came out to the balcony for direct sunlight, watched the morning life of the mall. The shops were closed, but garbage collectors were active in front of the closed shops. Little boys and girls with huge cement bags collected waste and garbage. They competed among themselves. However, a little ahead, unmindful of the competition, a girl aged around twelve and a boy of fifteen, out of sight and detached from the rest, didn't seem to be in a hurry. Both were not competing, they simply collected whatever came their way, but never stayed apart. They walked in steps and while chatting, glanced at each other. It brought a smile on my face, these two teens were in love that was the reason both were not competing with other garbage collectors and both had created the aura of love world among themselves. I thought how beautiful the world is. Everyone, from all walks of life fall in love, despite of all agony or let it be struggling to get daily needs too. What can we say to this? They found love in them or love found them? The roads were silent. I stared at them until they vanished from the corner of my eye and waited hoping that they may come back on the same path. But they did not come back.

Whenever I saw such lovers, I felt a strong desire to have Manav around me. All my thought processes transgressed to Manav's world. I gave a call to him, he picked it up on the first ring, "Yes, Pranami, tell me."

"You tell me, what are you doing? Are you waiting for someone's call?" I laughed and never expected he would pick the call so urgently.

"You called early in the morning, my heart missed a beat seeing your call," he explained the urgency in picking the call.

"It's early; half of the people in Delhi have already started their job."

"I am also working."

"Fine, you must be with your dream child, your website," I teased him.

He laughs, "No, I am on somebody else's site, on a social site."

"Facebook?" I asked and he answered with a smile, "Yeah."

I update myself on Facebook, but Manav was very keen about it. It had become a good means among them for communication, a mode of sharing, planning and executing the day's programs. He had a page of his website that had huge likes.

I asked, "What is the plan today?"

"Nothing, I will go to the office."

"That I know, I am asking after that, in the evening?"

"No plan for the evening, there is work in office," Manav was obstinate in his words.

"How, today is Friday?"

"So what, it is just like another day," again stubbornness reflected in his voice.

"It is not just another day for you, its party day," I was sure he couldn't obtrude himself from the weekend parties.

"Shall I come with you to the party?" I asked graciously. I showed as if I needed his permission.

"You?" he was shocked.

"Yes, am I secure at your parties?"

"Very much..." his unintended reply fixed him for answering me; otherwise, he usually preferred silence about the security of a girl at a gay party.

"Where is the party?" I asked.

"I will let you know."

"But when, what time will you tell me, I need to be back from office early?"

"I will give you a call, but you have to go to the bank tomorrow or is it a holiday for you?" Manav asked whether on the eve of a working day I could afford late night parties. These gay parties always last long.

"Don't worry. I will manage; we don't have holidays on Saturday. Now you tell me where I need to come," I asked to get assurance.

"Certainly I will call you and inform you."

He dropped the call. He was not in a position to have a dialogue with me anymore and seemed mystified.

--Ω--

I waited until two in the afternoon and then called him back. My guess was right; he had no intention to give me a call.

His tone articulated that he was thinking twice about it, "Yes, Pranami, I was about to call you."

"It's okay; now tell me where to come."

"You need your car for the weekend," Manav tried to deviate me from the dialogue.

"This is not what I am looking for. I don't need the car. You know I don't go alone anywhere, but where does the car come into this. I am asking you about the club, where to come?" I asked.

"Yeah...the party is at Pegs N Pints Pub, Chanakyapuri."

"But, normally you go to Hauz Khas?" I asked in surprise, I was very well prepared for the Hauz Khas party.

"No, today it's in Chanakyapuri," his voice seemed compelling.

"Right, I will be there at 7 p.m.," I was about to drop the call.

Manav replied hurriedly, "Listen, Pranami, I will pick you up."

"No...no why should you make a double round. I will reach there in a taxi and after the party ends, we will return to my place," I said intently, as Chanakyapuri is the centre point from both our homes.

"Okay, it will be done like this."

"No, tell me if you have any obligation after the party I will come back by taxi!" I asked him his plan.

"No...nothing...what I will do after the party? I will come back with you."

"Then see you at seven at Pegs N Pints," I hurried about the pending jobs to navigate my time ahead. If I start at five from the bank, I should be back home by five thirty, and if I start at six fifteen from Dwarka, I could reach Pegs N Pints easily by seven, calculating the traffic jam in the rush hour.

6

I thought many times before boarding to taxi, "Am I going in the right path?" Even though I was spontaneous and committed to attend the party, many thoughts disturbed me from inside. Again and again, I thought, "Will it be wise to attend gay parties with him?"

With conflicting thoughts between my heart and brain, I left for the party.

Special parties are organized on weekends to celebrate gayism. Manav was standing right at the entrance gate of the pub. This was the first such party that I was going to attend. I was a bit nervous, but Manav seemed tenser than I did. I reached there at 7.25.

"Am I late?" I asked.

"But tell me why did you want to join the party?" he was still in the state of mystification and probably the reason of his tension.

"You are not comfortable with me?" I cross-questioned him. You want me to join your community so I am here today that is what I actually wanted to tell him.

"Has this happened ever?" I nodded in reluctance, "Then why are you thinking so?" He forced me to be silent through his words.

Straightway, he took me to the vestibule, a waiter, as if he knew us very well gave us two colourful different bands. Manav had a designed black and white band and mine was plain pink. It was something like we used for friendship and love bands in our school days.

Manav frequently looked at his watch.

I asked, "We are waiting for someone?

He did not answer, perhaps he had not heard my whispering tone, I asked again, "Why are we standing here, is someone coming?" as we were standing for some time in the vestibule.

He nodded, but next moment holding my wrist, he said, "Come on...let us go."

We started walking for few meters and loud music was gradually audible. He stopped in front of an entrance point. Bouncers checked our colour bands and we entered into the hall. It's not a big hall, but can accommodate fifty people; the music was in full swing. The party had already started, and the hall seemed full, but still the entrance gate opened up and one-by-one people entered inside.

I whispered, "We are late, Manav."

To my surprise, Manav was not by my side; he had left my wrist and joined in the crowd. All were shaking their body to the beat of the music, whether they knew how to dance or not, thin or fat, tall or small; it did not matter. Dance...dance and dance, the only motto. It's not a formal office or family party so any sort of absurdity will not be taken as ridiculous. People were licensed to touch, grab, hug and kiss in the open. Moreover, it was with the same sex, so no alarm was raised about any stupidity.

I searched for Manav and felt very isolated. How can he become so irresponsible, after entering with me into the hall, he just vanished, so careless? He knew that it was my first such party. He was never like this before. Or did the man for whom he was waiting arrive? Is the man, Vardhman? I kept on guessing many probabilities.

I was the only one who was not on the dance floor. Standing for a long time in a place embarrassed me and I started walking on the sides, keeping a suitable distance from the dancing couples.

"Hi, Pranami," a strange voice surprised me and increased my sensitivity, made me stand still where I was. Who knows me here? Thanks god, it's not a gay's voice, a sweet chirpy girl's voice.

The girl came close to me, charming, curvy and in full makeup, "Why are you standing alone, Pranami? Come with me."

"You know me?" I asked without moving. My heart began pumping; the girl was very new to me.

"Of course, Pranami, very well."

"But I have never seen you," I asked, the pumping rate of my heart increased. I guessed her to be a customer of my branch. If it is so, then things will be worse. Some day she will take advantage to enter my cabin and the staff will smell it. These things were never possible to hide.

"We always talk about you in the office."

"Which office?" I almost snatched words from her to ask my question. My doubt doubled up.

"Manav sir has never told you about me?" the girl asked. She seems much younger, a 24-25 type girl.

"No, you work for Ericsson?"

"Yeah…we are good friends," my heartbeat came to normalization.

I cursed myself as I panicked soon. However, what to do, it was my nature; the bankers were quite concerned about issues, whereas a software girl is bolder and audacious. They don't have any fear about being exposed; they don't have to deal with the public.

"Come with me. Manav was saying it is your first party," she turned and walked on the sides towards the closest room. Adjacent to the hall, there was a big foyer, more spacious than the hall and less noisy, only the loud music of the hall was audible to some degree. The music gradually faded towards the end. We chose the last sofa. Before sitting, I gazed at all corners of the foyer.

The place was silent; people were enjoying cocktails with their partners and very often were kissing each other. No one even bothered to look at the other or frown on what the other was up to.

"Nice place na...enjoying," she enquired seeing me staring at partners.

"You have not told me your name?"

"I am Purba Saxena, MTech from MITS (Madhav Institute of Technology and Science), Gwalior. I am from Morena, just 30 odd minutes from Gwalior. I have already said I work for Ericsson," Purba extended her hand for the heartiest handshake.

"You hail from proper Morena."

"Yeah...you have been there? it's a nice place," she became nostalgic.

"Yes, it's a nice place, but I have not been there. I heard about the place. My forefathers were from Shivpuri, we have an ancestral house there, but I have never been there," I expressed memories of few conversations with my father.

"Waiter, two red wines," Purba called the waiter and gave the order

I stared at the partners once again. The subdued light formulated a conducive atmosphere for them. They talk, talk and talk like women. In fact, I was searching for Manav.

The waiter served the wine, Purba taking one glass, said "Cheers."

"Cheers."

"This is my second glass, I had one before you came. Wine is nontoxic and good for a lady. What do you prefer?"

"I like scotch or whisky."

"Wow... but those are strong and especially not good for a lady," she tumbled on my desire, "wine is the best friend of a lady, it suits her."

"Yeah, I like to be hung out," I told her and finished the glass in the second gulp. "Does it suit a woman, what you are doing?" I murmured to myself. I wanted to say this to her but didn't find courage to say so. She had also shown speed and finished the glass.

"Waiter," she called.

"One wine and one scotch."

The waiter left.

"Is it fine now?" she inquired.

I nodded and again stared at all sides and corners.

"You are looking for Manav?" Purba asked, seeing me staring repeatedly at others.

"Yeah...all partners looked like silhouettes and appeared hazy. I am finding it difficult to find Manav," I said. Still, I am not sure whether Manav is on the dance floor or here in the foyer.

She laughed and laughed aloud, "Manav will be with his partner, why are you searching him?"

"Partner who?" I nearly screamed, but realized later that I should not have it was not a party for straights.

"Stop fibbing, you don't know. Why are you making..." reason being I had not thought on the line of his thought.

I pretended to join him, but from where would I bring the natural instinct. The waiter saved my sorry figure.

The waiter held the tray in front of us. Picking her wine glass, Purba offered, "Your scotch."

"Thanks." I took the first large sip. I have to make my stand; Purba looked at me passionately, as to whether I faked to her or is it real.

"It's not a gay party?" I asked. I doubted watching partners of both genders.

"Not exactly, it's a mix party. Gay parties are exclusive ones and mostly hosted in CP and Hauz Khas, we are not allowed there. As we don't have exclusive parties, mixed parties are organized for us," Purba explained.

I saw partners who had finished their drinks move to the dance floor, after sweating in the chilled night; they returned and enjoyed their drink, again.

When she contented I had not faked, she commented about my intrepid behaviour, "You are strong."

"To me, every woman should become strong," I said.

"Exactly what I wanted to say, woman is the most beautiful and wonderful creation of god then why fall in love with gender inequality. Why not chose our love and life within ourselves. Why compromise with plenty of disparity between man and woman. A woman lives and walks in beauty with blossoms of flowers in every sphere of her life, then why bring this into danger with gender parity. Woman being the fairer sex revels in plenty of freedom and care and it amplifies being with a woman."

She looked straight, after the long dialogue to see my reaction, and when she found a blank on my face asked, "Am I right?"

"Yeah...absolutely, a woman is an unprecedented and a beautiful creation of all era and has the ability to get the strongest man on his knees begging and hoping for her love in a puddle of hapless desire then where is the comparison; woman is always on the top."

"No, I don't mean that." She felt I interpreted her words wrongly.

"When there is plenty of discrimination between a man and a woman's wish, desire, nature and thought process then why live with compromise."

"Yeah, you are right." I didn't allow her to speak anymore to make me understand further, she was pretending to me what she is. Bow down to his views and thoughts.

"That's why, Rekha and I stay together. She also works for 'Uniweb Solutions' a good software development, website designing, web-based solutions, e-commerce on line solutions company. She is a Manipuri girl."

"You love her?" I asked.

"Very much and we have wonderful days and nights. No compromise, no deviation of nature. We are enjoying life as partners and respect each other ..." Purba comes closer and puts her hand on my shoulder.

"Yeah, it's being nice to stay as partners."

"Absolutely, enjoying marvellous experience of sex."

The waiter served two glasses again.

"Your friend Rekha has not come?"

"She is out of station, gone to her native place Manipur."

"Yeah, I see."

Bordering our sofa, two gay partners were sitting and developing their intimacy. When I first looked at them, they were just talking with a cocktail, next they touched their fingers, got closer and spread their hands over each other's body. I kept observing them; they kiss, and then kiss gently and gradually it became vociferous and now both of them opened their shirts. They hugged each other and kissed on the neckline and chest.

Purba said, "I never wished to come out without her; it is Manav who asked me to do him a favour and requested me to come," her lip touches my cheek.

Two bouncers came and stood in front of the gay partners.

"No, not here..." forcefully they separated them. One bouncer lifted one man and walked down towards the entrance and the other bouncer followed him with the same action.

I asked, "What will they do to them?"

"Bouncers will throw them out. Open sex is not allowed. It makes the party dirty," Purba replied, but her lip touches my cheek again.

However, she did not check her advances, held my face in both hands and kissed my lip.

Throwing her apart from me, I nearly screamed in a whisper, "What nonsense?"

Purba looked at me strangely; she had thought I would not oppose her and asked finally, "What do you want to prove?"

"Nothing, but I am not like you."

"Certainly not, but I know you are a bisexual, and enjoy sex with Manav, but what is the harm in doing it with me," she tried to convince me and advanced to cuddle me again, and moved her hand to hold my face again.

"Stop it and just shut up, you don't know anything of me."

And I ran way.

--Ω--

I ran away in a single breath to the entrance. Seeing my horrified face, even the bouncers feared coming near me.

The organizing staff ran parallel with me, "Tell us, Madam, what went wrong with you. Who misbehaved with you, we will discard his membership, please, Madam, tell us?"

They kept on asking the probability of my anger, until I hired a taxi and left the place. It was 11 p.m., and I didn't feel it was right to inform Manav. I did not even call him once. He had shown his pathetic quality today.

The taxi took just twenty-five minutes; at that time the road seemed deserted, very less traffic and the red lights were blinking giving way for an unhindered flow of vehicles. Just ten minutes after my arrival, the doorbell rang and I was sure it must be Manav. Yes, it was Manav and entering inside, he said, "Why did you come back without informing me?"

I was not in a mood to answer to any of his questions. He asked again following me towards the bedroom, "Why did you become so furious?"

I again kept quiet.

But he kept on talking, "Tell me something?"

"She has not told you?" my patience lapsed and I yelled at him.

"You deployed her for me and how can she not say anything to you?"

"Believe me, I don't know anything."

"Will you go back again?" I asked, not sure of his intention, because these type of parties continues up to four or five o'clock in the morning.

"No..." he replied. "Just stop the pretence and go to bed. We will talk about this in the morning."

He followed like an obedient child.

--Ω--

I cannot say when I managed to sleep. However, I woke up fresh before the sunrays touched me, made tea and went to Manav to share it.

He was in deep sleep, occupying the entire double bed. Suddenly, a naughty idea erupted in me that I used to do in school days. I put a drop of the boiling hot tea on his cheek and he woke up abruptly, rising as if he saw a snake near his bedside.

He was about to scream, but stopped when he saw me smiling at his state of affairs. I used to put water in his ear and sometimes, he had beaten me, but now we had grown up.

"Go...go...wash your face, quick...otherwise, you will miss the taste," I said.

He went to the bathroom and I sat down on the bed waiting for him.

Both of us took our cups quietly.

After few minutes, he said, "Sorry Pranami, actually, Purba misjudged you."

"It means you have spoken to her in the night?"

Manav nodded in acceptance.

"Then sorry for what. It is one way of life and natural for everyone, the basic instinct. Don't ask forgiveness for it. To me, for a community of this type, quenching the thirst of their mind and body is a fanfare so they pretend everyone is in the same flight. Don't be sorry for it. It is obvious that their sex-craving minds always search for it as their mind didn't get satisfaction."

He listened to me and his face bowed down.

"Gone is the time, it's past now, drink your tea, it is getting cold," I said, as I couldn't watch his gloomy face. It is the problem with our women; we never wait and start a negotiation.

He was in heebie-jeebies and stopped drinking his tea with his face lowered.

I said again, "It was my fault. Why did you take me with you? You should have stopped me, as I was not accustomed about the system and should have had the intuition...now you drink the tea, yar."

I had also started sipping the tea.

Still when he did not say anything, I made myself sorry in front of him and say, "Purva must have told you I was drunk and two large pegs are more than enough for a woman."

"What was the need to reveal what you were there?" Finally, he said, but still would not make eye contact.

"Oh...you have not gone deaf; I thought you have become a stone," I teased him, but it failed to put any extra impact on him, he still did not smile.

"But you should not have left me alone," I said the innately burned emotion that troubled me 'now and then' and relieved.

"It's okay, yar...I told you forget it, it's nothing new for a single girl, but this time the difference is only the gender. If Purva would have a man I would not have screamed so much. I am habituated with men, but it will take time to be with women, now smile."

He looked at me, but without a smile.

"No, not this way...you smile," I said.

He smiled feebly, but that was enough for me.

I asked again, "What is the plan today, are you going somewhere?"

He thought a while and replied, "No...not going anywhere... no plan for the day yet."

"Nice, we will go shopping today."

"Shopping? Shopping for what?" he remarked surprised.

"I need to buy some winter clothes. Now you go to sleep again, I will wake you up as early as possible. I will come back from office soon. Don't go anywhere. The maid will cook for you, and if possible I will join you for lunch here," I said many things at a stretch.

The doorbell rang; it must be the maid.

Getting up from the bed, I asked again, "Do you understand?"

He nodded in acceptance. I gave instructions and guidelines like that a mother gives to her child, while leaving him alone in the house for some time.

He obeyed, only he did not say, "Yes, Mom."

I gave many instructions to the maid as well and entered into the bathroom. While going to office, I knocked the door and asked, "Have you slept, Manav?"

"No...I am not getting sleep again," replied Manav from inside.

"Then drop me at the bank."

"Okay, coming."

I waited for him at the dining table, meanwhile gave few more instructions to the maid. There were no dirty utensils of last night, so she had fewer jobs.

Manav came out in minutes in his nightclothes, "Okay, come."

I followed him.

--Ω--

After the night's incident, Purba never ever expected that she would get a courtesy call from me. In between our conversation, we had exchanged phone numbers. I insisted that I must have the phone number of persons of the LGBT community, who were close to Manav.

"Hello, Purba. How are you? Never expected my call na," I called her from the office.

"Yeah...you terrified me in the night."

"I know, probably you are still in bed."

"How do you know?" She was surprised at my beating about the bush.

I laughed, "Your voice says."

"Yes, after you left, I took scotch and I am feeling the hangover until now."

"So, it's better you take wine meant for girls to chill."

"What does that mean?" she was baffled.

"Feeling the absence of Rekha?"

"Yeah...exactly, she would have started caring for me by this time."

"Nice, I would like to meet her also when she is back."

"Sure," she gave a smirk that was well understood over the phone.

"Purba," I said, "I did call you to say sorry for my last night's behaviour."

"No...rather I feel sorry."

"It's okay," and I dropped the call, and expected that she will convey it to Manav soon. Oh...the content of a heavy heart has faded gradually and I get all the freshness I desired. It's so simple saying sorry.

--Ω--

Manav stayed at home the entire day. I called him twice before finally reaching him, at 6 p.m. First, before 12 o'clock, I was in a mood to join him at home for lunch, as the maid had prepared the food. However, once I was involved in the banking work, it looks difficult and it is obvious in a banker's life. There's no certainty of work schedule. The second time at 2 p.m., to know whether he had eaten his lunch or not. But the main concern was to know his whereabouts. Had he flown away or was still there?

The live-in boys have no bondage.

After two, I was nearly leaving the office, which I could not do until six.

"Sorry, sorry... Manav...you must be feeling bored," I repeated the words to emphasize my busy work schedule, which was obvious from my voice and attitude.

"What did you do the entire day?" I asked again, as I did not get a response from the initial question.

"Nothing, rather I enjoyed the day."

I looked at him straight, "How?"

His action seemed contradictory to his manner.

"I just slept the entire day and completed my quota of sleep." Manav really looked cool and asked, "Have you eaten your lunch or not?"

"Something...something...whatever Gopi fed me. Just five minutes, I will change over and we will go shopping, but where shall we go?" I left the decision to him.

"You say...you know better about these things," he threw back the ball into my court.

"Let me change first, we will decide on the way. Have you had tea?" I asked.

"No," he nodded in the negative.

"I felt a strong desire to have a cup. Let us have a cup of tea and then we will go." I headed the other direction, to the kitchen, rather than the bedroom to change.

"Pranami..." Manav called, "let me make the tea and you can change. It will be faster." He looked at the wall clock; it read 6.30 p.m.. In winter, it's dark already.

"Wow...great, good idea," I exclaimed with joy.

"But you have to take whatever the outcome?"

"Sure yar, but don't make bad tea I always make you good tea."

We both changed our direction. He headed to the kitchen and I, to my bedroom.

I am not the sort of girl who takes a long time for makeup, but Manav was prompt enough to bring tea before that. He came straightway inside the bedroom with two cups; he has the accessibility. I was at the jeans and bra stand in front of mirror for my light makeup.

"Sorry," Manav turned round seeing me and started walking towards the door with the cups in his hand.

"Oh... hello where are you going?" I asked.

"You finish up first then I will come."

"You are shy like a school girl. Have you not seen me before, naked?" Manav turned again and sat down on the bed. I did not hurry to put on my top.

"Where have you learned to keep distance?" I asked, without turning to him while putting on the eyeliner, watching his complete activity in the mirror.

"Finish it quick. The tea will get cold and then don't curse me for bad tea."

"Just few seconds." I was about to finish my makeup. Then I put on the top and sat down with him on the bed. I took my cup; he had already started.

"Nice tea," I commented. Manav had made good tea.

"Now tell me where shall we go?" I asked, as we had time to negotiate until the tea was over.

"It's your requirement, you know better. But if you ask me then I feel 'The Ambiance DLF mall' or 'The Great India Palace' will be best."

"Then let us go to DLF, Gurgaon, and we will have dinner there." I felt the excitement. It's been a long time since I was going for an outing with Manav. I was thrilled about the evening.

"Pranami," Manav called, his voice showed he had something to say.

"Yes."

"Vardhman wants to join with us."

The information was shocking. I took few seconds and this time, the persistence of vision was not lost, not given any chance to think otherwise and forced to give my verdict.

"Sure...what is there to ask me. He can join us, rather it will be more amazing."

Manav got up from the bed quickly finishing his tea. He seemed delighted, but the bright expression on my face faded gradually.

--Ω--

They say 'three S' are essential to always make a woman happy. The 'SSS', are shopping, spa and space. Shopping keeps her updated with the latest trends and changes in the market—keeps her desires satisfied. Spa brings out the tranquillity in her body and posture—adorns the beauty that is woman.

Space brings out a feeling of a beautiful home she can cherish and decorate in her own style, in the way she wants. Use that space to indulge in romance and sex, if she feels like, with the man she loves and enjoy a happy life. I have all 'three Ss', but it is in a mixed bag. I was happy about going shopping, but not as happy as I was a few hours earlier. Vardhman was waiting for us outside the parking. I got down and Manav took the car to the underground parking. That's what Manav wanted and I too respect this. Can't say how much the poor guy Vardhman waits for us? Manav must have told him very early; otherwise, I didn't remember when he called Vardhman to speak to him about shopping at DLF. Oh...as I told him in the morning about shopping he had the plan. Instead of using the lift from the parking, Manav will need to come back again here and we will have to walk down to the mall. Stupid ideas, but helpless and must say an unavoidable situation. I have to keep Vardhman company, until Manav returns. Well after his return, he will take care of him.

"Hi, Pranami...how are you?" Vardhman extended his hand for a handshake.

"I am fine; how you are, how is your landlord behaving?" He had a landlord problem, Manav once narrated to me. He did not own his own house. Obviously, no landlord would tolerate mischief and gayism in his house.

"I changed my landlord...perhaps Manav has not told you. I have shifted to an apartment."

"No...I did not know! But it's nice to have one's own apartment."

"No...no," he interrupted, "It's not mine, it is a rented one, but I have a two years agreement and may extend it for another one year. The house owner has gone to France with his family."

"Ooh...I see, but it's better to have one's own home, at least embarrassment can be avoided," I tried to be as formal as possible.

"Yes, I booked one with the Vatika group, but it will take at least two years to get possession."

"Yes, nowadays builders take even more time than the scheduled possession date, but you can go to a consumer forum if delayed," I added.

"What are you talking about?" Manav joined us and was surprised to see us indulging in conversation, which he felt was unusual. It was obvious we possess contradictory characters, he loves me and I hate him.

"Vardhman booked a flat with the Vatika group. Did you know? He was talking about the delay of possession," I threw a question at Manav, though I knew Manav was well aware of all the facts, but wanted to show my enthusiasm and show that I don't have any issues of confrontation with him.

We walked silently towards the mall and I led the convoy.

From that point, they held each other's hands and were so close to each other; it would be difficult for a mosquito to pass between them. Rather than caring about me, both cared for each other too much. What could I say, it is in their character.

Shopping is something that freshens up a woman and I am a woman, how could I differ. With the winter jacket that I came to buy, I also bought jeans, a T-shirt, formal office pants and a shirt, besides buying some kurtis, tops, innerwear and shoes. Both friends did not allow me to pay for anything. For some items, Manav paid and Vardhman paid for others. When their hands were full Manav asked, "Have you finished, Pranami?"

"Yes...yes, now you guys need something?" I asked formally, as we got out of many shops and headed downstairs.

"Yes," said Manav.

"What, do you want?" I was shocked, he had not said earlier.

"Yes, Pranami, help me choose a T-shirt," Manav said what he wanted.

"For you? I asked again.

"No...it's for Vardhman."

"No...no I don't need anything." Vardhman was shy.

"You may not need it, but Manav needs it," I teased.

We entered into Shoppers Stop. Manav chose a pink coloured, Lee Cooper T-shirt and asked me, "How is it, Pranami?"

"Nice, good choice for a love gift," I added fuel to Vardhman's shyness; he was more embarrassed.

I declared after getting out from Shopper stop, "Time for food. I'm hungry and it's my turn to treat you guys. What you would like to have?"

"Pizza...let's go to Pizza Hut. I am hungry too," said Manav.

I asked Vardhman, "You have not said what you want?"

"Anything," he said.

"What anything, don't you have a choice?" I asked him.

Vardhman looked at Manav and said, "I will also have pizza."

"But I won't," I declared profoundly, "I want a proper dinner. No pizza, burger, pasta business. Let us go to a proper restaurant."

Both looked at me strangely.

"What?" I asked, "I have not eaten at lunch as well."

They followed me to 'Fresco Co.'

At the table, they sat face-to-face, making eye contact.

The waiter came for the order and I asked them, "Tell him your orders."

"Order anything, Pranami, we will eat it," said Manav, without missing eye contact with Vardhman. They behaved as if they were eloped lovers meeting after many years.

I placed the order, "Chicken mushroom soup, butter nan, butterfly prawn. How do you make it?"

Ma'am, it's a Chinese recipe, a little spicy, you can choose the size of the prawns, if you want big, medium or small," the waiter gave details of the recipe.

"Give us the tiger prawns." I go wild and order some more dishes, "Chicken kabab and coconut chicken...and what else is better?" I asked the waiter.

"Ma'am, go for Handi Chicken, it's special today."

"Okay, give us a handi chicken."

"Anything for dessert, Ma'am?

"Gulab jamun."

The waiter took down the order neatly, and read it out again, to confirm the order. He turned to go, but I called him again, "Bhai, make it fast."

"Ma'am, your order will take time, all are special orders," the waiter clarified, before we got angry with him.

"Still try to hasten the order," I said. "You start with the soup, Ma'am, before you finish the main course will be served."

"Thanks," I said, not meaning to hold him for any longer. My order showed how hungry I was.

All this while, the lovebirds were mesmerized looking into each other's eyes. I didn't disturb them. The waiter lay down the soup bowls, still they did not respond. Looking around each corner and at each table, I whispered to them, "Hello, people are watching you."

It did not affect them. This time my voice got a little louder and aggressive, "What nonsense are you up to?"

"Ooh sorry," said Manav and sipped the soup.

With three heads bowed to the soup bowl, I whispered, "How do you gays forget a girl is also sitting with you?"

No one said anything and the atmosphere was gloomy around us.

To ease the situation, I started talking in a normal manner, "Do you remember, Manav, twelve years ago, we used to come here and sit for a long...long time."

Manav glimpsed at me and giggled, "Yes...and then there were no malls, nothing...deserted lands and rocks, where we used to sit."

"Yes, how fast it changed...unbelievable, no one imagined and we had never thought that where we sat twelve years ago, we would someday sit again for pleasure," I started imagining the scene twelve years earlier.

Manav had a silver line moustache and I was lean and thin. We found this place quiet and lovable. Rocks were surrounded with shrubbery, the beautiful and remarkable DLF building was in full front view, large aircraft took off in the background. We used to sit and talk for long hours a little ahead of the highway where no one could find us.

While eating our dinner, Manav started, "Pranami, do you remember, how we used to save money from our shopping?"

Manav looked at Vardhman; he raised his head to listen to him passionately, "When we got money for shopping from our parents, we used to come to Mahipalpur, the factory outlets. We bought branded products at lower prices, much less than the printed tag."

"Is that so?" asked Vardhman.

"Yes...and you won't believe the brands that were available; Lee, FM, Reebok, Addidas, Numero Uno...all brands at half price and we claimed the complete price of the tag from our parents," Manav laughed.

"What did you do with the money?" asked Vardhman.

"Haaaa...Big money seems less when you are with a girl."

"Oho...hello I also contributed in the same fashion," I intervened when it came to our age-old love tale.

--Ω--

It was past 11 p.m. by the time we finished our dinner. Vardhman asked, "It's really late now. Why drive to Dwarka! Let us go to my house, as I don't have a landlord issue now."

Though Manav kept quiet, he seemed interested.

"No...11 is not late night, the road is still crowded and moreover, tomorrow is Sunday, it is the ideal time that people come back after Saturday night parties," I resisted.

Manav was helpless and Vardhman could not argue with me.

We said goodbye to Vardhman; he could take a cab. Manav asked, "Can we drop him, it's hardly fifteen minutes' drive?"

"No...we will be late and I am feeling sleepy after the heavy food," I refused right away.

But Manav on the way still called him, "Have you reached?" Shows how much concerned he was for his partner.

The next moment, he dropped the call with, "Bye, good night, sweet dreams."

And fuelled my temper.

7

I was looking at homosexuality and its cure on Google. One needs to just type a word and there will be ten to fifteen related words and acronyms that follow. It is tiring, but the needy and possessive have no choice.

One website says, "*Homosexuality is a sexual orientation, not an action. Sexual activity and sexual orientation are not the same. Just as there are straight virgins, there are gay virgins. Because sexual orientation is not the same as sexual experience, being gay cannot be considered to be a sin, just as being straight cannot be considered to be a sin. Homosexuals feel long-term and fairly consistent sexual and emotional attraction to other people of the same sex or gender, and do not feel consistent sexual and emotional attraction toward people of the opposite sex or gender.*"

The website also says, "*Sexual orientation is not a disease so it does not need treatment. Attempting to cure homosexuality is like trying to cure having red hair. One can mask having red hair with dye and one can mask homosexuality by acting straight, but one does not cure homosexuality or red hair.*"

It upsets me, I felt disgusted and ruined. My entire endeavour had gone in vain. If gayism is not curable then I stand no chance. I keep on surfing through page after page and site after site my entire life going into a flash back mode.

I stopped on one point, which read, "*Gay people are good parents and do not need to change their sexual orientation to be parents. The American Psychiatric Association studies show that the children of gay and lesbian parents are not qualitatively different from the children of straight parents.*"

It also shows, "*There is no scientific evidence that reparative or conversion therapy is effective in changing a person's sexual orientation. There is, however, evidence that this type of therapy can be destructive. Some risks of therapy that attempts to change a gay person's sexual orientation include depression, anxiety and self-destructive behaviour.*"

I was amazed to see there are many things written about gayism, lesbianism and homosexuality, it's a never ending type. And after a two hour head on studies of all websites, I found things were contradictory. One cannot come to a certain conclusion based on the hypothesis of websites.

The sole purpose was defeated; I looked for some help from the websites so that it would reduce some weight of my heart; instead, it increased the weight. Manav had not spoken to me from the last four days, neither had I. He was upset after returning from shopping. He wanted to be with Vardhman, which I didn't allow. That maybe the reason for his anger. These days I was so busy in the bank I did not give it a second thought.

I called him; he picked up on the first ring, "Hello, Pranami, I am lucky. I was just thinking of you and was about to call you."

"Is that so, you were thinking of me...then I am lucky enough."

"Truly, Pranami, I promise...my call would have been just a second's difference as I was about to press the green button," Manav justified himself.

"It would have my pleasure."

"You don't believe me!"

"But how come today?" I know Manav never lies and never exaggerates things, but women have the birth right of swooning over men and the license to prove her presence in his life.

"You mean to say I don't think about you?"

"How do I know?" I teased him; I was really in search of him and wanted to prolong the conversations just like our juvenile love. No thread to the talk, no issues, no subject, no starting point and no ending point, but there was lots of arguments, low and high pitch voices, swooning, smirking and teasing, by all means love blossoms.

He went into silence but I couldn't, I said, "I believe, hundred per cent believe, but I am sure you did not remember me just like that, either you have some work and my presence simplified it. Or maybe you need something from me. Without a reason you won't remember me."

"How do you know, Pranami, I really need your help?"

He gave me a straight answer that's why he didn't reply to my roundabout query. At least, he should have shown some reluctance, some laughter, some sweet talk and lots of praise and then he could reveal the hidden agenda behind it. Though I always expect it from him, he never goes into a poetic mood.

"How can I, there is no magic. You remember me when there is a need," my tone was high pitched. Whoever is in my position would get angry, but I controlled myself, there was no means to show anger.

He preferred silence again, whenever he does not want to reply he goes into silent mode; the best way to avoid queries. But my problem is I cannot hide my curiosity, "Now tell me why you remembered me?"

"I sold my car."

"This is the reason you remembered me?" I raised my voice.

"You always insisted that I should sell it and now when I have sold it you do not want to listen to me. You are getting angry."

Within seconds, the heat in me comes down to zero, the child in him needs cuddling.

I smiled and said, "Who told you I am angry?" my voice lowered and tone showed that I cared for him.

"You are angry, don't hide it from me."

Women are always emotional whatever toughness they show. Tears flowed down my cheeks, but there was no one to see it. 'Perhaps, he was able to listen to all my heart beats as he heard today,' I said to myself in condolence.

I smiled again and said, "No, Manav, I am not angry. Have you ever seen me getting angry?"

He kept quiet; possibly, he tried to remember when last I had got angry.

"When did you sell it and at what price?" I asked, not giving time to rethink about my anger, when and why I was angry with him.

"Today, at 1.55 lakh. The person has given the money, but they will take the car on Sunday morning," said Manav.

"Fair deal...direct sale or is a middle man involved?" He drove a 'Santro Zing', 2005 model.

"Through an agent, he will take five thousand."

"Nice, 1.5 lakh in hand."

Pausing, Manav asked, "Pranami do you have any plan this weekend?"

"Plan means what?" I was perplexed at his query.

"Any outing, any shopping?"

"You know it very well, I don't go anywhere and by the way I get only Sundays. Not like you, all Saturdays and Sundays. Banks do not give many holidays. But tell me what is the necessity? Why do you want my holidays?" I laughed.

"We will go buy a new car...Sunday will do as we will not go for new purchase on Saturday."

His words 'we will go for a new car' echoed many times in my ear and heart. My heart felt pleased and satisfied. Perhaps, I had not felt this contentment ever before. If it did happen, I could not remember.

I realized that when the heart is in turmoil, how few words could fulfil it to enchantment. That moment, I was not able to think beyond this. A complete satisfaction carved inside me.

"What happened, Pranami, are you listening?" Manav awakens me from the hallucination, of my dream world.

"Yes...which car do you think?"

"Passat VW," I thought he would ask me, 'you tell me, Pranami, which car we should buy?' He knows my passion. I am very passionate about cars. First, I would show my reluctance to accept his view. I would say, 'What is the necessity, you can manage with my CRV. It is all right as I am managing to go to office by auto or taxi. Besides, going to the bank, I have nowhere to go. So it is fine the way it is going."

He would request further, "It does not seem good, as you also need a vehicle and it will be yours only, so tell me which car we should go for."

That is when I would suggest VW Passat. I also had that in mind. But all this did not happen. He zeroed in and just informed me of his choice.

The overwhelming pleasure that my heart was engulfed in vanished like a water bubble. But the contentment had not gone and it tried to surround the little unhappiness developed in it. I still looked cheerful.

"Where shall we buy it from?"

"I have not yet planned, if everything goes fine, then Frontier Autoworld, Gurgaon or Bhasin Motors South Ex."

'Zero it to Gurgaon, it will be cheaper, and the tax will be lower', actually, I wanted to say this, but I feared once I speak up things will come out automatically. He must have planned the address proof of Vardhman. I did not want to his name by any means, neither think of it nor allow it in any form into our conversation.

"Come down on Saturday, I will pick you," said Manav noticing my quietness.

"Not required, I will catch the Metro, you pick me up from the metro station."

"Pranami..." he asked again.

My heartbeats quickened when he called me like this. A questionnaire call, it seems as if a thousand unsolved queries were ready to attack,at once."... Please do me a favour!"

It was expected, he was waiting for my reply to say the toughest thing, I said, "Yes, tell...what favour do you need?"

"Promise, you will not get angry."

I laughed and laughed loud over the phone. I liked this attitude of his, he wants to kill you, but he begs permission from you. Still laughing, I said, "Promise, I won't be angry, now tell me."

"You need to take an interview."

My laughter stopped with a jerk, "What...interview for what and whom?" This favour is very new and I was absolutely surprised.

"For the website. The interview is of a woman...so I need your help. I will be there."

Taking an interview is not an easy task and I have no formal education on it. I was perplexed. Or gays are not cosy with girls, was that the reason?

He continued over my silence, "I have not finalized the time, before finalizing I wanted to speak to you once."

"Me...are you sure I can do it?" I doubted my ability.

"Pranami, there is no big deal and it's not as if it is any formal interview that will be telecast."

"Who knows, you will put it on the web?"

"Yes, Pranami, yes," his exuberance was exposed.

"What happened?" I asked.

"Good idea, Pranami, we will work on this. We will post videos also," the idea clicked with him.

"But what is the matter, who will be interviewed, what does she do? You have not told me anything."

"I will tell you tomorrow when we meet...okay, bye."

He dropped the call. My mobile showed call duration thirty-one minutes three seconds. Neither was I happy nor sad, after the phone call. A mixed feeling of both mounts in my thought process. Whom should I listen to, my heart or brain?

Heart says go...go...go... but my brain puts some barriers.

I don't know why people say when in love listen to your heart! But when love is purposeful listen to your brain not heart. However, it is very difficult to distinguish purposeful and spontaneous love when both works, heart as well as brain.

And mixed feeling always wins in this case.

--Ω--

The next day, on Saturday at 11 a.m., Manav called, "Pranami, the interview time is finalized for today at one p.m., I am coming to pick you up."

"I am in the bank and it's a hasty move?"

"Yesterday, when I spoke to her she said Sunday anytime, so I had fixed for 10 to 11 in the morning, she just called that she won't be available at that time. Tonight, they are leaving on a holiday package to Malaysia and she agreed for one o'clock interview. I am helpless, Pranami."

"Okay," I replied in a monosyllable.

"See you in one hour," but he took just forty minutes and it passed in a jiffy for me.

"You drive fast?" I asked him, staring at my watch.

"Less traffic."

"Wrong."

"Promise."

"Come out, Pranami, cannot say if there will be traffic on the way we need to reach on time," said Manav, standing in front of me. He expected that I should come out immediately.

"Come on, do it fast," he urged again.

"Just few minutes, let me clear some files...you have not said where we are going?"

"Rohini."

"Okay, you need coffee?"

"No, Pranami, we will be late. We can drink coffee on the way, you make it fast," he gets impatient.

"Okay, leaving," I called Gopi and told him to clear the table, and said I will look at the pending jobs on Monday, pending files came to me and I had to separate them.

"It's only 11.50," I said looking at my watch, "we have enough time why not have coffee and you can tell me something about the interviewer, shall I go blank to her?"

"I will tell you everything on the way and we will have coffee too."

"Why not coffee here, at my place?"

He thought, looked at the watch again, and then said, "Okay."

--Ω--

At CCD, he goes silent over coffee, so I asked again, "Tell me how and what do I need to ask at the interview?"

"I am thinking of that."

"At least, tell me about her and why you are taking her interview?"

He spoke up, taking a sip of the coffee, "She is a housewife and happy with the relationship with her husband..."

I laughed, "What is new in that! All wives are happy with their husbands."

"Despite knowing he is a gay man," he completes the sentence, perhaps got the clue to speak up, "her husband is a gay, a businessman. She does not obstruct his way of living and gayism. Rather her husband is proud of her, as she supports him. And because of her, he is able to proclaim loudly that he is a gay."

I was just listening to him, at the back of my mind a long thought process developed.

He continued, "To a man, his wife is the strength and for this man, his wife stands as a pillar of strength."

I had no mood to listen further, so I stopped him, "Her husband will be around?"

"No...she has taken permission from him, I have also spoken to him. He has no objection."

'How can it be?' I told myself.

"If we wish, we can take his interview over the phone, but the woman is important. I want to portray her significant character on the web. An attribute of applaud."

We left CCD at 12.15 p.m.

--Ω--

We were on time; she was waiting for us.

The drawing room was set for the interview, a huge drawing room of the huge house. A glimpse of the drawing room indicates that both are art-loving people.

On the way, Manav instructed me about all that we needed to ask for the website.

We, women sat on a sofa, facing each other, sidewise. Manav put a recording device near us and sat at a short distance to do the filming.

"Shall we start?" I asked.

"Okay, when I say ready, start."

He gets ready with his handycam to capture the sequence. The extra sound recording was for further precaution, if he has to add or mix anything there should not be a lack of resources.

"Okay, ready...start," the red light of the handycam is switched on.

"Your name please."

"Rupali...Rupali Raheja," she said it twice.

"Raheja is that your husband's title?"

"Yes."

"Is it a love marriage?"

"No, but we found love on our first date."

"It is not love marriage, then how did you date each other?"

"It was arranged by our family members; after our marriage was fixed, we then met each other on different dates."

"When did he tell you he is a gay?"

"On our first date...he told me his nature, likes and dislikes."

"You married him after knowing that he is a gay man?"

"Yes."

"Was there any compulsion, meaning family pressure or anything of that sort ... something like the marriage was fixed and breaking off would give a wrong message in the community and all. I mean were you forced to marry him?"

"Not at all, no strain and no pressure. Yogesh (Raheja) gave me freedom on the first date. He left it to me to decide."

"And you decided to go with him?"

"(Smiling) yes, I was bowled by his frankness and simplicity. He told me not to take the decision alone when I said, 'Yes' on the spot, he asked me to discuss with my parents and family."

"And your family agreed?"

"No...I told them about his love and unfussy character. He could have lied and acted as a straight until I discovered his gayism, but he did not do that. Nobody knew about his gayism, not even his parents. After all, a gay is a man. He is proud of his character and because of this, he lives happily, a stress-fre life. We all know how much stress these people do carry, though it is no more criminalization. However, before that (Delhi High Court's historical verdict on IPC section 377), it was treated as a criminal activity as well as a social evil. Still people live in stress and do not come out because of fear, fear about evil respect from society. He was happy he got an acceptance nod from his family and friends, as well as from my family (in-laws) which also plays a vital role in a man's life."

Though she finished, I paused for a while. My thought on the subject was mixed. I stared at the wall and then Manav; he kept on capturing the moments, his eyes make contact through the lens and he looked out from the viewfinder. His eyes sparkled spontaneously.

I asked Rupali, "You are happy being married to a gay man?"

"Obviously...sometimes, I thought had I been married to a straight man, I would not have got my pound of love and affection."

"How come, does he have a partner?" my impulsive question erupts.

"Yes."

"You know him?"

"Certainly, he is Yogesh's best friend."

"True..." Gay people always bat for their partners and say they are their best friend, because only he understands his emotions and thoughts. Where will a woman stand in between them and how can you judge love? Or it is you that sacrificed a lot more to be noble and exemplary?

I wanted to ask these lines, but asked, "He used to come home?"

"No...I have seen him once, Yogesh, he and I, had met over lunch before our marriage. It was a courtesy call, he wanted to show him to me and that was the end. It is their affair and they kept it out of the home. They go to parties and pubs. But yes, he talks about him."

"Have you asked him what they do at the gay parties and pubs?"

"No...I never enquire, never felt the need."

"You never felt like a second wife in his life?" I asked.

"No...never, he has given me everything what a woman; a wife is supposed to get, love, money respect...everything."

"You never felt like you are his co-wife. Your things are shared by someone else?

"No."

"Sex?" I asked an out of syllabus question, "I mean to say how is your sex life?"

Manav looked at me out of the viewfinder; I also looked at him, after asking the question. Our eyes met and I cut it down, I had raised the wrong question. I thought she would hesitate to reply, but she showed no such expression, rather she smiled, "Absolutely fine, we have a healthy sex life...four times a week. What else should I expect?"

"Nice, but is the intimacy real or a fake one?"

"I told you earlier also, he believes in frankness and truth and the truth is in front of you," she indicates towards her belly, "I am five months pregnant and Yogesh cares very much for both of us. You know what he expects?" she asked me and answered herself, "he expects a baby girl. He loves girls."

She continued. No need arise to ask the question, "I cannot speak about others, but I also believe your website's theory TCOWYA, the acronym is 'To Come Out What You Are'. Yogesh is a follower of your site. And what is gay? It just another element of man's nature, just like braveness or masculinity."

She had not left anything for me to ask. As per the guideline, I had asked everything that was meant to be asked, but personally, I was not convinced.

I asked further, "Right...but have you ever been embarrassed because of Mr Raheja's gayism? Don't just answer it, think and answer about any particular event or job."

She thought a while and answered, "See nothing goes wrong in a relationship if you tell the truth. We are all living in a relationship only. Mother-daughter, husband-wife, boyfriend-girlfriend...all these are relationships. It depends on each one, how he or she deals with that particular relationship."

"Does that mean according to you in all relationships, if truth prevails, it is pure." She nodded acceptance.

"You are never embarrassed about his nature?" I repeated.

"No...never, we enjoy our healthy relationship."

"What would you suggest, should all gays be treated in the way you care for Mr Raheja?"

"See, I cannot speak about others, there are differences in gays as well. They have been categorized, their nature differs and it is not wise to speak for others."

"What category is your husband Mr Raheja?"

"He is the 'top' one."

"How are these categories being made?"

"Simply by their nature."

"Girls, we have almost finished. Let us finish it quickly," Manav interrupted. We stared at him. The red light of the handycam was 'OFF'. I understood that I was going out of track and asking questions that were not part of the interview.

"Okay," I said.

"Right...okay...start," said Manav and the red light of the handycam is switched 'ON'.

We faced each other.

"The last one, Mrs Raheja. It's not a question. What you would like to say to these gay people...the LGBT group and above all to the people...we all are in a society...just express your view."

She smiled, relaxed and said, "You know, I am neither a leader nor will people follow me, but still I would like to say specially to the gay and LGBT people, listen to your heart, the solution lies in it and never feel suppressed about nature; it is not in one's hand. Apply TCOWYA (smiling), initially it may feel bitter, but it overcomes lifelong stress. And I will appeal to the people; the common people of our society don't treat these peoples like prostitutes...they love their nature the way you love yours."

She had finished, took a deep breath and sat in a more relaxed fashion. It seemed as if she narrated what was taught to her. Manav came closer to us and said, "Nice, Rupali, the discussion was absolutely fabulous and thanks for your co-operation and giving your valuable time."

"I must say thanks to you, Manav. You gave me the opportunity, otherwise what am I."

"Not to me alone, Rupali; it is again your husband Mr Yogesh's nobility. We were almost finished with writing your story, but he only suggested including your interview," said Manav.

"He is always nice."

"He is proud of you, always talks of you and thinks it is great having you as his wife," Manav moved one-step ahead, praising her.

She smiled, accepted all praises as authentic, but changed the topic, as she could not accept any more admiration.

"Both of us regularly look at the posts on your website; it has very good fan followers on Facebook as well. I must say your team is doing magnificent," she looked at me, when she said the team.

She asked again, "By the way what happened to Alwar's school headmaster? You have not posted further; I sent a mail to you about this."

"I reply all mails immediately," said Manav promptly, "Mr Sambhu is not in a good condition, so it has become difficult nowadays to get in touch with him. We cannot meet him, he does not come to the phone and he is not allowed to use the Internet. The last time he sent a mail was six days ago, where he wrote that his life has become worse after that post. People in Alwar have advanced and have access to the Internet. Someone saw it and told his wife, so she increased the security level and barred him using his mobile, Internet...

or any communication device. But he feels great, as the whole world knows his story now."

Rupali said, "How sad that this kind of a woman also lives in our world...but it's great work. Manav, keep it up."

She indicated that it was the end of the discussion. I was a mere spectator of them thanking and praising each other's work. Manav looked at his watch, so did Rupali and I; it showed 13.45.

Manav said, "Thanks again, Rupali, for allowing us a wonderful interaction and interview. We are wasting your time; you must have to take care of many things for your holiday trip."

"Yeah...sure," she said.

Manav collected his equipment. She seemed happy and came to see us off to my SUV.

--Ω--

Starting up the Honda CRV, Manav asked and I was expecting this one from him. "Pranami, you should not have gone so deep into their relationship?"

"Why? She claims everything is fine in her relationship and merely answered to all my questions."

"Still you should not have asked about their sexual life."

I laughed instead of answering it.

"You are laughing?"

"Yes, it seems appealing, love and sex Q&A, to Pooja Bedi and Varkha Chulani. After the complete narration, what was I supposed to do? Sometimes, I wonder if all these questions are real."

Real, Pranami! There are people who deal with bizarre relationships, you cannot even imagine them. I encounter the same Q&A's every day on the website and our website is the mirror of those relationships."

"Ohhh hello...amend it...this is not our website; it is yours, exclusively yours. Rupali felt I was a crew member and you carried on with it," I asked.

"Okay, babe."

"I bet she is faking, how can a man be true to both of his characters?"

"Sorry?" asked Manav.

He perhaps didn't understand what I was saying.

"It is a god gifted quality of a woman; during sexual intimacy, she easily understands the degree of affection even when she is cuddled. She is just lying to get popularity through your website, if this could happen then the world would not protest gayism and gays always live with their family happily."

Manav stared at me confused. He wanted to say a lot more, but finally asked, "What is its parameter?"

"Why, you want to apply it on me. You fool...there is no measurement defined yet, a woman can only measure it on the spot, no imagination works in it."

"She is not lying Pranami, it's a fact," he tried to make me understand in a soft voice.

"No way...either she is hungry for power and money, or she is trying to be noble."

"You mean the man cannot be faithful to both of them?"

"No way...but I am not talking about the man; I am talking about the woman. By the way, what do you want to prove? Yes...I have not asked you what your category is."

Perhaps the conversation would have lasted longer, if would not have asked about his category. A new terminology found on the interview process. He kept driving quietly, preferring silence to replying.

Whatever bitterness I have towardz him is his gayism, but I am always happy to be with him. You can say it's my internal thoughts and feelings. Despite all that I hate about his lifestyle, I still liked to be with him. And the SUV moved forward without any conversation inside.

Suddenly, I yelled out, "What we are doing on Parliament Street?"

"You want Dim Sum?" Manav asked politely smiling; the overcast face he had carried some time ago had vanished.

"Wow...feeling hungry...very hungry..." he knew I was a foodie.

"Where are we going?" I cannot wait any more, a few minutes' drive also seemed lengthy.

"Wait for few minutes."

"I can't...had you kept the secret from me, it would be fine...now I cannot resist myself."

Manav smiled, "That's why I was not telling you where we were going, at least, leave some secret to the man...no...you want everything to be finalized before a move."

"Don't lie, did I ask you before boarding the vehicle?"

"No...you had other topics," he defended himself.

I did not get annoyed or angry about it, but looked around for the spot, "You have planned?" He kept smiling noticing my eagerness.

Five minutes passed and we parked at 'Mist, The Park hotel'. These five minutes seemed like long hours for me, but the moment I got down, I was delighted. I looked at the watch; it was 3 p.m.

Before the waiter came for the order, Manav asked, "What do you want, chicken, prawn, crab meat or lamb meat?"

"Both prawn and crab meat," I said both, considering that my hunger was on a fast track from moment to moment.

"And for you?" I asked him.

"I will take lamb meat with spinach and mushroom."

"Yeah...nice, we will share."

He ordered for the same and looked at me again, "Do you want soup, wine or champagne with it?"

"What do you want?"

"Anything will do."

"Wine...Red wine." The waiter understood.

He served the Dim Sum in round decorated bamboo baskets on lotus and banana leaves. Four pieces in each basket served with Jacob's Creek Pinot Noir, an Australian wine. Hunger overtook me, as if I had not dined for many days.

After gulping the first sip of wine, I felt warm and cosy. When one is so hungry, it tastes delicious and you can relish it from the mood. For a foodie, good food is like a refresher and bliss to many displeasures.

"Strictly no talk on the website and gayism," I said, I had no intention to spoil this mood.

He agreed and we talked about beautiful moments from our school and college life. We analysed them and laughed a lot making fun of it. The strong Australian wine made other things clear and smooth. We came out of the hotel at 9 p.m., and it was chilly outside. I continuously reminded him, "Nice treat."

Everything seemed beautiful to me, it was the effect of the wine. He looked cool.

I had lost faith that I could drive, so I asked Manav, "Will you be able to drive Manav or shall we take a taxi?"

"No I will."

"Watch out for the Delhi police. They are tough with sozzled drivers, and they have this campaign launched."

"I will..."

He did not fear Delhi police, whereas I had this tremendous fear about the cops, but the terror of them diminished and vanished with wine.

As we came out, the chatter began and this time it was about where to go now, as the Parliament Street was almost equal distance from both of our homes.

He started the Honda CRV and I said, "Go to my place," as if I was the queen and I ordered the king to follow my orders. *Nights are for queens and days are for kings.* I feel I am the queen of the night.

Manav protested feebly, "We decided today was at my place."

"No...you live-in boys live in filth, there is always a pungent smell in your room...you don't clean your rooms daily."

Manav did not answer to my comment; he knew my comment was genuine. I normally spent two hours arranging and cleaning his rooms, whenever I visited his home.

I said again, "Is your job done?"

"Not yet, the car will be bought tomorrow."

"Have you decided from where to buy it?"

He searched his phone for a call or any miscalls, my sixth sense replied, "I know...I know what you are searching and why you are searching."

"Okay, tell me...what I am searching?" Manav teased me.

"Vardhman's call...right?"

I guessed right, so he did not reply.

I said again, "You buy it from Gurgaon or South Extension, as both will be nearer my place."

My justification was right and he turned the Honda CRV towards Dhaula Kuan.

"That's like my good babe " and I locked my lips to his.

--Ω--

Miniature kisses are very unsafe; its effect continues until the soul relishes it.

It started reacting on me.

In the Honda CRV, it is he, me, my thoughts and 92.7 FM's old melodies that play along with its wheel movement. My thoughts only stay calm on red lights, when the wheel has stopped. It again started running fast with the wheel after the green light. A nervous affair with my heart always dreaded the Delhi police.

We reached at 9.40. FM was last playing Anamika's *'Bahaome chae aa... Ooo... Hum se sanam kya parda...'* featuring Jaya Bachchan, by the time we stopped the CRV, the most romantic song touched the heart passionately.

Men take longer time while entering into a home; they loosen their shoelaces carefully and remove their shoes. It's vice versa as women take longer, while stepping out of the home.

He entered into the other room and by the time he entered, I had changed over into my pyjamas and taken out one for him. He was sitting on the bed, when I gave them to him to change into. He took it from me, kept it aside and still continued sitting.

I asked, "Oh hello...change over...or you are feeling ashamed of me? Okay, babe, I am turning in the opposite direction...now you change," I turned and looked at the wall.

"Pranami, I need to freshen up."

"So do it, who is stopping you...and come to the balcony." Again I acted as if I was the queen and the king had to obey my orders, it's night and it's mine.

"You won't sleep now?"

Queens do not like questions, which he did not know and made the mistake.

"We will talk about the unfinished memories."

The sweet past that we were talking about in the hotel is still not finished. Actually, it's never ending, but still I want to finish it.

"It's chilly outside."

"Not much...rather I find it's pleasant as a gentle breeze is blowing."

"You have taken more..."

"How much have we consumed?" I asked.

"Four bottles."

"So, my intake has increased."

"Obviously so." His facial expression shows that he wanted to say this, but somehow he controlled it, "You wait I am just coming."

He joined me in five minutes. I was in the other balcony adjacent to my bedroom, facing south. From there, the entrance of 32C was visible and beyond it the main road, with very little traffic movement as the night progressed and further the heavy growth of trees made it seem as if it was a jungle. I watched families coming through the entrance, wives ordering husbands and kids. It was night and they were the queens.

Manav sometimes watched the entrance, my nodal point of focus and me. He is surprised why I looked around, but didn't say anything then I thought why should I speak first? I was the queen. He ran a website and knew very well what women like.

Women like talking, and if it is romantic, there's nothing better than it. I waited for him to start; he started late when I feel the cold in my body, "Let's go, Pranami, it's chilling."

He talked late and when he spoke what does he speak 'about going back' made the queen furious.

I turned my cheek and then my lips touched his lips in momentum. I was about to fall down, but he held me tight with the support of his right arm. I felt weightless and swung on his arm. His breath blew over my face. I could see only his eyes, black, wide open and haunted. I was being raised higher and higher; the one-inch gap between our lips took several attempts and a long time to make contact. Our lips made contact and my eyes closed. When I stood up raised on tiptoe, both of his lips arrested my lower lip. It was then my turn. My lips opened and widened to get hold of his lips and my eyes opened up. The kiss got deeper and deeper; he held me firmly pressed to him; our tongues searched each other and we could taste each other and the wetness of our mouths. My lips became softer and my body firmer and stiffer.

He lifted up my T-shirt and gently moved his hand inside it, while he grasped and held my body firmly in his hand; I was braless underneath my T-shirt. He released my lips for a second; I whispered, "Manav," and closed my lips over his and this time opened up my mouth wider and bit his lips harder.

He took off my T-shirt in one quick movement. I stood bare-chested; my breasts firmed up, and I released myself from his embrace to catch the falling T-shirt that almost fell over the balcony.

"What are you doing? We are on the balcony. People are watching."

Both looked around cautiously to check if anyone was watching us.

"No one has time," I uttered.

He moved his lips again, but not to my lips but to my breast and held me tight to get closer to me.

Women are cosy in their own home; they become fearless.

We made love and my faith in our love was alive again with the intimacy of the lovemaking. In the early hours of the morning, we woke up to make love again. I thought was Rupali right? Do men change their stance accordingly? However, I was so mesmerized I could not judge any aversion in him. He seemed full of love, simple and honest. In our long relationship, for the first time we made love twice in a night and it seemed as if golden days were coming ahead.

--Ω--

I woke him up at 10 in the morning with tea. He did not make eye contact with me.

Giving him a cup, I said, "Comm on, babe this is not the first time we have made love."

He gradually raised his eyes, shyly. The child in him lured me. I wanted to kiss him once more, grab him as close as possible, if it was possible blend him with me and make us one. However, it will not happen.

I asked, "Have you forgotten to go for the car?"

"No." He looked at the watch.

"Where have you decided?"

"Bhasin...South Ex."

"Do you think you will get it today?"

"I had booked the day."

"Why didn't you tell me? Why did you keep things in abeyance and forced me to guess?" I acted as if I was angry, the birth right of a woman.

"How can I make fun of you?" he chuckled.

"You naughty babe," I jumped at him; luckily, he had finished his tea.

He fell flat on the bed as I was over him. He grabbed me, mounted kisses all over me and opened the robe. He watched a while and kissed me again; I loved seeing me in his eyes.

"No...we will be late for the car," I resisted feebly.

"Let it be."

"The maid will come; she has not come yet."

"Let her come," he advanced towards me and the doorbell rang.

He stopped advancing; I laughed and laughed, "It's the maid...I told you...get dressed quickly and go to the other room."

--Ω--

The day was fabulous. He drove back the Volkswagen Passat Trendline Mauritius Blue pearl. We had lunch at Amour, Hauz Khas, one of our old time and favourite restaurant. We went to the Basant Kunj mall and did some shopping, and again came back to my place. He had not even said that he wanted to go back to Ghaziabad in the night.

We got back at 9 p.m. He started cuddling me no sooner than we entered the house; he lifted me from the drawing room into the bedroom. He had not forgotten the unfinished act.

"Wait, babe...we have the entire night."

"You made me wait for eight hours, babe."

"Not me...it's the maid, my feeble resistance was not enough.

8

I renewed my membership in 'Push Up Gym and Spa'; a walk able distance from my residence, the building and signboard were clearly visible from my balcony. I needed to reduce the extra weight I had put on. I controlled my diet strictly to salads only.

After office, I used to go to the gym for a one-hour workout; and after a hot shower, everything seems lighter and cosy. I could have a peaceful sleep filled with pleasant dreams. I had always planned for a spa treatment on Sundays that never ever happened. It needed time. A spa was not possible on a working day for an employee like me. On Sundays because of the rush on the weekend, a prior appointment was required and one's time slot had to match with Push Up's time and I had kept Sundays reserved for Manav. I think a spa treatment was required to resettle body ache and refresh both body and mind. I could not remember when I had last given a good treat to my body. I had almost forgotten that I have a woman's body which needs caring.

I stood for a long time in front of the mirror. Even at 32, I still felt that juvenile love in me. I laughed looking at myself and said to myself, *'Love avalanche has no age bar and no boundaries'*. The best part about winter is that it makes me appear slimmer than usual.

"You weigh less," Manav noticed my effort the next weekend when he lifted me. Women are obsessed with praise and admiration and I was no exception.

--Ω--

Manav gave me a call on Friday morning. The love and stuff were enough to carry on until the day end. "What's the plan, Pranami?"

"Nothing, absolutely."

"I owe you a treat."

"Woh...but what for?"

"For the car."

"Of course...when?"

"Today...we will go to Gurgaon. The Pub in Sahara Mall."

"But tomorrow I have office." I showed my reluctance; the pub in Sahara meant a late night entry and an early hour exit and then the next day at the bank I cannot think about it?

"Nothing doing, I will pick you up," and suddenly, he was about to drop the call, when I intervened.

"Listen, Manav...is there any Vardhman business?" it showed my consent either way.

He smiled, "No, babe, not at all."

I exited early from the bank and worked out more at the gym. At nine, he called, "Pranami, are you geared up?"

"Yeah."

"Come down, I am reaching in five minutes."

"Okay," I was waiting for him only. I put on my jeans, as after the workout it felt comfortable.

At 9.10, his VW Passat arrived at 32C gate.

"Come, Pranami...drive," he got out from the driving seat. He knew my penchant; I am crazy about cars. I took a U-turn after 15 meters; Manav asked, "Which way?"

"Over the Palam over bridge, less red light," I replied, as it was a nice feeling to drive there. It was Friday and all the traffic was headed towards Gurgaon. We reached at 10. The entry had already started. On Friday nights, the pub was crowded; still we managed to enter inside and gulped three pegs of Blenders Pride one after another. Whisky works marvellous on a workout body and I had done a heavy workout at the gym in the evening; it further lightens the body and mind.

My favourite Hindi music was playing, disco and rap beats. In the chilly winter, we sweated out on the dance floor. The effect of BP disappeared after some time and we had two more pegs when the clock struck two.

Manav cautioned, "Pranami...no more...we have to return... and you have office too."

"Yeah...I know...but one more please," I realized, I had over drunk.

But when life is so blissful, now that it appears I have his hand in my hand, something that I had dreamed for a long time comes true, how can I resist myself without having a hangover! Moreover, after the gym, the spirit had less influence on my body too. Still I begged for one more, but Manav refused. I was surprised to see that my capacity had increased.

He was always like that, cautious. Women do not drink so often, but when they drink, they drink heavily.

We came out of the pub at four in the morning; he drove the car. Gurgaon Delhi highway never sleeps; vehicles were rushing around as if every vehicle had a delivery patient. It never seems as if a dark night has passed over. I slept on the move inside the car.

I woke up to the ringing of the doorbell. The clock showed 8.20, in the morning, I thought it must be the maid. I could not remember how I came out from the car. I was in my sleeping gown, whether I had changed into it or Manav did it, was a hard choice to remember. My jeans lay down near the side of the bed and I had slept on the most trusted lap and in safe hands.

I asked myself, had we made love as well? No, we had not had sex; I was sure. I put back the jeans into the cupboard, arranged the bed and stared at each item, giving it a last glance, before going to open the door. She pressed the bell again. Finally, I put the quilt over Manav again and I went to open the door.

"Babe has slept late today? Have you taken leave from office?" the maid entered saying.

"No...I worked late in the night, you woke me up; otherwise, I would have been late for office."

The maid straightaway entered into the kitchen for washing the utensils.

"Don't come to my room, clean up the other rooms and leave my room. I am going to have a bath. Manav is sleeping there."

The maid looked up and stared at me with eyes wide open.

"Okay," she nodded.

"Make breakfast for him, I won't have any breakfast."

I did not wait for any query or question and went straight to the bathroom.

I was feeling the hangover.

--Ω--

I thought about calling him at least ten times, at 10 in the morning, but then thought again, he must be sleeping and let him sleep. When I left at 9.15, he was deep in sleep.

Finally, I called him at 12.30; he was still sleeping, but took my call, "Hello, Pranami, have you gone to office?"

"You are still sleeping, look at the time," I fired him, without replying to his query.

"I have woken up, babe...how did I take your call?"

"Okay...fine...breakfast has been made for you, have it like a good babe."

Actually, I wanted to tell him by calling that there was breakfast and he must have it on time, but it was lunchtime now.

"When you will come?" he asked.

"Soon."

The 'soon' was possible only at six. I hurried, he must be bored. Sometimes, he complained also, "I was bored coming here" the reason being that I work on Saturdays, but it cannot be avoided.

I made him understand, "If I go to Ghaziabad then it will be on Saturdays and that too after working hours of the bank and you know there is no specific working hours for a banker. We even work on Sundays; our nature of job differs. When you come down here, I get company."

He kept the door open and was busy working on the laptop in the drawing room. He asked without even lifting his head, "Have you come?"

"No."

He just chuckled at my answer. He had not felt lonely; otherwise, he would not ask this. I wanted to wail, I drove the Honda CRV at a speed of 80 to 90, at least, to reach five minutes earlier, but it seems to have had no impact on him about my arrival.

"Working on some serious stuff?" I asked finally.

"Yeah," he answered precisely and kept on typing.

"Why did you keep the door open?" I asked because I never do.

"I am not a single woman," he smiled teasing me.

"Even men are not safe, especially gays," I also teased.

"I smelled your arrival, babe."

Now he became serious and did not smile even while answering. He stopped working and swiftly lifted me to bed. This is what actually I wanted; when I come home, he must take care of me. It's every woman's desire. Women never compete with men; we want our pound of love and care. Though the gloominess in me was removed instantly, we knew acting. Acting was the best way to keep things in order for a woman.

Then he commented about my weight loss. I may be weighing less to him, as he has been lifting me from childhood.

He kissed my lips; his hand touched my breast.

"Why...why do you want me? You don't care for me?" I turned my face and avoided his kiss.

He needed my company and me.

"I waited for you, babe; just replying some mail...promise."

I stared at him, convinced but acted again, "Mail has become important than me?"

"No, babe," he tried to kiss me again. Men do not want long discussions they come to the point straightaway, whereas, women want to talk and talk. Though he succeeds to land the kiss, I pushed him away, "No...not now...it's evening."

"So what? What's wrong in the evening?"

He became impatient. I wished to hug him tight. Conglomerate my wishes with his and sweep away with his desire. I also wished what he desired but women can act superbly and are blessed to hold the desire for a long time. He moved his lips to mine again, strong and firm.

"Evening is not for sex; gods and goddesses roam around this time. Have you not heard about this?"

His advances stopped.

He laughed, "In Delhi...you are talking mythology?"

"Yes, it is written in the Vedas."

"Where did you get to know it?"

"I know it."

"And you also know what to do in the evening? Party... Pub...bar...what else?" he asked.

"No...evening is prayer time."

"So, no sex in evening?"

"Yeah."

"And morning sex?"

"That is also not advisable...if you must have it, then it must be before the sun rises and better sex should be over when the last darkness leaves the earth."

"Nice...what should we do now?"

"Talk...discuss...with tea."

I released myself from his clutches and said, "In the night... promise..." before I went inside the kitchen to make some tea. While the water boiled, I changed over to an evening gown. He looked at me silently and stared at each of my activities.

--Ω--

The evening started with tea and the conversation moved onto spa, the buzzing and hot topic of my mind. Gradually, from spa it switched to Bollywood and Hollywood heroes, their physique and figure. We watched TV for some time, soap operas and the Filmfare awards, as I watched these passionately. I was passionate about the dances of Bollywood heroines, their makeup and attire.

When an Ad break came, he changed to other channels mainly English Movies. 'Apocalypto' was showing in 'Movies Now'. It had already started; the hero had put his wife and child in a well like cage before the entire family was caught to be slaves. Manav was stuck to it.

I yelled, "Manav change the channel the Ad must be over."

"Watch this movie, Pranami; it's a nice movie."

I am movie crazy, but only Hindi movies; reluctantly I asked, "What is the story?"

"Simple, it shows how he survived to rescue his wife and children, before the rain water supposedly washed them away. His wife was expecting a baby any moment and she gave birth to the new baby in neck deep water."

"What is new in it?" I was not interested in a Hollywood scientific movie style; they simply exaggerated things. But I like Hollywood thrillers and romantic movies.

"You watch it; you will definitely get attracted."

"How many times have you seen it?"

"Once the complete movie and ten times parts of it."

"Still interested!"

He did not answer rather watched it ardently. I also watched it for quite some time. They were being carried for an auction. No one takes the hero's mother, his brothers are killed and he ran away.

Manav asked, "Do you have something?"

"Only wine, white that too Indian...'Sula Brut'."

He did not ask further. I was bored of this English movie and went to bring it.

"I have only four," I said, placing the bottles on the side of the sofa.

"Okay fine," he said, without looking towards me.

"These are only 350ml...will it do?"

"Let's start."

I switched off the TV, "Now we can start," I wailed, "really it is disgusting...I am bored."

He played a trick with one Sula. He opened the seal and kept it for some moments, the cock opened up with a sound; he immediately poured it into a glass.

"There is nothing for dinner," I said after some time, as we were nearly finishing.

"What do you want to have...let me order for a home delivery."

"Pizza...I want pizza...order from Domino's."

He placed the order.

"One hour," he looked at the watch, the delivery time of the pizza.

"It's finished, Pranami." He showed the bottle upside down.

"I told you earlier, I only have this much."

"I have some, but it's in the car."

"Then...go and bring it...what is it?"

"Black Vodka."

He went to the open parking. His car was parked in the open, as he went for it, I looked at him returning from the balcony. Black Vodka tastes good. The pizza arrived as per schedule. At 1 a.m., we went to bed and probably, at two, we were asleep.

The next day, in the morning, I woke up to the sound of the doorbell ringing; it was 9.30 and must be the maid.

As I opened the door she came saying, "Babe has slept...I was about to return."

She had tried ringing the bell many times.

"Babe, more than ten times I rang the bell...tired babe... it was over yesterday? Hangover?" asked the maid, while entering the room.

The bottles were scattered in the drawing room and my mouth smelled.

"Yeah...I am going to sleep again...Don't come to the bedroom, Manav is there. You finish your job and before going just call me."

She nodded.

"Make breakfast for us, where will we go at this time?" I told her again, before entering the bedroom, I locked the door and snuggled deep inside the blanket.

"Who is it?" Manav was aware, as he had also woken up.

"The maid."

He held me close to his bare chest, and I went into assured sleep again.

--Ω--

At 2 p.m., I received a call from Roshni, my classmate from school, "Hi, Pranami. How are you?"

"I am fine...you tell?" I replied.

"Absolutely...enjoying life," she replied cheerfully.

"Nice to hear it," I have to reply something as I am not jealous of her.

Manav asked, "Who is it?"

Blocking the mouthpiece of the phone with my palm, I whispered 'Roshni'. He heard what he wanted to know and did not bother to listen to our discussion.

"Hello, buddy. What are you doing today?" she asked curiously.

I laughed, "One holiday, I get only one Sunday, guess what can one do...I just woke up, yar."

"Listen, Ajay is asking for an outing today."

"Outing...with me?" I was wired.

"I will also be there, yar...bloody dude is listening...he is laughing...see he is asking your consent...stop, yar, I am talking." Roshni half talks to her hubby Ajay.

She again said, "He saw you on Facebook...sent you a request, probably you have not checked your profile for many days..."

"Yeah...you know banking job."

"Okay, I was just kidding, but why not plan a trip to 'Great India Palace.' We will have fun and enjoy the evening on rides. Actually, I don't have your boyfriend's number, otherwise, I would have called him also, together we will enjoy."

Manav whispered and asked, "Is it the same girl from your class who had an affair which was broken, she got married to another guy and her initial marital life was not going so well?" Manav had not sat idle, rather he recollected the lost memory about Roshni.

"Same girl," I whispered replying him, while putting my palm on the mouthpiece.

"How is she?" Manav again whispered.

"She is doing fine," I whispered to Manav, keeping the palm on the mouthpiece of the mobile.

"Yeah...he is here, would you like to talk to him?" I asked her.

"Yeah...it's great, you are in a fun mood?" she said.

Meanwhile, I handed over the phone to Manav, "She wants to tell you something."

"Me...but why?" Manav hesitated to take the phone.

"She wants to talk you."

"Hi," Roshni talked to him.

"Hello," Manav was not comfortable with other girls.

"What's the plan...by the way do you recognize me. We

were in Tagore Shree International School. I am Pranami's classmate...we heard a lot about you from Pranami...so sweet."

"Yeah...sure," said Manav curtly.

"Then are we meeting at 'Great India Palace'?" asked Roshni.

Manav looked at me, I wired to Roshni, as he held the phone, "Yeah...Roshni...we are coming."

Manav cut the phone and asked me, "Why do you want to go, Pranami? It's chilled out...and that too with some other family."

"Come on, Manav...she is my classmate and certainly you would like to meet her when you would know about her." I chuckled and he looked at me nervously. He frowned and it showed 'tell me what the secret is?'

"She was a lesbian...a homosexual...but I don't know of her current status. She was practicing it, her love, affair and breakup was fake...this lesbianism was the root cause of the devastation of her married life. I don't know how things were settled and they started living together...happy. Things had become so bad, they had filed for divorce."

I wanted to see the colour changing on Manav's face, how he would react listening about a homosexual individual. He didn't answer, but accepted coolly, as if he knew each Delhi gay and lesbian's story.

Manav asked, "Does she know about me?"

"Not until now, but certainly when two class of titans meet they will come to know about themselves...why are you afraid of her or you don't want to reveal your secret?" I asked, as sometimes I loved to tease him. I wanted to see the pain in him.

But silence followed.

Sometimes, when I behaved abnormally his behaviour also became mysterious.

--Ω--

At 4 p.m., we were at 'The Great India Palace' Shopping mall. We took the Passat, as Manav had to come back to my place and the plan was that tomorrow morning we would go to Ghaziabad. The last time that I met Roshni was at Divyanshu's marriage party. That day she came alone. That was the period their marriage was in a rift. I met her husband Ajay on their marriage day and would now be meeting him again today. He had changed a lot in appearance from the wedding day. It had been two years or more.

Both guys met for the first time and mixed up well. We first went for some rides and then entered into the 'Fun World'. Being a Sunday it was very crowded, children and parents were packed in like sardines. Manav loved bowling and I enjoyed the game so we played until we sweated it out.

Whenever Roshni and I found time, we spoke about our past, our friends and where they were settled, about their life and how happy they were. When two women who have known each other meet, they have enough to talk about, and they can talk up to infinity.

It had been amazing talking with her; she knew many of my friends and had contact with them. In fact, they were all her Facebook friends and shared life's happy moments.

Though I have Facebook friends in thousands, I had never done research on them and had never searched any friend. The maximum number seemed fake to me.

After bowling, when both guys went to check out the simulator car racing, we had plenty of time.

I asked Roshni, "I heard your marriage was not a success?"

"Who told you?"

I thought I raised the wrong question; she seemed uncomfortable to answer it. The appearance on her face changed; she looked pale.

As I kept quiet, she asked again, "Let me know who told you?"

"Leave it...the gossip may be wrong," I tried to avoid embarrassing her.

"No...no you are right. Our relationship was not healthy, but I want to know who all knows about it."

"If it is true, what does it matter who all knows about it?" I saw she was ready to speak out the truth, but was only waiting for the right click.

"That is also correct...if the relationship is not good, what does it matter who all knows about it..."

"But why did this happen?"

Roshni took a deep breath before starting, "You know I had a long relationship with Mohan and after marriage Ajay came to know about it. In fact, Mohan blackmailed me. When I refused to pay him, he told everything about our relationship to Ajay. He showed him some photographs which he had taken in our close moments...you tell me which husband will accept after seeing all this?"

"But what I know is the other part of the story, that your relationship broke up with Mohan because of your lesbianism. I heard that your relationship with Mohan was namesake, so that no one ever suspects you. Yes, he blackmailed you because he needed money and when you refused he told Ajay everything about your lesbianism and your secret acts."

She guffaws and guffaws loud, there was nobody to bother about this in the crowd, but I was frightened of her swift action.

I asked wavering, "Was this wrong?"

She looked terrible, "So you know all this...and others must also know about it...so no point in lying."

"But how was the matter settled...you both look like perfect couples with lots of love and affection?" This is what I wanted to ask, everything else that she confessed I was sure about its truthfulness.

She laughed again, "Dad applied some patchwork."

I looked bemused, "What?"

"Dad gave Ajay one crore to start up his own business... but he is quite a good fellow, loves me and cares for me."

"And you are still active in your secret act?"

"Why do you ask, have you...?"

"No...I know two girls...they are lesbians."

"No...no I left all this," she vehemently refused.

"Really...you are not into the act?"

After a brief silence, she said, "Pranami, habit is such a stupid thing very difficult to leave...everyone knows I left this habit and stayed with the normal life...marriage life runs smoothly. But let me confess...by confessing I can relieve the heaviness within me... I am still into the act...Ajay is very kind, he believes me...sometimes I think I should chat with Ajay, I pity him and tried every way to get away from this habit...but it's very difficult, Pranami."

After a pause, Roshni said again, "It's better to be TCOWYA (pronounced T'kewya.)"

"What do you say...what is it?" I was bemused. I had heard this word somewhere.

"You know, a website '*myrelationship.com*'," she chuckled.

I got it, it had been associated with Manav, but I behaved in the same mysterious way.

"They are in lakhs. How many can one know?"

"No…it works especially for LGBT group."

My heartbeat increased. Does she know of Manav?

I vehemently refused, "No."

"It's amazing…" she gave a pleasant look at me and said again "…spare some time and look at the website, but it will be of no use to you as it speaks of the LGBT group."

It was amazing to listen to Roshni and especially the success of the website, so the success of Manav, but I tried to conceal the truth that I too know about the website.

"You know the guy?" I asked in a quiver.

Roshni nodded reluctantly, "How do I know the guy? I look at it secretly; I found lots of fun in it…the stories and queries seem real. I feel, if it happens…someday if I meet the guy, I will certainly request him to post my story," she smiled.

"Are you serious? Now you said you wanted to quit from the practice and still you are talking about credibility…it is clashing your thought process what exactly you want to do?" Roshni shows a contradiction in character.

"When I read the posts and thought about T'kewya my inner thoughts have risen. I intend to come out…enough is enough…whatever I am, I must accept it with pride. I tried hundred times, but I again indulge into the practice…it's something in my nature…I will not be able to be relieved from it, so I had better tell the truth…there is no other happiness than in telling the truth."

"Who stops you then?" I asked.

"It's my brain…that says no…let it be as it is going. There is enough stuff hidden on the earth. Did the earth come and say this is mine take it?"

"But if it is revealed, why not use what T'kewya speaks about and accept life as it comes, you can't always act double character like a cat, despite of knowing that the whole world knows about your behaviour vehemently you refused what is the truth?" I asked.

"To the world I have stopped it, but I practise it secretly... you know, Pranami." She showed great intimacy by addressing me and continued, "One can't just make a woman happy with sex and shopping. That is all rubbish that is written, which must have been thought of by a man, what a woman actually wants is 'Love and Power'. I feel proud and satisfied when I do it, so how can I eradicate it from my life...those moments were happy moments."

I did not understand why Roshni was telling me all this. Was this the reason she called me? She was getting emotional and the matter was becoming sensational. Because of my fear, I kept on asking her about her life to extract if she knew about Manav or not? These community people know each other well. And another factor I mingled with such type of discussion to extract some inner thoughts of the LGBT community. The Manav factor bounds me to act on this process.

Soon we could see both the guys and we stopped our discussion.

We stood quietly at the railing of the 'Fun World' waiting for both guys. Roshni went back into her memory lane and I was bursting with thoughts. The free flow momentum of our discussion had stopped.

Ajay came back and Roshni got back her charm. Both guys got along well together and simultaneously said, "Let's go...it's dinner time."

I also felt the same, "Okay...where shall we go?"

"KFC will do," said Manav.

"Roshni is vegetarian...she will not be able to handle the non-veg food and may puke at the sight or aftertaste of the food...find a restaurant," said Ajay.

We sat for a complete meal at a vegetarian restaurant.

Roshni became very comfortable with me. We were not good friends and just greeted each other with a customary hello, when we casually met each other, but now she tried to build up intimacy between us. I get suspicious particularly when Manav is involved.

We talked about food, and the dinner was finished on a quiet note.

Over coffee, Roshni asked, "Pranami..." Her voice had a questioning tone; everyone looked at her hopefully, expecting something new from her.

"When are you getting married? You have been in a live-in relationship for a long time...I heard about it right from school days."

Except Roshni, everyone laughed at her silly query. We expected something great from her, but she did not laugh or take what she said lightly and asked again, "What is wrong with it, why did you all laugh?"

"Nothing, Roshni...very soon...you tell us when to get married." I teased to make her relax.

Ajay intervened, "What is there in marriage...what is wrong with this live-in relationship?"

"Yeah...Ajay is right." I supported him.

"Legitimacy.!" Roshni still looked serious on her statement.

--Ω--

I was thinking about Roshni, she possessed a contradictory character. Her ideology and character did not match.

"What are you thinking, Pranami?" Manav asked, seeing me in a preoccupied mood. Usually, I was the one who spoks a lot; Manav was always the less talkative among the two of us.

I did not intend to tell him about Roshni's practice that she still continued as it was enough that he knew 'Roshni was a lesbian'. Actually, I was afraid to tell him, as there is a saying 'If you think good, good will follow; if you think evil, evil will follow'.

I never expected that Roshni would invite us for a casual visit and tell me her inner thoughts, though I knew she was a lesbian. I initially agreed with her thoughts, as I thought it would be fun to see what she says, but finally I was wounded, whomever I am meeting seems unchangeable in character. In all my thoughts, I thought of the same sex relationship and at every sphere, I met those other people. Roshni was ridiculous...On the one hand, she wanted to make her hubby happy and that their married life should be smooth, but on the other hand, she couldn't stop practicing lesbianism.

With a changed intention, I said, "I was thinking of Roshni and you."

"Roshni and me, about what?" Manav was surprised at my answer.

"Correlating both...on the same ferry."

Manav stared at me. "Are you okay?"

"Yeah...absolutely...I have good news for you."

He looked eagerly at me.

"You are a hit Manav."

He stared at me again, while his hand was on the driving wheel. This time, he chuckled, "Where am I a hit?"

"Everywhere...I mean your website; I told you that Roshni was lesbian..."

He interrupted, "Was?" He emphasized the word.

"Yes...she stopped after marriage...but she knows everything about your website...and gets inspiration from your website...she wants to meet you...I told her that I know the person; then she begged me, 'Please, Pranami, please...once... just once... fix a meeting with the guy."

"Are you kidding?"

"No way, why not take an interview of her?

"Are you crazy, she talks like a dunderhead?"

"Why can't we take an interview of her...tell me...because she stopped practicing...you will not include her in your group... LGBT group...or what?" I almost whirled towards him to know the answer.

"Who says no...I am ready to take her interview; rather I will be happy to project her story," said Manav.

"No, you won't," I was infuriated over my thought. So much thinking it made me angry and that reflects in my tone.

"It seems as if it is fun to you," he was annoyed and now wired.

"Not me, you people make these things funny...very funny," I was aggravated and turned my face. I looked at the traffic and the lights for some time. It did not affect Manav, and he drove quietly.

For the last few hours, I did not agree with my brain. It was agitated from the time Roshni said she still practices. My brain advised me profoundly that these people never give up their habits, never... But my heart said no...everything was not the same for everybody, there must be some exception.

I was confounded...whom should I listen to my heart or brain?

I lowered the glass, and the chilled air entered inside. It felt good. Manav just said once, "What are you doing, Pranami? The heater is on."

I did not heed him. He switched off the heater. It's not as if I was angry with him. I was annoyed with myself, for a reason I cannot find.

The chilled air numbed our faces. Without any words exchanged between us, we reached my apartment 32C.

And without uttering a single word, we went to bed. Manav slept with me as usual on my bed. Sometimes, I thought he should sleep in the other room and sometimes not. I slept facing opposite him.

Manav tried to cuddle me; it's in a man's nature. He kissed the back of my neck. He played with my hair with his fingertips. He kissed me again. When a man sees a woman is stressed, he opts for sex, and feels it's the panacea. Two things happen, tension is eased and he gets his share. It's not true, but who will teach these men?

To avoid his kisses, I slide, and by sliding, I reached the edge of the bed. Finally, I stopped his lips with my finger, "No...I do not feel like it today...I am not in the mood."

He withdrew and slept within seconds. But I could not sleep; my thoughts were scattered over all these people, Roshni's sudden emotional expression, her husband's thoughtful eyes and the most Manav's illogical behaviour. "At least, he could have asked why Pranami, why don't you feel like cuddling...why are you not in the mood... what happened, what makes you worried?"

But nothing of that sort of happened. When I stopped his advances, he simply went into deep sleep. Manav went back early in the morning hurting me again.

--Ω--

After two days, on Tuesday, Roshni called me around 5 p.m., while I was at office. "Hi, Pranami, you didn't call after Sunday evening?"

"Ha, yar...I was thinking of calling you, but somehow I got stuck somewhere and at some time with the job, you know how banking jobs are..." I replied, though I was never interested in calling her up.

"Are you free from the bank duty?" Roshni asked again.

I laughed at her question and said, "How can a banker get free before 8, but tell me do you want to say something. I am listening?"

"Pranami...Ajay has become a great fan of yours."

"Fan of me...is it true?" I asked and sitting erect on the chair. I kept aside the job I was doing. A dubious thought popped into my mind, being single at the age of 32 teaches me to think beyond my imagination and with a great hold of the sixth sense.

"Absolutely...since the Great India Palace meeting, he has all praise for your beauty."

"Fine...at least someone praises my beauty," I said.

"Why do you think so...you are beautiful?"

"But you took two days to tell me? I asked.

"Ajay was adamant and told me many times to call and tell you, but it was stupid me that took so much time...from that day he is just talking about you only."

"Oh...that's great." I was really enjoying her talk.

"Ajay invites you for dinner today," Roshni stopped awaiting my reply.

I was just waiting for this kind of request from her. Being single, I had learned so much from society, friends and from all my surroundings. My sixth sense iwas active all the time and acted promptly.

"What happened, Pranami...are you there?" Roshni asked, as I took few seconds to judge the situation.

"Ya...Ya...I am listening..." I said in a loud voice, to show my presence on the call.

"Come over for dinner...we will have lots of fun and amusement."

"Roshni, you know the banking job, I won't be free before 8 o'clock and unnecessarily I will be late."

"No problem...we will wait."

"No, Roshni, I will be too late after dinner."

"So what's the problem. It's my home not a market place. You stay back tonight at my home. What's the big deal! Rather we can talk the entire night about our school our friends." Roshni was too keen and her voice was enthusiastic. Perhaps, she had the feeling that she had convinced me.

"Not today, Roshni," I showed my reluctance with a grieved voice.

"What is wrong with today...you know I have all the contacts of our classmates few seniors and juniors too."

"That's great, how could you do it," I asked, trying to divert her from the dinner issue.

"Thanks to social media..." But she came back to her same question again, "You come today, Pranami... we will have lots of fun."

This time I strongly refused, "It may be here until 10 o'clock today. Let us plan for some other day."

"Okay...are you sure?" asked Roshni.

"Sure," I replied.

"Then come tomorrow."

"Okay done...tomorrow," I confirmed. But that tomorrow would come only on Friday and it was intentional. In the night, while speaking with Manav, I asked his plan for the weekend. He took time to say, "Can't say, and today is Tuesday only."

"If you don't have any commitment then we can go for dinner at Roshni's."

"But why me? She asked for you and she is your friend only. Don't drag me into your friendship." Manav was a bit reluctant.

"Who knows you may get some stuff there," I said.

"What stuff?"

"Masala...material...for your website...I mentioned about her, she was practicing lesbianism...have you forgotten?"

"But you told she is no more practicing?"

"Does this bad habit go away very often? It was intentional."

Manav laughed and said, "I know, I could read you very well"

"So you are coming?"

"Okay," Manav agreed.

I was afraid to go alone for dinner and at the same time, I did not want to show the reason of my fear to Manav, so I used his interest to drag him to accompany me. I was quite sure he would agree. Nowadays he was running after news and interviews for his website.

The next day on Wednesday, in the evening, I called Roshni to say, "Sorry, Roshni, today there's an audit going on at the bank. Can't say what time it will take, so cancel the dinner today and we will see tomorrow."

She seemed upset, took time to say 'okay', and dropped the call soon. But I called her at 10, in the night, "Sorry, Roshni, but see I just reached home..." knowingly I lied to her; I had finished my dinner and was in bed reading a book before sleeping, when I called her.

"It's okay...but come down tomorrow."

"What happened, you seemed nervous...in the evening too and that's why I called you again...what's the matter?"

"Nothing, yar," said Roshni.

"No, there is something, I know you very well...if there is something bothering you, cancel dinner we will have it some other time."

"No...no...there's nothing, Pranami...don't cancel dinner... actually, Ajay is pushing me and when he heard that you are not coming today he was annoyed too," Roshni came out with truth.

"Great, Roshni...your husband has a lot of interest in me... He didn't show it, when we met at the Great India Palace the last time," I said and smiling, hiding my concern of annoyance.

"He has become a diehard fan of yours."

"But why...I am not a celebrity," I asked.

"Okay, Pranami...come tomorrow positively without fail," Roshni cut the call, perhaps Ajay had come back, I guessed.

The next day Thursday, around 12 p.m., Roshni called me, "Sorry, Pranami, I cut the call yesterday night; Ajay came back at that time."

"Okay...I understand...that time you were saying something?"

"He says he loves you and says not to tell you...he is interested in calling you for dinner and when your program was cancelled for the last two days he started abusing me."

I laughed loud in the cabin before saying to her, "Great, Roshni...he must be a great man...those men who love me in the world I must say they are great."

"Are you coming today?... please come down yar, for my sake at least."

"Sorry, Roshni, I may not come today, but certainly tomorrow."

--Ω--

The next day was Friday and as scheduled Manav reached my place at seven in the evening and we started around eight to Roshni's home It took half an hour to reach her home at Paschim Vihar. On the way, I narrated everything to Manav and in reply, he just smiled. They were waiting, but did not feel pleasure on seeing us as I had expected.

Ajay seemed nervous and had not looked at me; he seemed like a juvenile lover full of shyness and talked very little with Manav.

Roshni brought scotch; she opened it and started pouring it into glasses. At that time, I stopped her, "Don't pour any for me."

"Why?" Roshni asked surprised.

"Why means...I don't drink," I said with a smile.

Perhaps, they did not believe me, as Roshni said again, "How is that possible?"

"Yes...I don't drink alcohol," I said with a smile again.

"This is impossible; being single and a working girl you don't drink liquor?" Roshni was not ready to believe me.

I said again with the smile, "Is it necessary for a working girl to drink liquor? You people start, I will drink water."

Roshni did not reply further, raised her glass in cheers... and after few minutes, I said, "Excuse me; I am just coming from the washroom."

Roshni promptly got up as soon as I spoke, "Come I will show you."

The moment we entered the bathroom she whispered, "Why did you bring Manav?"

I was shocked and filled with anger, but did not express it, Why? You know he is my friend."

Roshni looked puzzled, "I know, yar, but Ajay was annoyed."

"Okay, I will go back."

"No...no...he will simply kill me...please don't do it...I beg you." Roshni joined her hands together begging.

Assuring her, I came out of the bathroom, but I was exasperated to go out. However, before that I wanted to teach a lesson to Roshni. So in between their drinks, I proclaimed, "Roshni, do you know who Manav is?"

Everyone stared at me, their eyes wide open. All their eyes were red, but I wanted to see the fear in Roshni's eyes so I declared loudly, "He is the man who runs the so-called website *myrelationship.com,* the other day you asked for and wanted your story to be part of the website."

Roshni's eyes opened wide, but I did not stop and continued, "I narrated your story to Manav, Roshni, but he has something to ask you like your present relationship with your husband. How your husband supports you and how do you continue, who is your partner?"

I had to say this because this was unplanned and Manav too frowned at me.

Roshni's face became pale and she started saying with a broken voice, "That was my past, Pranami. I don't have any partner and our relationship is very good...you ask Ajay," she winked at Ajay and he took over, "Yes...yes we are fine."

"Pranami, I was never a lesbian, few jealous friends in school just spread the rumour...and people still carry on with the fallacy," Roshni tried to explain her innocence and her husband supported her with a firm yes.

That day the dinner was just a formality as no one enjoyed the food.

--Ω--

After listening to our conversation of the bathroom, Manav was furious while coming back to the car itself.

He cautioned me, "You should not have accepted her request at all and what is shocking is you predicted her intention too...but still went on."

Manav continued while driving, "You know, Pranami...this type of people suffer a lot in their life, if she had forgotten the past and continued with the present relationship is fine; otherwise, I bet her life will be disastrous."

"No, no...she is still in the practice. You have not seen her eyes, she was just lying; otherwise, she would not have an interest in your website."

"May be...these two-faced people don't live a normal life. Their lives are always full of mysteries and it leads them to tragedy.

The next two days, that is, Saturday and Sunday, we spent our time discussing Roshni's past and present probabilities.

My biggest surprise was on Monday evening, without calling me, I found her waiting in the compound of Shree Ganesh Apartment. I came back from office, around 8 p.m., in the evening and while entering inside, the security guard at the entrance told me, "Madam, someone is waiting for you for the past two hours."

"Where is he?" I asked.

It is a normal phenomenon that if we have to guess an unknown gender, obviously the male gender, comes to mind.

"She is a woman, Madam, and said she is your friend...I made her sit at the maintenance office."

"Okay, send her."

The guard brought her up to my flat entrance.

"Hi, Pranami," the voice terrified me; I was just drinking water from the fridge. It was Roshni and she looked exuberant.

"Sorry, Pranami...I misinterpreted you," Roshni said, while sitting on the sofa.

"Will you have water?" I asked.

"No, thanks, I had it in your corporate office...actually my husband pressed me very hard to call you."

"What was the intention then?" I asked, while occupying a seat on the sofa in front of her.

"I told you over the phone."

"What did you say?" I was a bit frantic.

"He loves you."

"Meaning it was not a joke...and you believed I would fall into your ploy."

"Perhaps, yes, and we used to do it...he thought you may be in need of someone's company."

"What?" I merely shouted, Roshni narrated it so simply that it made me furious.

"We have been doing it, Pranami," she got up and occupied a seat near me, close enough and whispered, "Many times."

"But why?" I was captivated about her words, which were beyond my thought process too.

"You know, Pranami, I am a lesbian, despite all my refusals, my parents arranged my marriage...they thought the problem was about age and I would quit it after marriage. You tell me is that just a habit that can be given up?"

She waited for my response and I was transfixed and nodded to her question.

She said again, "Our sex life was disastrous and headed towards divorce, when Ajay came to know about my past."

Roshni stopped and asked, "Shall we make tea; I am thirsty for it...you don't have a maid?"

"No...but I will make tea for you..." I stood up, with me she too stood up and walked down to the kitchen with her continuing speech, "My father gave him the compensation, but it did not bridge the gap of our relationship and then we decided to hunt women in need for Ajay. This way I saved my married life and he does not question my integrity further."

"And you succeeded too?" I asked.

"Yes, I developed a strong database. Ajay has a capsule and I used to induce it in her drink or food, where she develops a strong desire for sex suddenly...and things worked for us."

"What about the girl or woman?" I asked.

"I would film everything, so she is trapped further...she couldn't go to court as it was not a rape, the film showed her desire."

"And you intended to implement it on me?"

Roshni came closer to me, held my hand and said, "Sorry, actually Ajay was really interested in you."

"How many of our friends have been trapped by you? And this was the reason why you searched for old friends and get to know about them well and social media helped you a lot," I said in an angry voice.

"You are right. The social media helped me a lot in this regard."

"What did you achieve, Roshni?... you must have destroyed so many lives." I asked.

"Ajay allowed me to carry on with my partner. It is our deed. I hunt women for him and he lets me do whatever I wish to do."

"It is the same neighbour from your parental house is the partner," I said.

She held my hand too and started rubbing my palm.

The water had boiled to a rising point.

Roshni laughed loud, "Hundred changes... "

"Oh...the water has over boiled," I shouted and released my hand from hers.

I came with the tea and biscuits on a plate. Roshni headed towards the bedroom and said, "We will sit comfortably on the bed."

She sat closer to me; her body often touched mine.

She started again, "Ajay searches for my partner too... but that man Manav is handsome."

When her conversation returned to Manav, I listened to her carefully with full energy, so Roshni had complete chances to touch my parts often.

She said, "His website is a big hit, Pranami."

"But why did you lie on that day?" I asked.

"We don't want that people should know about us."

"The identity could be changed on request," I said.

"But Ajay was not aware of this site and I had never told him about it. He is a straight guy...but this Manav is a gay?" she asked.

I nodded in acceptance.

"He never seemed like that in school," Roshni started putting her hand on my neck and she often touched my breast.

"Why do all these people have pre-signs?" I asked.

Roshni laughed aloud and said, "I am just kidding."

While she was laughing, she started nibbling my breast, hugged me and when she moved her lips to kiss me. I threw her out, "What are you doing?"

Being a woman and my old friend too, I was tolerating her until now. I had never imagined, she would have a second objective too.

Roshni stared at me from top to bottom and asked, "You are not a lesbian?"

"You are really a disaster, get out...get lost from my home...and don't call me again."

I threw her out of my house.

--Ω--

A great lesson was learnt from this incident. First being a single girl, I needed to be more vigilant, especially from friends and close relatives too. The statistics say a woman is harassed more from near and dear ones, rather than by unknown people. Second, never act anything against your sixth sense, being adventurous is good, but knowingly inviting trouble is foolish. Everyone in the world is an opportunist, if one thing does not succeed then another thing is tried on speculation. First Ajay wanted to seduce me, and when he didn't succeed, Roshni tried her luck. What an amazing relationship in the world?

In the human mind, especially about a single working girl, many things are taken for granted, as if she could be thirsty for sex, she could be desperate for love, she could be eager for a companion, she must be drinking...and so many things.

When I narrated what happened to Manav, he was angry too and remarked, "I told you despite of knowing their intention if you fall to their prey, what can be said except question your foolishness...be cautious now."

My anger shifted from Roshni to Manav.

His remarks made me furious too, I thought, 'Instead of getting married to stop all other speculation, he is advising me to be cautious! Why could he not think that, no matter how cautious you are, people have their own ways to build their imaginary web world around you and make all efforts to make you fall into that.'

I was annoyed with him and stopped calling him for few days. I did not ask him to come home on the weekend and I did not visit him.

9

I hope you readers are not dazed over our relationship. It carried on in this manner for quite some time. After Manav left, I asked myself 'why did I get annoyed?' He had not done anything, he did not hide anything from me, then why should I be annoyed? I found some of my best moments with him; I spent all my emotional and passionate moments with him.

I gradually regretted when a few days passed by, but that was of no use.

Manav called me on the next week Wednesday, "Pranami, can you make yourself free for lunch?"

He spoke formally, whereas, on other days he just called me for lunch, without asking me whether I was free or not.

My inner heart was delighted, and spoke out, "Yes, yes I am ready...I was just waiting for this auspicious moment...I am free...free...tell me when, what time and where to come...I can even come to hell with you."

I thought he must have planned it, as I was annoyed.

Putting all emotions aside, I asked, "Why, what happened?"

"It's luncheon with two overseas clients."

"Then must be sponsored by the office?" I asked.

"No...I have invited them...they have been with me for the last two days and tonight they are going back to Germany."

"Why? Are they gays?" I do not know why I asked this, but it was spontaneous.

But he kept his cool, "No...they are a couple."

"Gay couple?"

"No...a man and a woman."

"Where?" I asked, as I did not want to prolong the discussion.

"QBA...CP at 12 O'clock," he took it for granted, when I asked 'where' and it is obvious.

I reached QBA on time. Everyone was waiting for me.

"Hi, I am Pranami," I introduced myself.

The woman seemed to be older than the man was; she said, "We know you...no need to introduce yourself, only didn't meet you. She is lovely, Manav." The woman addressed the last sentences to Manav.

"Yeah...from your words what we figured out about her found she is more than that, she seems more beautiful," the woman paid me a compliment in the second sentence and the man in all his words.

"Hi, I am Eva Halliwel," said the woman.

"I am Justin," said the man.

The man was in his thirties and the woman in her forties. They shook my hand and Eva continued, "It's nice to be here, Manav, you are real like the definition of Manav and the young woman is fabulous."

Both showed immense admiration for me, whereas, I had not even opened up until now. I looked at them, frowned and winked at Manav 'what is the matter?'

Eva perhaps comprehended my sparkling face and twinkling eyes, chuckled and said, "Don't be baffled miss...

Manav has all praise for you...it's your love that you left all your busy schedule and came down for lunch with us...we are unknown to you and thankful to you to give us company."

The waiter served mushroom and lamb meat soup. Eva after taking a sip continued, "It's been amazing...that's why India always fascinates us...your love makes us remember our love...Justine is always kind...was always ready to do any sort of damn thing for me."

She smiled and looked at Justine; he chuckled and listened to each word carefully.

Eva asked, "Am I right, Justine?" Justine nodded in acceptance.

Eva continued, "Once someone told Justine that I have gone to Saarbrucken, to my friend's house. Justine travelled by train from Hamburg to Saarbrucken without reservation and the foolish guy after reaching Saarbrucken called me and I had not even started from Hamburg."

Everyone laughed and I too laughed and laughed. Others had stopped and I alone kept laughing, and became the centre of attraction. When I stopped Justine looked down nervously, his foolishness was rediscovered.

Justine said this time, "But we enjoyed there."

Eva said, "Yeah...we stayed there for fifteen days...and I felt how passionate Justine was about me...I discovered my true love."

Both got emotional, by this time, they must have travelled to Saarbrucken in their memory lane, that's why people get emotional. The memory runs faster in the past. The waiter served the main course. With their love memories, we silently finished lunch. They looked at each other and their eyes showed as if yet again, they had fallen in love.

Soon after lunch, they went back to the hotel, saying thanks repeatedly...Manav had to drop them at their hotel in his new Passat. Manav smiled before taking them into the car. They were in a hurry to go back to the hotel. Manav gave a mischievous smile; I reciprocated in the same way seeing their hasty action.

Later, Manav said, "They wanted to share the feelings of those days now in Delhi and left for their hotel hurriedly, so that it should not disappear from their memory track."

Manav called in the night again and said, "Eva is Justine's senior, they are not married yet; Eva has three children, two from her first husband and one from Justine. They just live together. Her first husband died in a plane crash."

I guessed why Manav told their story.

--Ω--

The perpetual fear of losing Manav overcast me, at all times. I kept worrying about the fact that these people never change, if so one can never live a meaningful life. The fear that things may change tomorrow...the hope...and ambition of a family life, all fluctuated in the air.

Not that I have not asked him, but every time I asked, he went into dormant and speechless mode.

He cared for me, and loved me a lot, but still he loved to be a gay. Sometimes, I thought he felt duty bound. The responsibility my father had given him in his last moments. He is just following his last command.

He knew the importance of a single girl, a bank employee, whose respect and character are paramount. He did not show my face as the interviewer in Rupali's interview and used only my voice. I had even expressed my gratitude, after watching the interview post. After two days of the interview, I called him and thanked him, "Thanks, babe...for not showing my face in Rupali's interview."

"Have you finished, or are you drunk? What rubbish are you talking? Thanks...thanks to whom...me...what I am?" Manav was annoyed.

"That's what I want to know, what we are...what binds us?" he was speechless again.

He did not want any obligation.

--Ω--

On Friday, he did not call and my schedule was so hectic for the last two days that I returned at 11 at night, from the bank. On Saturday, too, he did not call; it was Christmas Eve. Despite my busy schedules, I never missed regular events. At the back of mind was the thought about why Manav had not called me. However, I did not get time to call him. I had to go to the bank even the next day on Sunday, despite the holiday. I called Gaurav Sharma and few others to join me, but only after eleven in the morning, as it was a holiday and we need not wake up so early.

On Saturday night at eleven, I checked my mails, as I had neglected checking my mails or Facebook for a month. I had two mail Ids. I use Google mail for my personal uses. I quickly browsed through the 87 unread mails. Many of them were promotion mails from Home Shop 18, Naaptol, Flipkart and Goodreads, as I do a lot of online shopping. I had developed this habit, because I hated shopping alone and had very little time for physical shopping because of my busy schedule. Few mails were from Facebook. I had not blocked any mails and had a long list of FB friends. Almost daily, I received a message reminding me of at least five or more friends' birthdays. I deleted them. There were many other unwanted notification mails from Facebook about people mentioning, commenting or inviting me, which I did not even bother to read.

Today, I received five mails from Facebook. The first one at 8.15 and the last one at 2100 hrs. The first mail read, 'Pranami, you have notifications pending'. The second one read, 'Vardhman changed his profile picture'. The third one read, 'Vardhman friend of Manav also commented on his photo'. The fourth mail read, 'Vardhman and Manav at Amber Fort of

Pink City, Jaipur'. The fifth mail read, 'Manav commented on Vardhman and his photo'. A new mail popped up on the right hand corner of laptop, time 11:25, from Facebook, 'Manav updated his profile picture'.

I clicked on the fourth mail, my heartbeat quickened in anticipation, as the Facebook window opened up. I quickly glanced at the profile – 25 friends requests, 12 messages and 58 notifications. Scrolling down quickly past n-number of posts, I saw Manav in it. A post showed that Vardhman had added a new photo and the next line showed that Vardhman commented on his own photo; Rahul Dhingra, Raaj Singh and 18 others had liked the post. Another post showed that Manav commented on his own photo, which showed Vardhman and him standing close to each other, against the backdrop of the Amber Fort.

Many other photographs posted showed that they were in Jaipur, the Pink City. Vardhman had commented on one of them 'enjoying vacation in Jaipur'. I was furious and did not know what to do. I could achieve nothing more by scrolling anymore.

I stopped scrolling the site and called him – the phone rang four times, but there was no answer. I felt dead and everything appeared dark to me. A few rings later, I heard a computerized voice. I cut the call. I tried once again, but after five more attempts, he had not picked the phone.

Manav never forgets his phone; he always had it by his side, even when he went to sleep. I could only think that either he had lost it or it was stolen. The thought consoled me, but only for a moment. I began to imagine and think about all possibilities of his actions, especially involving Vardhman and him in compromising positions. It was past one at night and sleep eluded me.

A phone call woke me at four in the morning; it was still dark outside. I looked at the phone and it showed that Manav was calling.

I pressed the green key to talk, but before I could say hello, Manav asked, "Pranami, you called me so many times, what happened, is anything wrong?" he sounded desperate on speculations.

"Tell me where you were?" I asked emotionally.

"I was with Vardhman, but the phone was in silent mode, not even in vibration mode so I didn't get it. I just saw your missed calls."

He had become shameless, without thinking for a moment that he was talking to a woman!

"You are out of Delhi?" I asked.

"Yeah, I am in Jaipur and Vardhman is also with me. We came on a holiday package."

"You didn't bother to tell me, I was waiting for you."

Manav preferred silence while speaking on the phone, but after few seconds, he said feebly, "Sorry, Pranami."

"It's simple 'sorry, Pranami'...do you know how terrified I was when you didn't pick up the call," knowingly I kept the FB issue in abeyance.

"Sorry, Pranami. Actually, Vardhman planned the tour and informed me at the last moment," he tried to cover up for himself.

"I know why you went with Vardhman, as I refused to have sex with you the last time we met and men can never accept this," my speculations poured out.

"That's not the fact," answered Manav.

"It's a fact, keep on feeding the men and they are happy, if one day the feeding is stopped they revolt," I cut his voice "I am coming...which hotel are you staying?" I was furious too.

The next moment, I wondered how I could be so mean.

Manav reacted quickly, "No...no...no...we have already left

the hotel. We are going to Goa. We are on the way to the airport...the flight is at 6.30."

"Nice...I am coming to Goa. Which hotel will you stay at?"

"Which hotel in Goa?" Manav asked someone and told me, "'Lotus'. It's a resort at Candolim."

"Then wait for me in Candolim." I cut the phone.

Probably, he asked Vardhman about the hotel they were going to stay at as part of the package. What pinched me was that I spoke rudely to him. If he was alone, it would have been okay, but Vardhman or many more must have accompanied him on the tour package. I regretted. But that made no difference. The next moment, I called my travel agent asking him to book a flight ticket to Goa.

He showed reluctance, "Madam, it's peak time and it will be very difficult to book for today."

"Not today...I need it now." The man was confounded.

I softened, "I mean as soon as possible by any means at any cost...and also book a room in the resort 'Lotus'."

"Let me try, Madam."

"Okay."

"You will go alone?" asked the man in a half-sleepy voice.

"Yeah."

Every time, I regret my decisions over my life. I always take decisions late and that too, when life had shown me its true colour, hoping that I had taken the decision earlier. I was pleased how I had made up my mind to go to Goa with such speed and audacity.

The next moment, I rang up Gaurav Sharma. He was still in bed.

"Yeah, Gaurav, I unable to come today and I will be on leave for a week, please manage everything."

"What happened, is anything serious?" he started speculating.

"Nothing serious."

"You are going out of Delhi," he enquired.

Men always pursue women's movements, even if they are married men with two children!

"I will be in Delhi, though I may go for some time to Shivpuri, my father's native place," I lied to decrease his speculations.

I cut the call and mailed Mr Ravindra Shukla, the regional head of my bank for a week's leave.

My travel agent somehow arranged the ticket for the evening flight on 'Go' airlines and booked a room in 'Lotus' which was not difficult.

--Ω--

In the evening at 0830, my flight landed in Goa. I felt alone on landing as neither had I informed Manav nor had he bothered to check if I was actually coming or not, he was not at the airport to receive me. I reached the resort at 10.

I called Manav. This was my first conversation with him after my earlier call to him early that morning.

After five or six rings, he picked the phone.

I was murmuring, "Com 'on, baby, pick it up."

"Hello," said Manav's, amidst plenty of background noise. He must have not looked at the display of the phone, so did not know it was my call.

"Where are you, babe?"

"Oh, Pranami...yeah...tell me what happened?" That meant he had not taken my trip to Goa seriously.

"I said where are you?" I repeated my question slowly.

"I am in Goa," he spoke loudly.

"I know where are you now?"

"I am at Pantem beach."

"I am in the resort...the same Lotus resort."

"What, you are in Goa, why didn't you inform me?" he was surprised.

"I told you, but you were not in the mood to heed me."

"Okay...okay...let me come and we will talk...there's plenty of noise I can't hear you properly."

"But I can hear you...no problem," before he heard me, he cut the connection.

I had made my appearance, calling him again would not be fruitful.

Nights in Goa are beautiful. I came out from my room and walked a long way on the seashore. I had not even bothered to change; I walked barefoot.

The weather in Delhi was freezing cold; while here the weather was so pleasant, one could roam barefooted. I wondered about what to do now. I had reached Goa, sure, but how could I be with him? Vardhman would be cordoning him always. Probably, they were in a group. The travel agencies these days make good profits arranging such trips. Gays are most interested in it; they search for partners and a crowd to follow them.

Sometimes, I feel their number is increasing. People are more inclined towards being gay. I start presuming about what they will be doing at the beach party.

I hate that man, Vardhman. He is the bottom man and I started taking him as my rival. After a long walk, I had come back to my cottage, yet they had not returned and the watch showed 11:30 p.m. Pantem beach is far away, they must have chosen it because of its seclusion. Restlessness gradually mounts over my patience, it is past 12 now, but still, they have not returned and I thought of calling him again. Just then, a Traveller roaring over the night's tranquillity came and stopped few metres ahead of my cottage. Gradually, fourteen men stepped out from the vehicle. Manav was the fourth of them to step out and Vardhman followed closely.

I watched them profoundly; Manav looked around and fished out his phone. Vardhman who was sticking to him murmured something.

The next moment my phone rang.

"Hello," I answered.

"Which cottage are you in, Pranami? Or have you gone to sleep? Should we meet tomorrow?"

"No chance, I am waiting for you. I am in the cottage just in front you. I can see you, but I cannot come to you. I hate those so-called masculine gay men, you know."

"Okay, I am coming."

He asked Vardhman something; the others had departed from the place, in pairs and some started kissing on the move as if thirsty for thousand years.

Vardhman walked alone, gloomy and unhappy. He must be feeling the sparks of hatred in my presence as I felt for him. Now I opened the cottage door and Manav walked straight into my room.

He started with the old question again, "Why didn't you inform me about you coming to Goa?"

Instead of answering to his question, I asked my same old question, "Why didn't you tell me about your move?"

Manav sat on the sofa and answered, "Vardhman planned it late."

"Or you feared to tell me," I intervened. "You are not a small kid and you don't have a phone to call? These are all excuses."

I was right, so he preferred to take the silence route.

"You have planned to go back to your cottage?" I asked, seeing him sitting on the sofa. Manav looked around and at my eyes, but didn't speak out. Perhaps, he had the plan to go back, but was perplexed to say so. I pretended he must have promised Vardhman he would come back.

"Come...come freshen up and changeover, I have not slept last night as well."

"I don't have anything to change into. I am drenched in perspiration in this outfit."

"Come on, babe. This is not first time you are staying with me, I have my pyjamas and T-shirt."

He had no choice, as he knew that now his chance of going back to Vardhman had diminished and his excuses were feeble. When he was in the bathroom, Vardhman called his mobile. I saw Vardhman calling, but ignored it as usual. He called again and this time Manav came out from the bathroom.

"Yeah," answered Manav. I couldn't hear the voice of the opponent, but Manav cut the phone shortly with monosyllables of no...no...yes...yes.

I was on the bed and when he came back, I asked, "Who was it?"

"Vardhman."

"Is he confirming whether you will stay here or go back to him?" Manav was silent.

I asked again, "He wants to be with you and you too want the same."

He slept beside me, but did not answer.

The burning smell of my heart reflected in my words. Manav knew it and preferred silence, anything he said would have led to unwarranted arguments. But what could I do, my heart was burning and sleep seemed a distant dream. I tried to make myself comfortable and after a deep breath, I turned towards him, and put my hand on his chest.

Manav's position was unchanged, and his eyes were closed.

I asked to overcome the silence, "Are you asleep?"

"No."

"Then why don't you talk with me? What are you thinking?" I asked for intimacy and moved my body closer to him, and put my palm inside his T-shirt to feel and play with his chest hair.

"Nothing," answered Manav.

"You want to go back to Vardhman?" I just said to tease him.

Manav opened his eyes, it felt as if Lord Siva opened the third eye and I corrected myself, "Sorry...sorry."

"What did you do the entire day?" I asked.

"Where was it the entire day? We reached the cottage at 11 a.m. After lunch, we went for some sightseeing of Portuguese monuments and then we had the beach party," he seemed more comfortable now.

"What exactly did you do at the beach party?" again the smell of my burning heart spoke out. Manav looked at me profoundly. I was not supposed to ask this! I had attended many gay parties, but not a beach gay party. Other parties were bounded with many rules, but the beach party was free and they loved to be free.

My fingers moved inside his T-shirt, first in search of the hair, which I would play with on many occasions. He had shaved off; it was clean now, and felt smooth.

"Wow...when did you shave this, it is as smooth as 'makhan'."

He simply laughed. I was waiting for some other reactions from him.

Finally, my endurance gave up and I asked shamelessly, "You don't want sex?"

"Pranami...it's too late, go to sleep."

"You had enough of it?"

"You have not slept last night also."

"Don't speak in circles, be straight...how many times did you make out with Vardhman...you must have finished your first session at the beach party and planned to have more in the cottage! But unfortunately, I came as an obstacle. You may have had many more in Jaipur as well...was it only with Vardhman or with the other gays too?"

My words had no effect. He just closed his eyes. I knew he had not slept and this was an act to avoid me, avoid the piercing words of my burning heart.

I withdrew from him, turned to the opposite side and tried to sleep, but sleep was against me. Hours later, I don't know when I dropped off to sleep..

--Ω--

I woke up as my phone rang. The time showed nine in the morning.

"Hello, Pranami...it's me, your brother, Subham."

I woke up completely and sat on the bed with the phone to my ear.

"I am calling from the London airport. I am coming to India; I didn't get a direct flight, my connecting flight is at seven a.m. What is the time there?"

I looked at the phone again to confirm the exact time, "It is 9.10 here."

"Yeah...you can add seven hours from that time...it's the flight duration."

"Why you didn't call me from the USA?" I asked.

"What is the big deal?"

"Bhai, I am out of Delhi and I would not have planned for it."

"Where are you?"

"I am in Goa."

"Nice...holidaying...but I don't need a warm welcome and don't think about coming to the airport; I am not going to stay with you. I have booked a hotel for me."

"Then why are you calling me from London, you could have called me after reaching Delhi," I raised my voice.

Manav woke up with the ringing of my phone, but didn't get up. Now he got up and sat crossed-legged in front of me and asked, "Who is it?"

"Someone is with you?"

"Yeah...its Manav."

"I knew it would be Manav only."

Bhai's teasing words irritated me. I asked in the same raised voice, "What are you coming for?"

"I need the property...I need the settlement...you know, Pranami, I have lost in business and it's downsizing now. I need money to restart my business."

Bhai's voice was appealing.

"Yes, you take your share who stops you and you had taken part of it, it's nothing new."

"But, it won't suffice my requirement...I need more money...I need the complete business."

"You cannot get that Bhai."

"There is no point talking to you...my lawyer will talk to you."

"Yes...it's not you; your lawyer was talking to me until now."

Bhai cut the connection. Our dialogues were gradually getting high pitched and headed towards infinity. No way things could be resolved in this fashion.

From our dialogue Manav understood who it was, until now, he was listening to us passionately and the moment the connection was cut, he went to the toilet.

--Ω--

When he came back from the toilet, I went inside. Many unwanted thoughts processed in my memory. It felt as if my brain was jam-packed. Earlier, it was Manav and now it was Subham Bhai. Things had occurred unnoticed and abruptly.

Perhaps, I had taken plenty of time in the toilet with my unthreaded thoughts. When I came out Manav was talking to a travel agent and two cups of coffee were served. The room was full of the coffee aroma.

Seeing me, Manav held the mouthpiece in one hand and told me, "Have the coffee." He was engaged in talking to the travel agent again.

I was desperately in need of the coffee, but was unable to express what my need was. I sat with the coffee mug. With one sip of it, I felt good. I heard he concluded with 'okay' and came and sat with me, taking his coffee mug.

"Probably, we will get tickets for the evening flight of Indigo," Manav said after taking a few sips of the coffee.

"Whatever."

We drank our coffee silently.

Suddenly, he stood up and said, "I am just coming."

Before I could even think of anything, he left.

I also came out to see what had happened, the nights Traveller was parked in front and the 13 masculine gays had assembled around it. Manav had joined them to say adieu to them.

I hid myself to see how they would act and especially to see Vardhman's reaction. With others, he did the formality of kissing on the cheeks, but with Vardhman, he hugged and kissed him. Manav talked with him quite briefly until everyone was settled down inside. Vardhman again hugged and kissed him, before getting inside. Manav waved his hand until the Traveller was out of vision.

Manav then came back with his baggage and kept it in the cottage, which he shared with Vardhman.

"Flight is confirmed for 5:30 p.m. Would you like to roam anywhere?" he asked.

"No," my answer was clear.

After watching their love scene, I felt all my thought processes were jammed. I had developed a heavy headache.

--Ω--

In the taxi, at 9 p.m., at Delhi, from T1, Manav asked, "Why is Subham Bhai coming?"

"He has already come."

In the last eight hours, we had not spoken a single word to each other.

"But why has he come?" Manav asked again.

"He wants his share."

The case was an old one and Manav knew everything, rather he had stood beside me for every bit of it.

My thoughts found words and I was spontaneous, "He wants that his lawyer should speak to me...he has not come to stay with me, rather he will stay in a hotel...he wants to maintain proper rivalry. It's okay...fine...I will also maintain the same...let my lawyer also speak to him," my tone was tense and my voice rose.

Manav came closer, put his hand around my shoulder, when we crossed the Palam over bridge he said, "The industry is closed, the machines are getting rusted and value of the company is gradually getting low. If the dispute continues few more years, it will become zero. Why don't you let go...let Subham Bhai take it and utilize it in his bankrupt business."

"No way...who told him to go back the USA, marry his gay partner...what was his name...Russell...check out that bastard must have come, that's why he didn't come to stay with me."

"Pranami, think about our customs. If he had been here, all the property would have gone to him...the business...the house, everything, after Uncle's death."

"Fuck the customs...our law says that I have equal share in dad's property...and yes, he sold our Green Park house as the hierarchy transfer, after dad's death. He had not listened to me...if dad had not gifted me this Dwarka house today; I would have been on the streets."

Rarely do I use the f word, it showed my desperation. Manav was afraid of saying anything to me, but I had not finished, "It's not Subham Bhai, that bastard Russell's mind must be working behind him. So who wants to do a job, I too could sell the property and eat by sitting idle, he would want his own business, so why shouldn't I?"

My frustration was not yet over, "He sold most of the properties but I had not objected, only left over the factory and his share is half in it. I am ready to give it but not the entire property. And this time I am warning you, Manav, don't support him. I would have given him everything if he had obeyed father." Manav too listened me carefully.

The taxi stopped in front of Shri Ganesh Apartment and I had to rush my unsaid words.

While mounting the stairs, I said again, "I have spoiled your Christmas mood...no?" I asked something from him, but he had no answer for it.

HE

10

A message flashed on my Facebook account. It was an invitation that read 'Soul Satisfaction' the venue given was 'SSKY Lounge and Bar 42', Antriksh Bhawan, KG Marg, Connaught Place, New Delhi.

The invitation continued, "Let's quench our thirst, dance a lot, hop around, make some friends, sing while drunk, burn the dance floor, make some noise, dap in the air groove with zeal, move to the beats, sway with the lights, wear some tights, drench our soul with all the ingredients for a yummy soul curry. At the end, let's keep a count of the satisfied souls and all party to glory."

I consented for attending the party. Usually, these types of parties are organized on Friday's and Saturday's and in some locations on Wednesday, as well. Organizers have a clear motive of profit nothing else. But gays have their fun and increase the social community status.

"Hi, buddy," said a well-known voice near me. I looked back to confirm who I thought it was; yes, it was Subham Bhai. Not much of a surprise, he must have been invited. He was on my Facebook list as well as on the 'Gay Delhi's list.

"Surprised?" he asked.

"No," I nodded.

"How can I forget Delhi, wherever I may be, I am always in touch with Delhi...*Delhi meri jaan,*" he laughed introducing a man accompanying him, he said, "Meet Russell, he is my fiancée."

Russell came closer and hugged me. We kissed each other on the cheeks as that was our way of greeting each other.

"I know him. I had met him earlier on your last visit to India. He is on my FB list also," I clarified, Subham Bhai laughed aloud.

"New York is advanced. We have not married yet, but we stay together and there the law governs it," Subham Bhai continued laughing aloud.

Being an NRI, he had all the rights to bat for New York. I didn't heed him much, I was looking for Vardhman, as he had not come yet.

"Manav," Subham Bhai called tenderly, "I wanted to talk to you." We walked towards the sofa in the other room. Russell mingled with somebody else.

"Before coming to India, I thought of calling you many times, but then I didn't call thinking that what you will think about me. Perhaps, if I would have talked to you this situation may not have arisen."

I looked with a frown at Subham Bhai; I was not aware of what situation he was talking about.

"Have your drink," Subham Bhai said, as I had not sipped my drink even once, since the time he was talking to me.

Perhaps, it was the fear towards him that I carried from childhood. Once he was a terror to us, but today's stance is different, we are friends on the same boat sailing with the tide in an unknown river. And this gave me the audacity to have a drink with him. I finished the glass in one go.

"Waiter," Subham Bhai called.

"Yes, sir."

"Refill it," Subham Bhai indicated towards my glass.

"Yes, sir...whisky or rum?" asked the waiter.

"Vodka and normal water."

I asked Subham Bhai, "You won't drink another one?"

"Yeah...sure," he made the waiter stay as he refilled my glass, "just wait dear." He finished the remaining drink.

"Get me a whisky with soda," Subham Bhai ordered the waiter.

He took the glass and said 'cheers,' then he continued "even after coming to India, I had thought of calling you, but still don't know the reason why I didn't call you...but luckily today we met."

I did not wait for any more speculations and asked, "You want something from me?"

Not heeding me, he continued, "You are close to Pranami, rather I would say that you are the only one close to Pranami... please help me. You know I came to India for the sole purpose of settling the issue, but six days have passed, but she is not bothered to listen to me. Even today, she has not taken my call."

After coming from Goa, we spent the night without noticing each other. I joined office on Monday and five days had passed, I had not talked to Pranami, very much unaware of the latest development between the siblings.

"How can I help you?"

"Yeah...she will listen to you, make her understand just how much I am in need of the money."

"She won't listen. I have tried."

"Then tell her to meet me once, after all, she is my sister. I will make her understand my situation."

"You annoyed her by your coming; you should have visited her place first," I said.

"What can I do with Russell; she is damn against him and would not even want to see his face."

"He could have stayed back at the hotel."

"Yeah...that could have been done...but it's too late and I am leaving tomorrow...do something, Manav," Subham Bhai's voice was on the verge of tears. I couldn't see him suffering anymore. He was remorseful that he made a mistake.

"I cannot be sure whether Pranami will be willing or not to broach or talk about this topic, still let me try."

I dialled Pranami's number. Subham Bhai finished the glass in one go and asked the waiter for a top up and looked at me longingly, hoping for something good to come out from the phone call.

--Ω--

She picked the phone late.

"Hello Pranami, have you gone to bed?" I asked, before she said anything.

"What is the time...it's nine only...? I just came back from the bank and had gone to freshen up, so I was late taking your call," Pranami replied, while I was clueless what to ask.

Over my hush silence, she said again, "What happened, you are not coming?"

Her first reaction about asking this, was because we have a usual way of spending our weekends. In between if we get call means there was some deviation in the plan.

"No...actually, I need to talk on some other issue."

"Yeah, tell me," she was spontaneous over the phone.

"Subham Bhai is with me, he wants to meet you."

She was quiet for some time and this was painful. I cannot

even divert the talk. After few seconds, Pranami said, "Finally, he has reached you?"

"Pranami, listen he is in trouble..."

"All this is drama."

"This is not drama, I know it."

She was silent for a long time, and then said, "Where are you now?"

"Me...in my room," I told her a lie and it was intentional.

"Okay... but tomorrow my bank is open."

"Right, I will bring Subham Bhai to you and you talk over lunch at CCD."

"No...not at my place. I don't want to make any nuisance here, you decide somewhere at Connaught Place and tell me where. I will come down there, but it must be after 1 p.m." Pranami cut the phone.

Subham Bhai was enthusiastically listening to our talk so I did not need to explain the entire conversation. He got up, and before leaving from me, said, "Thank you...I shall call you tomorrow morning."

I get relief from the stress and whatever will happen it will be tomorrow. But the next moment, I jumped up from the sofa with a jerk. It was 09:15 and Vardhman had not yet come. I stepped out from the room quickly; the hall was densely packed and in the subdued light, it would be difficult to search for him.

I tried to call him. When I switched on the phone, I saw four missed calls and all were from Vardhman. Oh, he had tried to contact me when he did not find me in the hall. I called him...he stood alone where I could see him, he took the call in one go, "Where are you?" he stirred anxiously.

"Just behind you."

--Ω--

Subham Bhai called me at 8 a.m., in the morning. My eyes were barely open; we had left the party at one in the morning and Vardhman had accompanied me to my place. We had drunk vodka again and had gone to bed at four in the morning.

"Still sleeping?" Subham Bhai asked.

"Yeah...we left the party late."

"Where have you planned for the meeting?" He came straight to the point.

"Not yet thought on this."

"Ignis, in the inner circle will do."

"Okay, fine, I will tell her."

I tried to sleep again, but I could not. Vardhman slept profoundly, the call and my discussion had not affected his sleep. I made coffee, as it suits me in winter. There was no reason in waking up Vardhman. Before I forget, I must tell Pranami about the venue. Taking a sip of the coffee, I called Pranami.

"Where are you?" I heard some noise over her phone.

"Reaching the bank soon...I am driving," replied Pranami.

"So early, it's not even nine in the morning!"

"It is the bank and today is Saturday, but you have woken up early, so what is the deal?"

"I slept early and woke up early...I am taking coffee."

"So nice."

My heart was contented at her kindness. At last, my lie had managed some positive remarks from her.

"Subham Bhai called in the morning...it's at the 'Ignis', in the inner circle of CP."

"Okay, fine."

"What is the noise?" I asked.

"It's traffic on the over bridge."

"Traffic, so early!"

"You have not looked outside; it's the first thick fog in Delhi."

"No...I have not looked."

The phone got disconnected; I came to the balcony with my coffee mug. It's the first thick fog of this winter. The sky-high buildings of Ghaziabad looked dim and hazy.

--Ω--

Siblings' rivalry was tough to digest.

At Ignis, we booked a three-seater table from one p.m., and waited for her.

Pranami's SMS came at 1.30 p.m., "I won't be free before two."

I showed it to Subham Bhai. He did not make any remark. We ordered coffee to kill the time and he was telling me about the up's and down's of his business in New York.

I replied to Pranami, "We are waiting at Ignis."

The gist of Subham Bhai's talk was that the retail chain business in New York was going through a tough period, and was doing very badly. Russell and he in partnership opened a supermarket, which was doing well, but when they opened another store, they were short of money that affected the entire business. And the first store also suffered because of this. No bank, no investor was ready to invest in trading now. So they were running around to fetch millions of rupees for restarting their business. Machinery would not cost much, but the factory and the land in Gurgaon would be in millions. He had talked to a builder who was ready to give ten crores for the entire deal, machinery, building and land though machines and building were of no use.

Pranami came at 3 p.m.

The siblings hugged. I had ordered lunch and we finished lunch silently.

Washing his hands, Subham Bhai said, "Pranami, do you want that your brother should die for money."

"Not at all," Pranami wasn't carried over by his emotional words.

"Then why are you reluctant about selling the Gurgaon property?"

"Earlier, I was reluctant for the sale, now I agree, we can sell."

Subham Bhai's face blossomed; he had never thought the dream would come true so easily. But I could not see it easily, I knew Pranami better than anyone else. Something must be going on in her mind.

"Sell it and take your 50 per cent share. I have no objection," Pranami declared, when the flower in Subham Bhai's face had fully blossomed.

Subham Bhai seemed clueless. The merriment on his face suddenly dropped to dismal, "How? We have already five millions in debt and we need another five millions to restart it, you know it...huge money is required for retail trading."

"It's your business and you are not alone, your partner can help with funding."

"He has nothing, he put all his resources in it and still we are short of ten millions."

"I am not here to fund it; legally you can have 50 per cent. I know 50 per cent of the land may not fetch you good money, but I want half of the entire money. If you feel so, go ahead."

"I am your brother, Pranami, and I am in trouble."

"I know it."

"Still you insist to make me suffer."

"Who told you to suffer, who told you to stay back in America? You come back it's all yours," Pranami's tone was raised.

"It's not possible."

"Then this is also not possible, you leave that bloody gay friend of yours and the property is all yours...ten crore is huge money to start a business in India... why just money; we have the infrastructure and the reputation of dad...you just need to build that...come back, Bhai."

"Don't say anything about Russell," Subham Bhai intervened.

"Why it pinched?" Pranami's tone amplified.

"Have I said anything about you, your relationship...what you feel, I don't know anything about you...I know each and every moment of yours..."

"What's the big deal and you ask...ask me what wrong did I do?... I am not a lesbian and I love Manav...I will marry him."

Until now, I was just a spectator in the scuffle between the siblings. Whom should I support? But when my name came in their scuffle my inner soul woke up.

Before I could say anything, the manager came to preserve the peaceful ambience of the restaurant, "Sir, madam please...others are also having their lunch and they are getting disturbed."

"Come Manav there is no use talking to him," said Pranami, taking her purse to leave.

I was bewildered about what to do and stayed back. Pranami walked few steps and said, "Okay, you stay back with him I am going."

She walked out.

"Why Subham Bhai, she had agreed for the sale, now the sole purpose is defeated," I said.

"But how can I tolerate those things about Russell?"

"Is Russell listening? What do you expect from your sister, she would welcome Russell and you? You don't know your sister...few seconds of your anger turned around things."

"Yes," Subham Bhai snatched his hair in regret, "but she was talking about 50 per cent only and that alone won't be enough to solve my problem," again he tried to define that he had not done wrong.

"Initially, she was not ready to sell, but now she agreed, in time she might have given you the complete amount, but you lost everything...what is the time of your flight?" I was irritated.

"20:00 hrs." Both looked at the time, it was 4:15.

"Get ready, I will drop you at T3."

"Okay."

--Ω--

Subham Bhai was disappointed.

While departing, he said, "I don't know what to do after reaching America. The bank may snatch our store." However, I had nothing to say to console him.

Saying bye to Subham Bhai and Russell at the airport, I reached Pranami at 9 p.m.

"Coming from the airport... said goodbye to him?" Pranami asked, closing the door.

"Yes... Subham Bhai was upset and, Pranami, he was not acting, he is in real trouble."

"He invited the trouble only and please don't say anything about him...I warned you earlier too, I am not in the mood to hear about him and his friend...I hate gays."

I knew she was fuming about her brother.

She was furious. She had not looked into my eyes as well. Quietly, I entered the other room. Then Pranami came straight and asked, "Anyone stopped you entering the other room (her bed room.)"

"No."

"Then why did you come here." She took my bag and the jacket that I opened up and I had to follow her. Usually, I wear her pyjamas and T-shirt.

Pranami asked, "What was Subham Bhai asking?"

I laughed, after all, they have blood relations, it attracts.

"Nothing...but he was worried about you."

She laughed, "Not for me, for the money...the man, who had not come back on mama's death, but came on papa's death, so that he could take the rest of his share, can't be worried about me."

She was not ready to accept anything.

She cooked for me, and did not order anything through home delivery.

At the dinner table, I asked, "You knew that I would be back?"

"Yeah."

"How do you..."

"Everything is not told..."

"You said you hate gays."

"There it struck you...yes I do... but I love you damn fool." Her mood changed gradually.

11

The other day I met a guy named 'Shashikant'. He narrated how he became gay and I penned it down which later I posted on my website.

I gave it a heading of 'Butterflies' life'.

The post read:

"No one is born gay. It is not a mental disorder and science does not say anything about it.

Deciding you are gay often happens gradually, it may not be something you can initially put a name to, and it can feel very confusing. Mr Shashikant said it is an adaptive process.

Like his friends, he also was attracted to girls, in fact, and he had a girlfriend. However, things changed when he joined engineering and started living in the hostel. He shared the hostel room with 'Varun', his ultimate partner. They saw porn movies and one day landed up having a physical interaction. From that day, sex was made easy for them. A four-year stint in engineering in a far-flung area from the city brought them closer. They started caring for each other and behaved like lovers.

Those days, he had not thought 'he is a gay'. In the final year, he thought seriously, when the buzzword 'gay' showed its profound presence in the air.

Many people feel attracted to people of the same sex and wonder whether this means that they are gay? Shashikant vehemently opposed this question. He felt that he was in a situation, where this was just a phase. Eventually, he was going to start finding women attractive. But it never happened. He finished engineering, and took up a job, but the gay phase did not change. Gradually, he was more attracted to men, and still had not gotten attracted to women.

He started asking himself, "Am I gay?" He kept on denying, saying, "No...I am not."

But at the age of 30, he began to accept the fact that he is gay. Shashikant said, the feeling was very intense and alienating. He had tried hard to change himself and he had visited the whorehouse many times, but never found the pleasure he intended. His parents started pressurizing him to get married the moment they came to know of Shasikant's changed interest. However, Shashikant was not convinced and visited Varun in the other city to find out how his life was going on.

To his surprise, Varun was living a normal life, was married and had a family.

Shashikant asked him, "You never feel attracted to the same sex?"

Varun laughed and replied, "Yes, sometimes...but I am happy with my family."

Shashikant said some people are 'transitional gays'. Some people are bisexual, meaning they are attracted to both men and women, and have relationships with both. Like Varun, they were bisexual.

Shashikant is now 43 and lives as a single. He was branded as a gay in his locality and no girl was ready to marry him. He changed his area, town, city and state, but did not marry. In his youth days, there was no law protecting gays rather it was taken as sin and an evil in society. Nobody could ever think about a marriage with the same sex.

Mr Shashikant still carries many doubts with him. He attends gay parties, participates in pride parades and asks questions. Will Varun be called as 'Gay'? Some people are not attracted to anyone and wonder if this is a sign that they are gay?

When this website asked him what is your answer to your question that Varun be called as gay or bisexual or straight he replied, "With time, someone who is gay will realise that not only are they sexually attracted to members of the same sex, but the attraction is not transitional. This realisation could come at any time during anyone's life. Many people become aware of gay feelings during their teenage years, as this is when they begin to learn more about their sexuality and identity. However, the difficulties associated with accepting these feelings and coming out mean that many gay people don't identify themselves as gay until much later on in one's life."

Shashikant said, "A small stint or passing phase of the same sex relationship does not bring the man to gayism."

He also agrees with our motto T'kewya.

And when this website convinced him what TCOWYA means, he smiled and replied, "This is what I am saying."

--Ω--

One thing Pranami didn't mention in our life cycle that both are fond of theatre. Indian Habitat Centre and Shri Ram Centre were our aaddas. Last Sunday, at the 7 p.m., we had seen 'Ramkali' a Hindi drama by Arvind Gaur, at Shri Ram centre. After dinner, I took a taxi and returned to my place. On Monday, I needed to go to office early; I had a meeting with some overseas client at 9 a.m. And if I stayed back at Dwarka, I may fail to reach on time. The long distance as well as the traffic problem is increasing in Delhi, especially because of the thick fog. I convinced Pranami about this problem and she agreed. She was in a good mood after the show and dinner at 'De Villa' in our old area of operation, Hauz Khas.

We had not been to the theatre together for almost nine months. My case is different, I had been to multiplexes with Vardhman and other friends, but Pranami is a filmy girl, loves film, soap operas, and drama very much. It was her interest to see a play. She was happy, so she accepted my proposal and returned alone in her Honda CRV.

The next morning, I was on time at office. Pranami's call came at 09:15 a.m. But I was unable to attend it as the conference was in full swing. Pranami's call went unattended. Again, it came in 09:30 and went unattended. She called for the third time at 10 a.m. I still could not attend to it and she did not call again.

I was free at 11 a.m., there were two missed called that I had not noticed. One from a landline, a Delhi number and the other one from Pranami, again at 10:42 a.m.

I called Pranami first, "Hello, Pranami, I was in a meeting so could not take your call. Tell me anything urgent. You called so many times!"

"Manav, I am at Green Park police station."

My heart beat quickened and speculations were even stronger than that.

I started thinking, "Did she come across an accident? I should not have left her alone, it was a foggy night."

"Manav, you know Mr Sambhu is dead?"

"Mr Sambhu...the Alwar school headmaster...is dead?" my question was loaded with surprise.

"Yes, he is dead. He has committed suicide."

"I knew this would happen...you remember I told you that day he would be killed or will commit suicide...and the same thing happened...this is the fate of these people..." I could not stop myself, if I was not in office I may have wept a lot.

"But why are you in the police station and how do you know Mr Sambhu is dead?"

"The police called me in the night."

"So you did not go to the bank and why didn't you inform me in the night?"

"It was late...they called me, at 12 in the night."

"But why did they call you, neither do you know Mr Sambhu nor do you have any relationship with him?" The thing struck me late, why Pranami, she had no cause for his death.

"His wife mentioned my Honda CRV number in her statement."

Now things were clear to me, I said, "I am dropping the call and just reaching to you...okay...I am just coming...don't panic."

It took 40 minutes to reach Green Park Police Station, by the fastest means in the traffic rush. Pranami sat in a chair and looked gloomy and depressed. Seeing me, she rushed and held me tight and started weeping.

Wiping her tears, I said, "Nothing to worry I am here okay...you are here from the night?"

"No... I came in the morning, at nine...they asked me to reach the police station, at nine in the morning," said Pranami, controlling her tears.

I sat where Pranami was sitting beside her. The police inspector was busy asking something to another fellow.

I asked Pranami in a whisper, "What did they ask you?"

"Whether I know Mr Sambhu, why the Honda CRV had gone to Alwar, who drove it and whether I run the website or not?" Pranami told me in brief.

Before I could ask Pranami anything more, the police inspector signalled us to come and sit in front of him. The man he was questioning had left.

"Sir, it's me who had taken the Honda CRV to Alwar. Pranami has nothing to do with this...leave her sir...she has no connection," I started as soon as I sat in front of the police officer.

He asked me to keep quiet on his signal.

"You are Mr Manav and you run the website?" asked the police inspector.

"Yes, sir."

"You took the Honda CRV to Alwar?"

"Yes, sir."

"Why? Why not your car?"

"That day, my car had engine problems so I took her car."

"Yeah...that's the way you brought her into trouble," said the police inspector.

"Sorry...I don't understand," I said.

"The woman is simply crying from 9 a.m., and many times I told her it's a formal investigation, a simple questionnaire that I have to do. Nothing is generated by us. We have to submit a report to the Rajasthan police also. She has been crying for two and half hours. What is your relationship with her?"

The police officer's question put me in jeopardy; I had not thought on this line and had never given a definition to our relationship. I looked at Pranami; she also gave me the same bemused expression.

"Don't say you are friends. Your relationship and her concern for you indicate beyond friendship," commented the police officer.

"We are family friends and she is my fiancée."

I knew it would surprise Pranami and that happened. She looked at me profoundly.

"That's why she was worried for you," remarked the police officer.

"Will you please tell me what happened, sir?" The preface is over and I am keen to know what happened exactly.

"Yes...Mr Sambhu, whom you showed as a heroic figure in your article...on your website, committed suicide 15 days ago."

"It can't be suicide, sir. They must have killed him."

"How do you say this?"

"I know him, I met him and he was not a person to commit suicide...they must have killed him in the name of honour killing."

The police officer went into silence for a while and then said, "Why do you want embroil yourself into trouble?"

"I...I don't understand, sir." eagerness came to a halt and I asked perplexed.

"Yar...nowadays honour killing is deeply present in the air and why you want to give a new name to this...by the way, if you know he had a life threat then why didn't you inform the police?" The police officer seemed annoyed. I was really frightened on his stance.

"How could I, sir! It is the case of a gay and the entire world is against them," that's what I wanted to say, but I could not.

Restoring faith and courage in me, I spoke in silence to the police inspector, "He had told me and I have the evidence. You see the website...I can show you," I tried to open the laptop from my bag.

"Mr Manav, I have seen it all and the police have come to know that it's not a suicide case. In the autopsy, it has clearly come out he had not died of hanging himself. His death was caused by poison. He had died much before he was hanged. So it was a clear case of murder. The police have taken his wife, brother-in-law and a neighbour into custody. The purpose of murder is not yet known."

Pranami and I listened to him carefully.

With a pause, he said again, "Why we called you is that in the FIR, his wife mentioned about your website and your article, which put him under stress and as one of the reasons for suicide. She mentioned the Honda CRV and gave the description of the man who met him. And it's you Mr Manav... the sketch matches with you. Do you want to see it?"

The police officer showed a sketch and it really matched my face.

The police officer said again, "I told the lady also nothing to worry; now it's not a suicidal case. It's a clear cut murder, but his wife and others have not accepted it. We will send the report; let us see what else the Rajasthan police wants."

I was relieved; I never believed police officers could be so kind. My obligation clearly showed in my attitude, "Thank you...thank you very much, sir, shall we go now?"

Things were clear; if not today, tomorrow the truth would come out.

"One thing...don't leave Delhi until I say so and in the next few months, don't visit Alwar... especially you Mr Manav," the police officer clearly voiced his instructions to me so that I could be called to police station anytime any day for further investigation on Mr Sambhu's murder case.

"Sure, sir...now we can leave?"

He winked. The clock showed 12.30.

Pranami was so frightened; she was not able to speak properly. She had not even breathed properly at the police station, and now took a long breath coming into the open air. She feared the police, police stations and crime, but loved to see those films.

I asked, "Are you okay?"

"Yeah...I am fine."

"What should we do now?" I asked.

I could not go back to office now, but Pranami may have to go to her bank, so I asked.

"I will go home."

"Are you sure you don't want to go bank," I asked repeatedly.

"No...I will go back home."

"Will you able to drive?"

"Yeah."

But I felt she would not be able to drive, she was not even looking at me. She was giving all the answers by looking down or sideways, instead of at me.

"No...you will not, you come with me."

"But my vehicle?"

"I will arrange someone to drop it."

The Hauz Khaus and Green Park areas were our childhood playground. We had many friends. I called Sandeep, luckily, he was available in the shop. He agreed to drop the Honda CRV to Pranami's apartment.

He was eager to know what happened and why the Honda CRV was in the police station.

I told him in brief, but lied, "It was a minor accident...no harm...nothing, but Pranami is still frightened, so I am taking her with me. I need your help to drop the vehicle."

"Why didn't you tell me earlier? The police inspector is a close friend of mine...I would have done something for you," said Sandeep. "Thanks...he is a very kind person."

"Then do one thing...give the Honda CRV keys to him...I will drop it."

"Okay."

Again, I returned inside the police station, and gave the Honda CRV keys to the inspector and said, "My friend Sandeep will take the keys to drop it."

He took the keys smiling.

--Ω--

Pranami did not speak a single word on the entire journey from Green Park to Dwarka. I felt very sorry for Mr Sambhu. Is this the fate of a gay? I asked myself. I wanted to speak about many things about Sambhu with Pranami, but she had gone into a deep silence.

"What will you take?" I asked.

"Nothing...I want to sleep for a while."

"Sure," I did not object, and took her to the bedroom. She lay on the bed and I sat next to her head. I knew she would not get sleep; it was her fear that made her nervous.

"Why are you so frightened?" I asked.

She looked at my eyes; I could still see fear in her eyes.

"It's a silly thing, Pranami...and the police officer said also nothing to worry... police have come to know that it's murder...so why are you so scared?"

She did not even reply.

"Let me order something for your lunch, what do you want?" I asked.

"Water."

"Water?"

"Give me some water."

"Shall I make it warm?" I asked.

"No...normal water."

I gave her a glass of water and ordered for two pizzas. When I came back to her and sat again near her head, she took her head and placed it on my lap.

Pranami said, her voice was feeble; "You know Manav in this entire world there is no one except you, whom I can say is mine. Then why you behave like this?"

She opened up her eyes, the love and care for me reflected in those eyes.

"What did I do?" I asked.

"The police case is never ending Manav. It is like a spider's net, once trapped you won't able to get out from that."

I laughed. Laughed to find the reason of her fear and said, "What happened, you are in the twenty-first century and that too in Delhi. Unless you have committed a crime, no one can punish you. Silly fear, Pranami, it has no base...I thought you are a brave girl the way you handled those two and half hours...but you are stuck in a stupid thought."

Pranami woke up and sat upright.

"It's not that easy the way you think, Manav...have you ever thought you could be brought into some charge like this."

"You are serious about silly things."

She was to say something and at that time the doorbell started ringing, "Who is it at this time?"

"Must be Sandeep or the security...let me check."

It was Sandeep; he had come with one of his boys from the shop.

"I parked it outside. How is Pranami feeling now?" Sandeep asked, entering inside the house.

"She is taking rest...come...sit for a while," I said.

215

"No...No the shop is open, that's why I brought him, he came with my car, we will go back now."

"Will you have something?"

"No...but the inspector was saying you run some website that writes about all this nonsense... you never told me, which website do you run?" asked Sandeep.

"It's nothing, yar...a small interactive website."

"Okay...you tell me about it some other day...let me go, the shop is open."

Sandeep left and the moment I entered into Pranami's room, she was ready to speak out, "How many people will you convince, Manav? Others will also come to know."

"But what is wrong in it, Pranami?"

"You have seen what can go wrong."

"It's your imagination, Pranami...the system never runs on thoughts...and you are thinking too much...co-relating facts. It was a courtesy questionnaire. Finally, the inspector said it's murder so means nothing to fear," my voice was raised.

She looked at me for a while and said softly, "That is the fear Manav."

I had never seen Pranami so terrified. I felt bad for raising my voice. Before I hugged her and consoled her again, the doorbell rang again.

Oh...it's the pizza man. My hunger was accelerated with its aroma. Putting it on the table, I called, "Pranami...come... come take a bite."

No answer, no movement came out from her so I called again, "Come on...fast, babe...it will get cold."

This time she answered, "You have it. I don't feel hungry."

I threw myself abruptly at her, "Why? Why don't you feel hungry? Come on... nothing doing," I almost pushed her outside the room.

On my insistence, she took half of it and the rest I consumed. A foodie girl takes only half of the delicious food means that something serious is going on inside her, which I could not understand.

"Will you sleep for a while? It will make you feel better."

Pranami didn't say anything. I asked again, "Will you go to the bank?"

"I wish, but I won't... have you planned to go?" asked Pranami feebly.

"How can I go leaving you in this condition?"

"I will be fine...you go...you may have pending work."

"Okay I will go, but you get well soon," I insisted that she should sleep and forcefully made her sleep. She then woke up at 8 p.m., and looked much better. Now she insisted that I go back. Tomorrow is a working day and I may not reach office on time was the only reason not to stay back in Dwarka.

I started at 8.30 p.m. from Dwarka.

--Ω--

Exactly after 40 minutes, at 9:10, Pranami called. I was opening the flat door.

Earlier, she had come down to the street to say bye and before I started the car, she cautioned me three times, "Drive carefully; it's a foggy night, don't take any call while driving and ring me the moment you reach."

I was about to call, when she called, "Yes, babe...I reached and reached safely."

"Where did it take more time?"

"Nowhere, the road was absolutely free from traffic," I replied.

"Then why were you so late...it usually takes 30 to 35 minutes?"

"I was driving cautiously, babe."

"Don't joke...what will you do for dinner?"

"I may order from a restaurant," I said.

"Do it first, they will also take time for delivery and what time will you eat, you had not eaten lunch properly."

"I just came, let me change then I will order."

"First, you give the order then you go and change, what is the harm in it?"

"Okay, babe, okay...I will do as you say...how do you feel now?" I asked.

"I am fine," said Pranami.

--Ω--

The entire day, I was thinking about Sambhu's murder, it was shocking news for me. Sambhu had kept saying that he may be killed, but I never took it seriously that someone might actually be killed because of gayism.

Sometimes, I felt guilty that this may have happened because of me. Somehow, he was pulling through his life, but I induced the sparkle of dignity and honour in him that led him to his death!

I needed to share the fact with the followers of myrelationship.com. I uploaded the picture of Mr Sambhu on the Facebook page of myrelationship and started sharing my views.

"The photograph shown is of Late Mr Sambhu, who was murdered fifteen days ago by his family members. He was a member of the LGBT group, who fought for his pride and dignity and because of the fight he lost his life."

I tweeted the same message on Twitter as well.

However, I could not get peace; my heart was crushed with the thought, "Is this the ultimate destiny of a gay?"

Gays march for their pride just to show their existence, fight with society at every step of life for their dignity, but people pay them lip sympathy conceding that 'Yes, these different creatures also exist together with us, give them some consideration'. But in reality, they are hated everywhere.

I tried to call Gopalji. But it was 11:30 p.m. I was afraid that he must have slept, but he responded on the first ring of my call. I always spoke to him, whenever I was troubled and my heart bled and felt crushed with the weight of my problems and I would open up my heart to relieve all the stress of my broken heart that was not at peace. He was a man of diversity and a treasure chest of social guidance. His experience had matured with his age and the many new experiences that he had faced in life in dealing with society.

I asked, "You have not slept yet?"

"If I had gone to sleep, how would I able hear your voice now? God desires and knows... an unknown power kept me awake until now. I am a working man," he said jubilantly.

"New poem?"

"Yes...this is the right time, when everyone goes to sleep and the night's tranquillity is overpowering, I start doing my job. Again, I have to wake up at 5 a.m., in the morning. I was completing a long pending job, you know at this time I am busy in exam duties...today somehow, I found time."

"Have you seen Facebook now?" I asked.

"No...I have been working on my poem, from the last two days I have not been on the internet."

"Do you know Mr Sambhu from Alwar, whom I had written about a few months ago, on the website is dead now?"

"Oh, sorry to hear it."

"He was killed, murdered...by his family members."

"So sad...how could this happen?"

I narrated everything to him from the meeting with Mr Sambhu to the police station. I narrated how Pranami was framed into the picture and her fear too. And finally my desperation showed in my words, "A little more vigilant and I could have saved his life if I could have gone to Alwar police. But what was the surety that the police would help him?" I regretted what I could not do.

He took a long breath.

I asked again, "Tell me, Gopalji, is this the ultimate destiny?

Gopalji laughed, "A simple police case and you are afraid?"

"No...I am not afraid of the police."

"What do you feel; it is a path of roses?"

"No, I never thought," I was reluctant to accept the allegation on me.

"What do you think proclaiming oneself as a gay, attending pride parades and gay parties will bring the decisive consequence that you feel? My dear Manav, remember it will take years and years to stand firm on the street of straights. Revolution does not happen in one day, but changes occur gradually. I feel proud to be a gay, but to come up to this stage I have passed many obstacles, even I had tried to commit suicide once. Like others, I had also visited a psychiatrist and counsellor. So, ultimately it's the individual who makes the difference between living and dying. How firm you stand matters," Gopalji stopped.

I was listening to him carefully. Gopalji asked, "Did you get your answer?"

"Yes."

"Should we go to sleep now?" he asked.

"Yeah sure...I felt relieved talking to you, but I wasted your time and stopped you from working on your poem," I apologised for keeping him awake and taking so much of his time away from his poem.

"Not at all, dear. Rather, I am thankful that you listened to me, and respected my words."

"Good night," he said and disconnected the line.

I felt stress-free and could get a good sleep. Switching off the laptop, I checked my posts as it was open. There were 540 likes, 83 comments and 17 shares on the picture and post.

Sometimes, Facebook seems funny, someone's death is liked the most and this kind of news spreads fast. It is 12:30 a.m., and within an hour, a minimum 640 people have seen it.

I had a sound stress free sleep.

12

I woke up very early at six in the morning. I switched on the Internet and logged in to Facebook, even before I could freshen up. I brewed myself some coffee, and I sat sipping it, while I browsed through my Facebook account. I was amazed to see that there were 9678 likes, 1989 comments and 226 shares on the photograph and the post.

I now looked at the website and checked my mails to find 31 new mails in my mailbox. Most of the mails wanted to know about the recent post 'Butterflies' Life' and its hero Mr Shashikant. I replied to each of the mails.

A person called JP Thakur asked, "Sir, will you please mention the engineering college, I think I know the man well."

I replied, "Dear JP Thakur, sorry, I had mentioned the real name (no name change for privacy) of the friends, their activity and thoughts. But I have been requested to keep the college name anonymous. You will need to respect this and make your own presumptions."

Sonali Mishra, a regular visitor to the site, had written, "Dear Manav, thanks again for uploading an interesting true life story. Keep up the good work."

I replied her, "Thanks, dear."

Varun Bagchi who had written two earlier mails to me had sent me one more mail today.

"Dear Manav, I am writing to you again with respect to your mail and the recent article posted on the website 'Butterflies' Life'. The story appears to be the same that I had narrated about my son and I felt as if you are mocking me, but after reading it completely I realized my mistake. This is not exactly my son's story. To my surprise not only my son but also it happens to many students in their hostel life.

But think about me, as he is my only son, my wife and I have all expectations for him that are obvious. We need him to carry forward our lineage and our next generation.
You tell me son what I should do, whenever he receives a marriage proposal, he just refuses and he is over 33 years. I am an old man of 67, when will I see my grand child?

Now people suspect him, as when marriage proposals are declined people make enquiries to get to the truth. People in the society have started spreading the message and once he is recognized as a homosexual no woman will agree to marry him. Parents are now willing to offer their daughters to him, as he works for a prestigious firm 'Navratan Company' in India. But once he gets branded neither a high status nor huge emoluments will attract parents anymore.

I have done all that I am supposed to do. I had not touched liquor in my 67 years, but started drinking it, only because my son drinks it. I thought I could spend time with him, when we both sit down together for a drink and in these moments, he may listen to the pain of an old man. He sat with me, but did not drink with me and did not oppose me as well. I asked him as you had told me in your reply, but he had not given a single answer. He refused to give any response to my questions. He has not come home for 13 days since our last conversation on this subject.

You tell me, son, what I should do? Help me son.

Regards,

A poor father Varun Bagchi"

He had written this in connection with two of our previous mails that we had exchanged. I am producing those other two mails so that you can pick up the trend of what transpired earlier and I do not have to spell out the details.

I had received the first mail 17 days earlier. The mail from him read as below.

"Dear Manav,

I am an old man from Sindri near Puruliya, WB, writing to you because my son follows you on Facebook, Twitter and is a regular visitor of your website. He thinks he is gay. He is my only son and no one in our family history had ever been gay. He was normal, but suddenly I find him reluctant for marriage. I feel he must have developed some homosexuality feelings during his stay in the hostel or spending his bachelor life in a PSU company, away from Sindri and us.

I have tried all means to get him married, but he refuses vehemently and refuses directly to the girl's parents. I even threatened him that if he does not marry, his mother and I would commit suicide, and then he could do whatever he wanted to do. But it had no impact on him.

He did not say a single word about it.

Help me son... perhaps he may listen to you, and your advice. He follows you at every step. Or you give me an alternative solution that I can adopt.

Think son, if he does not marry our generation will end after him and all the property will go to a trust or someone who is not from the Bagchi family.

If you want, I can give you his phone number.

He will feel good to talk you.

Regards

Varun Bagchi"

The mail was not a simple mail of praise or comments on certain issues; it was a mail of problems, which the Bagchi family encounters and needs help. The mail was written with the hope of a solution to their problem. Otherwise, a mail of this intimacy level is not easy to write to someone who is unknown and suffers the same problem that his son does.

I had to think before I wrote this mail and took two days to reply the mail.

"Dear Varun Bagchi,

You sought my help, but I don't know how I can help you. My website helps and supports gays as well as homosexual people to overcome stress and trauma. You are asking me to do just the opposite of it.

I am not against you; you have all rights to bring back your child into becoming straight, again. But think before doing it, sometimes excess pressure makes a cane break into two pieces. There are people who happily exist on both sides of the coin, living both sides…meaning being bisexual…in their life. Marriage and raising children is not the ultimate goal of life and could be adopted if you wished.

You talk to him the way he understands, this is the only way you can satisfy your desires.

With best wishes from myrelationship.com."

The reply was rather tough for me to write, but when I sat to reply an old face appeared in front of me, appealing to a child with whom he wants to spend time. Again, his mail put me in a dilemma, where I could not find a proper solution to the situation.

My mobile that was near my bed rang. I picked it up and saw that it was from Pranami. I looked at the watch; it was only 07.30 a.m.

I took the call, "Hello, Pranami."

"Ohoo, the bad boy has woken up." Pranami teased me.

"How do you know? It's wrong, I am still in bed."

She laughed, "There are many ways to know, Mr Manav. I have fixed a camera in your bedroom ."

I actually looked around at all corners in fear, 'Is she really telling the truth?'

She laughed again, "You fool; don't you think that I cannot distinguish your tone and voice? Moreover, I could see you are online on the net."

I admit to myself, "I am a fool, it was so simple."

Pranami said again, "Babe, yesterday I asked you to sleep early, but what was mister doing so late at night?"

I cannot hide anything from Pranami and in this technology savvy era, your sleep hours are counted through various measures. Is it not amazing? I laughed.

"And again you woke up early to see the response of your post, am I right?"

She was right so I didn't say anything.

"It was the reason you wanted to go back?"

I maintained my silence to all her queries. She must have got fed-up with me and cut the connection. I felt sorry for her. She cared for me in all respects, but I had never been able to rise to her standard.

The clock struck eight. I needed to prepare for office, and I would check other mails, after coming back from the office, and probably, give a suitable reply to Varun Bagchi. I checked my Facebook page again; the likes, comments and share list had risen even more: 9926 likes, 2102 comments and 248 shares.

--Ω--

By evening at 9 p.m., there was a dramatic increase in the likes, comments and share list. There were 59,999 likes, 17,652 comments and 11,083 shares of the profile.

The next moment, I had not even completed smiling on seeing the response when Pranami called, "Yes, Pranami, tell me."

"The police officer just called me," her voice was nervous.

I really panicked, "What did he say?"

"Stop posting anything about Mr Sambhu, at least until the murderers go behind bars, otherwise...!"

"Otherwise what?" I interrupted in between.

"You are inviting trouble."

I thought for a while and asked, "But why did the police call you?"

"He doesn't have your number."

"No... I had given it to him; you remember I noted it down in a writing pad while coming back...then why did he call you?"

"Let it be anything...please, Manav, don't create a nuisance now," she got irritated at my question. "Calling you or me is no difference; can't you stop yourself for a few days?"

The police officer didn't call me then and now also, it is simple intention driven, but who will make Pranami understand?

"Have you had dinner?" Pranami asked over my silence.

"No."

"What time you will have it?"

"I have given the order, and it might come any moment."

"Nice... have dinner and go to sleep...okay."

"Okay."

"Listen," she called, before cutting the connection, "Are you coming or shall I come to your place tomorrow?"

I thought what was tomorrow.

She replied, "Thursday is a holiday, don't you have one?"

"I have not checked."

"Yes, you have, once a bank has a holiday means all other offices must have the same," she laughed and said again after a pause, "I may take two days leave and stay with you. Are you listening?"

"Yes... I am listening," I replied hurriedly.

"Are you worried about my coming or do you have any commitment?"

"No...no I don't have any commitment."

"Sweet boy," Pranami cut the connection.

As soon as I put down the phone, the delivery boy came with the order. I thought I would check my mails and reply them in the morning, so I finished dinner and tried to sleep but could not, as thoughts about Pranami kept swirling through my mind. The audacious girl was frightened about the police; otherwise, she had never stopped me from my activities.

When you cannot sleep, the adrenalin increases and the saga of old memories begin to flood your mind and occupy every corner of your mind. The startled face of Pranami in the police station first flashed and then moved to the hospital when she had lost her parents. The girl had no one left in the world except me; the presence of the far away brother had no meaning in her life.

I was an orphan already, who better than I could understand her stifled heart.

When I thought about her; memories of how she would scold me continuously for my carelessness and untidiness filled my thoughts. Though, I felt the rooms were neatly arranged, she would find abundant loose ends and places that were not up to her standards to rebuke me. I actually relished and enjoyed those admonishments that she made; they are like memorable memoirs and just go into re-enforcing the fact that I have someone who cares for me.

The fond memories give me peace of mind and relax me; I drop off into a sound sleep and wake up fresh in the morning.

--Ω--

The entire day this freshness stayed with me. In the morning, instead of switching on my laptop the fond memories of her rebuking me about the untidiness of my home, made me start cleaning and arranging the rooms. I collected and threw out around ten empty bottles of vodka and whisky scattered around in different rooms, but most of the empty bottles were in the drawing room. She would have found these on her first glance.

I neatly arranged my room and called Gouri, my house cleaner, before leaving for office. Gouri had a key to my flat. She usually came at 12 or 1:00, depending when she got free, after clearing other flats. She cleaned my rooms and washed my utensils, if there were any unclean ones.

"Gouri, today clean all rooms with extra care."

"Why, bhaiya, don't I clean them properly?" She called me bhaiya and treated me as her elder brother.

"No...no I am not complaining, Gouri...you clean thoroughly, but today Pranami is coming, so you need to be more thorough and remove every speck of dirt or dust, you know her."

She smiled, "Understood, bhaiya... today Pranami Didi won't find any reason to scold you."

"Fine."

In the office, I first checked whether tomorrow was a holiday or not? Yes, it was a holiday. I had two overseas meetings and a meeting with the team members.

The first meeting would end by 1 p.m., and the second meeting was at 2 p.m. I had an hour. Should I call Pranami to find out what time she was coming? She always reaches late after nine, after finishing all her job, and then sets out for my place. I connected the call once, but stopped, she must be busy; otherwise, she would have called me. The bank may have an avalanche of workload, as tomorrow was a holiday.

Ordering a coffee, I checked my Google mail account. Two mails were in the inbox, one was from Subham Bhai and the other one was from Vardhman.

Vardhman's mail was written last night at 11 p.m.

"Hello buddy?

How are you?

There is no news from you.

I read your recent story on the website and saw the post on FB and Twitter. It is really sad to know about Mr Sambhu. Truly a poor fellow, when he strived to get over his anxiety destiny had its own way to take him.

After coming back from Goa, you have just vanished, not even cared for me at the party. You have not even remembered me once. I had called you once, but Pranami picked the phone and from that day, I was scared to call you. I don't know where you are and with whom?

It was really a good trip to Goa, had you been there for all the time it would have been fantastic.

Let us plan a trip to the northeast.

Or if the Philippines, nothing can beat it. One travel agent has approached me for the trip, what do say about it.

Vardhman"

I felt sorry; it was true, after coming back from Goa abruptly; I had not had much contact with him, perhaps, we met at a party. First, Subham Bhai was around and then the police case, I had really overlooked him. He was hurt, but never opposed my care and love for Pranami; in fact, he loved Pranami and feared her terribly.

Before opening the other mail, I called him.

As he took the call, I started with infinity, "Yar, can't you just call me? Why write a mail at 11 in the night. Who stops you doing that? You very well know where I stay on working days. You are hurt, I know, but you also know I cannot say no to Pranami and that's how she reached Goa."

Vardhman was blank at the speed that I talked and he was speechless, even after I stopped.

I asked again, "What happened? Are you there? Say something."

He laughed, "What can I say, you are only speaking."

I laughed at his admiration, "Okay, tell me."

"There are two offers from the travel agent one is for the northeast and the other is to Philippines..."

I interrupted, "But when?"

"It starts in mid-February to the northeast and the end of February to the Philippines."

"But how can it be possible to go in a month?" I was excited so I asked for a solution.

He observed my enthusiasm, so said promptly, "Why go for both we can choose one."

"Yes...but where can we go in the northeast?" I nodded and asked.

Vardhman added, "The agent was showing some photographs of the place, I will forward the photographs to you. They have developed a resort in the far-flung state of Arunachal Pradesh, near Along. The flight only goes up to Dibrugarh and then it's a 8 to 10 hours taxi journey. It is beautiful...we need to book today."

"Why today... why such hurry, let us think and plan I don't want a repetition of the Goa issue," I said.

"They only have eight cottages and in the slot we want it's all full."

"Which slot, you have not mentioned?" I added I am not aware of it.

"It's a weeklong plan from 11 March to 17 March... if you say, I can come down today. Tomorrow is a holiday and we can discuss...I feel this is the best suited."

I hurriedly said, "No...No, don't come today. Pranami is coming today."

He took a pause then asked anxiously and feebly, "But we need to give our consent today or tomorrow...he has booked it for me, if I don't say probably, he will give it to someone else...it's in high demand."

"Okay, let me plan out in office and I will tell you by evening."

"Sure, you tell me by tomorrow," he extended the time limit. He was hopeful of going to Along, as I had not been negative about the trip.

Vardhman said again, "You will be amazed to know the other four cottages are booked from Delhi only."

"It's nice," and I cut the connection.

--Ω--

With the beautiful scenery of northeast in mind, I opened the other mail.

Subham Bhai had written at 4.15 a.m., our time.

"My dear Manav,

What I guessed has come true.

One bank has already captured half of our business.

Russell is not talking to me. He thinks it happened because of me. I didn't put enough money in the business. But the truth is I had invested 70 per cent and he had invested 30 per cent, whereas, the partnership was made based on a fifty-fifty sharing basis.

He is planning to start some other business with some other partner. He had money, but he does not want to put it into retail. It's his country; he has the advantage and freedom to do so more than people from another country.

He is not staying with me now, probably dating some other guy. We have not legally married yet, so I cannot even go to court.

Sometimes, I feel Pranami was right in not giving me the Gurgaon property. Had I put in that amount too, my condition would not have changed much.

Again, I would have been left forlorn.

I feel lonely and regret leaving Delhi.

I can only curse my fate.

Subham"

This was to happen; even though he was questioning why he had left the country, he had no justification in his favour to save the situation. I looked at my watch; I was running short of time, it was 1.45 and hardly any time was left for the meeting,

I quickly sit down to reply.

"Dear Subham Bhai,

Delhi was yours and will always be yours.

You left Delhi but Delhi has not left you.

Now it's still open to you...

Don't feel lonely; someone here still awaits you coming back.

Manav"

It's the best I could console him. I finished the last sip of the coffee that had gone cold and closed the mail account. I drank some water, closed my eyes for a while, took a deep breath and pushed myself away from all old thoughts and got ready mentally too for the meeting.

--Ω--

The team meeting lasted up to nine in the evening. I hurried up, as it was just a ten-minute drive from my office to my flat, but I wanted to check Pranami's position. When I was out of the parking lot, I switched on my mobile to call Pranami and found two missed calls from her, the last called was four minutes ago.

I called and asked, "Where have you reached?"

In return, she laughed.

"What happened, why are you laughing?"

"I am standing underneath your tower."

"You reached?" I asked amazed.

"Yeah...I returned from your flat as well, it's locked and now I am waiting for you to come back."

"But why you wait in open, why don't you go inside?" I asked.

"I have forgotten to put the key in my purse."

"Oh...sorry, I had not imagined you would be back before nine, otherwise, I would have given the flat key at 506...I am just coming, will be there in five minutes," I felt apologetic as she was waiting in the open.

"It's okay...come coolly, I am not going anywhere...don't drive in a rush."

She had not finished, but I cut the connection.

It took me exactly five minutes; Pranami was standing outside. She had a packet.

"You drove hastily, I told you not to do."

Without heeding her, I asked, "It's cold and were you waiting for a long time?"

"No. Hardly 15 minutes and it's been a long time since I waited for you. It was nice Manav, it brought back remembrance of your coaching class, where I waited for your class to get over. I wished you had come a little later."

She walked towards the lift and I followed. Other than her vanity bag, she was clinging on to a packet she carried.

 In the lift I asked, "What is it?"

She smiled and said, "Vegetables, I knew you won't have anything."

"But what do you want to do with it?" I asked surprised.

"Why... I will cook," she said so innocently, I believed her.

"It's already 9.30; if you start cooking then we will dine at 2...fine I can wait up to two. Absolutely, I have no problem tomorrow is a holiday," I said coming out from the lift.

"You order for dinner today or let's go and dine out, tomorrow I will cook; we have the entire day."

"Sure," I nodded and we went to one of the bathrooms to freshen up and change, finally, we decided to dine out. But Pranami came out halfway from the bathroom in a T-shirt and asked promptly, as if she was practising what to ask, "Do you have vodka or whisky, Manav?"

I looked at her as if I saw a stranger who asks for a forbidden thing.

"Why do you look at me, I asked something...do you have vodka or whisky?" she repeated.

I wished to say, "I have both, which one do you want?" but I only asked, "What do you want to do with vodka?"

She laughed, "You fool, what do you do with vodka? We won't go out to dine out, you order the food home."

"And..."

"We will have it here. It's been a long time that I have not had a drink with you... give me five minutes...we will sit together. It will be fun."

She closed the other half of the bathroom door to take five more minutes to freshen up.

I had already dressed up; it took another two minutes to get into the situation. After that, I hurried to unfasten my buttons and come back in my evening outfit.

I went closer to the bathroom door, "What do you want vodka or whisky?"

"Anything will do," she replied from behind the door.

"Any particular brand you wish?"

"Whatever you drink...it will be amazing if you have black vodka."

I could hear the musical sound of the shower as the water flowed overhead behind her closed door.

--Ω--

She took extra time in the bathroom. I was ready with a glass and bottle, and had not poured it into the glass, as I was waiting to know what she would prefer, normal water or soda.

She seemed in an exuberant mood today, as she came out and asked, "Not yet ready?"

"Ready...what will you take with your vodka?"

"Oh...you have black vodka! I will take soda but no lemon," she said, sitting comfortably on the sofa.

Pranami commented after taking two sips, "Nice taste."

It surprised me; she had taken it, "You had this before?"

"But long back...it was not that tasty as today...you added something extra? she questioned.

I thought, but did not say anything to her, "Liquor has no taste, it tastes best as per the mood of the taker...and she proved this also."

She did not ask anything further but smiled.

I asked, "What happened something funny?"

She smiled more brightly, "Yeah...listen to the joke that happened today."

I waited for her to begin it, curiously; she started with the same smile, "I was talking about the story of a Major..."

My facial expression changed, I tried to recollect when and what the story was that she had told me about a Major.

She understood. "I didn't tell you? The Major who is on my FB proposed to me once."

"Yes...yes," I remember that story and eagerly asked, "He proposed again or what?"

"Proposed! He planned a lot more than that. He is no more a Major; he is now Lt. Col. He brought his parents from Chennai. A couple of days ago, the old couple visited my bank anonymously and today they came to my cabin."

"How Gopi didn't stop them?" I knew every person of the bank.

"He stopped them, but I let them come inside...old fellows, who knew their intention?"

"What did they do, any mischievous thing?" I was curious.

"No, yar, what can they do, they are bounded by their son's wish," she was cool and took her sip in between.

"The woman said, 'Beti, Pranami,' they knew my name and everything about me... 'we came to Delhi to ask your hand for my son Lt. Col. Madhavendu Nair. For the last two days, we were coming to your branch but did not have the audacity to come to your cabin. You must be wondering why we travelled from such a long distance, from Chennai...Madhavendu loves you Beti and is not ready to marry any other girl. We have business Beti, we have 20 acres of coconut fields and 50 acres of paddy fields, high-class families and their educated daughters are willing to marry my Madhavendu, but he has no interest in any other girl, we know about you, still if you have any guardian then please allow us to talk with him. "

The food arrived and she stopped. After paying the delivery man, when I came back she had finished the freshly poured glass much faster than me; my glass was untouched. I was fascinated enough to listen to her but my heartbeat rose faster.

Refilling her glass again, I asked, "How dare they ask you?"

"Why? Then whom should they ask? Who is there that they can ask for me?" Pranami seemed unbelievable to me.

"What did you tell them?" My heart was not ready to listen to what my thought process retrieves from her conversation.

She laughed, "You guess?"

My question boomeranged on me. I looked at her blank and in reality. I must say I feared inside and finished half of the glass in a sip.

"You are going faster, babe."

She also finished half of the glass.

Without heeding me, she asked, "Guess what, I would have told them?"

"How can I say? I am not god, neither do I know magic. I showed my irritation.

"But I know what you wish and I said the same to them, now you guess."

The toxicities of vodka in me reduced to zero within a moment.

"The old fellows travelled a long distance for me with lots of wishes and hope; I could not disappoint them," Pranami said with a smile, looking at my plain face, it must have become white, without a thought.

"You said yes to them?" I asked quickly, as waiting kills me.

"I said, yes, it would have my pleasure to marry your son, but unfortunately, I love another guy..."

I feel a bit relaxed, "What did they say then?"

"They were still reluctant to accept, and said we know this, Beti. Madhavendu told us about this...he speaks only about you nothing else."

"Then?" my heart became restless again.

"Then what, I have to bow down to their wish...they were ready to accept me with all my nitty-gritty."

"You told them you are ready to marry him?" I was broken.

"Who else will speak for me? I have to find everything for me even the match."

I wanted to say, "How can you do this, Pranami! Can't you read the love for you in my eyes? For every small thing, you ask me before doing it and you had taken such vital decision of life alone. I know why you have taken the decision; you feel I am a vagabond, but you do not know the truth Pranami...I am on a mission...'Mission for total sanitation' of a truthful life. How many people live a truthful life in the world? You do not know the mystery behind Pranab Bhai's death and about Subham Bhai's exile in America."

But I was not able to speak a single word, I seemed speechless and hapless. I am a man so I did not weep, if I was a woman tears might flow like a continuous stream over my cheeks.

"Oh...hello, where have you been?" She rubbed my shoulder, to wake me from my thoughts. I just gave her a blank look; really, I did not have a single word to say.

She laughed and laughed for almost one minute and when she stopped, my look was pathetic.

"You are so down by just hearing of a separation, what you will do if really I go away from your life?"

My sixth sense smelled some ploy and I looked at her meaningfully.

"You are so scared, babe...the last part of the story is not true and it did not happen today, but last week. When they were ready to accept me, knowing that I love another guy I said, 'I am pregnant with his child'. Still they were not ready to believe and asked 'is it possible?' I said, 'Yes, I am carrying his child and we have all the relationship of a married couple, only thing we have not married yet.'"

I got back to normalcy and manhood, and asked, "They believed this time?"

I wanted to show her that I was still enjoying the joke. It's the specialty of a man, at one time, I was dying and now I wanted to show that it's fun for a man.

"Who will take a pregnant woman as a bride...but poor guys...they did not ask a single word after that and silently left my cabin."

"This is what is needed for these types of people," I remarked proudly.

"Sometimes, I feel sorry for them. They must have come with an aspiration that they will be able to convince me and take me away as their bride, but left empty handed."

The last part showed that it was not simply a joke; it expressed her inner thoughts. Perhaps she asked for the drink to narrate the happening; otherwise, it was kept within her for the last one week. She had already finished four pegs and she emptied the glass to pour another one, whereas, my fourth one was still untouched. She was going fast. I did not fill her one and made her wait until I finished mine.

We did not have many topics to discuss. I never speak about my office work. She hates to discuss about my website and gay activity. We don't have any relations to discuss. So the maximum time she talks about her office people and her work.

Pranami asked, "Fill it."

I ignored her.

She changed the topic to Neha, the new girl in her office and her activity.

She spoke about Sandeep Duga, about his laziness and how he slept right there on his chair after lunch. Gopi would come into her cabin whispering all these little bits of gossip and information about the staff.

She asked again, "What happened, you are slow and not even refilling my glass?"

"Yeah...sure," I finished mine and refilled both our glasses. She finished half of it in one swig.

The wall clock struck 11; both of us looked at it.

She started about Gaurav Sharma, her deputy in the bank. This is the unfinished story...he feels he is the boss and carries the bias. But but as the head office placed her above him, he is forced to obey her commands in public. Other than this, he has a cruel intensity and feels the single girl Pranami must share love and sex with him. So he looks at her with narrow and lusty eyes. But a woman is able to read through all these avaricious, lusty looks of a man as it's god gifted.

She was talking, when she abruptly asked me, "Why don't you take your bride?"

I was traumatized, her pitch changed.

Finishing the rest of the glass, she asked again, "Why Manav, why don't you take me as your bride? You don't take me; that's why people comment, look at me with craving eyes, have lusty desires and have the audacity to propose me. A single girl is forced to face conjecture of manhood and it's all because of you."

I accepted it was because of me. But I could not accept the tears in Pranami's eye. It was not a joke. She was deeply hurt about the matter.

I went close to her and wiped the tears from her cheek. She held my hand on her cheek and asked again, "I don't know when and how you became gay, but I know you love me...then why do you insist that I marry others and that bloody Vardhman, I hate him and I will hate him until the end of the world."

Tears flowed from her cheeks continuously. First, she is a woman; tears are a weapon for her; second, she is drunk.

"Sorry, I will never ask you to marry anyone." It came from the core of my heart. I regretted why I ever said such a thing to her.

She smiled and acted like a child, "Promise."

"Promise."

"You will marry me," she asked.

I was unable to answer this, and took some time.

But she replied to it, "I know you will not ask me to marry you."

She looked into my eyes, "Okay...don't worry...you don't marry me, I will marry you."

The atmosphere became relaxed.

Pranami asked, "Why have you left my glass empty?"

"It's too late we have to dine also."

"What's the time?" she looked at the wall clock, "only 12, okay let me put the food into the oven you fix me one more drink."

"We have finished the bottle," I said.

"No...it can't be," she was disinclined to believe it, she got up and sat down again.

"Yes, babe...you see it." I held the bottle and showed it to her. The 750 ml bottle was finished. No, the bottle was not empty; some vodka was still left inside, almost one peg.

She exclaimed, "Yes...yes...it's there."

"No...you have had enough."

"See...does it look like enough...I have just started."

"We have to dine, babe."

"Sorry...let me put the food in the oven."

Again, she got up, but fell down and sat down again. She tried again to get up and walked a few steps; her steps fell far apart, as she staggered, absolutely drunk.

I stopped her and stood up, "You have the drink, let me heat up the food."

She obliged, "Thanks, babe."

I put the food into the oven and came back, Pranami urged again, "One more please."

"No way."

"Please...see I am alright."

"No way, Pranami...you have had enough."

"You make me cry a lot...I lost the great taste of vodka and see I have no feeling of being drunk...so please...I promise one more only."

"I don't have any, it was the last bottle," I poured the leftover vodka in her glass and turned to get the food.

Pranami called from behind, "You are lying."

I knew she would not able to sit at the dining table, so I brought the food to the centre table. She had finished her glass, but she kept repeating the same words, "You are lying, Manav...I know you care for me...love me...tell me you love me."

"Yes...I love..."

"Then why you became a gay...why? I hate gays...what's this top bottom business... I never understand it...you are lying."

She had not touched food and slept on the sofa. She was sozzled and said, "You are lying" in her sleep as well. I did not feel like waking her up for food. I held her in my arms, and took her to the bed.

--Ω--

I woke up, at nine in the morning. Pranami still slept profoundly, quilt over her body, and the T-shirt pulled over that showed her waist and belly. She showed no signs of getting up. I looked at her for quite some time and got away from the bed with gratification in my heart and a smile on my face.

I sat with my laptop; mails and other things had been piling up. Yesterday, I did not get time to even call Vardhman; he must be waiting for my call. If I call him, now, Pranami may wake up and the morning, rather an entire day would be ruined. I needed to reply Mr Bagchi also.

I opened my Google account first; the inbox showed a reply from Subham Bhai.

I must write to Vardhman first, so I opened the compose box and wrote:

Hello Buddy,

Please cancel it, if you have not booked the resort.

It may not be possible to go at that time.

I was relieved from an unknown load.

Next, I opened the reply from Subham Bhai, he had written:

Dear Manav,

I know Delhi is humble enough to accept its disguised child.

But there is no place for me in Delhi, I am the one who lost it.

I mentioned in the other mail that Russell is dating someone else. It's true. The guy is Nick Canon, a model and anchor. Russell plans to withdraw his share. As you know, the second store is in the hands of the bank and at this juncture, if the partnership is breached I will lose everything. He will take his share of 50 per cent and my share will be taken by the bank.

It was the way the agreement was made.

My signature was taken fraudulently.

They are planning for a reality show in American TV, where Nick will play as anchor.

I am finished Manav. The day is not far away.

You and Pranami will always be in my heart. I remember those days when Pranami, Pranab, you and I played together.

Subham

I thought for long hours about Subham Bhai. His condition was pathetic. The person for whom he had left his parents, sister, property and country had now left him with nothing. That's why it is said, 'a mouse is always safe in its domain and man is in its place'. Love had ruined him.

He cut out all connections from everybody for Russell and Russell had now lost all connection with him.

His mail showed he was depressed.

Something needed to be done; otherwise, we may lose Subham Bhai. Gay people are very tough outwardly, but sensitive by heart. For his love, once he had left his parents and country, so losing life would not be a big deal. A mail would not do, he needed to be talked to, but how? If Pranami knew, she would screw me.

Still I replied:

Dear Subham Bhai,

Don't lose heart; we are always here for you.

Let me talk to Pranami, something will come out."

Manav

I sent it, saw the message sent caption that came and vanished.

"What are you doing, Manav?" the sleepy voice of Pranami echoed in the background. She came tightening her hair with a clip. I became cautious and switched to checking the website mails.

She came and sat beside me, looked at the screen, and remarked, "What are you doing?"

"Checking mails... it's long pending. "

"You are unchanged," her voice was dismayed.

"I need to work, babe...people have sent mails that I must respond to them."

She did not talk in this regard again and asked after a little pause, "When did you get up?"

"Long back."

"Why didn't you wake me...I drank heavily yesterday... no...why didn't you stop me? And the food...you threw it? What is the time...10:30...oh god!" she questioned and answered.

"What happened, it's only 10:30...You have to go somewhere?" I asked popping my head out of the laptop screen.

"No, yar...I had planned to make breakfast...when will I mak and when will you eat? she looked annoyed.

"What is the problem, its 10:30 only...there's enough time to eat...by the way, what will you cook?" I asked.

"Upama."

"Nice."

"Then come and help me," she shut the laptop screen and dragged me to the kitchen.

"Have you had tea?" Pranami asked; she was still drowsy.

"No."

"Let me make some good tea first and then we will cook upama...but be here with me, if you go back to your laptop then I will not make tea or upama...is that clear?"

"Yes...babe I won't go," we drank tea standing in the kitchen; she would not let me move an inch out from the kitchen and many times said, 'Sorry, I should not have got sozzled and because of me the food was wasted'."

I also wanted to be with her in search of an intimate moment to speak about Subham Bhai. Many times, I thought about speaking to her about him, but again stepped back with the thought 'she is hungry now, she had not eaten anything yesterday, what if suddenly she gets angry?' The moment did not come until breakfast.

At 12 o'clock, we sat for breakfast, and at 12:15, we finished it silently. We were too hungry, and concentrated on only eating.

"It was marvellous...delicious," I commented on the upama.

"Don't praise me, somehow it came out good."

She is a foodie, once she says it's nice means it is really nice or it tasted good because we were really hungry.

Pranami relaxed a bit on the chair, after the heavy breakfast, she looked normal and in a jubilant mood. I started gathering courage to talk about Subham Bhai, before I could do it, she got up and said, "Let me have a bath first then we will cook lunch."

She walked out of the room.

I sat at the dining table without a thought, until I heard the bathroom door slam shut with the sound of thunder, as she slammed the door hard.

--Ω--

I sat with my website mails; she took quite some time in the bathroom.

First, I replied to Mr Bagachi.

"Dear Mr Bagachi,

Sorry, I took time to reply you. Actually, I was in search of words about how and what to tell you. I thought repeatedly about the facts, co-related with other truth-values and finally came out that, it's only a talk that can guide your son to your way. He may avoid you many times, but you don't avoid him. I am sure some solution will come out.

Finally, I have to tell you that gayism is not bad, it's accepted in society. Until now, no science has understood the reason or the remedy for gayism. There is no reason or cause why one man became a gay and one man remained straight.

I am eager to know what happens next. Please let me know.

Best regards,

Myrelationship.com"

I read the mail once again, the lines seemed strange to me. I thought it's not my lines rather they were Pranami's thoughts. Her ideology had been incorporated into me and I was carried by it to write to him for the first time. I sent it.

On the other hand, it was the best that I could write to the father of a gay.

Vardhman had not sent me either a mail or message. How could that be? I checked the mobile. Shit...it had two missed calls and one message. All were from Vardhman. The phone was in silent mode from last night.

Vardhman tried to call me twice and sent a message, "Yesterday you didn't respond, so I booked it. No meaning in cancelling today, so let's wait, if the condition permits we will go or simply quit."

He must be annoyed. I always make him unhappy. But once Pranami was around, she got things done in her way.

I messaged him immediately, as the bathroom door opened like thunder again, "Okay, I will try to come, it's still far away."

His message came instantly, "Thanks."

Pranami entered like a storm into the drawing room, "Oh... you are still here...I thought you would have taken your bath... leave the laptop; otherwise, I will throw it."

"Okay, babe...okay," I just surrendered.

"Come...help me in the kitchen and then go for your bath, come on."

She left and I followed her as a calf does a cow.

"Only veg...no non-veg...okay," she proclaimed.

I had to obey her orders and nod at her command.

We sat for lunch at 4 p.m.

"It's nice...the aroma fills half the stomach," putting a spoon full into my mouth I declared, "Absolutely delicious."

I hardly got home-cooked food and it's only when Pranami was in a mood like today. So naturally, it tasted good to me. I was telling the truth, it was well cooked.

Pranami took very little in her spoon with her head down, as if she was thinking something seriously.

I asked, "What happened, why are you eating so little?"

"You are simply praising me...it's not cooked that well."

"Oh...you won't believe how good it tastes...awesome food...actually you directly came from the heat, so wait for a while and then start, it's really nice."

"Truth!"

"Yeah...100 per cent...promise."

"So, foodies can cook good food also!" she exclaimed.

As soon as she started taking a few spoons, I merely whispered, "Pranami..."

"Yes," she listened and replied in a dramatic voice.

"Subham Bhai is in trouble."

"He invites trouble, gets into trouble and invented trouble, so what, it's nothing new for him."

"He is in serious problems."

"He was always in serious problems. The day he decided to reside in America; actually, he called the problem to himself."

"He has gone into bankruptcy; the bank has captured one of his stores and his partner Russell withdrew his shares from the partnership. He had created a fraudulent agreement."

"Please, Manav; I don't want to hear anything about them. If you want that I should not eat peacefully then you talk... right...okay." She left the spoon on the plate and looked at me.

There was no option left for me other than to keep quiet.

--Ω--

In the evening, at seven, Pranami came to balcony where I was sitting with two cups of tea. We had not exchanged a single word from our last conversation about Shubam Bhai until now. I was thinking deeply about what could be done for Subham Bhai.

Giving me one cup, she asked, "What were you saying about Subham Bhai?"

I did not answer; I was searching for words about how to tell her.

Pranami asked again, "What will he do then?"

I was convinced that Pranami was serious, as she kept her eyes focussed on me waiting for an answer.

"Subham Bhai is ready to come to Delhi, but he is scared..."

"Scared of what?

"Don't know...maybe you...you are the fear factor for him."

She laughed feebly, revealing the pain in her, "Tell him to come back."

"He won't listen to me."

"Tell him, I have asked him to come back."

"Why don't you talk then...he will feel good," I asked.

"No...I won't," she got up, asked the empty cup from me and went back.

The next moment, I called Subham Bhai. He cried on receiving my call. I saw Pranami listening to our talk. Subham Bhai wanted to speak to Pranami, but she did not come out.

Finally, I had to say, "You come down, Bhai, then you can talk for a thousand days with Pranami...you plan quickly and then tell me your date of arrival?"

13

Pranami and I were sitting in the beautiful drawing room of Shobhaban Khare at G-28, behind Hotel Park Residency, Green Park.

The house had extra tranquillity; the interior of the house was superbly designed. A Honda City car was parked in the portico, but nobody else seemed to be in the house. Mrs Shobhaban had gone to make us coffee.

Mrs Shobhaban was in her forties and a professor of history. She was the Head of the Department of History of a college she had not mentioned to us. She wrote about the ancient history of India and had many books to her credit.

Finding the house was easy; we knew every inch of Green Park. We remembered that a Mr Khare resided in this house. Structurally, the house was unchanged, except for the colour of the paint; now it was painted yellow, while earlier it was green. We may have come across him and would probably recognize him, if we saw him.

Pranami and I were speechless. We looked at each other making presumptions about the calmness of the surrounding.

After fifteen minutes, Mrs Shobhaban came with three coffee mugs on a tray. She placed the tray on the tea table and sat comfortably in front us.

"Guys, please help yourself." She picked up one coffee mug.

"Sorry for the long wait. You must be wondering why I made the coffee instead of the maid."

We desperately needed that coffee and eagerly picked our mugs.

I said, "Exactly."

She laughed, "I don't keep a maid...yes, a girl comes on a daily basis to clean the house, but I don't keep a permanent servant, not even my driver. When needed, I intimate him a day prior; otherwise, I drive my own car and I cook as well."

It surprised us; Pranami frowned and asked, "Why is that?"

"What can I tell you... you are aware of the situation in Delhi and the brutal attacks on old aged people?" said Mrs Shobhaban.

That was a well-known fact and I thought she had taken the right step. There was an increasing trend of killing older people in Delhi.

She continued, "For a single woman like me, it's very difficult to pull on and the probability of attack is even more."

Her words addled us. Pranami exchanged looks with me, thinking that perhaps, I knew about her single hood, but I was in the same perplexed boat sinking on the wave of probability.

Perhaps, Mrs Shobhaban noticed our confused stage, she said, "Oh...you don't know Mr Khare is no more...he left me long ago...sorry, I didn't mention it first, as I thought you were aware of it."

"No...We don't know anything," I said.

"When you say you were a resident of Green Park, I thought you may know that Mr Khare is dead because everyone here knows it. He died in a road accident. It's been 21 years... and I stay alone here since 21 years."

"Sorry aunty, that time we were kids...we saw your house earlier, it was painted green, but did not know of the fact." I called her aunty, as I felt some binding of closeness being a Green Parkian. Mrs Shobhaban did not mind it, but Pranami noticed it and frowned at me.

"Yes...the house was painted green, only this year I painted it yellow," Mrs Shobhaban said, after taking a long breath.

"Guys, let us start with the purpose you came for...I know you must have many questions, but you will get all the answers in our conversation, so let's hurry up, as I have very little time."

Before getting into the conversation, I have to relate the earlier story because of which we were here today. On the website 'myrelationship.com' and in the contact tag, we had made a provision 'about telling own story' to the world. There, the individual fills in his or her personal data, contact number and hundred words narration about the practices he or she opts for. If the matter has an impact, I contact and fix a meeting, discussion or interview according to the convenience of the person. That was one way I used for getting stories. Sometimes, I got clues for a story in the mails as well, and developed the story by regular follow up.

When I contacted Mrs Shobhaban, she gave few guidelines, and was only willing to talk and narrate her story, if those guidelines could be adhered to. It was quite difficult, but I felt her part of the story was unique.

Her guidelines meant that we could not reveal her name, residential address, profession, area of concern and the organization that she worked for. Her reasons were quite clear, 'if you give some clue technology savvy people will find you'.

She was not afraid of herself, she was afraid of her profession and the organization that respected her and secured her future. It was against my website policy, but I still accepted it.

When I had shown my reluctance, she was forthright, "It's up to you, Manav, because in our society people who are quite educated still feel gayism or lesbianism is a sin, despite the historical verdict of the high court."

Another condition was there we could not take photographs or a video, which meant we could not show her face on the website. I could record our conversation, but I could not upload the audio on the website and for doing so I had asked her permission too and explained that it will help me analyse the story for the write-up for the website post.

Her third condition was that, we could not reveal the name of the person with whom she had the long relationship. Once we had accepted her first condition, it was pointless arguing on the third point.

Her final condition was that we were not to ask any questions on her professional front, for which I had no objections.

Of course, she assured me that when she retired from her professional service, I could use her name. Apparently, she had planned to take voluntary retirement from her service, quite soon.

As Mrs Shobhaban revealed this long list of guidelines, I asked, "Will you be comfortable with me or would you prefer a female for the discussion..."

She asked, "What is your age 30,-35?"

"I am 33," I was amazed at her guess.

She said, "I have no problem with you, but if a woman is around us, I can express my views freely...if not, absolutely no issue...but keep my points in mind."

Before coming, another amazing thing happened.

When I asked Pranami to accompany me, she asked, "Why me? You take your friend Purba Saxena; she is always there to help you."

"Pranami, are you coming with me or not? I am not taking anyone with me...I will go alone."

"You know I can't refuse you."

"I have done many cases alone...this time also, I will do it alone...it's not a big deal."

"Oh...you think the atmosphere will be conducive? She is not even your age...a long gap of age and gender, and you think she will be free to tell you everything...no way. When there is gender bias, people never open up and you are not going to take an interview of a sports person or awarder? You gay people have all slang and vernacular talks...how can a woman be comfortable talking to you...though you may be in the same group."

I laughed; it meant she was coming.

"I have fixed the time for six in the evening..."

"Where will we meet?" I asked Pranami.

"You come down; we will go from here."

"I have some work at Nehru Place, so I won't come."

"Then I will wait for you at the turning to Green Park... you come under the flyover...I will be there by 5.45 p.m...will that be fine?"

"Yeah," I was happy she did not bargain to come and take her from Dwarka.

--Ω--

Pranami finished the coffee first and got ready to be the interviewer; the filmy woman enjoys it very much. I switched on the recorder.

Pranami asked the first question, "When did you come to know you are a lesbian?"

Mrs Shobhaban said, "Actually, I am not a lesbian. I practice the sexuality of lesbianism. So, I don't treat myself as a lesbian"

"What is the difference?" Pranami asked promptly.

"Difference is there and you will come to know. I have never attended any pride parade...I keep myself away from these activities," said Shobhaban.

"And your partner?"

"She too..."

"Why the fear? Once you practice the thing, you can't bat for it?"

Mrs Shobhaban thought for a while, then said, "May be fear...fear of status...fear of profession."

"Okay...you said you are not a lesbian. When and how do you practice it...what circumstances made you do so?" asked Pranami.

Pranami educated herself in the act of taking interviews. Amazingly, she transgressed herself to be a good interviewer, and knew exactly how to extract facts...not giving me a chance to speak.

"After my marriage," said Mrs Shobhaban.

"Wow...after marriage...means your sexual life with Mr Khare was not successful, but what made you opt for lesbianism?"

Mrs Shobhaban thought for a while, took a deep breath, and prepared herself well. The discussion became intrinsic and dialectic.

"Yes...my physical relationship with Mr Khare was not healthy...according to your words not successful."

"Why...you did not like each other...any stress...he had some affair or he did not like sex...there exists some people that are not interested in sex...cold customer of sex."

Mrs Shobhaban smiled. "These were not the causes."

"But there must be some cause...if a husband and wife do not enjoy their sexual life then there must be some cause...any inability?"

"Yes, the inability was with me; I didn't enjoy sex with him," said Mrs Shobhaban and this time she did not smile.

"Exactly...what was the cause, did he have some affair?" asked Pranami.

"No...the affair developed after my inability showed up. Listen, I was married at the age of 18. I told you I had never had a successful intercourse with him...It was painful for me... each day I suffered..." Mrs Shobhaban stopped in between, perhaps remembering the pain. Her body stormed into pain again and the extra tranquillity was ramified.

Pranami was wordless, but Mrs Shobhaban continued, "I couldn't sleep the entire night because of pain. Mr Khare and I thought it was because of early marriage, but after two years of marriage, one night I was admitted, at Safdarjung Hospital. That night, Mr Khare had transgressed from a human to an animal. He gradually lost interest in me and developed a relationship with one of his cousins, a distant relative. Both died in the road accident. This is my story."

Pranami cornered her then, "Fine...but how did you develop lesbianism in you, was the harassed sexual relationship the cause of lesbianism?"

"Yes...one of the causes."

"You did not consult a doctor?" asked Pranami.

"I consulted a doctor, but the inability was with me; he had a normal life as a man has."

This time, I asked the question, as I wanted to extract the exact science behind it, which is the motto of my website.

"When Mr Khare developed an illicit relationship, you could have thought about getting into a relationship with another man, if not Mr Khare. Don't misunderstand me, as all I want to know is the theory behind every human thought and the path it leads…"

Pranami looked at me astounded; a true woman cannot bear an illicit relationship in any form of conversation. I smiled at her.

She thought Mrs Shobhaban may get angry, but she laughed at my question, "It can be imagined…can be asked, but it is very difficult to handle any illicit relationship."

She continued, "I accepted their relationship, but she could not become his wife with my acceptance…their relationship could not be legitimate like that of a husband and wife."

"You could have taken divorce?" I asked.

"Yes, we could…but we were afraid about our social status."

"When did Mr Khare die?

"In 1991, after four years of our marriage."

"You would have been hardly 22…you could have remarried?"

"Sure…but I had started hating men."

"This is how your lesbianism started?"

"Yes…though my sexual life with a man was not successful, I had sexual desires. I had feelings…yes my body urged me to take to lesbianism."

"Then why do you say you are not a lesbian?" I asked.

"Because I don't have feelings of lesbianism, it was the requirement of my body nothing else that's why I said I am not a lesbian, I practice the sexuality of lesbianism."

"Okay...your sexual relationship with one man was a disaster...I am again emphasizing, you could have remarried and led a normal straight life."

"Why are lesbians not normal?"

I laughed, "You only said that they have different feelings."

"Yes, I said...they have different feelings, but they are very normal. In my case, I am normal but I opted for lesbianism, not because of desire, but for a need. You may not understand this Mr Manav, your friend Pranami will understand me...she understands better, she is a woman."

I looked at Pranami, she had mixed feelings and there was confusion in her expression.

I said, "What I wanted to say is that you had that different feeling that's why you had opted for lesbianism...and your partner?"

"She did not hate men...she had a successful marriage life...but her husband was always on a tour. She had children. She was exercising her fantasy and desire."

"How did you find her? I asked.

"It was co-incidence."

I could not ask anything more about her partner, as per the guideline.

I took time to ask her further. "I understand, everyone has different characteristics. Did you practise lesbianism before Mr Khare's death or after it."

"It was before."

"This may be the reason why you didn't get remarried?"

"May be."

We had taken more time than scheduled, so I asked a few more random questions, looking at my watch, "You never felt the desire for a child of your own?"

She laughed, "Who said I don't have a child...I have a son, Rohan. He is studying in London."

Pranami and I exchanged our confused look, "Adopted?"

"No...he is Mr Khare's son from his cousin. He is 24 years old."

"He knows about your practise?"

"No."

"You would like to tell him this, one day?"

"No"

"If he caught you red handed?"

"I will react according to his reaction."

"You love him?"

"More than anything else in the world."

"Do you ever feel you are doing wrong...maybe committing a sin?"

"I told you I am not a lesbian...and I never give a second thought to it...once you start thinking you cannot get pleasure from it."

"Our last question," I asked, "what do you say about lesbianism...to our website to our readers and viewers."

She laughed, changed her sitting stance, took a deep breath then said, "Again, you are coming to the same point. I do not know much about lesbianism...I read about all the happenings of it in and around...I am not a follower of your website...it's Priyanka, who sent you the mail."

"Who is Priyanka?"

"My partner...she is a regular viewer and follower of your website. I wanted to just share my story with others. You will take the essence and interpret it according to your desire. I don't know chemistry...no science...no theory behind it, but certainly I would like to see your next post...what you write about me."

She sent us with smiles, and came up to the portico to say bye. Before saying bye, I asked, "If I need you at any time, can I call you aunty?"

"Sure...but not at night time. I don't take calls at night and certainly not for a story again," she laughed.

--Ω--

Pranami asked before boarding the vehicle, "You will go back? What is the plan?" I laughed, as I was expecting the same question from her.

She asked again, "Why are you laughing? Have I asked anything wrong or anything funny?" she gazed at her belongings.

"It's nothing; let's go."

"You tell me first why you laughed?" she became adamant.

"Okay, babe...I laughed as I was thinking the same thing, when you asked."

"What is wrong? I had planned not to ask you, but could not control it...I know you will go back to Ghaziabad, you need to write and post it on the website, but still I asked... it came out spontaneously." Pranami emotionally broke down; I had never thought she would take such minor things so sensitively.

"Who told you I am going to Ghaziabad? You just predicted it; this is wrong with women. I am coming to Dwarka and will stay for two days...okay...fine."

She smiled.

--Ω--

As soon as we entered into her flat, Pranami asked, "What do you think of Mrs Shobhaban?"

"What's there to think, it was her part of the story."

"I mean is there anything like not being a lesbian, but practising lesbianism?"

I smiled. "It only struck you...have you not observed she is practicing lesbianism for the last 21 or 22 years continuously, when no law or no morals governed it."

"Very clever woman."

"I will not comment...for me, she is the right choice."

"Obviously...you fall in her group."

She never hesitated to take a dig at me whenever she got a chance. Quietly, we changed over. It was a hectic day for me. Before coming to Mrs Shobhaban, I met 'Raju Gay' at Nehru Palace. He was hardly 17 and on my Facebook friend list. Unlike others, I did not receive any message or mail for their story; I was chasing them. 'Raju Gay' is his Facebook name. His real name is 'Rajendra Chug'. Last week, I met 'Yuvi Gay' in Janak Puri, it is also his Facebook name, and his real name is 'Yugandhar Hooda'. He is in his twenties. 'Yuvi Gay' gave the lead to 'Raju Gay'. These young boys opened up on social websites and mostly used Facebook as their tool of communication.

"You feel my words?" Pranami's voice echoed in my heart.

"Oh...hello, where are you...have you slept?" Pranami awakened me by pulling my shoulder.

Rewinding the day's work on the sofa, when I dropped off to sleep, I cannot say.

"Yeah...just snoozed." The aroma of tea intensified all my sensation.

"Tired?" asked Pranami.

"Yeah."

"Why, had you gone to extinguish a fire in the sea?"

Sometimes, she jokes and when she jokes, it comes heavily.

"I mean there are no new posts or no great news on your website; it means you are not working extra time then why do you get tired?" She did not even give me time to answer her, and asked again, "Have tea, if it gets cold all my hard work will be in vain."

I took the cup in my hand, after having one sip of it, I praised it, "Nice tea." The tea she makes is always worthy of praise, one could easily understand this from the expression on my face, but still it was necessary to praise it.

I looked at her, she seemed jubilant, "Don't praise I know...what do you want?"

"Nothing," I said, stretching both hands, coming out of my drowsiness.

"I know what you will ask...Pranami, do you have anything left...I am tired."

I laughed aloud. She was right; I intended to ask the same.ʾ

"But no," she came closer to me, "you will not get anything..." she held me in her arms "today no..." put her head on my shoulder, "that's why I made tea at this time."

"Okay, babe, as you feel."

"That's like a good babe," she pressed me to her body, and closed her eyes.

"When will you change, Manav?" she whispered this time, resting her head on my chest and closing her eyes.

"What is wrong with me...what do I need to change!" I asked, in auto motion. I raised my hand and started caressing her hair.

"Your gayness...I can't even imagine whether I am doing wrong or right...I am just helping where your happiness lies. Sometimes, I feel by helping I am encouraging you...but I am afraid to say 'no' to you...I get frightened it may hurt you...and even in my imagination I don't want to hurt you," her voice dropped lower and lower, she was surrounded by a sensory emotion of binding...her head pressed against my chest, firmly.

"I also feel the same," I whispered, caressing her hair gently.

"Then why do you harass me always?"

"Me!"

"Yes...why are you involved with Vardhman? I don't like that fellow."

"You have said this a hundred times," I said, intending to tease her.

"I will say it a thousand times...many times...what a cruel man...he knows I love you, still he wanted to marry me?"

"It's over, why do you repeat it?"

"Because you had supported him, you are also a cruel man."

"So, you don't love me?" I held her face in front of mine; her eyes were still closed.

"That's the problem...I can't live without you."

I moved my lips to arrest hers that were speaking a lot today; she didn't resist. My hand ran over her neck and moved downward, when it tried to unhook her bra, she abruptly released her hand and jumped over the sofa, "You naughty... not now...let us finish our dinner...every time we skip it."

I looked at her passionately.

"I said no...not now...what are you looking...the maid has made dinner. I will just put it into the oven and make an omelette for you."

She left with a smile.

14

I woke up early for checking my mails. Around 4 a.m., in the morning, I woke up once to write about Mrs Shobhaban, but was afraid if Pranami woke up and saw me, the sweet night's lovely dreams would be ruined in seconds. I went back to sleep again. I was right, the next moment Pranami engulfed me in her hands, the quilt was away from our bodies, but in the wee hours, she felt the cold and pulled over the quilt to get some warmth. It showed that Delhi's winter was at a diminishing phase.

As I sat and switched on the laptop and went through the mails, Pranami's sleepy voice sounded, "Where are you, babe?"

"Just coming, babe," I stood up.

"What happened?" I asked.

"You have woken up?" Pranami asked, with her eyes still closed.

"Yes."

"Why do you wake up so early, babe?"

"It's not early, it's already nine."

"Then why am I late always...it's because of you...you kept me awake until late night, then dropped off to sleep first, you know after that I could not get sleep for more than two hours...

and in those two hours, it appeared as if the entire world's problem came to me for solving them."

I was not interested in her talk, I said, "Wake up...come and see Subham Bhai has sent a mail."

"What has he written, why is he not coming?"

"I have not read it; you called me so I came back to you first."

"Okay...give me five minutes...I am just coming from the bathroom," she got up reluctantly.

Until Pranami came back, I read the mail.

He had written...

Dear Manav,

I am really thankful to you; I received your money... thanks again for helping me out. All the settlement will be over by Wednesday, I kept one day with me to say good-bye to America.

I am coming on the next Friday's flight on the 2nd of March.

You have done plenty of favours for me and this time I beg you, please arrange a rented house for me and if possible a job.

I have no place in the world to stay.

See you on the third.

Subham Bhai

I contemplated that Subham Bhai would have written his date of arrival that was why I called Pranami to see it. But his gestures of thanks would open up a storm in Pranami. Very soon, she would become a detective and would start questioning about all the details of the mail that I would not be able to answer and I would get bullshit from her. Before I could think of anything to avoid showing her the mail or do some editing Pranami sat beside me, "Show me what Subham Bhai has written...has he written about his arrival date?" Pranami pulled the laptop towards her.

She read the mail and I saw her changed expression. My position was that of a terrified rabbit that sees death at both ends. When a rabbit saw the lion near it, it was unable to move, if it moved it would be caught, if not, then too the lion would capture it.

She took some time. In this case, the anxiety of waiting for her to react was stronger than the expectations and the anxiety of a pregnant woman waiting to deliver her baby.

She pushed the laptop towards me and asked, "You have sent money to him?"

I nodded like a child confessing his crime in front of his father.

"Why didn't you tell me? I would have sent the money to him."

"It's the same...he is my brother also and what difference does it make whether you send it or I!" me was somewhat relieved at the manner that she responded to me.

"Money was the reason of his delaying?" she asked.

"Yes...and other settlements as well...In the settlement he has some amount to pay back to Russell also."

"How much was the amount?" Pranami intervened and asked profoundly.

"Some 50 US dollar."

"No...you are lying to me."

I cursed myself, why had I called and invited trouble? Women always have detective thoughts, and she read and knew me deeply.

"It's fifty thousand USD."

"How much does that convert into Indian rupee?"

"Some 33 lakh 59 thousand plus in Indian Rupees."

"And you think it's a small amount."

"Pranami, it's not big compared to a life...they would not let him leave the country, until all the money is paid to the US government."

"This way you become noble and for the man who didn't bother to come to the funeral of my mother and came after the demise of my father for settlement of the property."

"Pranami, he has regretted his deed."

"Regret at the cost of money. By the way, where you get such a huge amount, you purchased the car recently with hard cash and it's a high-end luxury car?"

I said women have detective minds, they can presume and assume many things and correlate it to many things.

"I took a personal loan...this is the fastest means to get a loan approved and I had some amount in the bank."

"From where did you take the loan?"

"From the bank."

"Which bank...I must know."

"Why, because you are a bank manager...not only your bank, even other banks give personal loans," I said to ease the atmosphere.

"Fine I am not interested from which bank you took the loan, but at least you should have spoken to me first."

"Don't worry, I have taken the loan from your bank only, but from the Ghaziabad branch," I tried to ease the conversation.

"I told you I am not interested. What I said is it's not a small amount and you have given it to such a person who wanted money desperately...it may be a ploy."

"No, Pranami...he is not gimmicking, this time he is not lying about anything...have faith in your brother."

Pranami gave a smirk, it's painful, "I don't believe gays."

Tranquillity mounts over both of our faces.

I intended to ask, "You don't have trust on me!" But could not, as suddenly a cold wave captured my heart. Was Subham Bhai finally playing a trick with me? He was desperately in need of money, who cares from where the money came? Thousand unwanted thoughts of these kinds suffocated me.

She took a long time to break the serenity, "I mean you should have discussed with me, we could have sold some property of Gurgaon factory or I could manage some amount."

"It's fine, Pranami... let him come back to India safely... and he needs something to do...so he can start the factory again and I am sure he will succeed."

"Hope so."

She moved into silent mode again, leaving me with hundreds of unbelievable thoughts.

After few minutes, Pranami asked again, "Why has he written for a rented house?"

"I told him...he could stay with me, but he feels it would be an extra burden again for me...he is writing stupidly...I won't allow him to stay outside... you be sure," I proclaimed with a strong belief in me.

She did not say anything. It's very painful when you expect some quick answer and the person you expect something from goes into meditation. She closed her eyes in deep thought.

I was amazed, when she started speaking hastily, "Why can't he stay with me?"

Yes, he can...but I was not prepared for the question, so preferred to be silent.

"What is the problem with staying with me...tell me...why can't he stay with me?" Pranami questioned.

When she questions I get frightened. It's unusual.

"No problem...but he was afraid to stay with you," I said half-heartedly.

"Afraid of what? He will not able to practise gayness here... tell him he is coming back for survival not for enjoyment?

She goes into deep thoughts again; I sat like the little child whose master goes into deep sleep after assigning class work. The child has completed the class work, but was frightened to wake up the master.

Pranami again woke up suddenly, "Nothing doing...he is staying with me...it's final...okay."

I nodded like the most obedient child.

--Ω--

A new message flashed on my mobile, it's from Ronit Bali, my new friend from DU, Rajendra Chug had given him the lead. The message read, "If U wish to C can come to CP inner circle." The time was 7 p.m., in the evening.

It's Saturday and their meeting day at CP, I understand.

I messaged him back, "How do I spot U?" I had not met him yet and the photo he uploaded on FB was not his, I was sure. I had spoken with him twice over the telephone.

His replied to me immediately through a new message, "I can find you, come alone."

I replied him, "Okay," and hurried to CP. The 30 minutes' drive took me almost an hour until I parked the car. It was rush hour everywhere. I reached the inner circle; it was nothing new for me. I looked for Ronit Bali; I could not see anyone that I thought could be him standing around, so I called him. He picked up the phone on the third ring. I asked, "Where are you?"

"Have you reached?"

"Yes...I am standing under a light post adjacent to the fence and in front of the Titan show room, near gate number 4 of the metro gate," I narrated my location.

"Okay...just two minutes," and he cut the connection.

I had been here twice, a long time ago, but the purpose on that day and today was different. We start our pride parades from here; this place is conducive to all. In the crowd, you cannot distinguish who is what, there are men-men, men-women, women-women and eunuchs roam around for a safe haven. There are policemen in civil clothes as well.

After two minutes, a well-built muscular man in his twenties stood in front and asked me, "Yes?"

I understood he was the man, I asked, "Ronit Bali?"

"Yes."

"I am Manav and I called you," I tried to explain my position.

"I know."

"Okay, fine," I gulped my saliva baffled.

"Now...tell me what you want?" he seemed intrepid and bold compared to me.

"Can we sit over coffee and talk...but not here...lets go to some other place, if you have no objection and have you finished all your commitments here?" I asked.

"Sure, I have no problem...but I have very little time, I must reach my home before 10," answered Ronit.

I looked at my wristwatch; it was only 08:20 in the evening, and we have enough time. I said, "No issue, I will drop you...which place?"

"No...no I have my own bike...I can go," he vehemently refused to take help.

The next moment, we ordered two coffees and sandwiches at the 'Night Safari restaurant' in the outer circle of CP.

The order takes some time and our time passes quietly.

I spoke first, "Every Saturday you come to this place?"

"Not exactly, but almost."

"What you do here?" I asked naively.

Ronit gazed at my face for few seconds and rather than answering me, he asked, "Are you gay?"

It shocked me, "What does that mean?"

"My answer would be accordingly."

I had never been in such a confused or mixed up state, I said, "Yes, I am."

Ronit laughed, "I know...I was just kidding...who does not know about you...your website is a hit."

He eased up the atmosphere and I felt very comfortable.

The waiter served the coffee and sandwiches.

Taking a sip, I asked, "Now you answer."

"We come in search of partners."

"But you have partners...I met your friend Raju and Yuvi?"

Ronit answered with a smile, "We are not exactly partners, we are in a friend circle and we need to expand it."

"Love happens with one to one relationships then why create a group?" I asked.

"You know gay sex is not easy, a new partner may add some fantasy. Sometimes, one partner is not always available."

"Then?" I asked.

"Then what?"

"Did you get a partner today?"

"No...that's why I am sitting with you."

"Okay, fine...suppose you would have got a partner today...then?"

"I would not be here...I am kidding...it's not easy to find a gay partner, and if sometimes it happens there is no guarantee it will sustain for long."

"I know...I know," I nodded, giving him space to open up.

"There are lots of ifs and buts...sometimes, the problems are top and bottom problems... sometimes fear of AIDS, age difference and the police is also a threat...the biggest threat is the mind...if both minds are not surreal, gay sex is not enjoyable. "

"If it has problems, threats and obstacles then why gayism, why not be straight?" I asked.

Ronit's face became pale, he looked insipid and fumbled for an answer. I intervened then, he had not come up to the state where he could answer this question, as they were simply enjoying gay life.

I changed what he loved to do and asked, "I mean what you do when you get a partner?"

"We go to discos, parties and pubs...drink...dance."

"If the partner does not drink, meaning someone who does not drink liquor, then what?"

"It's rare...I have not come across anyone...yes, there are people who only drink cold drinks...but enjoy party time just like others," Ronit answered smartly and seemed to return to his juvenile energetic mood.

"Who pays, what is the rule?"

He laughed at my question, "The rule is whoever invites."

"And you pay for sex also?" I asked.

"Not exactly."

"WhatIhavecometoknowthatpayingforsexisrampantnow."

"They are a different community."

"It's been a long debate at every corner." I said.

"Actually, these people make gays dirty...they are an operated group and handled by masterminds...but why are you asking me all this?" Ronit reverted to me with this question, "You know everything...you are also a gay...you want a new story for your site?" he waited for my answer, with fear and eagerness. He looked at his watch.

Finally, he had caught me on the wrong foot, "I am doing research work on youth...their mental state and their thought process...certainly, it will be posted on the website," I said.

"But don't mention my name."

"Are you afraid?"

"Yes."

"Don't worry I will not mention anyone's name...happy...I know you are getting late, but give me a few rapid answers to my questions...okay?"

"Okay," said Ronit reluctantly.

"Your family knows about it?"

"No."

"If they came to know, how would you react?"

"Can't say...I have not thought about it.'"Do you have a girl friend?"

"No...Yes," he was puzzled to answer.

"Means yes...have you gone out for a date with her?"

"Yes."

"She invited you or you invited her?"

"She invited me."

"You had sex with her?"

"No...not even we kissed each other."

"Okay, final question what if your parents were to ask you to marry that girl?"

He looked blank and said, "Don't know..."

Our conversation ended, he seemed in a hurry to leave, I paid the bill and then left the restaurant, it was 9:30 p.m. Before leaving, he again requested me not to mention his name. Coming out from the restaurant, I stared at the way he took for a long time until he vanished from my eye as well as mind. Thought these gays have not grown up to be shared intellectual rights so they found their own way of enjoyment, where they are heading, they mapped gayness in all conducive means to them. I felt pity for these so called gays.

After coming back from CP, I thought about them too. Their attitude and thought process made me concerned about them.

When I found a catch-22 situation within me and called Gopalji or met him at his residence. I felt it is too late to visit him so phoned him and narrated my follow up about Ronit Bali and Rajendra Chug type new generation upcoming gays, their FB gang, fun and gay sex haunting experiments.

Gopalji listened to me silently; waited until I finished all my desperate narration with harsh words. When I felt that I have expressed myself fully, I kept quiet and waited for him to say something.

After a long pause, he said, "Have you finished?"

"Means..." I was perplexed.

"I mean you have said whatever you wanted to say?"

"Yes."

"Then listen, a well-known intellectual had four sons and all were brilliant too, though he was dubious about his younger son. The younger one was intelligent, but had a fickle mind. He wished all his sons to get selected for the kingdoms ministry and the elder one to become as chief minister, but the king examined them all before selecting. The man was sure all the elder sons would pass but was doubtful about the younger one. But when the results came the father was surprised the king chose the younger one as chief minister and declared why 'the position needs to be experimental rather instrumental'."

Pausing from his story, Gopalji asked, "Now think these upcoming, young ones are experimental rather than instrumental. They have power and will one day change the way society thinks about gayism."

"You mean it's a good sign?" I asked puzzled over his narration.

"I have not said it's a good or bad sign, I just said their power will change the society," replied Gopalji.

I understand he is welcoming the change, I did not say anything just dropped the call by saying good night.

--Ω--

On the morning of the 2 March , Pranami called me, "Do you remember or not?"

"What?"

"Subham Bhai is boarding the flight or not, has he confirmed again?" she still had doubts.

"He is coming and it's certain," I confirmed.

"Okay," she dropped the call, but again called me at mid-day, "What is the plan?"

"Nothing...what's the plan?"

"Are you coming tonight?"

"Yes."

"Okay...come early."

Again, she called me at 5 p.m., "I am leaving office, have you started?"

"I am in office and I will take time. I have a meeting."

"Complete it first and come early I have something for you."

Before I could ask, she dropped the call. I reached Dwarka at 10 p.m.; Pranami opened the door with an apron on and a long knife in her hand. The room was filled with the aroma of the cooking masalas. She was probably chopping something.

"Something is cooking?" I asked.

"Yes," she looked exuberant.

"It is the surprise for me?" I thought what other thing could I expect from a foodie girl!

"Yes, I am making a chicken dish for you."

"Oh...really...will it be eatable?"

"Don't joke...I have made corn chicken...its easy...actually the maid taught me...she was here, she just left few minutes before...you must have been in the parking at that time."

"Nice fragrance," I had to comment.

"Go and change, everything is ready. The maid has made rotis as well. You must be hungry. Why did you make it so late? What was so important that you could not come early today at least," she questioned, remarked and answered—her queries and what she wanted to convey—all coming out in quick succession, while nurturing the chicken bowl with care.

"What are you looking? Go and change, don't you feel hungry!" she ordered, as I looked at her passionately.

"Yes...yes...I am."

Coming back from the bathroom, I said, "Subham Bhai confirmed his boarding and the flight is reaching tomorrow at 2 p.m."

Pranami did not say anything; she was sitting with the food arranged on the dining table.

Pranami said, "Manav..."

I looked at her enthusiastically.

When she asked, she would ask if not for the sun then for the moon, "Just one...one sip...I have your favourite black vodka."

"No...you go out of control," I refused vehemently.

"Only two pegs...promise...I swear." She swore as we did in childhood holding the skin of the neck. If anyone knew her better then he would agree with me, it was baseless to refuse her again.

"Come...come to the sofa."

She had arranged everything for the drink. She took two pegs as promised then slept on my lap, putting her head on it.

She cooed softly, "Manav..." My heart beat rises faster when she calls like this. "...Tell me one thing; yesterday, I was looking at some facts on gayism, where one website says the human body is not designed to accommodate anal sex. The rectum is radically different from the woman's part for intercourse and basically it's not meant for sex. It's meant for exit only...vagaira...vagaira...(etc.). I hope you get me...they are very much prone to HIV and many other diseases like anal cancer, Chlamydia Trachomatis and many more. What I say if god has not made the body structure to have sex between men and men then why do men opt for it?"

"You are searching websites now for gayism?" I asked.

"Shall I say one thing, Manav?"

"Yes, tell me."

"The victim only knows how much pain is evoked when he encounters it every day, so it forced me to search what is in it? I know you don't have any answer; no gay can answer it. On the other side of it, God has put the desire for anal sex into a man. Gayness does not develop in practise, what I feel it is intrinsic, then why all these contradictions? Where and how does it develop in men?"

I was dumbfounded by her question as no one knows the origin and why do some people deviate from the masses? The theory was as debatable as the theory of what comes first the hen or the egg. Mythology also speaks about homosexuality. From the time of human evolution, straight and homosexuality existed side-by-side, like two sides of the same coin. Not only in human beings it is found in animals as well. So, it has nothing to do with education. But I did not want to debate anything with Pranami.

I asked her casually, "What happened, why you are taking so much interest in gayism?"

Pranami was serious, and said, "I know you don't have the answers...even if someone would try to answer, there will be contradictory answers."

"If you know there are no answers then why are you asking?" I said.

"That's what I don't understand...why I am thinking so much of it. Am I asking too much Manav?" her voice emphasized.

"No...Pranami...no."

She used a woman's best weapon; tears flowed freely over her cheeks. Vodka made her more sentimental.

She said wiping her tears, "Tomorrow Subham Bhai will come and we won't be able to stay together more."

I understood, she was thinking about the future, so I said casually again, "Why, you can just come down to my place."

I thought she would bite me for the casual joke, but it worked reverse, she wept more, tears flowed as if it was showering on a rainy day. I had spoken the wrong thing, as it would not be possible to leave her brother alone, as she could not come and stay with me on any day she felt like. What answer would she give him, if he asked her where she was going?

"Be cool, I was just kidding, Pranami."

"I will find out some way where we can meet," I tried to make her not weep.

"Imagine those days when we met full of fear, avoiding all our family's watchful eyes...that time has come again, we will again meet like the way we used to meet."

Suddenly, she said, "It won't possible...we are not teenagers anymore... and our requirements have changed," she got up and sat as close as possible keeping hardly any distance between our faces; I could feel her breath on my face.

Tears still flowed over her cheeks, her hair fell down on her face and she tried to put it back over her head, but failed. Her hair grew wet with her tears. When next she tried to wipe the tears from her cheeks, with her palm and fingers, I stopped her. I soaked the tears with my lips and closed her eyelids down slowly. Her salty face tasted marvellous. I mouthed her parted lips and her hands held me tight.

$$--\Omega--$$

"You are stupid and because of your stupidity I have to put everything into the oven again," Pranami murmured, while putting the chicken dish into the oven. I had to oblige, "Yes, I was stupid."

"I have made the dish with so much care and because of your stupidity everything has been ruined. Will it taste good, It's 12:30 a.m., and we will now have our dinner...how funny?" she murmured, while setting the micro-oven knob.

Like a dissident child looking at her, I enjoyed her euphony.

"What happened to you, why you are so silent say something?"

"Yes...yes," I said, as if coming out from some other deep thought.

"What yes...yes?"

"Yes...I am stupid."

"Nice...at least you agree you are stupid...is it time to have dinner...it is all because of you. If the chicken dish does not taste good, I will break your head...the original taste vanishes when you put it again into the oven."

I nodded, by the time she again arranged the table and called me, "Come...come...I am feeling very hungry."

"Nice...awesome," I said, taking one bite of the corn chicken.

"Don't joke, it's not that tasty."

"It's marvellous, Pranami...really awesome...god promise," I said, and it's not just undeserved praise, it's really a tasty dish. It showed how much care she had put to make it. That's why she was worried. When you are confident of any dish's taste, eagerness remains until the person for whom you make it tastes it and gives the judgment.

Pranami came to her flow, "One day, I will make prawn with sweet corn. It tastes good with nan and is best in summer... it is a little spicy and a little sweet taste and can be relished more in summer."

Her conversation continued and she seemed exuberant. That's what a woman is, every moment they change, and change in such a way that they don't leave any sign of the previous instant.

We finished dinner at 01:30. Until then, she was sluggish, but the moment she started collecting the utensils, she hurried up, "Oh...we are too late...when we will sleep and when we will wake up?"

15

The flight to Mohanbari was uneventful. A mini bus took us from Mohanbari to a hotel in Dibrugarh, around 15 Kms away. Dibrugarh is the district and the main town, Mohanbari is the airport. I had never been to a northeast state; I was fascinated as the first draught of cold air brushed against my face. It was mid-March and the climate seemed colder than Delhi. A clear blue sky with tiny white clouds and our mini bus crawled on the dark grey road in between the tea gardens. The road was adjacent to the railway tracks. A Delhi bound train joined us from the side and moved parallel. Tea garden workers were plucking the green leaves and putting them into the large bamboo baskets on their backs. It looked like a scene out of a movie; it was aesthetic.

A gay couple from Chandigarh also accompanied us in the bus. We were on the same flight, but got to know each other inside the mini bus. They had started yesterday from Chandigarh. Initially, they travelled by train, next stayed the night at a hotel in Delhi and then in the morning, they had boarded the same flight. For them too, this was their first trip to a northeast state and they were equally fascinated. Vardhman was busy talking to them.

We stayed for an hour at a hotel in Dibrugarh, freshened up and then boarded a 'Scorpio'. We were eight couples and we drove in four Scorpios.

Vardhman asked the driver, "How much time will it take?"

"Eight hours, but if it rains along the way, we will be delayed, further," replied the driver.

"How late?" asked Vardhman, again.

"Can't say, sir, it depends on how much rain. If it is heavy rain, we may have to stay back somewhere on the way."

"But where, in the vehicle itself?"

The driver didn't reply, he was cautious on a blind curve. Vardhman looked at the sky again and asked, "The sky is pretty clear, there is no sign of rain clouds, are you scaring us?"

The driver gave a sweet smile and replied, "You don't know, sir; in Assam the rain can come anytime anywhere."

Everyone joined him with great laughter.

It's really amazing to be in the northeast; incredible northeast. From the beginning of my entry into the northeast, the greenery and beautiful people mesmerized me. Trees were tall, almost touching the sky, roads were narrow, dark grey and serpentine—all together giving an illusion of reading a thriller novel, where the hero had whisked his heroine and they escaped from the heroine's father.

I asked Vardhman, "You were saying some Bollywood picture was shot here?"

"It's Koyla, starring Shahrukh and Madhuri."

On the way, we stopped at many 'Dhaba's' for tea, snacks and lunch and were amazed to see all the dhaba owners were Punjabi. But they serve food mostly eastern-Indian style rice, dal and curry. Vardhman faced the food problem. A pure Punjabi by nature, he wanted roti with and spice curry. I am acquainted with all types of food from my hostel life from Delhi IIT.

We reached the spot at ten, in the night, which happened to be the moon's dark phase. Moonlight just reached the earth, but was not enough to reach the cottage roofs, as tall trees surrounded the area. A large area was cleaned and cordoned with bamboo sticks. The cottages were at a distance and were positioned in a U shape in between the tall trees. Each cottage was made up of mud with a grass roof. The entire landscape looked heavenly in the moon light. The moon light gave a heavenly touch to it. This was a rare experience for we the north Indians and we thanked our tour operator for introducing us to such a beautiful and amazing place.

As we stepped out of the vehicle, we explored the beautiful landscape for some time, quenching all our desires. The cottage manager welcomed us with roses and beside him stood a man with a 'lantern', the only source of light. We gathered to listen to him.

The cottage manager addressed us, "I, Subodhkant Mittra, cottage manager on behalf of 'Sikhar Group' welcomes you all to this beautiful place 'Along'. It is in Arunachal Pradesh. As you can see all the cottages are independent, hope you will enjoy the privacy. It has one room, with an attached latrine and bathroom, but you can indulge in the experience of the open as the locals, if you feel like."

Everyone laughed, but not Mr Mittra.

He continued, "No light here, so you have to make use of lanterns in the night. Breakfast, lunch, dinner will be served in the cottages; however, if the entire group wishes, they can have it in the open; here it is called 'jungle bhoj'. But you need to intimate the staff, at least four hours before. It needs plenty of arrangement. You have one jungle bhoj in your package. We are four staff members and four drivers. Vehicles will be parked here for all days. The nearest town Along and the hospital are eight kilometres away. No phones and no network are possible here. The next day's itinerary will be intimated on the previous night. One caution, 'no teasing, no '*Chedkhani*'? with the localities'. Tomorrow, we will have a bath and go fishing in the river, just five hundred meters away from here. Dinner will be served in your cottages soon. Anyone wish to ask anything?"

No one wanted to waste any time; everyone was eager to go to the cottages, as everyone was tired.

Mr Mittra said, "So I am clear to all. Enjoy your stay. Good night."

Vardhman was excited; he checked the surrounding and each room.

I asked, "What are you doing?"

"Yar, I belong to a village background, I know how these mud houses are made."

"So?"

He examined the wall and replied, "It's hardly two inches thickness...they have put bamboo with cross-connected sticks and have applied mud to make the wall...even our whispers will be audible outside...but our northern mud walls are thicker and are more than 15 inches."

I understood his worry and replied, "That's the reason they have separated each cottage and built them at a distance."

"That's not my intention, I was just educating you," said Vardhman with a smile on his face.

Simple dinner was served in a thali, and the food was tasty. We were so tired and hungry we ate double of what we normally had in our routine dinner. Temperature is quite low here, Vardhman slept by hugging me under the blanket and sleep came faster.

We slept well and woke up only at eight in the morning. The sun rises early here and much above the sky. The sunrays were stronger and the illusion made it look as if it was midday.

Everyone stepped out of their cottage to take in the pleasures of nature.

On the first day, we had a river bath and visited the local market.

On the second day, we visited the nearby 'Boudh Pitha'.

On the third day, we visited 'Zero', a place covered with a thick forest. Mr Mittra announced it, on the night of the second day and requested us to wake up early so that we could cover the distance and come back safely before night.

On the fourth day, we had that 'jungle bhoj'. The food was cooked on dry woods, collected on the spot from the forest. The food had a delicious flavour and everyone relished it. That's the reason why Mr Mittra had emphasized about it on the very first day. This jungle bhoj had become so famous that the Sikhar group had started marketing it in their package. When we took the package, we had not paid much attention about it, thinking it may be just some promotion technique. But it turned out to be incredulous and added real spice to the stay. The jungle bhoj was a great opportunity to interact with each other, exchange phone numbers and learn about each other's profession.

An odd pair that was aged 40 and 20 had all eyebrows raised in a frown and for the last four days became the centre of gossip at the jungle bhoj.

Vardhman showed his dissidence over them on the first day, and asked, "Do you think they have a relationship?"

"Obviously, why not?"

"Okay, they have a relationship, but are they lovers?" he emphasized why he asked.

"Why, love cannot happen between two people aged 20 and 40?" I knew why he was asking, he had been spying on them before and trying to correlate their attitude to come to a conclusion and give his verdict.

He was suppressed at my reluctance to chat on the topic so, asked without much diversion, "You feel the 20-year-old man is the lover of the 40-year-old man? I feel the other way. He is either the supplied man or the hired man!"

"Why you think so?" I smiled and asked.

"I have enough evidence...the old man orders him for everything and he does it politely. If you have noticed, the young man even carries the luggage for both of them."

"The evidence is not enough to prove the young man is hired."

"There is no meaning talking with you," Vardhman was annoyed and dropped the talk.

This man has womanly qualities in him that I loved most.

"Okay, babe...the young man is hired, but what does it mean to us! When did I disagree with you...from the first point I agreed with you that's why I cross questioned. And if I had not done that how could I watch your annoyance, which is lovable," I said.

We came closer. This annoyance and love had symbolism for better lovemaking.

Vardhman disclosed whispering, "He is the supplied man from the traveller, I asked him and he didn't hide anything."

"That's good, when you feel alone you can hire him, what did he say, is he top or bottom?"

"What rubbish, why do I need him? And for your information a hired man has no choice," Vardhman got impatient, his lips started quivering and his body got stiff.

He did not need any more time, he closed his eyes, I kissed him and a cold wave entered the room.

Rain had just started outside; huge drops were falling on the grass roof and there was a sound of a musical beat on the roof. This was the first rain since we had come to the northeast. Vardhman opened his eyes, rushed to the door and suddenly walked out of the room. The rain waves chilled the room again. He waited for a while in the corridor; a few wet drops soaked his body. The raindrops were flowing down his neck making me feel that it was a newly bloomed rose soaked in the first rain. He had a beautiful face with sharp features, his lips were rosy, and eyes were like rose petals, some pink some white. I could not control myself and ran behind him, and some unknown force within compelled me to hug him tight.

I was also soaked in water; both our muscular bodies were exposed to the rain. My fingers caressed his hair; he loved to grow long hair like the 90s Bollywood hero's'. I first kissed his neckline. He hugged me tighter. He is well aware of me and my moves, fixed his eye gazing at his feet. His eyeball gradually moved upwards and lips shivered. I kissed his lips and slowly bit them; he started responding by moving his lips.

The rain had a free flow, sometimes thunder and lightning made their presence felt, but it did not affect us. The cold wind that was followed by heavy rain made wet the corridors and drenched our bodies again.

He turned back and made me kiss his wide well-built back. The thunder roared, but we did not listen to it, the frightening sound of heavy rain on the roofs and leaves, created a musical hum in the surroundings.

It appeared as if the rain was not going to stop tonight.

The wind together with the heavy raindrops cooled the atmosphere.

While wiping off the raindrops from his body, Vardhman asked, "Did you ask Pranami?"

"About what!"

"Don't be silly...of course our marriage," he sat by my side on the bed.

"Have you gone mad?"

"Why...you only assured me...and what happened now?"

"Don't be foolish...sleep now I am tired."

I got into bed with a light quilt on. He waited, hoping that I would say something, again... when it did not happen, he said again, "You have fallen in love with her, again?"

He waited for a few minutes and then slept facing the other side. I tried to get some sleep, but would not get it for few more hours.

Vardhman did not talk to me, until we came back after two days.

--Ω--

"I am a 19-year-old college student doing my degree in biology. My life is weird but simple. I must say I am probably bisexual. I never thought of myself as a full-blown gay because I do have a strong liking for women and I do hope one day to be married to a woman and to have children of my own, once I get a good job. I've had many gay sexual encounters and the first one at the age of 14. It was with my friend who is the same age and I guess you can say we were experimenting or whatever. This friend and I were having sexual encounters a lot all the way up, until I was 16 and I moved away from the previous college. We are still in "love" with each other; I've had three sexual partners until now in my life, two being guys and one being a girl."

This was a confession by Somveer Singh Yadav, a final year student of biology, and we were sitting on one of the benches of Mandi House Metro Station, it was less crowded than Rajiv Chowk.

I met him at the Rajiv Chowk Metro Station, where he changed the metro towards Vaishali. We travelled some distance to enable a better conversation.

"So, you still have a relationship with your first love?" I asked.

"Yes, but we get very little time after we have shifted from Janak Puri and my college has also changed, but we try to meet at least once in a month. That day we talk a lot."

"What do you talk normally?"

"About the entire world like any lover."

"Does he know about your relationship with the other guy and girl?"

Somveer gave a smile, "Yes, he knows, in fact we talk about this."

"Does he not get jealous of your new love?"

"No, why should he? He also shares his experience."

"Has he also found his partner...is it a guy or a girl? I asked.

"It's a guy."

"Why, does he not like girls?"

"Not exactly, I have not asked him, but he listens carefully when I talk about my girlfriend."

"May be he has not found a suitable girl for him or he may be shy enough to propose to a girl!" I said.

Somveer laughs, "Maybe."

"So, the moment he gets a girl, he may forget you."

"Probably not, we have a long relationship and that counts. When we meet we don't go for sex, we have overcome that phase. We are now good friends," said Somveer.

"No one objected, your parents, friends...or did someone find you in your intimate times?" I asked.

"No one knows it...and if you have control over your emotions, it's easy. All guy friends are not gay friends."

"You participate in the pride parades."

"Yes."

"Alone."

"No...always with my first friend."

"Why then?"

"To know what exactly is being done in a pride parade and for excitement."

"One final question, as you know the Delhi High Court has legalized gay relationship then why do you fear...you can practice gayism and stay with it...even other countries have legalized gay and lesbian marriages...in years to come Indian gay couples may apply for marriage also...so why do you stay apart from it?"

He laughs, "I told you in the beginning, I am not a gay; I am a bisexual. And it's one life; we enjoy what comes to us, why think for years to come, which is highly unpredictable."

He did not show any hurry to go back, rather enjoyed our talk. But as I said my last question stick to it. I am not here to know what they do; I am here to know what these young lads have in their mind.

So, finally I had to say, "It's nice talking to you."

He stood up and shook my hand, "Me also."

"You are free to contact and share your feelings, and experience with us."

"Sure."

The metro train for Vaishali arrived and he boarded it, and said goodbye. I kept on looking at him in a hallucination, even after the train passed off and another train arrived.

This way my truth with youth continued.

--Ω--

Subham Bhai landed safely and it seemed as if he had gone for a weight loss program; probably, lost ten kilos and looked thin. Pranami was quite confused, about how she would talk to him, how Subham Bhai would behave and many things. But when he came out from the airport, Pranami was spontaneous.

She had arranged the room for him on her own. For one week, Subham Bhai had not gone anywhere out of his room, sometimes he came out to the balcony, but did not stay for a long time. He was just like a sea fish that heads out of water for a while to take a breath and then goes deep inside.

He had his breakfast and dinner in the room only and hardly had a chat with Pranami. Pranami gave me the last 24 hours report between 1 to 2 p.m.

On Thursday, Pranami asked, "Can you come down tomorrow, Manav?"

"No, Pranami, it will not look good, he may not endure it, after all, he is your brother," I said.

"I am helpless, Manav, and besides, he knows everything about us? We will go shopping, if you come early, I feel he needs a wardrobe...but he won't come out."

"Okay, let me see what I can do."

"Nothing doing you have to come...at least, he will talk to you."

I reached Dwarka on Friday at 5 p.m., and both brother and sister were ready for shopping. Pranami came back from the bank after 2 p.m. We started from Dwarka at 5:30 p.m., in my Passat, Pranami first sat in the back seat. So, I had to offer Subham Bhai to sit along with me in the front.

He had really gone into equanimity; over the Mahipalpur flyover, he asked, "Where are we going Manav?"

I looked at Pranami enthusiastically.

She said from the back, "We are going to the mall Bhai; you buy whatever you like."

"But I don't need anything," answered Subham Bhai.

"I know, Bhai, you need many things, but you hesitate to ask," said Pranami.

Subham Bhai did not say anything; perhaps, he had gone into equanimity again. He must be thinking, if the things are expressible through facial expressions then what is the necessity of dialogues.

Pranami purchased jeans, T-shirts, trousers and shoes for Subham Bhai forcefully. When she was satisfied, "Yes, this much is enough for today's purchasing for Subham Bhai," she asked me, "You won't take anything?"

I smiled, "If you have finished for Subham Bhai then only!"

Pranami also laughed at her selfish behaviour, "Sorry... sorry."

I asked, "You don't need anything?"

"Yes...but," Pranami was addled over her own words. How come, a woman has nothing to buy from a mall? If a woman visits a mall thousand times, she has ten thousand things on her wish list.

I bought a T-shirt only and Pranami again started her endless purchasing...vanity, shoes, tops and small items like hair-bands, hair clips and many more until I intervened, "Enough Pranami it's 10 oclock."

"Yes...yes, let's go," she finally realized she needed to hurry.

I stopped her, "Where we will have dinner? Let's dine here and go."

She refused vehemently, "No, it will be too late, we will reach home at 12 o'clock. Better we take a carry home dinner," she thought a while and then replied, "Okay, come on, let's go."

"Okay, let's also take a parcel," I asked.

"Don't worry...I will make the arrangement." Pranami was confident about her words.

When we crossed the tollgate, she made a call to 'Supper Art' and ordered dinner for home delivery. Keeping her hand on the mouthpiece of the phone, she asked, "Anything you want?"

"Anything you order will do for me, you ask Subham Bhai," I said.

"Nothing...anything will do for me also," said Subham Bhai.

Pranami ordered, "Chicken Mughlai, chicken 65, mushroom masala and nan...okay nan eight...Shri Ganesh Apartment, Plot no 32C, Sector-7, Dwarka, Tower – II, First Floor, Room no 108...but deliver it after 1 hour at least...we are out and will reach in an hour...okay fine."

I looked at the time; it was 10:30. By 11 p.m., we would reach Dwarka, but why had she said in one hour, she could only tell, I tried and failed in guessing it.

And we reached at 11 p.m. Subham Bhai went to his room straight away, Pranami came closer and whispered, "After one week Subham Bhai talked something...he still has not come out from the trauma...you talk to him, he will open up to you."

Pranami also went to change; she looked exuberant... after all, it's 'blood calling blood'...I saw it and felt it, but I was hapless...I stood alone, as I had no blood relation in the entire world. I also went to freshen up.

Pranami's intelligence showed vividly, when we all came back to the drawing room and that time the doorbell rang loudly. It's the delivery man. We felt the hunger inside, immediately everyone sat at the dining table.

When we were halfway, Subham Bhai said, "Manav, I need a job...I can't sit idle...it hurts."

I looked at Pranami, she put down the food and listened to him carefully and said, "Why a job? Why don't you restart the factory Bhai?" Pranami tried to make eye contact with Subham Bhai, so he may feel confident.

She said again, "After papa's demise, I had not visited the factory even once; it's our lawyer who settled everything with the managers and workers. You go Bhai first you visit the factory and then meet the lawyer...Manav will help you, you go with him."

Pranami had taken me for granted; she said, "Tomorrow are you free Manav?"

She did not wait for my answer and said, "If you don't mind, please accompany Subham Bhai to Gurgaon."

"It's okay...I will go," I had to say yes finally.

"But it needs a huge investment," asked Subham Bhai.

"First you go and have a look, Bhai, then we will approach the banks and venture capitalists...investment will come, don't worry about it," assured Pranami.

We finished dinner by 12:30 p.m., and went to bed at 1 a.m., in three separate rooms.

--Ω--

In the morning, Pranami woke up early as well. I had never seen her getting up earlier than I do, but today was exceptional. At eight in the morning, she knocked the door, "Come on...the tea will get cold."

Within a minute, Subham Bhai and I came out of our rooms. We knew her very well, so delay in her command would cost us heavily, thus there was no risk taking. Pranami had taken a bath and got ready for the bank. She sat on the sofa with three teacups on the centre table steaming hot with the aroma of the freshly brewed tea. Pranami waited for us.

We took our cups and sat down, "You are very early Pranami?" I asked.

"I need to go to the bank early...but you people get ready that's why I woke you up after making tea and after tea, don't sleep again."

I nodded in acceptance, and she said again, "The maid will come soon and make breakfast...have your breakfast and then go."

Pranami left at 8:30 a.m., and gave us today's newspaper from the doorstep. We quietly read the newspaper; I took the main paper and Subham Bhai the supplementary one. And after some time, we exchanged them.

Subham Bhai asked keeping an eye on the paper, "You know Manav, why I was reluctant to come to Delhi? I never get peace here. It's the reason I left Delhi and visited rarely in all unavoidable circumstances. When I think of Delhi Pranab's face appears before it. Delhi had taken my Pranab from me."

I didn't say anything to him, old memories flashed back in my mind. Sometimes, he is right Delhi had taken Pranab Bhai's life. Had they not been caught red-handed by the Delhi police and had not Subham Bhai succumbed to them by refusing his love to Pranab Bhai, perhaps Pranab Bhai would have alive today among us.

Despite knowing all this, I could not hate him. Still, I feel he is Pranab Bhai's love. Pranab Bhai would be watching him from heaven.

One can judge oneself from its action and activity but no one can judge anyone's mind.

Perhaps, Subham Bhai was lamenting his deed.

Perhaps, it was the fate of Pranab Bhai.

The doorbell rang and I got up to open the door, it's the

maid. Coming back from the door, I said, "We will be late, I am going to the bathroom."

My voice modulation had changed.

--Ω--

I took more than an hour under the cold shower. Still the heat on my head did not get cold. Things of my life cycle flashed before me; sometimes in slow mode and sometimes, in fast mode.

The truth from which I wanted to keep away from always fastens me in it tautly. Some nights I had been unable to sleep with the bad dream.

Flash of that scene seems never wiping up from my memory. No liquor, no gayism and no party could ever confiscate it from me. It was the initial years of my time in IIT Delhi, I was not staying in a hostel and it was a Friday, evening around seven. I saw few people were gathered in front of my house. My cycle fell down, People were calm and looked at me pathetically and made way for me to enter inside. Inside the house, it was heart breaking. Papa was holding the dead body of Pranam Bhai in his lap. Papa mourned his eyelids closed once on seeing me, he wanted to speak something but was not able to speak out anything.

And before I could understand anything, the police came inside our house and took Papa and Bua in the van and Pranam Bhai's body in the ambulance.

I was a mere spectator.

And within two years from that day disaster captivated my entire life. I became an orphan in the vast world.

Pranab Bhai's death face flashed back heavily in front of me. The shower was not able to quench the heat inside my brain and my body started quivering.

Subham Bhai knocked the door and brought me back to the present "You are still in the bathroom, Manav?"

"Just coming, Subham Bhai," I hurried and came out with a towel around me. Subham Bhai was waiting; he had dressed up and sat on the bed.

"I will take two minutes, Bhai...sorry I took more time."

"No problem, you get ready, I am waiting," Subham Bhai had not shown any significant change in his stance. He stared at me with eyes wide open. I was hesitant first, but there was no option left for me, I cannot tell a man to stay away when I was changing. Subham Bhai still looked at me profoundly.

"You know, Manav, you have the same physique like your bother Pranab," he finally speaks out overcoming his watchful eyes.

I felt embarrassed to look at him and come out with my Passat key.

He followed then...

--Ω--

The Passat sped over 100 km per hour on the Gurgaon Jaipur highway. It showed my uncontrolled mind-set.

Over a long silence, Subham Bhai spoke, "Pranab should not have adopted his own fate. He broke down easily." The pressure on the accelerator increased, it touched down to 140.

"People obviously treats gays like the scum of the earth... but see today we have identity, recognition and many more changes will come gradually...perhaps, Pranab would have been alive today?"

He took a deep breath. The speedometer touched down to 160. My mind was unstable, it seems someone is hammering my heart.

I was supposed to hate this guy. Where I stood today is because of him only. Pranab bhai died because of him. My father did not last much longer with Pranab bhai's death. Bhai was his elder and loving son. He had much more faith and aspiration on him.

The next day the police released him from custody, he was behaving as a half mad man after losing his beloved son and survived for few days only. One day a strong cardiac arrest ended my father's chapter forever. After a year, my Bua too died making me an orphan in the big bad world.

This happened only because of him. Bhai and Subham bhai had a gay relationship, one day the police caught them red-handed in our car near Janpath. Those were dismal days for gay couples. They were harrassed and paid the huge ransom and were brought to our parents' notice. When our parents asked them Subhaim bhai vehemently refused and said it was a forceful act by Pranab bhai. Pranab bhai is a gay not he. Papa scolded him so rudely he hanged himself. Pranab was at an age where he could not bear anyone yelling at him.

A simple lie of Subham bhai made me an orphan today and devasted my family. Even if I tried to I was not able to hate Subham Bhai. I had read the sucide note of Pranab bhai, in the end, he had written I love Subham very much. This may be the reason even if I try, would not be able to generate hate in me towards him.

"What are you doing, Manav...why are you driving so fast?"

The speedometer decreased to 150 and then 120.

"Pranab was like you...never bothered about life. What is the hurry? After seeing the factory, we will go for a party."

"Sorry, Subham Bhai, here there are no gay parties in the day time."

Finally, I intervened in his thought process.

"Yeah...I have forgotten it's India not the USA."

"Hmm," I replied and he calmed down.

Suddenly, he erupted, "No problem we will have a few drinks and wait for the evening...here in Gurgaon."

This suggestion sounded good, I nodded in acceptance.

Subham Bhai looked very casually at the abandoned building and the factory area spread over three acres of land.

While walking along the fence he said, "Why don't you call your friend...he stays in Gurgaon only, what's his name... Vardhman...to join us for few drinks!"

It sounded good as I would be relieved from the flashback of Pranab Bhai and Subham Bhai, but still it astounded me the way he approached things.

I thought, "My friend is in his mind...He had only met with him once?"

Without any fuss, I called Vardhman.

As soon as I dropped the call, Subham Bhai asked, "Is he coming?"

I nodded.

"Then let's move...why waste time?"

I was surprised and asked, "But we are not half way through the area."

"What is there to see here Manav...I had seen all this from my childhood, all the way it is the same...come, let us move."

And I followed him towards the main gate where my car was parked.

--Ω--

While getting into the Passat, Subham Bhai asked, "Where is the party?"

"Hauz Khas."

Subham Bhai sat in front and Vardhman went to the back seat, which I did not like, but could not oppose. It was 7 p.m.

On the Mahipalpur flyover, Subham Bhai called Pranami and put the phone on the loud speaker. The ring bell was irritating, after a long call, she picked up, "Yes Bhai have you seen the site?"

"Yes...you are still in the bank?"

"Ha...Bhai, I was about to move when your call came again, I sat down," perhaps, she smiled.

"Actually, I called that we have started from Gurgaon now."

She intervened, "It took so much time; I thought you people must have come back, so I hurried."

"Ya...it took time and we are straight going to Ghaziabad, Manav has some important work...so I thought I would accompany him."

I was shocked, Pranami was also reluctant to accept it, she hesitantly said, "It's okay."

While dropping the call, Subham Bhai made an excuse, "It won't be wise to go back to her after the drinks."

16

Pranami called only on Monday and that too while I was parking the car.

"Have you reached office?"

"Ya...just parking the car...you are in office?"

"Yes."

"You have come really early today. It's only 9 o'clock."

"Ya...but what to do at home; yesterday the entire day I was bored...you have become my addiction."

I just smirked, did not find the audacity to laugh, comment or tease her as I usually do.

"What happened? You did not say anything."

"The truth is I felt the same inclination..." I wanted to tell these lines, murmured to myself, but I would not be able to tell this to her. She knew it very well, I cannot express it in the simplified way that she expresses. She did not know all the trauma that had happened to me in the last two days.
"Let me call you in the afternoon, I have a meeting right now," I said.

"It's okay," she obliged.

--Ω--

The story two days earlier...

We sat for a drink in a roadside restaurant in Gurgaon. Pranami called on my mobile so I made everyone to keep silent and specially Vardhman.

Pranami asked, "Where are you?'

I looked around and said, "We are at the factory site."

She thought a while and said, "It does not seem like, were you struck somewhere?"

"We are on the site only, inside the factory, it's calm."

"Okay, did Bhai agree on starting the factory again?" she was eager to know.

"I have not asked him, he is just checking every inch..." I had to tell a lie to cover a lie to make us safe.

"Where is Bhai, his voice is not audible?" Pranami enquired.

"He is here only would you like to talk to him?"

"No, it's fine; we will talk the moment you come back..." Pranami dropped the call and everyone was relieved and took long breaths, as if Vardhman and Subham Bhai were holding their breath.

We drank until evening.

The story from the time, we entered the Pub in Hauz Khas...

Subham Bhai and Vardhman entered the pub with holding hands of each other and I had to follow them. We sat for drinks together. They sat side by side and I sat in front of them. They drank with hands crossed and I was a mere spectator. After few drinks, they hit the dance floor and I was not able to gulp the second sip from my first peg at the pub.

To add to the drama, in the car, they sat in the back seat, while coming back and started hugging and kissing.

I felt ashamed about Subham Bhai, as so soon he had whisked away my partner.

After coming to my flat, they just said goodbye and goodnight, while entering into a room and locked themselves from inside. They forced me to feel lonely and alone. Flashbacks of childhood and the current scenario now ruptured my mind in such a fashion that I could not sleep the entire night. Pranab Bhai's dead face kept me awake the entire night. To deviate myself from the thought process, I browsed through the website and checked the mails. There were 230 unread mails in the inbox within these two days. People had asked opinions and suggestions. I opened up a few, but did not reply even one because I was afraid that I may not do justice to the mails since I was so stressed out.

The next day they woke up late and stayed together the entire day, not bothering that a third person was with them.

At the evening tea, I asked Subham Bhai, "Why did you tell a lie to Pranami?" My voice was precise and loud, not the normal voice that I used with Subham Bhai.

He was courteous and looked at me straight. I repeated the question again.

"When did I tell a lie to Pranami, you too and I just carried on your voice? Subham Bhai laughed. I was stunned the way he expressed his lie.

My tone softened, "Bhai, Pranami is anxious about the development and restructuring of the factory."

"You have also seen it, tell me can the factory be restructured, or anything can be done in that place?" he threw back the question to me.

"Pranami expects many things from you...but you have not even visited the inside of the building. What is the plan what do you want?"

"Where is the need to go inside, the outside shows the way," said Subham Bhai.

"But, Bhai?"

Subham Bhai stopped me with his words, "Please Manav, you have also seen it, rather I request you to convince Pranami to sell it. Builders are ready to pay a hefty amount and with that amount, I can start a retail chain in India and I am sure it will succeed, the market in India is not as saturated as the USA."

Things had worked in the reverse for me; my intention was not to know about his work ahead, but to deviate both of them from the actions because of which I was stressed.

Pranami handed over Subham Bhai to me for his wellbeing, settlement with life and job. But this was not exactly in my mind now.

We had not yet finished our discussion, when Vardhman asked, "Manav, do you have a bottle with you?"

Promptly and vehemently, I refused, "No," though I had a bottle, unlike my nature I refused, but I did this because of stress. I never kept my cupboard empty; there were plenty of black vodkas.

"Okay...I will come with a bottle," he stood up and walked out, but Subham Bhai called him, "Wait I am also coming."

Still I did not say, "Don't go I have a bottle."

I started watching TV.

After an hour, they came back with a Black Dog Whisky and food for dinner. We sat for a drink, but I was able to consume only the first peg. After the quiet dinner, they again locked themselves in the room and I watched TV until one at night. The room door was not opened up, until I came out to go to office, in the morning 8:30.

--Ω--

Pranami was happy and accepted Subham Bhai, forgetting all his misdeeds and the devil in him, after all, they were siblings. Her look in her eyes gave the credit to me. Her happiness showed she was free from all thoughts and concentrated on me.

At 4 p.m., Vardhman called, "Hi, Manav, we hope you will be back home on time..."

"Why so?" speculations ramified in me.

"Actually we are going..."

"Going where...?" my distressed heart was soothed.

"Along...the same place, the resort."

I was surprised because I had not imagined they would go so soon and it reflected in my voice, "Along...now, and with whom?" I asked intentionally.

"With Subham Bhai, who else and I knew you would ask the same thing. We are going via Guwahati, a night halt there and then by road. I was really mesmerized by the beauty of the northeast."

"It's okay."

"So are you coming, our flight is at 8:30 in the evening and we have planned to move by 5:30," he said.

"No...I cannot...it will take time," I replied. If I wished, I could have gone, but I was furious and did not want to see their faces now.

"Then, what should we do with the flat key?"

The key bounded him to call me; otherwise, he would not have done so.

"You hand over the key to the neighbour Mrs Sharma and tell them I will collect it."

"Okay."

Our conversation ended and he cut the line.

The next moment, I rang up Pranami and she picked up the mobile on the first ring. It showed her concern.

"Your meeting is over now?" she asked.

"I am coming to you Pranami."

"What?" she was not ready to believe it.

"Yes...I am coming to you."

"Are you serious?"

"Yes...you are my addiction too," I told her and it came out spontaneously

I did not waste a single moment, it was not yet 5 p.m., but I closed my cabin and started the Passat. My heart has never bound me so much. The feeling was quite different. It seemed as if I have not seen Pranami for long years.

It's ME again

Pranami

The story is now nearing its conclusion; though life never ends and neither do all incidents and matters related to it, but the subject relevant to the story nearly ends. That's the reason I took the opportunity to express myself in the final part. It is my story, my thought and feelings would be valued more than expressing it from the view of others.

The human life cycle is full of speculations; no one knows what will happen in the next moment. Sometimes, your heart does not agree with your mind so we ask ourselves thousands of questions whose answers lie within us only.

I also asked myself, is Manav mine? Has he left gayness completely? Does he love me? Should we get married? Should I get pregnant once again?

It's a kind of conundrum.

I became pregnant again; after all, I am a woman how can I give up my nature? I need to raise and nurture up my kids too.

I asked myself again, is marriage required to be pregnant? What is marriage? A one day affair, few moments' ritual, bounded by law or the believe of a hallucination or just a social obligation?

Whatever it may be, it did not stop me from getting pregnant again.

This time I was prepared to declare to the society, 'we were married in the temple'.

I took two days break, took Manav for a holiday and when we were back from holidaying, I started using 'sindur' on my forehead for some days then a small 'kum-kum' spot for life long.

Sindur and kum kum are customary symbols of being married. Would you like to know what Manav commented when he discovered this after a long time, "Pranami, you look cute; it suits you."

But misery does not end here; perhaps God does not wish so for me.

Things around me changed drastically, everyone hurried in their mission...and so did I.

17

I had never seen desperation in Manav; he is a cool headed man. He said I am coming and dropped the call that raised many speculations. I was afraid to ask him again confirming the news. Enigma in me ramified, his tone was not normal, but was Bhai with him also?

It was better to call Bhai; I thought and called him next moment. Bhai's phone rang many times, he did not pick up and after that it gets switched off.

The bank had its internal audit in progress, and the auditors would leave after few hours, but waiting for minutes also killed me. Manav would not come to the bank, and would go to the flat directly, I was well aware of his nature. With some instructions to my deputy, Mr Gaurav, I left the bank.

My presumption was right, Manav's Passat was parked and he was nowhere visible. I hurried and did not wait for the lift, climbed the staircase and simultaneously cursed myself; I should not have wasted time over thinking after getting his call. My shoe heels made a drastic sound and I just hopped up. Manav was standing in front of the flat listening and widening his eyes towards the sound of the heels. He did not call me a second time, the distraction on his face was widely visible. He looked pale as if had not eaten anything for few days.

My appearance was visible before a few stairs of my flat; he moved to me and grasped me, even before I stepped up the last one, hugged me tightly and only uttered my name, Pranami...

From day one, men are called strong and this is the reason why men do not cry. If Manav had been a woman, he would have cried for more than half an hour.

This moment was a captured moment for me, as I had always dreamt about this. When Manav would stay connected with his heart, putting his head on my breast, he would get peace and my soul would be gratified with all the womanish desire.

"Babe, what happened?" I asked and his hug tightened without uttering a word.

"Come on, babe, nothing to worry I am there." He was not ready to let go of me.

"Okay, babe, let me open the door." Still this had no effect on him.

I wished to hold him like this for lifelong, but his body weight gradually augmented on me. I dragged myself and somehow opened the door. His hug loosened a bit to facilitate us for entering into the room, which I did not wish. From the day Subham Bhai had come, I craved for a touch of him.

He did not move to the bedroom, just pushed me to sit on the sofa.

"Cool babe, tell me what happened," I held his face in my palm. I was a bit nervous, he did not make eye contact with me, was it so serious that he was not able to express it?

"Babe, I am there, tell me what is the matter?" I nearly begged.

"Pranami," he spoke only my name again. A lot of passion was concealed in him by calling my name.

"Ha, babe, tell me." This way he would not express himself. I almost compressed him, taking him firmly into my bosom. A man always searches for a safe place to open up and this worked.

"Pranami, Subham Bhai and Vardhman have ruined me. Both are now associated and have gone on a honeymoon package to the northeast."

"What?" I was dazed by his words.

"Yes, Pranami, Vardhman is no more mine, when and how Subham Bhai had taken him from me I cannot even guess it. But it is the truth."

I was shocked, amazed and thought, "This is the reason for his bizarre behaviour?" I was complete with internal happiness. My prayer had worked. On the other hand, there was my brother; I felt pity for him. He would never change. I squeezed Manav more to my breast and he started rubbing his head on it.

I could not find any words to console him, but actions speaks more than thousand words. I took his face in my palm and started kissing every part of it and when my lips found his, my complete body shivered; the sensation I had craved for many days. I started unbuttoning his shirt and so did he; we did not find time to move to the bedroom. Complete surrendering was so fascinating; I had encountered this for the first time, an appeal that I had been looking for. I got the feeling 'my man' for the first time.

Most men have stress relieved after sex; whereas, it is the opposite for women. Manav looked a bit relaxed, but I had jumped into the spiders net. Desperation on his face gradually faded away and within few minutes, he came out as very normal.

He sat coolly on the sofa and asked, "Pranami, coffee?"

"Ya...sure," I did not feel like getting up, laziness doused me, but with my mind, I promptly replied.

Nowadays, I listen to my heart, but act according to what my mind says. I just put one button of my shirt and started collecting my trouser and my inner wear. I got up and moved halfway holding the trouser and inner wear, when Manav held my hand and pulled me back again, to him, I nearly fell down on him, but he held me up near his face. His breath touched my face; today all his actions mesmerized me. He kissed my lips, then neck and moved lower.

"Naughty boy..." somehow, I released myself and rushed to change. I looked at myself in the mirror repeatedly like a teenage girl falling in love for the first time. Every time, I looked, a new face appeared in the mirror, happy, jubilant full of variant hues of Pranami. I am past thirty, but today it seemed as if I am just sweet sixteen.

I asked myself in the mirror, "Pranami, you are really happy today; god is so kind and listened to all your prayers."

I changed over into a pyjama and T-shirt and while moving to the kitchen, I saw Manav was still sitting on the sofa, naked.

"Go and change, I am making coffee," I almost gave the order.

After few minutes, Manav called from the bedroom, "Where is the pyjama?"

"It's there, babe, in the same place."

"It's all your printed pyjamas," he replied.

"Okay, just a moment I am coming."

I thought it must be his ploy to get me into the bedroom, sometimes; he used to do this, and get naughty. Things of his choice were lying in the same place, but he would not able to see it and asked promptly, "Pranami, where it is? I cannot find it. It is not in the same place?"

I do not know whether it happens to all men or not, but Manav always does this, both intentionally and unintentionally. I loved to be there for him, but it always happened at a time when I was busy making something like putting milk in the coffee or adding salt to the vegetables, the last moment of the event, the moment lost and you forget!

So with anxiety, I always entered with a mouthful of words to murmur, "You can't do a single thing alone, so why God has given you two eyes? You won't marry me, but that stupid guy, the gay Vardhman...you love him."

Wherever I am and whatever the reason; somehow, the link comes to my soul, I wished not to associate Vardhman with us, but it comes to my mind spontaneously.

However, after few seconds, Manav's reply came back from the bedroom, "Ya...got it?"

My attention towards the probabilities and the threads I linked with the past lapse. He was cool, though still not completely out from the trauma. When I reached the drawing room with two coffee mugs, he had positioned himself calmly. Handing over a coffee mug, I watched him for some time and chuckled. It acted so heavily on him that , he did not resist himself from a giggle before asking, "What is wrong with me?"

"Nothing," before telling him the fact I thought let it be...he is cool, looks amazing and I always imagine seeing him in my clothes. It is one of my hidden desires.

"No something has gone terribly wrong," he turned the question around again.

"It's nothing."

"There is something you are hiding from me, what is the joke?"

"Drink your coffee first."

"No...no first you tell me then I will drink the coffee."

"Means you will waste the tasty coffee," I had taken a sip, but he just held it until now.

"No...you tell me I will drink it," he held the mug to his lips.

"My foolish man...when I said I am coming, bravely and proudly you said 'ya.. got it'. And what have you worn? It's an exclusively women's t-shirt, you will not feel it as it has a cup shape?"

Manav laughed at his foolishness. "Yes, that's the reason...I asked why it is so uncomfortable today." He looked at himself again and started drinking the coffee. It showed he was still in stress; otherwise, he would have taken off the T-shirt immediately and thrown it towards me.

Both silently finished the coffee with our own thoughts, he had not given any compliment, which he used to do and put the coffee mug down.

I asked, "How was the coffee?"

"Ya it's good."

"Just good."

"It's nice," he replied again. I understood, I could not extract anything more from him on this topic.

So, I changed the topic, "Let's go out, we will buy some new T-shirts and pyjamas for you."

"Marketing now, we will find some other time to go," he showed his reluctance.

I was expecting the same thing, so I said coolly again, "We will walk, here in sector 7, some good shops have opened up nowadays."

Manav looked into my eyes, perhaps, trying to extract something from my eyes and his silence voiced all words for me.

I said again, "Come on."

"Okay, babe, coming...give me a T-shirt."

"No problem with the one you are wearing...you are looking cool, too pretty."

He took out the T-shirt, "Give me, otherwise I am not going..." and I rushed to pick a T-shirt for him.

--Ω--

Manav showed some interest in shopping. I wished to purchase whatever he liked, but it would not happen. Finally, we shopped three T-shirts, two pyjamas, a pair of casuals from Woodland for him and two tops for me. As the evening progressed, the glow restored back on to his face.

While stepping back on the staircase, I asked, "Do you have vodka?"

He gave me a glimpse, as if he had forgotten about it and I brought back the remembrance.

"May be," he answered and quickly returned with the question, "why you don't have?"

"No," From the day Subham Bhai has come I do not keep any liquor in the flat.

"I need to check the car; probably there will be one bottle."

"It's fine, let's buy one, as we are still in the market," I insisted.

"No...No...not required...it is there."

It was not just one, he had three bottles of black vodka, and a half consumed bottle kept inside his car and he was just picking one.

"Take them all, no need for them to be kept in the vehicle..." and I helped him to carry two bottles.

His reluctance was feeble, "See...it worked in urgency... some other day also it may help out."

317

"Nothing doing, from today onwards it won't be kept in the vehicle..." I said loudly and walked out of the car; Manav locked the vehicle and followed me.

The maid had cooked dinner and was about to leave, seeing us she said, "Didi, I have cooked for two."

Perhaps, she sensed the presence of Manav. She knew his car and his clothes hung around on my bed. But I was pleased. I had no mood to dine outside today.

"Thank you very much; I was just thinking about you, while climbing the staircase.

Earlier, I thought about calling you and telling you to cook for two, and then forgot about it. I thought about adding omelette or something instant if there would be less."

The maid said, "While coming, I had seen Bhai's car parked outside and saw the shoes here so I guess Bhai is around here," she emphasized her stance and left when I chuckled at her curious behaviour.

When you make up the mood and the substance is in front of you, it is hardly resistible. As soon as the maid left, we sat down with a sealed bottle, on the pretext, it would be heavy with the opened bottle. It is customary for those who sit with bottles; if a small quantity is left it urges you to finish it by any means.

His mood was getting better with time. We talked about our college life and old memories. I used to tease him with a drink, but today I cautioned myself not to utter a single word about gayness and homosexuality.

Instead of getting absolutely sozzled, we took three pegs each stretched over a longer time to energize our body and mind, after dinner, Manav insisted for a walk too.

When we came back after the walk, our mind was free from jumbles and the body felt weightless. Good to see Manav throw himself on my bed and wait for my arrival.

An internal pleasure bond my heart, a feeling that was very difficult to express. Something happened that had not happened for the last many years and I had been always craving for it. I took a longer time in the bathroom and changed into a maxi.

I switched off the bed light and slept with my face opposite to Manav, though I knew he had not slept and waited for me. After few seconds, his breath touched my neckline. Slowly, he removed my hairclip and moved his finger into my hair. My entire body sizzled with his caress. He started kissing my neckline and then swung me towards him. I was speechless and my body felt like resisting and then completely surrendered within few minutes.

I was fascinated and happy the way Manav cared for me, the happiness made me awake, but Manav was fast asleep after few minutes and slept like a relaxed man. I gazed at him for a long time and I cannot say when I slept and woke up uninterrupted at 7 a.m., in the morning. A fearless sleep, satisfactory, but Manav still slept profoundly. First, I thought of making tea and waking him up, as I, could not say whether he will go to office or not? Then thought may not be or else he would have got ready by now. I slept again encircling him in my arms.

I then woke up on Manav's call, "Pranami...Pranami...wake up, it's already nine..."

The sleep was so deep he had to shake my body with the call.

When I woke up, he said, "Come for tea."

"Just one minute, I will make it. But why didn't you wake me up early?"

He corrected me, "No...no...I have made tea...come down first."

The aroma of tea was coming up to the bedroom; it enthralled me.

I looked at his face passionately and said, "Just coming."

"Come first," he left and I entered the bathroom.

When I came back to the drawing room, Manav was just coming out from the kitchen with two cups of tea.

"When did you get up?" I asked, taking one cup from him.

"Few minutes before," he replied.

"Then you could have woken me up and I would have made tea."

"Why it doesn't taste good?" he had put more tealeaves and made it strong.

"No...no it taste fabulous," I chuckled.

Manav had not taken a sip yet, perhaps, he understood my smile, taking a sip, he said, "Why did you lie, it is too strong!"

"But it tastes good! Your first tea in the day should be strong, it energies all the dormant sensations, I like it," I had all praise for him; I bet it was from the bottom of my heart, not because he put an effort to make tea; it is because of his care for me and his changing attitude.

But he was not happy with the tea, opened up the newspaper and let the tea get cold.

I said, "Don't worry I will make good tea for you...has the maid come?

"No," he replied with his head in the newspaper and I enjoyed drinking the tea. I was so happy; if the tea had had a sour taste then also I would have loved to drink it. Quickly, I understood he had no intention to go to office, no need to ask him also as the time had passed.

"Where is my phone?" I searched and asked, as I used to carry it always even in my lower pocket.

Manav simply got up and brought back the phone from the bedroom.

"Thank you," he again was engrossed in reading the newspaper.

I quickly texted to GM about my sickness and asked for a day's leave. I was eager to talk to him and searched for a way about how the conversation could be developed.

"What will you have for breakfast?" I asked, rather tried to link up a thread for a long discussion.

"Anything," he answered.

"Anything means what? The maid has not come; otherwise, I would have requested her to make some breakfast...cornflakes will do?" I said.

"Okay...fine," he answered, with his face still stuck into the newspaper.

I got up and entered into the kitchen, opened the fridge door for boiling milk. But there was no milk. Manav had finished all of it in the tea.

From the kitchen only, I called, "Manav can you bring milk?"

"Okay," he put aside the newspaper and got up and before opening the door asked again, "How much?"

"Two packets," I answered from the kitchen.

Manav delayed bringing the milk, so while I waited for him to return, I thought I would oil my hair and have an hour-long bath and shampoo my hair. I managed to get some unplanned free time that I could utilise to derive some pleasure and indulgence that was long overdue. Just as I sat with the oil bottle on the carpet, Manav arrived; all the lights were switched off and as he was just coming in from the sun light he was unable to see properly, so he asked, "What are you doing on the floor?"

"Nothing, you were delayed so I thought I would oil my hair, a long pending task that I had been contemplating for the last two months and did not find any time."

Meanwhile, I took the oil in my palm and rubbed it over my head.

"Oh...'champi' let me give it to you."

He put the milk packets into the fridge and sat down on the sofa behind me, where he had easy access to my head.

"You will give it to me?" I turned to ask. I was shocked.

"Hm," he sounded nice.

First, he put the oil in his palm and started rubbing it gently on my head. My body vibrated from the top to the bottom with sensational waves that tickled every nerve in my body, giving me immense pleasure. My oily palm was sticky so I applied it on my leg, while sliding up my gown. I would never forget this day as it would linger in my sweet memories forever.

"Do you remember in your school days how you use to make two 'choties'" said Manav.

"Ha, Mama used to make it for me." Old memories are always fascinating and get amplified with your dearest one. "... but I used to get angry with her."

After completely applying a heavy amount of oil, Manav ran his fingers inside my hair, rubbed it and energized my entire body.

"Why?" asked Manav.

"That time I felt bad with two 'choties', Mama applied oil too and it seemed old fashioned to me...whereas I wanted to shampoo my hair every day."

He asked again, "Why so?"

"I was a filmy kid...I wanted to walk like the film stars."

Manav laughed loudly and started massaging my hair. My entire body started stiffening with the sensation.

"Those days I used to pull your 'çhoties' like this," he pulled my hair to two sides gripping it in two bunches.

"Aaha," I screamed, "it hurts Manav."

"Those days you cried...and tears fell down like a stream and now when you are a grown up girl you are crying just as much."

"Where did I cry...should I pull your hair and let me see how you won't scream," I turned back and pulled his hair angrily with my pain, but he did not scream.

"Did I cry?"

"You are a man, and your small hair does not even come into my full grip."

"So you didn't pull it properly."

"Yes," I said still nursing my pain.

"Okay...cool down. I don't like your anger. Those days also when you complained to aunty I felt bad," said Manav, with this, he massaged my neckline and rubbed his fingers at the side of my ear.

I was amazed where he had learnt all this; probably, they practise all this in their gay sex. The moment I thought of this, I immediately wanted to get rid of this disgusting thoughts about gays, at least not today, as I wanted to enjoy every pleasant thought as my mind was fresh and vibrant today and I did not want anything to ruin these pleasant thoughts and sensations of pure pleasure. He pressed my neckline and shoulder blades with his thumb; my entire body responded to his touch, but as women we can control our physical impulses, so I stayed as normal as possible.

"But where did Mama listen to me...she always batted for you," I still wonder why Mama did this. I was annoyed, Manav smiled, but with my fumbled mood, his fingers ran faster. With all his fingers, he massaged my forehead, head and neckline.

"Mama never listened about anything against you...either she said 'it all happens in play or Manav cannot do this, you are baselessly complaining against him'... you created such an innocent image that Mama was never ever ready to listen to anything against you."

I had gone back to the old memory lane; Manav took advantage while massaging my shoulders, he now moved his hand inside my T-shirt. I had not worn a bra since last night.

I turned to him, "Manav, what are you doing? The maid will come anytime."

He took out my T-shirt with a jerk. I was enjoying the massage and craving for more; every cell in my body was enjoying the sensation so my resistance was feeble.

"See...the maid has come...I hear her footsteps."

"This is the drawing room Manav, the windows are open. "

"It is all visible to the outside."

All my fake resistance was useless as it had not affected his movement, and he did not react at all to my words, rather I reciprocated with a deep lip kiss.

Finally, he smiled when I said, "This is for you, as you were a volunteer for 'champi'."

--Ω--

Luckily, the maid arrived, when I was dressed up. She was astonished to see me at home and asked whether I was fine and would not be going to office today.

"I have taken leave," I was happy to discuss with the maid, unlike other days. My internal happiness allowed me to do that.

"Planning to go for a vacation or what?"

"Aree...no...no...where is the time for vacation! Manav stayed back today so I felt like keeping him company."

She knew everything about us, so no point in hiding anything from her; rather I opened up with her, which pays back as an obligation. She does whatever is being asked, and does whatever she feels good to do. With many other talks of her life and family (she used to share with me), I guided her to clean the corners and underneath the beds, which she happily performed.

"Didi shall I make lunch for you?" she asked after dusting the entire flat.

I was delighted to hear this, "Why not, if you can."

She made some curry and rotis; I thought I would make something else before lunch; I put a green note in her hand and said, "This is for your children; buy some ice-cream for them."

Manav sat down with the newspaper until the maid finished the job and went back.

"Hello, mister, won't you have a bath!" I said, the moment the maid closed the door and left.

"Coming," like a good boy he entered the bathroom.

I thought a while then knocked his bathroom door, "Manav, I am also taking a bath, it will take time."

"Okay," he replied.

"If you come first make the cornflakes and eat, don't simply sit and wait for me."

"Okay."

When I came back after a long shower and shampoo I found Manav in the kitchen, he had made two bowls of cornflakes and was spicing it up with kaju, badam and strawberries. I loved to have this kind of breakfast. Finding the kaju and badam must have been difficult for him.

"Impressed."

"Oh...you have come back, I was about to knock your bathroom door...come fast." He lifted both bowls and started moving.

"Two seconds, Manav, let me put the saucepan on the burner to boil water for tea."

He had taken care of all my wishes, and had put some sugar into my cornflakes, but he had his without sugar.

While drinking tea, he praised my hair and said, "After a shower you look charming."

These words made my day.

Perhaps, in my entire life, he had praised my beauty for the first time. I was happy that he noticed my beauty.

The entire day he worked alongside me, helping me in all the jobs on hand.

I don't know how quickly and where time passed. Around 5 o'clock, I sat to paint my nails; Manav sat next to me and applied the nail remover to take off the peeled off old nail polish, and even helped in selecting the colour of the nail polish.

We cooked the dinner together, but around nine p.m., he looked gloomy and dull.

I asked, "Interested in some vodka?"

He refused vehemently "No."

I didn't insist anymore.

Quietly, we finished dinner and went to bed. Giving a last glimpse at the phone, I saw a new message, it was official and from the Zonal Manager, 'We have audit tomorrow so be prepared'.

I do not know about Manav, but I was not interested in going to office tomorrow. The message cluttered the beautiful mood that was present throughout the day. I could not predict if Manav would go to office, but could only guess he would not, thinking about his present condition that would take time to heal the wounds. I was afraid to ask him too, whether he would stay back, or go to office. Going back to office meant, he might not come back here. Once he stays back in his flat alone, it would charge him with the website and gayness, which I did not want.

If I tell him that tomorrow, I am going to office; he might go back, which again I did not want.

But this was the time I could get back Manav as 'mine'. To get him as mine I needed quality time to spend with him. How could I manage? For the first time, I bow down under time.

With a fumbled mind, when I looked at him I noticed that he was already fast asleep; I too fell asleep into a deep sleep, shortly after.

18

My eyes opened up directly at seven in the morning, giving a glimpse of him, I got out from the bed. My heart was content, filled with the satisfaction and happiness that 'he is my man'.

While preparing for office, very often, I opened the cupboard, and made sounds, but still he slept uninterruptedly. So, while moving to office at eight, first I thought of waking him up and telling him that I was going then I thought. 'Let him sleep. He is not new to the flat.'

But I was continuously thinking about him while driving and to the office too. First, I thought of calling him, at nine a.m., but again, I thought 'he might not wake up why disturb him?' Finally, I called him at ten and on the first ring; he picked up the phone.

"When did you wake up?" I asked.

"Just after you left."

"Then why didn't you call me?"

"Hmm...hmm," was all I heard; otherwise, he said nothing beyond that. "Have you had tea?"

"Yes, from outside."

"That's fine...the maid has come?"

"Perhaps, she is the one."

I heard the doorbell ring, Manav moved to open the door with the phone to his ear.

"Is it the maid?" I asked again.

"Yes."

I heard further, the maid asked, "Didi is not there?"

"No," Manav replied, while hearing me too.

"Didi has gone to office?" she asked again.

"Yes."

"Listen, Manav," I intervened, "tell her to cook something for you for breakfast."

"No problem, I will manage with cornflakes."

"That's like a good boy. Okay, Manav, I will call you in half an hour," and I disconnected the phone as few people entered into my cabin.

Next, I called him around 12 O'clock, "What are you doing?"

"Nothing."

'Empty mind is the home of the devil,' I thought.

"Have you eaten breakfast?" I asked.

"Yes."

"Manav, will you do a small thing for me," my voice changed to appealing.

"Yes, tell me."

"Yar...actually, I didn't want to come to the bank, I had planned for shopping today."

"Yesterday, only you had gone shopping?" Manav interrupted, with surprise.

"It was for daily wear. I need to do shopping for office and party wear and you know I won't get it from sector 7 market."

"So."

"Please help me and do my shopping for me..."

"But how can I do this, size...choice...all matters."

"For the 27 years you have held me, grabbed me...you don't know my size...my choice," I was annoyed over the phone.

"Okay...Okay, babe, tell me where to buy all this?"

"DLF Mall...when you reach there just give me a call I will guide you and yes have your lunch there."

It was the best idea at that time which suited me to keep him engaged. Very obediently, he called me after reaching the mall. Over the phone, I told him which shops to visit, what to buy, where and what to dine.

In this way, I kept him engaged until six in the evening and when I was on the verge of moving out from the bank, I told him, "It's enough come back now."

But again due to some reason, I was held up and Manav reached before me. "Wow," it spontaneously came out as I entered inside. He displayed all the bags in the drawing room.

"You have only ordered this much, Madam."

"Very nice...lovely," I did not heed his words and kept on opening one bag after another.

"You have good choice, Manav."

He replied with, "Hmm."

After looking at the last bag, I almost hung onto his neck, and kissed him, "You are a sweet boy."

"Madam...can I get a cup of coffee?"

"Why not...special coffee on your order my majesty," I changed and then entered the kitchen.

--Ω--

The next day, in the morning, he also woke up with me, it was obvious but still I asked, "Will you go to office?"

"Yes."

"I will make breakfast, eat and then go."

I made cornflakes then entered into the bathroom and he had left before I came out, but as an obedient boy, he finished his share of the breakfast.

I was contemplating the same; all these ideas will not bind him for a long time, but being a working woman I couldn't stay with him all the time!

But to my surprise, he came back before me. He had not even given a call; when I parked my vehicle, I found that Manav standing in front of his car. I felt sorry.

"Why are you standing here?" I asked, as I knew he had a key.

"It left it in my flat and didn't visit," he replied.

I asked again, "When did you come?"

"One hour before."

"And you didn't bother to call me," I was angry and annoyed and walked up faster on the staircase and Manav followed me at the same speed.

'It was my fault I didn't call him once,' I thought. But I was very much pleased inside. The next day in the morning, when I handed over an extra key of the flat, he had not shown any reluctance rather kept it in the bag safely. I was assured he would return. Every day in the morning, I would get up early and make breakfast. Even if I wished, I was unable to cook for lunch at home that we could carry with us. Sometimes, I felt sorry about it. It would have better if I could manage to wake up one hour early than the scheduled time, but I could not, it was almost past midnight before we managed to sleep. Those days and nights were the most cherished ones in my life. I always had a smile on my lips.

This trend continued for almost twenty to twenty-five days until the day that Subham Bhai returned to my flat. It was not that he came back from the northeast after honeymooning on that day. He was back in Delhi much before. It was a trip of only one week, but neither Subham Bhai called me once nor I bothered to do so. I sympathized with Manav. And after that he started staying with Vardhman in his flat at Gurgaon. I got all information from his social media profile that he updated on those pages regularly.

If I remember that night, it seemed like a dreaded, fearful and twisted night, more like a Bollywood movie scene. It was before dinner, Manav and I were in the kitchen cooking for the night. Manav was unveiling an untold chapter of our school time. Manav had completely erased the trauma from his mind. I am always passionate about listening to love stories and this time too I was exuberantly listening to him.

Sanghmitra, a Bengali girl's 'Prem Kahani'. She had sent three love letters to Manav, but when he did not respond to any of them, she switched her love to a senior Sikh boy. Both were working with him, now in Ericsson. Both were married, but not to each other, and became close again in the company.

Manav asked, "You know, Pranami, I am playing a mediator between them."

"Wow...you," it seemed unbelievable to me.

"Yes...and Sanghmitra still asks me why I had not replied to her letters."

"Then...what did you say?"

"Where do women allow you time to reply, she answered to her question and asked where is Pranami?"

"She knows me, and remembers me too?" I was stunned.

"Yes...why not, you got famous after hitting 'Archana Mallick'."

"Hm...joking."

The doorbell rang up and we looked at each other 'who could it be at this time?' I moved with the smile on my face that was carried forward from the topic and suddenly, the smile dropped when I opened up the door. Manav too moved behind me. It was Subham Bhai.

From that time, no one had spoken a single word; we all became mourners, as if observing someone was nearing one's death. Dinner was finished quietly and with that, my anger ramified as Manav moved to the other room to sleep.

I opposed in a whisper voice, "Why are you moving?"

"What Subham Bhai will think?" he said

"Let him think whatever he wishes, don't go he is not a noble man," I said.

"It will be absurd," and he moved up.

I keep on turning left to right and right to left, to get some sleep, as it was hard to get, thousands of thoughts popped up and ruptured like water bubbles. I had got used to sleeping with Manav, with my hands and feet all over him.

The next day, in the morning, Manav left very early and I came to know as his clothes were kept in my cupboard; otherwise, he would not tell me and leave. I too left for the bank early, before Subham Bhai woke up.

--Ω--

The entire day I waited for Manav's call and finally I called him when his call did not come, "Are you coming?"

"No...No."

Exactly what I was afraid of had happened.

I was contemplating the same thing, and asked him, "Why?"

"What nonsense...what will he think?"

"Is anything left behind after he has taken your love Vardhman, when he could do it shamelessly then why should we fear," I said.

"No, Pranami, it won't be good, whatever he may be we must respect Subham Bhai."

"Okay...take care," he was right in his thinking. I hung the connection.

I came home late, but Subham Bhai was not there, in the entire day neither had he called me once nor had I. This time, he had not left any message where he had gone. It's was past ten in the night. Once I thought about calling and asking him his whereabouts, but in the next moment sympathizing with Manav, hatred overcame deliberation and I quickly finished dinner, without waiting for Bhai. Not only did I miss the presence of Manav at the dining table, but every corner of the home screamed the absence of Manav, as I had got used to his presence that had touched every corner of the home.

Perhaps, Subham Bhai will not come, and must be at some rave party with Vardhman, but why did he come back to me then? My thought process extended in search of the reason and I could not get sleep.

In one way, I was happy, due to him only Manav returned to me. Then why am I getting annoyed on Bhai? Being a gay he will not change his quality, the person who left everyone and rushed to America only for his gayness, how could he stay back without a partner? And taking away Vardhman from Manav's life had come out as a boon for me.

My stance towards Bhai was getting softer and I was feeling better. Heavy venom from yesterday creates havoc inside me, but happiness lasts for a few minutes, the next moment doorbell rang up. It was Bhai, he had drunk heavily and his steps were staggering, Vardhman held him firmly and paved the way for him to the sofa.

I just stood there and witnessed the mock drill. He made Bhai sit properly on the sofa and stood up to leave. Then Bhai promptly asked, "Why do you stand V... sit here on the sofa."

Vardhman perhaps wanted to occupy the seat next to him, but before that, his eyes moved in my direction. I was fuming; my eyes were on fire and at any time, the fire rings could erupt to burn him.

Everything made me furious; my seeing him with Bhai, his intimacy with Bhai and the fact that Bhai had begun to care for him so much so soon.

"Oh...V...you won't listen to me, why are you standing?" Bhai spoke again, seeing Vardhman still standing like an erect school boy.

"V...are you listening to me?"

It was too much now, Vardhman was in a catch 22 situation and he had to say something. Vardhman looked at Bhai and then at me; I was still fuming heavily.

"No...Su, I have to go back."

"At this time, no way V...you have parked your car inside, no problem stay back here today, and tomorrow you may go..."

Vardhman looked at me, my eyes were burning such that he would burn in it.

He said finally, "No...no...Su, I need to go I have office tomorrow."

"Oh V...you leave early in the morning, what is the problem?"

They had become so close that they nick named each

other...the fire inside me was about to explode. I wanted to move and throw him out of my home, but before that he spoke out and this time with action, "No, Su, I am moving... you take care."

Vardhman turned and left quickly, I caught up at the same speed and closed the door heavily as though giving him a heavy slap on his face.

When I turned back, Bhai was hissing like a snake, "He won't stay because of you?"

I laughed in agony, "Why am I terrifying him?"

"Yes...he fears you."

"That's good...at least, he fears someone."

"But what was the problem if he would have stayed back today?"

"No problem...what would have been the problem with me."

"Then why didn't he stay today?"

"How can I say? You are questioning and answering, go and sleep you have drunk too much."

"No...I am absolutely fine. Let me make it clear to you, he loves you and wants to marry you."

It felt as if someone had put burning charcoal on my hand and someone was hammering my head. It started pumping in anger.

Bhai said again, "If he had stayed back here, your intimacy with him would have increased; otherwise, who will marry you? He loves you despite knowing your relationship with Manav."

"That bastard will never stop chasing me," I murmured in anger.

"What did you say?" asked Bhai.

"Nothing, go and sleep...and don't interfere in my relationship, stay away from it, I know better what I am."

My entire body was shivering with anger; I listened to nothing more after that, as Bhai continued saying something.

I entered my room and closed the door.

That night it took me many hours to get sleep.

--Ω--

The next day, in the morning, Bhai woke up along with me; I made tea and was about to sit in the living room to take the first sip, when he came out from his assigned room. I had a pumping head due to the late night sleep. For the first time ever, I was frightened on seeing Bhai, frightened because I had stopped thinking of Vardhman now and was in no mood to discuss about him. If Bhai starts with him, I contemplated to burst.

I asked, "Will you have tea?"

"Ya."

With reluctance, I stood up and entered the kitchen again. Some left over tea was there in the teapot; I poured my cup of tea; added some milk, tealeaves and a little sugar then put it on the full burner of the gas. Within few seconds, it started to boil, two to three times, I slowed down the regulator and took out the pot out of the burner, put it in two cups and came back to the living room.

I had no intention to check whether tea was prepared well or not. Bhai looked at my face, while taking the teacup; he was astounded, as the entire process might have taken one to two minutes.

Holding the cup Bhai said, "Pranami, sit. I have something to discuss with you."

He was right, I was about to take a U-turn to leave the living room, his voice was quite normal to me. Either Bhai was in a good mood or it was the morning effect.

I sat down on the sofa taking a sip from the cup. Few seconds had gone; Bhai too took the tea, without talking a word. Internally, I was afraid; he should not start with Vardhman again. Moreover, I thought again if he starts with Vardhman's advocacy, I will throw the cup and leave the living room.

"Bhai, I need to go to office too, what is the matter?" I asked, after a long wait to hear from Bhai and this long waiting period was about one minute only. That one minute seemed like a long hour.

Still Bhai was wordless; I asked, "If your discussion is about Vardhman, then I am sorry."

Bhai perhaps finished his cup of tea, kept it on the sofa and said, "He is secondary."

"Then what is primary?" I asked restlessly, as I was bored with the silence and speculations.

"Pranami, what to do with the Gurgaon factory?" Bhai had broken his silence.

"Means! I had already told you about my views. Manav and you had gone to the factory point also...Ya...that day I had not asked you about the factory."

"Pranami, it is not in a condition to restart, it needs huge money to renovate."

"Where is the problem with money? I will give you the money...you just start."

"But I am not interested with that."

"Then what do you wish to do?" I asked.

"I will get into retail."

"Who stops you...you have experience, go ahead," I looked at the watch and pondered if I would be late, if I didn't cut short the discussion as a lot of time was wasted in silence.

"But I need money."

"Certainly, you need money to start a business...it's your business you arrange it... I am not interested in retail...I told you earlier too...if you wished I would be a patron or partner to you then I am sorry," I stood up and walked towards my room to get prepared for office.

But before entering into it, I turned again, Bhai sat on the sofa with his face down.

I called him, "Bhai, if you have made up your mind to go with retail, then I will support you from my savings with a return policy. I need my money back with interest and it will be in a legal way."

I didn't wait for his reply and entered the room.

After around 40 minutes, when I came out from the room to go to office, I saw Bhai was still sitting in the same position with his face down. He had raised his face, when I called him back, while entering my room 40 minutes before and now raised his face seeing me going out.

He called, "Pranami, why don't you then be a co-founder?"

"Sorry, I told you earlier too that I am not interested in retail and yes I will support after seeing the business plan and model both, then too a small amount, not so huge," I narrated my entire wish towards his start up I had envisaged, while dressing up to go to office.

I departed as Bhai looked at me and followed, until I closed the door from outside.

--Ω--

I had rung up Manav, as soon as I entered into my cabin in the bank.

"Ya," he picked up on the first ring.

"Where are you...you are driving?" I enquired.

"Ya...on the way to office."

"Then let me call you after some time," I said.

"No...no...it's fine, tell me," said Manav.

"Absolutely not...no talk while driving, you reach office then call me."

"I am waiting, as there is traffic, no problem tell me what's the matter?" said Manav.

Perhaps, he told a lie, he had caught up my tone, as I was really in a hurry to express myself.

I asked, "Tell me what happened on the day Bhai and you had both gone to see the Gurgaon factory?"

Manav thought a while and answered, "Nothing happened, what's the matter?"

I came to the point straightaway, "This morning, Bhai again started with me."

"What did he say?"

"He is not interested in our old business; he wants to go for retail again...and you know he was a failure."

"So what, he must have tremendous experience, once failed does not mean that he won't succeed, Pranami rather going with a fresh start up in which he is not interested and experienced it's better to go with the thing in which he has expertise."

"I knew you will tell me the exact the same thing, I had finally told him that I will support him with a small amount, but with my money back...It will be like a loan to him... it seems fine, I have done justice to him?" I merely asked whether I had done the perfect thing or not?

Perhaps, he smiled at the other end and said, "It's absolutely fine, but did he agree with it?"

"Where have I asked him? I had just projected my vision towards his start up, but why do you ask, you know what he wants?" I was surprised at his remarks.

"No...no, how do I know?" Manav refused vehemently.

"Tell me, it will be fine with Bhai?"

I had no intention to go deep into it; I called him to ask whether I have done justice or not telling Bhai that I would support his start up with money only, not as a partner and with money return policy.

The person repeats the question when there is a doubt in his mind. Though I am angry with his gayness and dating with Vardhman, building his work life better also falls in my responsibility. That is the reason why I asked Manav whether I had done justice agreeing to support his start up or something else I need to do?

"Yes...absolutely," replied Manav.

"But Bhai wants I would rather go with him as a co-founder."

"It is also fine."

"But the loss will be mine too, I never ever presumed he would succeed...his intention and goals are different. He is not focused," I told him.

"Why do you think so...he is very much focused Pranami... he would do very good at retailing."

Manav always supports Bhai despite of his misdeeds with him. This is the quality of Manav I always appreciate, he never thinks of negativity. Customers started entering inside the bank and few had peeped inside my cabin too.

"Have you reached office?" I asked.

"Ya...parking the car."

One customer entered my cabin and despite of seeing that I was talking over the phone, he started saying, "Madam... there is no one at the cash counter, I need to send the money urgently. My family is waiting for money in my home town.

"Manav, just wait a minute," I covered the mouthpiece with my palm and asked the customer, "Do you have internet banking?"

"No," there was a big no from the customer's voice.

"You have a cheque book?"

"Yes."

"Then transfer the money," I said.

"How do I? I need to deposit money in my account first." The customer seemed a bit anxious. I understood where the basic problem lay.

"Okay...just give me two minutes."

The customer went out from my cabin.

I removed the palm from over the mouthpiece and said, "Manav, I will call you in the evening."

"Okay," he replied promptly. He was holding the call until then.

I came out from the cabin. Yes, there was no one at the cash counter. Two big queues had built up in the meantime.

I asked Mr Pramod Gupta, the new assistant to me, "Where are both of them?"

Ma'am, Ansari is on leave and no news about Preeti."

"Did you call Preeti?"

"Yes, first her phone was coming unreachable, now it is switched off."

"Okay...arrange for the makeshift; we can't make the people wait."

"But Mam...whom shall I send?" he expressed his disability and looked at every counter.

I smirked at his remarks, my voice was raised, "You got thirty minutes to arrange for a makeshift and until you manage it, I will come and sit at the counter."

He looked down. I moved to the demat counter and asked Smita to move on to the cash counter. She promptly moved and I returned to my cabin as there was no customer in the demat counter and opened the mail.

After few minutes, Mr Gupta entered and said, "Mam… before you, I had asked Smita to move over to the cash counter, but she was reluctant."

"It's okay, Mr Gupta."

The evening passed and I didn't find a single moment to call back Manav. I remembered while driving back at 9 p.m., but decided to wait to make the call after dinner, once I was in bed. At that time, I would be free mentally and physically to have a long conversation. I hurried to reach home, the sooner I reach home, the sooner I could finish dinner and the sooner I could go to bed and talk with Manav…so I drove faster.

--Ω--

Bhai was not at home, but reached just as I sat for dinner. He opened the door and slammed it shut with a bang, when he entered. His steps were staggering and he was almost falling down, as he was totally drunk. I looked at his back repeatedly and wondered whether if that stupid guy Vardhman was around or not. For few moments, my heartbeats moved at a faster pace and thoughts of him made me restless. I was relieved when Bhai sat at the dining table.

"You are looking for Vardhman?" asked Bhai; perhaps, he assumed the fact through my actions. I did not reply, but got up to serve Bhai dinner.

As I put the plate in front of him, he refused vehemently, "Don't serve me, Pranami. I have had my dinner." I stopped serving him and started my dinner, quietly.

Bhai said, "Vardhman is a nice guy. You know, Pranami, I told him I would take an auto, but he refused out rightly and said he would drop me. Every day, he would give me a lift and drop me here too."

I just thought, but did not express my views in words, "Obviously you are his partner, what is so great about doing that?"

"He feeds me, takes care of all my expenses."

"You are shameless so someone has to bear your expenses and he must have some reason for doing this. Earlier, Manav did it and now Vardhman, what is new in it?" I thought, but had not told him.

"He is a wonderful person."

"Certainly, as he bears all your expenses and takes care of all your needs too."

"He loves you, Pranami, and wants to marry you too."

Until now, I was answering mentally to myself to all his remarks, but this time, I let my burning eyes answer him. I looked at him leaving my dinner, a few seconds later, he got back on his stance and repeated the same, "He wants to marry you Pranami and don't ignore him. I am your brother I will always think better for you."

Though he was drunk and his voice was faltering, Bhai seemed determined, despite my silence, and changed the expression with my burning eyes, which he used to get afraid of; he was firm on his stance.

I was getting irritated listening to Bhai's advocacy of Vardhman and got up leaving the food.

Bhai said, "Pranami, sit, let me say what I feel."

His voice held me there, and he said, "If you think Manav will marry you one day you are wrong...he will never marry you, even if you force him to marry, you will never be happy."

I sat down on the chair again. My inner conscious asked me not to listen to him and go away, whereas, my brain made me sit down and suggested; 'listen to him; you don't know what your future holds for you'.

Bhai said, "You know where I am coming from...the party which was led by Manav, the entire gay and lesbian community of Delhi gathered at the party to celebrate the US Supreme Court's ruling in favour of same sex marriage. He was the narrator and conveyor of the party."

This time too, I did not say anything to Bhai, but answered him in my mind, "You are getting jealous about his popularity."

However, the next moment, I was afraid; it showed Manav's activity had increased again. He was fine with me, but as soon as he has moments alone, his actions towards gayness increase manifold. I cursed myself for not being with him. I had not checked his posts on his website too.

Bhai unaware of the turmoil inside me, continued his speech, "Do you know the truth? You may not be aware of it. I am sure Manav would not have told you and at that time, you were too young to judge the truth. Do you remember Pranab's death? It was not just a death, it was suicide."

"Stop it, Bhai, you are the culprit and the sole cause of his death, I knew everything, Manav never hides anything from me and I know too why he tolerates you always. He always finds his dead brother's love in you and always bats for you," my anger burst out because sometimes, I saw Manav very upset and disturbed whenever Pranab's name was mentioned. After all, Pranab was his elder brother and he loved Manav very much. Pranab Bhai saved us on many occasions from the JNU students and told lies to their father for us. Manav and he had spent their childhood and youth together, played together and studied together. Pranab Bhai was very much affectionate and loveable.

"It means you don't know the truth," Bhai though drunk seemed calm as usual.

"What is the truth?" I listened to him carefully, as his action and words worked in tandem to unfold an untold and unknown truth about Manav's life.

"Everyone thinks that he died because of me and when I was blamed I had no option left, other than to quit India. However, the fact is that he died because of stress. He was under tremendous pressure, when he came to know that his father was a gay and his mother had committed suicide."

I looked straight at Bhai to judge whether he was bluffing or what. My thought process had stopped working. But his last sentences made me worried too it means his mother had committed suicide, she was not staying apart by getting divorced. Bhai answered to my anxiety and tried all ways to convince me, "Do you remember the woman in their family Pranab and Manav called her 'bua' not mother. Those kids were brought up by their widowed 'bua'. Their entire family is gay and it happened by virtue of nature Pranami. I am afraid if you get married to Manav, one day your child would also be a gay or lesbian."

"And what about you, is any of your family member gay or lesbian? Then why you came out as gay? Do you know what you did? You just devastated the entire family. You are a coward."

He preferred to be silent over my fuming voice.

"Whatever their family may be, they are not like you, a coward by nature?"

"You are calling me a coward, your brother," he seemed irritated.

"Stop it Bhai, I know everyone it's enough, even now if you ask me whom I want to marry I will say it's Manav," I was fuming too.

"But why what is wrong with Vardhman?"

"Nothing is wrong with him, it's simple I just don't like him."

"But he loves you, Pranami, and is ready to marry you despite knowing everything."

"What does he know about me? That I had sexual relationships with Manav, and that I had become pregnant... is that what you are talking about?" My listening capacity was over and I fumed. Every day Bhai kept talking in the same parlance emphasizing the mistakes that I had made.

"Is that not enough? In our society, no man will agree to marry you."

"You are crossing the limit, Bhai...so the person whom you advocate for my marriage will be a gay too and what about his relationship? He had sex with Manav and now with you... and this our society will accept! Where are you living my dear brother... you won't feel ashamed to choose such a man for your sister? At least, I slept with the man whom I loved and what about him, he slept with two men for sexual orientation only. Who knows he may have many more partners and slept with many more?" My anger reached to such extent that my entire body was trembling and my voice was stammering.

"Pranami, you have no right to say anything about Vardhman's personal life."

"Why, because he is your partner? And who gave you the right to talk about my personal life?"`

"Mind your words, Pranami; I am your brother."

"Brother my foot, where were you when Dad died, when Mom died, when I was desperately in need of a male member in my family, that time your brotherhood didn't came forward. You left me alone to suffer; you left everyone for your gayness...just for your gayness."

I wept, and tears fell down calmly over my cheeks, Dad and Mom's death toll rolled over in my memory lane.

I left all the utensils on the dining table and rushed towards my room, shut the door with a bang and fell down on the bed weeping. I wept and wept and wept...

--Ω--

That night I hardly got any sleep, perhaps, I slept at four in the morning and woke up at six. I wept the entire night. First, I wept remembering my parents, then Subham Bhai's atrocious behaviour, further on Manav's gayness and subsequently, what Bhai told me about their family, about Vardhman and his affection towards me. I then thought about the down to earth reality, judged the pros and cons, and tried to console my heart.

I woke up early and wanted to go to the bank early too, as I did not find a single peaceful moment here.

It was just 7:30 in the morning, when I was completely dressed up for office, but it seemed too early to go, so I entered kitchen for a cup of coffee. As I came with the coffee mug, I found Bhai was sitting on the sofa. My heartbeat ran faster for a moment and I cursed myself as to why I had stayed back for the sake of a coffee.

I sat down at the dining table, yesterday night's utensils were still scattered on it. I did not feel like even asking him if he wanted coffee.

Bhai said, "Sorry, Pranami, my intention was not to hurt you; I felt that you were unaware of the fact so I told you, now the decision is yours."

Neither had I looked at Bhai nor did I answer him; I tried to be calm and cool and took a sip of the coffee. It tasted better that day.

"What have you thought about money?" asked Bhai soon after, pausing the talk of yesterday's incident.

For the last few days, all he talked about concerned Vardhman in the night and money in the morning. The sympathy that had built over time to support him for his start-up had vanished and I promptly answered, "I don't have money and don't ask me about money further."

"I knew you would answer the same," said Bhai.

"If you knew it, then why did you ask me? "I tried to make eye contact with him to know what was going on with him.

Perhaps, my words did not make any impact on him; he was on his predetermined words "If you have no money, why don't you sell the Gurgaon property?"

"It's my wish...it's my property, and why should I give you the money?"

"It's mine too...in our society daughters have no right on parental property."

"But they have a right in our law and you have taken all your shares."

"I don't know anything, I need money and today the builder will meet you in your office," said Bhai.

I was angry and my voice rose further, "Mind it, Bhai, if any builder comes to my office, he would have his day and you would have your day."

"I will file a suit against you."

I smirked and said, "From the last three years, you are saying the same thing...and you know better what will be the outcome."

I finished the coffee and got up, any further stay would lead the confrontation to catastrophe, but before leaving the room, I said, "This flat is mine and it will be better if you search for your own."

19

Though I told Bhai to stay away from my house, I did not return that evening. I left office early and reached Manav's house in Ghaziabad. I did not inform Manav about my coming to his place neither did I call him the entire day.

I was determined not to come back to my flat as long as Bhai was there.

From the last mock up now, I always carry a duplicate key of Manav's flat. The sun was still shining when I reached Ghaziabad. I was feeling better. After a gap, I was going to meet Manav so I started thinking of Manav and left the confrontation matter with Bhai behind. When I opened the door a pungent smell came out of his flat. As usual, the items were scattered, towels were lying on his bed and the kitchen was in a very bad condition. I asked myself, "How do these men stay alone?"

First, I opened up all the windows; let the smell go out, as I was feeling restive with that smell. This may be because of long days of closing of the windows and doors, while running the air condition; Manav must not have opened up the windows for months long.

Changing to nightwear or clothes to wear inside the flat had never been a problem in either of our homes. I changed over and came out in one of Manav's shorts and T-shirt, with a broomstick in my hand. It took me more than an hour to clean and arrange the items; I changed the bed sheet and pillow covers in all rooms and when I was satisfied with the cleanness, I sprayed room freshener in all corners.

Then I took a shower and a long shower made me feel fresh. After the shower, when I sat on the sofa and rested my head on its back, a glimpse fell on the wall clock; it was 9:30. I was shocked and stretched erect like a spring-loaded doll. Until now, Manav had not come.

I called him, but he did not pick up the phone. I called him repeatedly, but it was the same reply from the service provider 'the number you are calling is not available to take your call'. Again, I slid back, but it was in slow motion. Thousand thought processes simultaneously processed in my mind, so the action-reaction time was delayed.

Why he is late today?

Does he come every day like this?

This is the biggest problem with men staying alone.

Why didn't he pick up my phone?

He never does that, is he with trouble?

What sort of trouble or is he still in office?

He may be in office and busy in some project.

My eyes automatically dropped down with so many other probabilities. The entire days' work along with cleaning of Manav's flat and almost yesterday's sleepless night made me drop off to sleep quickly and it was such a deep sleep, that even when Manav came I did not get aware of his presence.

Perhaps, he called me three to four times and when I did not wake up, he shook my shoulder and tweaking my nose Manav said, "Hey, Pranami, wake up, what a deep sleep you have slept."

I woke up with a sudden start and seeing Manav in front of me, I asked, "When did you come?"

Manav gave a smile and said, "Now."

"What is the time?" I asked and glimpsed at the watch too, it was almost 12 o'clock in the morning; just another five minutes were left.

"It's 12 o'clock yar...you are coming now? Where were you?" I asked.

"When did you come, Pranami, why didn't you inform me in the morning?" Manav asked me, without bothering to answer my questions.

He moved to his bedroom and I followed him saying, "I thought I would give you a surprise, but I called you so many times, where were you?" I was back to my basic point again.

Manav changed his clothes, came in shorts and while changing over asked, "Why didn't you switch on the AC's, you didn't feel hot?"

"Do you think human beings stay here?"

Manav moved to the bathroom, washing his hand he replied, "Why, who stays here then?" I followed him up to the bathroom door and made me stand at the door only saying, "Animals."

"That's good...animals do stay in flats...the world is changing."

"What a mess...everywhere dirt, dust...complete filth around. It took me two hours to clean," I said.

"It can be seen everywhere."

"I have not cleaned the bathrooms...see the amount of filthiness, do humans stay here?" I said entering the bathroom, pointing towards the spider webs and dirty floor.

Manav came out from it, "Who said humans stays here... only animals stay here."

I followed him closing the bathroom door.

"What you have eaten?" he asked, while coming out of the room.

"Nothing, yar." Suddenly, I felt hunger inside, until now, I had not felt any sensation of hunger, but the moment he spoke about eating, it had arisen inside me.

"But what will we get now?"

"You have not eaten your dinner too."

He shook his head in reluctance.

"Your maid is not coming nowadays, why were all the rooms full of dust?" I asked.

"She has gone to her village, and will take a few days to come back."

"At least, you could have cleaned your bedroom...won't you fall sick if you stay in this filth. But where were you up to so late at night?"

He did not answer me, but moved to kitchen and said, "We will have an omelette..."

"Bread omelette?" I asked.

"No...only omelette," he said, opening the fridge.

I peeped inside, it was almost empty; there were only few water bottles and six eggs on the tray, which he removed now.

"You don't even have onions or tomatoes?" I asked.

"Tomato...no."

"That I can see."

"But there is some onion," he looked to his left side and picked up a basket, where few potatoes and onions were available, to say, 'yes, we are existing'. They were all ruptured and not in a condition to eat.

"Do you have salt in your kitchen or not?" I asked in anger.

"Let me search," he started searching.

"Oh...what shall I do to you, get away from here, let me search."

"You won't find, let me help you."

"Do you have oil? "I asked.

"Perhaps there is some oil," said Manav, with all probability, he was afraid to tell the truth. Even the throttle speeded up with hunger and anger; I smiled at his remark.

After a meticulous search, I found there was plenty of salt available in a jar, but only few drops of oil were left. Scrupulously, I searched all the racks and cupboards because it would help me to bring the grocery tomorrow. Almost all the jars and bottles were empty.

When I put the salt jar and oil bottle on the kitchen platform, Manav said, "You take rest, Pranami, I will make it."

"So that it won't be in a condition to eat and we will have to sleep in hunger, you take rest." I put the gas burner on and with the residual oil; I made two omelettes, with three eggs each.

He stayed back in the kitchen only and looked at how I whisked the eggs in the bowl. After few minutes of silent observing, he whispered, "Will you have a drink, Pranami?"

"Which brand?"

He had enthusiasm in his voice, "All brands, what you want, whiskey or vodka?"

"Aa...ha...ha...you don't have oil in your kitchen, but you have all sorts of brands of liquor, nice going."

Though I craved for few drinks, I controlled my interest because of time. It was late at night.

He put his head down, understood my joke and was quiet until I asked him at the dining table, "You didn't tell me where you were? What was the important thing that you were doing that you didn't even take my call?"

He divided his omelette into two and put the half portion on my plate.

"What happened, you won't have?" I asked.

"You are hungry."

"You are not...have you had your dinner?"

He nodded.

"You are coming from a party?"

He again nodded in acceptance.

"Gay party."

He nodded putting his head down.

"That's why I don't leave you alone...Bhai was there?"

He nodded, "Ya."

Few minutes passed in silence and we finished omelette, silently.

While washing my hands I asked again, "Vardhman?"

"Ya."

We went to bed and quietly slept at two ends, with a wide gap in between us. Manav waited for few minutes and then dragged me towards him. Taking me in his arms he asked, "Is there anything, Pranami, you do not want to tell me? You are hiding something?"

I was waiting for the moment. I moved closer as near as possible to him; put my face on his chest, which was a powerful assurance in the world for me. I started sobbing getting the trust and conviction to express myself. Tears made his chest wet and I was weeping and weeping while rubbing my face on it.

Manav assured me and started caressing my hair moving his fingers through it and said, "You are a brave girl, Pranami. I am with you, forever, tell me what the matter is?"

That night I told him everything. How Bhai would bring Vardhman to the flat and insisted that he stay back with him. How he insisted that I marry him and how he repeatedly kept asking me to sell the Gurgaon factory to a builder and handover all the money to him for his start up.

Manav listened to me and gently kissed my forehead then held my face in his palm and said, "You are crying because of these simple reasons."

"It seems simple to you?" I asked.

"Nothing will happen, only that will happen what you wish for, now are you happy?"

I nodded, a smile appeared on my face again; my heart was content and blossomed with happiness; I slept on his chest throughout the night. When I woke up, I felt it was too late. I made Manav wake up too, shaking his shoulder, "Wake up Manav aren't you going to office?"

He woke up with a jerk asked, "What is the time?"

I brought my phone to see the time and shouted out, "Its nine."

"Won't you go to office?" asked Manav.

"Yes, I will."

While answering him, I saw there were ten missed calls from Manav, promptly I asked, "You had called me ten times; I was sleeping so deeply that I didn't hear a single call."

"Ya...you slept so profoundly, if someone had wished to kidnap you, they would have done it without any hindrance," replied Manav, but I did not heed his joke, instead checked the phone settings and shouted out again, "Oh...shit...it is in vibration mode."

We entered two bathrooms and within half an hour got ready for office. While coming out I said, "You don't even have a juice bottle, what would one drink in the morning...your liquor as an antidote."

He smiled, but did not say anything, but said in the parking, "Don't speed up, Pranami, it does not matter if you a bit late, go calmly...okay."

"Okay," I smiled and replied, "See you in the evening."

--Ω--

I was late, but it did not put any impact on the daily routine work of the bank.

It was Friday and the beginning of the month, the salary was credited on the last day of the June for Army personnel's, so the branch was a little crowded. Army personnel going on leave were lined up for withdrawal, as they needed all the savings for those long days of leave.

I was exuberant, and did not show any lethargy because of the sleepless nights. In the office too, I was listing out all the items I needed and finally decided I needed all grocery and vegetables.

When I turned the pages of the newspaper, the news in HT city of Hindustan Times made me laugh. How foolish I was? How could I forget the Delhi High courts judgemental day? Yesterday was 2 July and Delhi's LGBT community celebrated the judgemental day, by holding a public demonstration in the inner circle of Connaught Place. Even if I wished to, I could not have barred Manav from attending those functions. He definitely was there yesterday.

Perhaps, I was the happiest person and celebrated silently, when in 2013, December the Supreme Court overturned the High Court's decision on section 377, but it did not have any impact on the LGBT group, or on Manav. They held demonstrations against it too; I remembered Manav was hurt by the police lathi charge, while on a demonstration in the inner circle of Connaught Place, after the Supreme Court's judgement.

The day before yesterday, they celebrated the US gay marriage ruling. It gave them a ray of hope and felt that someday a fresh wave of positivity towards gay and lesbian marriages will flow and the court will change its verdicts.

I thought for a while and wanted to call Manav and ask about it, he said he was at a gay party, but did not mention about the anniversary celebration. In the next moment, I withdrew from that thought; in the end, it would hurt me only.

In the afternoon, I started marketing; first, I purchased grocery then vegetables, fruits and put it on the back seat of my Honda CRV. I departed early from the bank, at 04:30, I started from the Gopinath Bazar, as at this time I would get less traffic, but I could manage to reach Ghaziabad at six o'clock in the evening.

Manav had reached by that time, his car was parked in the parking, for a while I thought of calling Manav, the items were many and heavy too; he would help me out. However, the next moment, I thought let me take it, as by the time he comes and we move it will definitely take more time. Moreover, I was not ready to wait a single moment; somehow, I managed to hold all the carry bags and started moving. Fortunately, the lift was open as I reached; someone got down from it, so one hurdle cleared. Somehow, I pressed the floor button, but kept on holding onto the bags and did not put it down; as again, it would be difficult to collect. The flat door was open too, another hurdle was clear; I was relieved, but very soon was angry with Manav, why did he keep the door open ?

Putting down the bags right there, I closed the door first.

On the closing sound of the door, Manav came out from the kitchen and declared, "See Pranami, I have brought all the items, fruits, vegetables, juice."

He was arranging all those items in the fridge.

A smile lit up my face, I was grasping out, but asked in a teasing voice, "Babe...you have not brought the groceries?"

"I have brought it, come and see."

"First, you come here and help me out."

"What happened?" he asked curiously and rushed towards me. Seeing the items, he also started laughing and for the next five minutes, we could not stop laughing. That evening was spent in arranging all the items and it was necessary that we ordered food, at nine in the evening. By ten, the food was delivered, but my arrangement was not over, it seemed unfinished.

Manav called me twice, "Pranami, let us have food, and the rest we will do tomorrow." Manav was tired helping me out and I kept saying, "Just five minutes."

Manav made two drinks, handed over one glass to me where I was working, when I was just contemplating stopping.

"Oh...you are so sweet...just what I wished for," I hugged him and kissed him. I was just wishing for and thinking of asking for a drink, the moment he handed over the peg.

I hurried to finish the drink and food, so after three pegs, I asked, "Let us have the food."

"What is the hurry?"

"Aha...you have a holiday tomorrow, but I have to go to office."

Still Manav made another peg and that night too we slept, at two in the morning. I had forgotten to put the alarm, and woke up only at nine, in the morning. While I dressed up,

Manav in his sleep asked, "Why do you have to go Pranami, today is half day, take leave."

"That's why I am going; I will be back by three p.m., in the afternoon."

I came back to the bank and Manav went back to sleep.

At 11 a.m., in the morning, I called him, "Babe, have you woken up?"

"Ya."

"That is like a good boy...have you had your breakfast?" I asked.

"Uh...I just woke up and was going through the newspaper."

"Okay...have your breakfast on time."

Just before hanging up the call, Manav asked, "Hey Pranami...I was just thinking of calling you; should we plan for a movie in the evening."

"No...no...no," I refused vehemently, "Don't book any movie tickets, I have to do lots of marketing, I need to purchase office wear, from the last two days I am wearing the same dress and I don't want to go back to Dwarka for collecting them."

"Okay," said Manav.

That evening, we went shopping and the next day, we had a complete outing with a movie. These few days of my life were the most cherished and treasured days. While writing my memoirs, I felt the sensation because of the twists and turns that life had taken that I could not have even imagined.

--Ω--

My menstruation was delayed for more than fifteen days and I was not concerned about it. Luckily, doctor Sobha visited the bank for some of her work; we met and sat down for a long discussion. She is my doctor friend, who had done the abortion and from that day, she is in my high regard.

She said I had put on weight and I agreed the irregular eating habit made it.

She asked about Manav. I laughed and asked, "You remember him?"

"Ya."

"Did you people get married or not, still dating each other?" asked Dr Sobha.

"We got married and I am staying with him in Ghaziabad, every day I travel up and down," I told her what I had envisaged to tell the world. It's enough now, let the entire world know we are married, if marriage is everything.

"Congrats."

And in our talk. I told her about my delayed menses period.

She laughed so I got curious, "Is anything wrong?"

"You don't feel so."

"No...nothing...it's as usual."

She was annoyed and a little edgy too, "How can it be, it is not your first time and you are a matured girl."

I was tensed at her voice, "Is there anything wrong Sobha?"

"Nothing wrong, you just come to my clinic, I will do certain checks."

I was edgy now and curiously asked, "When?"

"Come anytime...I will take another half or an hour, then straightway I will go to the clinic," said Dr Sobha.

"Sure."

And I met her at 5 p.m., at her clinic, in Dwarka. I smelled something fishy from her words. She did the pregnancy test first and then some check-ups and declared finally, but before that, my heartbeat was running faster than a racing track horse, "Congrats, Pranami, you are pregnant again."

She cautioned me too, "It's fine nothing to worry, but this time, don't go for an abortion for any reason; otherwise, it will land you into big trouble, and you may not become a mother forever."

Out of the clinic, I was so excited even I could not understand what to do next. I thought, while getting into the vehicle, "Shall I call Manav and tell him...no...no the excitement will be over then, I will tell him in proper time."

It had been over a month since I left Dwarka, neither Bhai searched me nor I had called him once. But I used to call my neighbour Mrs Raghav to know what was happening in my flat in my absence.

She said, "Your brother never stays in it in the day time. He always comes late at night and sometimes his friend stays back with him."

I was expecting the same, in my absence they will make merry.

The day light was still vivid; streetlights were on, it would take time for the dark to win over the light completely and my vehicle entered through the main gate of Shri Ganesh Apartment. I entered on a thought that since I have come up to Dwarka, let me see in what condition the flat is with Bhai living there, and I will take some clothes too.

The security opened the gate with a salute and asked, "How are you Madam, coming after a long time, you were out of the city?"

I smiled and replied, "Yes."

--Ω--

The flat door was closed not locked, which surprised me. Who is there at this time or has Bhai forgotten to lock the door? Putting the key back into the vanity bag, I entered inside in slow motion and quiet steps. It was completely dark inside and some sound was coming from Bhai's room.

Bhai's room door was half-open, but dark, as he had not put on the light. With quiet steps from the sides, I reached the side of the door of his room avoiding a direct look through the door entrance.

Few moments passed in silence and what I observed was that Bhai and Vardhman were inside and they were 'on' from the daytime. I was contemplating scolding them by entering inside and putting the lights on, when Bhai spoke out, "Pranami is not agreeing...what should I do?"

I retrieved my steps backwards, again and I leant on the wall to hear their voices. I was their topic of discussion.

With a pause, Vardhman said, "You don't do anything? For Pranami only, I left Manav and joined with you, that stupid guy was never ever smelled what a trick you played to bring yourself back from America," he taunted on Bhai's words. Both were sozzled, words were dropping from their speech. I was shocked.

Bhai said, "I know, how many times will you tell me this, I am trying but Pranami has to agree also?"

"I had not told you I will try when you approached me, then why are you reluctant today?" said Vardhman.

Bhai's voice softened, "You also saw that Pranami scolds me, hates me and despite that I stayed with her only to convince her for you, I am trying."

"You just keep on trying, but the end result is zero... waiting for her is becoming intolerable."

"Shut up."

"What shut up...how many days you will keep on trying... there ought to be some end point," said Vardhman.

Their arguing voices were clearly audible to me. I thought about Manav, the poor guy was not aware of the big ploy behind him. Bhai lured Vardhman swiftly to act against him. And that bloody bastard Vardhman whisked away from Manav to Bhai for the sake of me, to marry me. I laughed in pain.

Bhai's voice rose, "Do you think that I don't want...I feel ashamed taking this drink from your money... every day, for every need I have to beg you, and I have to beg Pranami."

"Why don't you fight your case legally?" asked Vardhman.

"What type of CA are you? How many times should I tell you that I can't legally claim from her? On the first hearing, I will lose the battle...Besides, paying for the advocate's fee, I had sold out all my shares. Both the properties are in her name now."

"Hmm...then what will you do?" asked Vardhman.

"I will kill her."

"What?" Vardhman jumped up.

My entire body shivered in fear and my heartbeat ran faster.

"Yes...I will kill her, as a legal heir, I can be the only claimant of her property," Bhai was firm on his stand again.

"What will happen if she has made a will? Do you think that Manav will leave you? asked Vardhman.

"In fact, I will kill them both," Bhai was firm again on his stand.

My entire body was shaken up again.

"Both?" asked Vardhman.

"Yes...both."

"But what you will get on Manav's death, he has nominated

Pranami in all the bank documents and he has a will too that says if both of them die his property will be given to a trust," said Vardhman.

Bhai laughed, "It seems you know much more about him."

"I was with him too," said Vardhman.

Bhai's laughter continued, he took out some paper and waving it in his hand, Bhai declared, "It was old...now legally I am the only claimant of his property if he dies."

"You have changed the will? How?" asked Vardhman.

"Yes...I was with him too and he does it for the sake of his brother. Foolish guy he still believes I am the love of his brother and his brother will be annoyed in heaven if he does not obey me ...but I need your help V."

"Sorry, I can't help you...what will I get, why I would help you...shall I f**k her corpse?"

"Bloody hell, I am doing all this for you only."

Pouring two more pegs into the glasses, Vardhman asked, "How?"

"You are not going to get Pranami in this entire life, I bet...you do whatever you want to do and then we will kill her."

I was stiff and clung to the wall in fear.

Vardhman nodded in acceptance, Bhai said again, "Do you know what is the cost of the Gurgaon property."

Vardhman had shaken his head in annoyance.

"It is five hundred crore, when I sold my share it was just 50 crore...that foolish woman does not understand the value of the land...and after her death, everything will be ours... this flat...her bank balance, Manav's flat his bank balance, everything will be ours...this flat costs more than two crore. And we will stay happily together, forever."

"But how Su...there was hope after the Delhi High Court's verdict, but after the Supreme Court reinstated it, life became horrendous in Delhi. Two friends of mine were caught near Barakhamba road; the police dragged them from their car, and they were out by giving all their cash, gold chains, rings, but still the police were not happy they took the duo to a nearby ATM and made a cash withdrawal to its upper limit; otherwise, their life would have been finished."

"Still there is hope V...someday the Supreme Court may change its verdict."

"Wow...if that will happen life will be so beautiful," Vardhman was excited and amused at his thoughts.

"If that does not happen we will go back to the United States, it is legalised there and with this much money we can stay happily in any corner of the world."

Bhai came closer to Vardhman and started caressing him; Vardhman whispered further, "How will you do that?"

"We will first sedate them with sleeping pills then inject them with poison."

Vardhman laughed, "The police won't suspect a killing?"

"It will seem like suicide by consuming poison, when they are unconscious you do whatever you wish to do with Pranami and I will write the suicide note on their social profiles...I know Manav's entire social profiles password, Facebook, Twitter and LinkedIn. He kept one password for everything and I know his website admin password too. While Pranami has never kept her password secret, we can access her social profile from her smart phone, I know the pattern she used to open the phone and after that, we can access her profile directly. Though the contents of the suicide note will be different, the reason will be the same. Manav will show the reason as being a gay, as our law does not permit living with his partner and he cannot give up gayness, as it is in his blood so he decided to end his life, if this could open up the eyes of the law. All this must be posted within two minutes time span, because when the police investigate they will check every bit and seconds."

"What will Pranami write in her suicidal note?" asked Vardhman.

"I am ending my life because I am in love with a gay man...who it seems will never change."

"You have made it full proof."

"It will be a sensational suicide case V; social media will react in such a manner that the police won't find time to investigate the killing."

"Your mind works beautifully, Su...but remember Pranami is mine," Vardhman got closer to Bhai.

I left when their breath got deeper and not a single word was uttered from inside.

--Ω--

I was very late reaching Ghaziabad, though I started up the vehicle and got out from the Shri Ganesh Apartment I was not able to hold the steering wheel properly. My entire body was trembling with fear.

I sped the vehicle towards Dwarka Sector 9 Metro crossing, where it joined the Gurgaon link road. It was always less crowded.

In a whim, I drove out the vehicle from the apartment, but did not contain myself for long; I parked the vehicle on the roadside and cried. First, I screamed and then kept on sobbing and weeping for more than an hour until Manav's called me, "Where are you Pranami, still in the bank?"

"No...no I am on the way," I replied wiping my tears.

"Stuck somewhere in a traffic jam?

"Ya... I am still at Dhaula Kuan. Perhaps, the traffic jam is for some foreign delegates," I told him a lie, whereas, I was still on the Gurgaon link road.

"Okay, come slowly don't do rush," cautioned Manav.

"Ya."

I reached after 10 p.m., Manav was ready with dinner on the table, seeing me he said, "You came very late, okay just freshen up and come down, as you must be hungry."

I was not hungry before, but with Manav's words, hunger amplified in me.

I asked, "Are you hungry?"

"Ya...too much."

"Then you start, I will come after having a bath."

"Okay come soon, I am waiting."

I took time in the bathroom, as the pressure of the water hit me; Bhai's words hit me even harder. I was not able to think beyond that how could Bhai do this? He wants to kill me for money and that bastard wants to f**k my corpse. And that to Bhai advocated him. This ploy they were playing long before, Manav and I, helping them to act against us. Perhaps they have gone mad, it could not be the intention of a sound mind.

Manav knocked on the bathroom door, "Pranami, are you okay?"

"Ya, fine just coming..." I replied and soon came out from the bathroom.

Though I was hungry, I could not eat much, Manav asked, "Is the food not good, I ordered it from a newly opened restaurant."

"It's good."

"Then why didn't you eat properly was it because it had gone cold?"

"I had heavy snacks in the evening at the bank," I lied to him.

"Okay."

"Something wrong, Pranami, you look hassled?" asked Manav.

"No...I am tired," I lied to him, again, but I was amazed, as he was never so concerned.

He had dropped off to sleep first, with his arms around me. It took a long time for me to fall asleep, and I woke up early too. I gazed at his face at length and woke him up, "Manav, wake up."

He replied, "Hu."

"Wake up, Manav, someone is calling you?" I said.

"Who...Pranami Sharma," he replied in the same position as he slept.

"So you have woken up too?" I asked.

In reply, he came closer, took me into his arms and asked, "Who is calling, Pranami?"

"No...it is someone else whom you don't know."

"Who is he...where is he?" Manav opened his eyes now.

"Here," I took his arm and moved his palm around my belly.

"Here, is it so?"

I nodded, "Ya."

He hugged me tight and asked, "When, why didn't you tell me earlier?"

"Yesterday only I visited Dr Sobha's clinic in Dwarka to confirm, that's why I was late."

"You are so sweet...so nice." He kissed me all over madly and did not bother to listen to what I was saying.

I was happy, too happy at least he did not ask me this time, "Who is the lucky father?"

Manav kissed me repeatedly and put his ear on my belly... I had never imagined he would be so happy.

His changing behaviour was a surprise to me, but I enjoyed it, as it was desirous.

--Ω--

It was August 14, Friday, every banker hurried to avail two holidays on the weekend. At around 4 p.m., I received a call from an unknown number, but the true caller showed it as police, "Is it Miss Pranami Sharma?" The man's voice was rough and rude.

"Ya."

"This is Sub Inspector DK Pradhan from Ghaziabad police... is Subham Sharma your brother?"

"What happened, how had Bhai reached Ghaziabad ? And what is the matter?" I was curious to know what happened and why the Ghaziabad police were calling me.

Instead of answering my queries, he asked me again, "Do you know Manav Agrawal?"

"Yes...what happened to him?" my voice became wobbly.

"Madam please come down to Manav's flat, I hope you know it," asked the sub inspector.

"Yes...yes...I know, but what is the matter inspector?"

"Sorry, Madam, we can't tell you over the telephone please come down."

"I am just reaching."

Despite fast driving, I reached the spot late, at many places there were route diversions because of 15 August. The police cordoned off the entire flat; two dead bodies were lying in a pool of blood on the floor and Manav was sitting like a statue. Others were not allowed on the spot.

I asked Manav, "Manav, how did it happen, who did it?"

He did not answer; he became silent and sat like a statue.

The neighbour woman Mrs Khattana said, "I called the police, while I was coming with my son from the bus stop. I saw a blood stream was coming from the flat. When I had gone to pick up my son from the bus stop, it was not there. In suspicion, I had called the police and Manav too."

I cried, but the police did not allow me to go beyond a certain point. Sub Inspector DK Pradhan came forward and said, "We were waiting for you, Miss Pranami, we have to take the bodies for autopsy."

Wiping off my tears, I asked, "Can anyone tell me what happened and who did the brutal killing?"

"Madam, we can't say anything before the autopsy, we have done our prime investigation, only two mobile phones have been recovered from them as their belongings...it seems they have been called here for the killing...you know the other guy?" asked Sub inspector Pradhan.

"Yes...he is Bhai's friend."

"And Manav's too."

"Yes."

Meanwhile, the police had taken the bodies to the ambulance and sealed the flat and two policemen got hold of Manav to take him to the police vehicle, then I asked, "Why you are taking Manav?"

"He is the prime suspect madam, he called them here, there was a missed call and test message found in your brother's mobile from Manav's number. Though it is not clear who is the killer, we have to take him into custody so that he does not abscond. It seems a case of betrayed love madam, vendetta and vengeance seem to be the cause."

"But did you find the message from Manav's mobile? It may be a cross connection, at least, you should wait until the autopsy report comes?"

The inspector smiled and said, "He is an IITian, madam, and we don't expect that he will do foolish things; it is a well-planned murder. Though all the messages and calls have been deleted we will take the statement from the subscriber and we need to question you too madam, please come with us."

"Me...to the police station?" I was shocked.

"Yes, madam, you are close to the accused and the sister of the deceased man, so we need to question you about their relationship and the involvement of the third person. We had inquired from neighbours and many suspicious things have come out."

The ambulance with the dead bodies departed, but the inspector waited for me until I boarded into my vehicle, he followed my vehicle up to the police station.

I did not hide any fact of their relationship. I narrated everything, starting from Pranab Bhai's suicide, Subham Bhai's departure to America and Manav's gay relationship with Vardhman, his helping Bhai to come back to India, and about Bhai's relationship with Vardhman...everything...

"It's simple, madam, a case of revenge," the inspector listened to me carefully and proclaimed finally, "but still, let the autopsy report come tomorrow...and let Mr Manav open up his mouth."

I came back to my Dwarka flat. I was concerned about Manav; he had gone drastically silent.

The next day, in the morning, I purchased almost all the newspapers, walked down to the market and had tea from the stall. Almost all the leading local newspapers, both English and Hindi had published the news. Some of the captions were heart breaking like, "Gay man killed a gay man..."

"Twin murder in the triangular love of a gay man..."

"Double Murder: a gay man's revenge..."

And inside the same story what I had narrated to the police inspector. In some story, Bhai was being portrayed as the lover of Manav too. It was immaterial now...

I reached the Ghaziabad police station in the afternoon. The police inspector seemed happy.

I asked, "Has the autopsy report come?"

"Please be seated, Madam...the report has come and Manav has made a confession," said the police inspector.

I looked at him astounded.

He said again, "First, he had sedated them with sleeping pills by offering coffee and then cut their throat with a sharp substance, probably with a blade. All this happened around 11 a.m. He had gone to office marked his presence and then came back to kill them...coffee mugs were recovered, but it was all washed. It's a cold blooded murder madam, well planned and well executed, but being the first time he had left many clues behind."

I kept on weeping and weeping.

Then the police said, "Sustain yourself, Madam. Who has gone will not come back, but let the culprit get punished."

"Can I meet Manav?" I asked.

"Yes, but for a few minutes."

"Okay," I nodded in acceptance.

They didn't allow me to enter inside the jail. The iron bars were in between us.

I said, "Manav, I..." he interrupted and stopped me from saying my words.

"No, Pranami...don't say anything...just let me see you," and Manav gazed at me for a long time and then smiled and asked, "It is my baby."

"Yes."

For the first time, I saw the passion of fatherhood in his eyes.

On Monday, he was brought into court and within twenty-four court working days and four hearings, the court gave its judgement. Manav was sentenced to life imprisonment, 14 years in jail. All the newspapers were in high praise of the Ghaziabad police. The Ghaziabad police cleared the air of the twin murder case within a month's time.

My Confession

But there is a twist to the story and unless I confess what actually happened, the truth will not be revealed.

On 29 March 2016, I had delivered a baby boy, little premature because the doctor had given the date as 11 April. The baby boy was healthy and the moment I saw his face, I felt I was on the top of the world. Today, on 10 April, I took him to Manav for the first time; he is now in Tihar Jail. Within these eight months, he has been shifted to two jails and I always meet him on all Sundays come hail or storm.

However, my last visit was to him on 20 March, the next Sunday on 27th, I could not go because of false labour pains and in the evening, the doctor had admitted me to her clinic. These few days gap haunted me and it felt as if I had not met him for years.

When Manav saw the boy's face, he was speechless for fifteen minutes and tears fell down from his eyes silently. I had never seen him crying and weeping silently is really dangerous, the other person can't guess what is going on inside him. I felt irresistible watching him for those fifteen minutes and asked, "Manav, why are you crying? Tell me something. Don't be so silent." I too wept

The baby boy was comfortable in Manav's arms.

Manav said, "*Dhut Pagli ye ashu khusi ka hai* (you have gone mad, these are tears of joy). I cannot express, Pranami, how happy I am. When I hold the little boy in my arms, it seems as if I have everything in the world."

I saw pleasure in his eyes.

He was so glad; he keeps watching the face of the baby boy for a long long time, sometimes, holds his little finger and sometimes, the little feet.

Seeing this, the guilt that haunted me from the day Manav was sentenced gradually faded away.

--Ω--

I met Manav, the day after he was convicted of the charge of double murder to avenge love.

I said, "Sorry, Manav, I had no other option left to save my baby."

He said, "Don't say sorry, Pranami, I know everything."

"You don't know anything, Manav...you just know that I had killed them, so you accepted everything that goes against me. You had the motive to save me that was obvious, you wanted to save your child but you don't know what exactly happened and why I took the extreme step," I whispered.

He looked a little puzzled.

I asked, "Do you remember the day I told you about our baby?"

"Ya."

"I was late, "I said.

"Hu."

"I was there, in my apartment for some time."

I then narrated the entire incident of that day, the ploy they were playing for long , Vardhman's whisked away to Bhai, everything and asked, "I thought thousand times before taking the drastic step Manav, but I didn't find any other way to save my baby. I know despite of all his sins, you always forgive him. You went into debt for bringing him back from America, otherwise, he would have been in a USA jail, struggling for his life, batted for him with me, supported him all the way but what did he give to you? He made Vardhman go against you, harassed you mentally and you never reacted against him?"

I wanted to see the reaction on his face but he was so calm simply smiled. And I knew he won't react of Bhai's stance. What a love! His brother Pranab died for his love and he continued from where he left…

I said, "I know if he was to kill you openly you would not have resisted. So, If I had not done that, we would have been killed and I would not let my child die this time. Their plan was full proof…I have killed them on their plan…and planned it meticulously. I had seen the fear of death in their eyes. When I poisoned them, I was not sure, that they might be alive, so I cut their throat by using your used blade. Sorry I used your phone, messaged them and trapped them. I am not regretting what I did, but I had no other option left. Sorry…"

He simply listened to me and his reaction was normal.

I said again, "How could people become so greedy for money I could have never imagined."

"Bhai had the purpose and that stupid man Vardhman… just because of my body."

Sometimes, I felt bad for Vardhman, but sometimes anger mounted about it, especially when I thought how desperate he was that he wanted to have my body even when I was dead and a corpse.

Though Manav listened to me, no significant change was visible on his face; he said at last, "Whatever is done is done, Pranami…forget it and let us live with our little child."

"What sort of a man he is? Never found regret on his face...I put his whole life in jail but he never blames me for a single thing," I thought.

"Are you not angry with me?" I asked.

"Why...have I ever got angry at you?" Manav asked me. "Other than you who else is there in this big world to call me his, and the little world of mine has brought many hopes in life...and you bring this little world to the world of mine."

For the first time, I saw Manav carried over emotionally.

It is a fact; he never ever got angry with me for any reason.

"But why. Manav...why are you not angry with me?"

"How could someone get angry on his fate? In this entire, big wide world, whom can I call my own? I would have been finished long ago, if you were not with me."

Those few words narrated all the untold stories of his life. Coming back to the flat, that evening, I cried as much as I wished, until I fell asleep.

--Ω--

The next morning I was fresh, with a cup of tea I sat down with his website. He had uploaded the last post one day prior to the killing, unaware of the upcoming circumstances. The post read, "Someone beyond the Rainbow."

I saw a dream in my dream, eyes wide open, but my mind was in a different world. Thousands of people decked in the colours of the rainbow gathered, at India Gate to celebrate the Supreme Court's historical verdict, overruling its earlier verdict of 2013 criminalising homosexuality. The crowd increases as time passes, where plenty of journalists and supporters were also part of the gathering. Film stars, corporate leaders, social activist and many more high profile people across India gathered in support. There are MLA's, MP's across all parties and some cabinet ministers joined the rally, and showed their support and felt grateful about the apex courts historical verdict. The gathering marched peacefully through the heart of Delhi's Connaught Place to Jantar Mantar, expressing their grateful attitude to the apex court, shouting slogans, "We had faith, we have faith in the Supreme Court, only justice was delivered late...we are thankful."

Not only gay and lesbians gathered, the third gender, transgender were present in large numbers. Their faith was once again restored by the apex court in 2014 and one way was found to show loyalty towards the apex court. The landmark judgement in 2014 offered a newfound liberation for a huge community of lives in India. Their respect was restored and they are now into corporate jobs, government positions and high-profile portfolios, leaving begging on street red lights and trains. Thousands and thousands from Delhi alone gathered to pay homage to the apex courts judgement.

A TV journalist with its well-known brand name of the channel logo asked a question to a eunuch, "What is your feeling about the Supreme Court's judgement?"

"Great...it has restored our respect; we were struggling with our existence, now our aim will be achieving success in all spectrums of life and every sector of our society. The biggest challenge ahead is educating the third gender and working towards the feeling of their parents. Parents should not throw them out of their house, rather accept them and respect them inside the house."

One journalist shouted, "Here come the supporters."

Everyone including the police looked back, a contingent of older people marched forward behind the mass. They were parents. A wave of delight spread in the crowd. They are the greatest supporter of the deeds or misdeeds of their children, once they are out in support it means a lot to the society.

Journalists raced down to cover the event. Few anchors declared over the speaker on live telecast about the entire celebration being a double bonanza. There may be thousand laws to protect you, but parents are the first to protect you, guide you and hold your hand until you cross the barrier. They are the first to know your character and their support means a lot to society and the individual.

And in Jantar Mantar, they threw out the rainbow masks, and came out as open people, without masks. The daily struggle for their existence was over.

What a day it is, everyone seems happy, cheerful and felicitate each other on achieving freedom. The same joy and blissful aura existed as if it was 15 and 16 August 1947, when the country achieved the freedom to rule.

A three bench of justices, comprising Mr Radhakrishan Nair, Mr Prasant Bhusan Majhi and Mrs Somvati Sharma come out with the landmark verdict reinstating Delhi High Courts historical verdict of 2009 decriminalising homosexuality.

The khandpith enumerated, "After a long debate over homosexuality, the apex court comes out with the verdict that Section 377 of IPC needs to be reconsidered as the situation demands. There is no science involved in homosexuality, to safeguard the increasing interest of the LGBT group and to avoid further debacles over reservation, minority class declaration and riots, strengthen the constitutional rights to minimize the misuse of the law, this court reinstates Delhi High Court's verdict of decriminalizing homosexuality."

Wow...my eyelids were closed to get me into my thinking world. That would be the day, when this dream would come out as true; millions of people would get justice. The world gradually recognizes its truthfulness and perhaps India may take few more years to recognize them.

A British voluntary organization once said in its report that, "The country such as India that is secular about many religions must adopt decriminalizing homosexuality. It would minimise communal and casteism violence, as the main binding force is same sex in them and no community or caste."

Many countries have come out with legalizing same sex marriage strengthening love between them. The day will come when India won't stay far behind them. The journey has been long, and there are still miles to go and that will only happen when you come out about what you are without any hesitance. Let us gather the momentum, don't stay back within the colours of the rainbow...come out as a clean person and proclaim I am gay...I am lesbian...strengthen our unity... show our strength and I am sure the D-day will not be far away.

The next when I visited him, I asked, "Give me your admin user ID and password."

"What?"

"Give me your admin rights."

"Okay...but what will you do?" asked Manav.

I laughed and tapping his head, I said slowly, "That is none of your business."

From that day onwards, I write for his website, answer questions asked on the website, attend all pride parades and did not let the gay Manav die without a reason anonymously and stand firm to narrate the story of us to you.